BARGAINING FOR BABY

BY
ROBYN GRADY

AND

THE BILLIONAIRE'S BABY ARRANGEMENT

BY
CHARLENE SANDS

"I don't need you to understand me. Believe me, you don't want to."

"But know this. I want you to keep your promise. I want to do right by this boy. I want to give him a home." Under the artificial light, his green eyes sparkled. "Come back with us to Leadeebrook."

A choking breath caught in her chest.

Infuriating. Insufferable. How dare he be charming and sincere now!

But although she'd like to deny it, the note of caring in his voice had touched her. Maybe there was an ounce of human in Jack Prescott, after all.

Sensing her slide, he moved to take over the carriage's handles. Still wary, she shook her head. "I'm not sure…"

But then he actually smiled—a damnable slow, bone-melting smile. "I think you are, Maddy." He began to walk, and when she relented and followed, he added, "I'll give you two weeks."

Dear Reader,

At a recent family wedding, I enjoyed the company of a wise lady who said, "If you're lucky enough to find the one person in this world who really 'gets who you are,' you should hang on tight and never let them go." Years earlier, this lady had met and married the man of *her* dreams. They were beyond suited and immeasurably happy, particularly when their beautiful dark-eyed daughter was born. Sadly, when that little girl was only four, her loving father was taken from them.

To look into this woman's eyes is to know she will love her husband forever. And logic says…if you've already gifted your heart to another, you haven't another to give. For some I believe this is true.

But not for all.

When his wife passed away, Jack Prescott—my hero in *Bargaining for Baby*—felt as if his life was over, too. Knowing that their unborn baby had died at the same time seemed to cement the headstone over those emotions. But when Jack's nephew needs a permanent guardian, the baby's temporary caregiver, Madison Tyler, finds an unsuspecting chink in this wealthy cowboy's cast-iron armour.

However, Jack is unwilling to gamble on love…as unwilling as Maddy is to live in Australia's harsh Outback. And yet an increasingly vulnerable part of this savvy city girl continues to wish that their mutual smouldering attraction will heat Jack's heart enough for him to realise that he still has love enough to give.

I hope you enjoy *Bargaining for Baby* series!

Best wishes,

Robyn

BARGAINING FOR BABY

BY
ROBYN GRADY

Published in Great Britain 2011
by Mills & Boon, an imprint of Harlequin (UK) Limited,
Eton House, 18-24 Paradise Road, Richmond, Surrey TW9 1SR

© Robyn Grady 2010

ISBN: 978 0 263 88312 1

51-0811

Harlequin (UK) policy is to use papers that are natural, renewable and
recyclable products and made from wood grown in sustainable forests. The
logging and manufacturing processes conform to the legal environmental
regulations of the country of origin.

Printed and bound in Spain
by Blackprint CPI, Barcelona

Robyn Grady left a fifteen-year career in television production knowing that the time was right to pursue her dream of writing romance. She adores cats, clever movies and spending time with her wonderful husband and their three precious daughters. Living on Australia's glorious Sunshine Coast, she says her perfect day includes a beach, a book and no laundry when she gets home. Robyn loves to hear from readers. You can contact her at www.robyngrady.com.

This story is for Maxine, Katie and dear Aunt Jenn.
Three generations of smiles,
spunk and unfailing devotion.

With thanks to "Snow"
from Jondaryan Woolshed for your entertaining stories
and fascinating inside info, and also to my fabulous
editor, Shana Smith.
Go us!

One

Jack Prescott wandered out from the public hospital room, his senses locked in a mind-numbing daze.

He'd received the call at ten that morning. He'd immediately jumped in his twin engine Piper Navajo and had flown to Sydney with his heart in his mouth the whole way. He and Dahlia hadn't spoken in three years. Now he'd missed the chance to say goodbye.

Or I'm sorry.

Through stinging eyes he took in the busy corridor. The air smelled of antiseptic and, beneath that, death. As of today, he was the last surviving Prescott and there wasn't a soul to blame but himself.

A passing doctor, deep in conversation, knocked Jack's shoulder. He swayed, braced his legs then spread out his remarkably steady hands to examine the calloused palms. How long before the nightmare truly hit? Before he fell to his knees and cursed this godless world? Where was the mercy? Dahlia had only been twenty-three.

A woman in the crowded waiting room caught his eye, her fair hair streaming over one side of a red summer dress. She held a bundle. A swaddled child.

Jack rubbed a gritty eye and refocused.

Beneath fluorescent lights, tears glistened on her lashes, and as she gazed back down the corridor at him, Jack wondered if they'd met before. When her mouth pressed into an I'm-so-sorry smile, his gut hollowed out.

One of Dahlia's friends.

But he wasn't sure he could put words together yet. Those token pleasantries like, "Oh, you knew my sister. Yes, she was very beautiful. Sorry, but I have to leave… make arrangements."

When the woman continued to wait, her pale hand supporting the baby's head, Jack couldn't avoid a meeting. He forced one leaden foot in front of the other and, an eternity later, stopped before her.

"You're Dahlia's brother, aren't you?" she asked. "You're Jack." Her flushed cheeks were tearstained, her nails bitten to the quick and her eyes…

Her eyes were periwinkle blue.

Jack sucked in a breath. When was the last time he'd noticed something like that? He wasn't sure he even knew the color of Tara's eyes. Perhaps he should take note when he got back. Not that theirs would be that kind of marriage. Not from his perspective, in any case.

After the death of his wife three years ago, Tara Anderson had spent increasing amounts of time at Leadeebrook, the Queensland sheep station where he lived. Jack had been slow to appreciate Tara's company; he wasn't much of one for talking these days. But as close as his deceased wife and this woman had once been, so he and Tara had become good friends, too.

Then, last week, Tara had offered more.

He'd been straight. He would never love another woman. His wedding band was threaded on a gold chain that never left his neck while his wife's ring lay at the foot of a photo he kept on his bedroom chest of drawers. Sue had not only been his wife, she'd been the other half of his soul. The better half.

Still Tara had put her argument forward. He needed someone steady in his life, she'd said. She needed someone to help manage her property. That had gotten Jack's attention. Twenty years ago, Jack's father buckled under hard times and had sold half his land to a neighbor, Tara's great-uncle. Later, he'd tried to buy the land back but Dwight Anderson wasn't interested.

After Sue's death, Jack's life had seemed pointless. He'd found no joy in occupations that had once caused the blood to charge hot and fast through his veins. Even throwing a saddle over Herc and giving his stallion free rein down a beloved Leadeebrook plain had seemed a chore. But the idea of fulfilling his father's dream of regaining those choice acres had offered Jack's darker days a glimmer of meaning.

Tara was a good woman and attractive by any man's standards. Perhaps they *could* help each other out. But before he married again, a matter needed sorting.

The human race relied on the power of maternal instinct—women wanted children and Tara would make an excellent mother. But he had no wish to become a father.

He'd made mistakes—one error unforgivable. He thought about it often and not only when he visited the tiny grave which lay beside his wife's in the Leadeebrook family plot. Having your heart ripped from your chest once was enough for any man. He wouldn't tempt fate by siring another child.

If Tara wanted a marriage of convenience, it would be without plans of a family. Although she had acquiesced with a nod when he'd told her as much, the mist in her eyes had said that she hoped he'd change his mind. Not tomorrow. Not ten years from now. On that point he was firm.

Jack's gaze had settled on the lightly-swaddled bundle when the woman in the red dress spoke again.

"Dahlia and I were friends," she murmured in a thready voice. "Good friends."

He inhaled, rushed a hand through hair that was overdue a cut and got his thoughts in order. "The doctor said it was a hit-and-run."

At a pedestrian crossing, of all places. Dahlia had died of internal injuries only minutes before he'd arrived. He'd touched her hand, still warm, and remembered how he'd taught her to ride Jasper, his first mount, and how he'd consoled her when her pet lamb had passed away. When she'd reached out and had begged him to understand...when his sister had needed him most...

"She regained consciousness briefly."

The woman's words took Jack off guard. The back of his knees caved and he sat, wishing he hadn't. Taking a seat implied he wanted to talk. What he wanted was to take off his boots, down a stiff Scotch and...

He looked up too quickly and the light faded in and out.

And *what?* Face forms, funeral directors, a choice of clothes for the coffin?

"She spoke to me before...before she slipped away." The woman's lips were full and pink now, the bottom trembling the barest amount. "I'm Madison Tyler." She repositioned the baby and lowered to sit beside him. "Friends call me Maddy."

He swallowed hard against a closed, dry throat. "You said she regained consciousness…spoke to you."

Surely not about him. Dahlia had been a wreck after their parents' deaths. Not even his wife's patience and support had gotten through to her. That final night, Dahlia had shouted she didn't want another thing to do with her brother, his stupid rules or Leadeebrook. She'd come to Sue's funeral but he'd been too dazed to speak. Over the years, he'd received Christmas cards, but no forwarding address.

His hands clenched on his thighs.

Lord and Holy Father, he should have set pride aside and *found* her. Protected her. Brought her back home.

The baby stirred and Jack took in the sleeping face, the shadow of tiny lashes on plump healthy cheeks. So new and full of promise.

Full of life.

Clearing his mind and the thickness from his throat, he found his feet and the bulk of his control.

"We can talk at the wake, Miss…"

"Maddy."

He drew his wallet from his back pocket and dug out a card. "I'll see that the notices are posted. You can get me on this number if there's anything."

Finding her feet, too, she searched his eyes.

"I need to speak with you, Jack. I need to speak with you now." She stole a glance at her baby. "I didn't know… Well, Dahlia hadn't spoken about you before."

When her gaze meshed with his again, her eyes were round and pleading, as if she wanted an explanation. She seemed sweet enough, and understandably shaken, but whatever Dahlia had said, he wasn't about to justify himself to a stranger. To anyone, for that matter.

His gaze broke away as he waved the card. "I really ought to go."

"She told me that she loved you," she blurted out, jerking half a step closer. "That she forgave you."

Bent over, placing his card on the chair, he stopped, clamped his eyes shut and willed away the thumping heartbeat in his ears. He wanted this week to be over. Wanted to get back home. Back to his land. What he knew. What he could keep.

He straightened slowly and kicked up a firm chin. The baby was stirring, beginning to squeak and complain. A part of Jack was drawn to the sound while another only wanted to plug his ears and stalk away. The last straw would be to hear an infant cry.

Exhaling, he shoved the wallet in his back pocket. "There's nothing you can do here. You should get that baby home."

"I'm trying."

When she purposely held his gaze, he shook his head then shrugged. "Sorry. You've lost me."

But she only rolled her teeth over her bottom lip, her eyes huge and…

Frightened?

He assessed her classic bone structure—flawless porcelain complexion, the delicate curve of her jaw—and, despite the day, an instinctive flicker of arousal licked over his skin.

Was she implying that the child was his?

Some time after his wife's death, concerned friends had tried to lure him out from behind the walls he'd built around himself. They'd invite him to Sydney, to introduce him to suitable ladies within their circles. Although his heart had remained closed, there'd been a time or two he'd invited a date back to his inner city penthouse.

Was that why this woman seemed familiar? Had he slept with her sometime in the past?

He shucked back tense shoulders.

No. He'd have remembered those lips.

"Look, Miss—"

"Maddy."

He spared a tight smile. "Maddy. Neither of us is in any mood for games. Whatever you have to say, I'd appreciate it if you would spit it out."

She didn't flinch or coil away from his candor. Rather her expression took on a steely air.

"Dahlia left the baby with me today," she said. "He's not my son. This baby is your nephew."

Two beats of roaring silence passed before her words hit his chest, winding him as surely as if he'd been rammed by a twenty-foot log. He blinked rapidly, tried to find his breath. He must've heard wrong.

"That's…not possible."

A tear rolled down her cheek, catching and beading on the bunny blanket's blue hood while her periwinkle eyes gleamed with quiet strength.

"Your sister's last wish was for me to introduce you to one another. She wanted you to take him, Jack. Take him home with you to Leadeebrook."

Two

Fifteen minutes later, sitting across the table from Jack Prescott, Maddy brought the china cup to her lips, certain that she'd never seen anyone look more drawn.

Or more handsome.

With the shadow on his strong square jaw—as well as his demeanor—growing darker by the minute, his teaspoon click-clacked as he stirred sugar into his cup.

Over the intercom, someone called for Dr. Grant to go to ward 10. An elderly woman at a nearby table smiled at the baby before tasting her scone. By the cashier, a nurse dropped a full plate. The clattering echo bounced off the walls yet Jack Prescott seemed oblivious to it all. His hooded yet intense gaze was focused only inward.

From beneath her lashes, Maddy analyzed the planes of his rugged, Hollywood face—the cleft chin, the straight proud nose. How he managed to look both passionate and detached at the same time she couldn't guess. She sensed a fierce, almost frightening energy broiling beneath the mask. He was the kind of man who could single-handedly beat a bushfire in forty knot gusts and refuse to let anything he cared for suffer or die.

The million dollar question was: What *did* Jack Prescott care about? He'd barely looked at the baby, the orphaned darling he'd only just met. The man sitting at this table seemed to be made of stone, a perfect enigma. She might never know why Dahlia had excluded her brother from her life. If it weren't for little Beau, Maddy wouldn't *want* to know.

Jack settled his cup in its saucer, and then slid a bland expression toward the baby, who was settled again, asleep on his side in the carriage with a tiny fist bunched up near his button nose. Jack had been the one to suggest coffee, but after so long of a silence, Maddy couldn't stand his chilly calm a moment more. She had a task to complete—a promise to keep—and a finite amount of time in which to do it.

"Dahlia was a great mother," she told him. "She'd finished her degree in business marketing before the baby was born. She was taking a year off before finding and settling down to a good job." Maddy's gaze dropped to her cup as a withering feeling fell through her center. Now was the time to say it. Now was the time to confess.

"Dahlia had barely been out of the apartment since bringing him home," she went on. "I'd talked her into going to the hairdressers, having her nails done—"

Maddy's stomach muscles gripped and she grimaced under the weight of her guilt.

If she hadn't suggested it, hadn't made the appointment and practically pushed her friend out the door, Dahlia would still be alive. This baby would still have his mother and have no need to rely on this brusque man who seemed set on ignoring him.

"He's three months old today," she added, in case he was interested, but Jack only concentrated on stirring more sugar into his drink.

Maddy blinked several times then pushed her cup away and glanced, sick at heart, around the noisy room. This exchange was never going to be easy, but could it have gone any worse? What was she supposed to do now? The man was as sensitive as a slab of cold steel.

"Where's the father?"

Maddy jumped at his graveled question. But the query was an obvious one, even if he wouldn't like the answer.

She lowered her voice. "Dahlia was the victim of a rape." His face darkened before he swore and shoveled a hand though hair black as ink. "And before you ask," she continued, "she didn't report it."

Flecks of gold ignited in the depths of his hostile green eyes. "Why the hell not?"

"Does it matter now?"

Like so many in her situation, Dahlia hadn't wanted the misery of a trial. She hadn't known her assailant and preferred to keep it that way. She'd needed to heal as best she could and bury the horror as well as the hurt. Then Dahlia had discovered she was pregnant.

Choking on raw emotion, Maddy focused and straightened her spine. "What matters is she had a beautiful baby." This bright little boy she'd loved very much.

Jack studied the baby, the single line between his dark brows deepening as a pulse ticked at one side of thick, tanned neck. His next question was a grudging growl.

"What's his name?"

"Beauford James."

Jack Prescott's nostrils flared and his gaze slid away.

Maddy smothered a humorless laugh. Was this man a *machine?* Certainly these were special circumstances—he'd lost his only sibling today. But did he *ever* deign to show the world any emotion other than irritation?

Hot tears pricked behind Maddy's eyes as her hand tightened around her cup and rising emotion blocked off her air. She couldn't hold her tongue. No decent person would. Nothing had mattered more in her life than the outcome of this meeting—fulfilling the promise that she'd made—and if she had to brush an over-indulged ego the wrong way to get results, then by God, that's precisely what she'd do.

"He's your flesh and blood," she challenged. "Don't you want to pick him up and hold him?"

Promise him everything will be all right? That he'll be safe?

A dreadful thought struck and the fine hairs on her arms stood up at the same time as she slumped back. "Or would you rather he go straight to foster care?"

Not that she would let that happen. She'd take Beau herself first. Her own mother had died when Maddy was five. Growing up she'd longed for someone to braid her hair in the morning, burrow down beneath the covers with and read to her at night.

Maddy's father was a good man but obsessed with his business—sometimes it seemed as if Tyler Advertising was more Drew Tyler's child than his only daughter. He ran his corporate castle with an iron fist and didn't see a place on its staff for a "delicate girl" like Maddy. She disagreed. After serious and extended debate, she'd won and had gone to work at the firm.

These past weeks her father had become understandably edgy over his daughter closing her first big solo deal. Beneath the brave face, Maddy was nervous, too. But, come hell or high water, she'd have the signatures she needed and by the date promised. One month from today.

No one would guess how painfully shy she'd been as a girl, how hard she'd worked on her flaws in order to reflect her father's celebrated style of business savvy and determination. Now, not a day went by that Drew didn't in some way acknowledge his daughter's efforts. Still, there were times she wished she'd known a mother's love.

Her gaze fell to the baby.

How would this little one fare?

Jack's long, tanned fingers reached for the sugar bowl. "I don't recall saying I wouldn't take him," he drawled.

"You hardly seem gripped by the idea." Maddy slid back and one inky black brow arched.

"You'd do better not to be so hostile," he said.

"You'd do better not to be such a cold fish."

While her heart pumped madly, his expression didn't change. Those lidded sexy-as-sin eyes merely peered into hers until a not unpleasant shiver rippled over her skin, heating her from crown to curling-toe.

Blinking rapidly, she shifted back into the hard plastic seat.

Not only was this man dripping with bad-boy sex appeal, in that last point he'd been right. He might be as demonstrative as a stunned salmon, but now was the time for calm, not commotion. No matter how difficult, for the baby's sake, she must keep her emotions in check.

All of them.

Maddy loosened the grip on her cup and found the calm place inside that served her well in trying situations.

"This day has been a shock for us both," she admitted, "but, believe me, I only have one objective in mind, and that's to make certain Beau is cared for the way Dahlia would've wanted." She leaned in again, praying her heart would be there for him to see in her eyes. "Jack…he needs you."

A muscle in his cheek flexed twice. "So it would seem."

When he downed the rest of his coffee that must be three parts sugar and stone cold by now, Maddy's hackles went up.

All her life she'd mingled with powerful men, business associates from her father's advertising firm, influential patriarchs of the boys she'd dated in university. She'd seen an investment banker multimillionaire for a while. But never had she met anyone who stirred such strong emotions within her.

Both negative and shamelessly positive.

The hot pulse that kicked off low and deep inside whenever she looked at Jack Prescott was real. His presence was so commanding, despite the day, she couldn't help but be intrigued. The breadth of his shoulders, the strength in his neck…his man-of-the-land build was magnificent. His gestures, his speech, everything about him whispered confidence. Intelligence. Superiority.

Detachment.

The angel asleep in that carriage hadn't another living relative left in the world. Yet this specimen of masculine perfection, this emotional *ice man,* couldn't bring himself to even ask to hold him. She wouldn't have been able to leave Beau with his uncle and simply walk away, even if she had a choice.

Her stomach churning, Maddy nudged the blanket higher on the baby's shoulder and kept her eyes on the soft rise and fall of his little chest. There was never going to be a right time. Might as well bite the bullet and get the final bombshell out in the open.

"There's something else I need to say," she murmured. "About a promise I made."

Jack consulted his Omega platinum wristwatch. "I'm listening."

"I promised that I wouldn't hand Beau over until you were ready."

While her heart jack hammered against her ribs, the man across from her slowly frowned and folded his arms. Eventually he tugged his ear.

"I admit it'll take time to adjust to the idea of having…" His words ran dry, but then he cleared his throat and put more grunt into his voice. "You only need to know that I don't renege on my responsibilities. My nephew won't want for a thing."

It wasn't enough. If he'd greeted the baby with open arms, she'd still need to keep her word. She'd promised on her mother's grave to make certain Beau was settled.

Turning from the baby, Maddy clasped her hands in her lap and met Jack's superior gaze square on.

"I promised Dahlia that I'd stay with Beau until you were comfortable with each other. I imagine you have plenty of room," she hastened to add, "and I'm happy to pay for any expenses incurred."

The haunting cool in his eyes turned to flickering questions. He cocked his head and a lock of black hair fell over his suntanned brow while the corners of his mouth lifted in a parody of a smile.

"I need to have my ears checked. Am I getting this straight? You're inviting yourself to stay with me?"

"I'm not inviting myself anywhere. I'm passing on your sister's wishes. I'm telling you I made a promise."

"Well, it won't work." He shook his head, almost amused. "Not in a million years."

Maddy drew back her shoulders. He might be big. He

might be intimidating. But if he thought *he* was inflexible, these days stubborn was her middle name.

She'd try a different tack.

"This baby knows me. I know him. His routine, his cries." *Hopefully what to do when he wakes up, wanting his mummy.* "It's in your best interest to let me help you both adjust."

"I'll have help."

He'd said it without blinking and her heart missed several beats.

Dahlia said this morning that she'd followed what she could of her brother's life, really only that he still lived at Leadeebrook and hadn't remarried since the death of his wife. Of course he would need to hire a nanny. But what kind of person would be looking after Beau? Would she be severe and by-the-book or would she use her heart as well as her skills? Would she encourage him with gentle words of praise, or rap his knuckles if he forgot to say please?

"Miss Tyler..." A glimmer of warmth shone in his eyes when he amended, "Maddy. Are you sure this isn't more about your inability to let go?"

A dark emotion she couldn't name spiked and she kicked her chin up. "Rest assured, if I could be certain he'd be happy, if I could walk away with a clear conscience, nothing would please me more than to give you both my blessing."

That glimmer froze over. "Only I don't need your blessing, do I?"

Given that he was this baby's sole surviving relative, she conceded, "I suppose you don't. But then you don't appear to need anything—" she dammed her words then let them spill out anyway "—particularly this hassle." Lashing her arms over her chest, she challenged his hard gaze. "Am I right?"

When he didn't answer—merely assessed her with those striking gold-flecked eyes—her core contracted around a hot glowing knot. Before the heat flared any higher, she doused the flame and pushed to her feet.

Walking out wouldn't help matters, but she'd had all she could take for one day. The term *animal magnetism* was invented for this man: Jack Prescott was uniquely, powerfully attractive, but no way was he human. And before she left, damned if she wouldn't tell him just that.

"I respected Dahlia," she got out over the painful lump in her throat. "I loved her like a sister, but I can't imagine what she was thinking choosing you to care for this precious child."

With unshed tears burning her eyes, Maddy readied the carriage and headed for the exit. Jack called her name, but he could go to hell. He was no more interested in this baby's welfare than she cared what team won the national dart competition. If he was so uninspired, he could fly back to the scorched red plains of the Australian outback and leave Beau here in civilization with her. No child should need to grow up in a wasteland anyway.

One moment the cafeteria doorway was an arm's length away, the next Jack's impressive frame was blocking her escape. His legs braced shoulder-width apart, he deliberately set his fists low on his hips.

Maddy huffed over a smirk.

Well, whaddaya know. I got a reaction.

His head slanted. "Where are you going?"

"What do you care?"

She angled the carriage to swerve around him, but he

shifted to block her path again. "I care more than you'll ever know."

But she was done with words. She moved again. He moved, too. Narrowing her eyes, she let out a jaded sigh. "I've tried being reasonable. I tried understanding. I've even tried appealing to your better nature. Now I give in. You beat me, Jack Prescott." She raised her hands. "You win."

"I didn't realize we were in competition."

Oh, please. "Only from the moment you laid eyes on me." He'd wanted her gone? He could clap himself on the back. *Mission accomplished.* If Dahlia had heard this exchange, she wouldn't blame her friend for walking out.

"So, you've made up your mind?" he asked and she smiled sweetly.

"If you'd kindly step aside."

"And the baby?"

"We both know how you feel about raising Beau." It was in every curl of his lip.

A sardonic grin tugged one corner of his mouth. "You think you have me figured out, don't you?"

"I wish I could say I had the slightest interest, but I'm afraid I have as much curiosity about your workings as you've shown toward your nephew today."

While she simmered inside, his gaze drilled hers for a protracted, tense moment before his regal bearing loosened slightly. "What are you proposing?"

"What you're dying to have me propose. I'll relieve you of any obligation and take Beau off your hands." She would raise him, and show him love and loyalty and a million other values of which this man was clearly devoid. She'd work it out somehow with her job, with her father. "And if you're worried that I'll ask for financial support, don't be. I'd rather wash dishes fifteen hours a day than take one penny from you."

The air heated more, crackling and sparking between them before those big bronzed hands lowered from his belt.

"How are you in small aircraft?"

Her mouth fell open then snapped shut again. What was he talking about? Hadn't he heard a word she'd said?

"I flew down in a twin engine," he went on. "There's room for passengers but some people get queasy about small planes." His mouth twitched. "Though I have a feeling you're not the queasy type."

"I meant what I said—"

"You meant what you said to Dahlia," he cut in, but then dropped his voice as a curious older couple wove around them. "I don't need you to understand me. Believe me, you don't want to. But know this. I want you to keep your promise. I want to do right by this boy. I want to give him a home." Under the artificial light, his green eyes sparkled. "Come back with us to Leadeebrook."

A choking breath caught in her chest.

Infuriating. Insufferable. How dare he be charming and sincere now!

But, although she'd like to deny it, the note of caring in his voice had touched her. Maybe there was an ounce of human in Jack Prescott, after all.

Sensing her slide, he moved to take over the carriage's handles. Still wary, she shook her head. "I'm not sure…"

But then he actually smiled—a damnable slow, bone-melting smile. "I think you are, Maddy." He began to walk and when she relented and followed, he added, "You've got two weeks."

Three

Four days later, Maddy clutched her passenger seat armrest as Jack Prescott's private aircraft touched down on Leadeebrook Station's unsealed airstrip.

Jack had given her two weeks to fulfil her promise to Dahlia. Two weeks, no more, to have Beau settled in his new home with his new guardian. She would've liked more time, or at least the option to discuss the possibility of an extension should she deem one necessary. But, in the short period she'd known Jack, of one thing she was certain—he didn't speak for the sake of hearing his own voice. He was prepared to tolerate her company for precisely fourteen days. She supposed she ought to be grateful he'd seen the light and had relented at all.

When she stepped out from the plane onto the floor of the open ended hanger, the heat hit her like the long breath off a fire. The urge to spin around and crawl back inside the cool of the sumptuous cabin was overwhelming.

Instead she gritted her teeth and edged out into the blinding white sunshine.

Shading her brow, she cast a curious glance around the endless isolated plains—miles of bleached dry grass, parched scattered gum trees, lazy rolling hills shimmering a hazy purple in the distance.

She worked her dry throat enough to swallow.

Practically any part of Australia could get hot enough to fry eggs on the pavement. A serious summer's day in Sydney could rival a stint in a sauna. But out here the heat was different—bone dry—as if any sign of moisture would evaporate off a person's skin as soon as it surfaced. Within a week she'd be as dehydrated as the lifeless leaves hanging from those tired eucalypts.

Something bit her calf. She slapped at a beast of a fly then cringed at the red dust clinging to her new Keds. Who would choose to live in this godforsaken wilderness? No wonder Dahlia had escaped.

"Welcome to Leadeebrook."

At the husky voice at her back, Maddy angled around. Jack had followed her off the plane, aviator sunglasses perched upon his proud nose, carrying the diaper bag with one arm and Beau in the other.

Grinning, Maddy set her hands on her hips.

Heck, her iron cowboy looked almost relaxed. Nestled against that hard chest, Beau certainly did, which was a good sign. She'd been so worried.

Since the accident, she'd taken time off work to be with the baby 24/7. While her father sympathized with the situation, he wasn't pleased that his star junior account executive had asked for a leave of absence. He was less pleased when she'd told him she needed an additional two weeks out of the office. He needed the national deal she was working on bagged, no excuses.

She'd worked to reassure him. The Pompadour Shoe and Accessory campaign and media schedule were a wink away from being polished to a "simply-sign-here" shine. She'd be back in plenty of time to tidy loose ends. But these two weeks belonged to Beau, and today, in this unfamiliar environment, she felt more responsible for that baby than she could ever have dreamed possible.

When Jack had insisted she leave the plane cabin first—that he would bring the sleeping baby out directly—she'd automatically gone to object. She'd grown so used to the weight of him, his powdery scent, his smile; she ought to be the one to carry the baby out to greet his new home. But her friend's final request had echoed again in Maddy's mind.

Her job here was to do everything in her power to nurture an environment in which these two could connect and she could walk away knowing that Beau would be happy and cared for…that, God willing, he'd be loved and appreciated for the special little person he was.

That meant stepping back.

Watching the baby blink open his sleepy blue eyes and frown questioningly up into Jack's suntanned face—seeing Jack shift the nappy bag higher on his arm in order to push the sunglasses back into his thick hair and return the curious look—a cord in Maddy's chest pulled tight.

There'd been a slight shift in Jack's attitude toward his nephew. It seemed that now the funeral was behind them, he'd begun to show a tentative interest in his ward. Tender looks. Once the barest hint of a smile. But this was the first time he'd carried the baby, and while his wall was still steadfastly up, hopefully these small steps were seeds that would grow into a lasting, mutually loving relationship. Maybe, despite her misgivings and the sinking feeling that had minced around in Maddy's belly the whole uncommunicative flight here, Dahlia's wish would come true. That by the time she returned to Sydney, this aloof lone cowboy would have opened up, not only his home but also his heart to the person who needed him most.

Maddy stepped forward. But rather than take the baby, she cupped Beau's soft warm crown and smiled.

"He's awake. I can't believe he slept the whole flight."

"Isn't that what babies do? Sleep?"

When Jack's dubious gaze met hers, a frisson of awareness shot like the crack of a pistol through her blood. His sex appeal went beyond powerful; it was mesmerizing. The urge to tip close and savor that hypnotic lure was near irresistible.

Clearly Jack didn't mean for her to melt whenever they came within arm's distance. He had not the slightest interest in her *that* way. But she could do without him looking at her like that—as if she puzzled or intrigued him. As if he needed to know how her mouth might fit beneath his.

Her insides twinged and, guilty, she averted her gaze.

Those kinds of feelings were not only misplaced, they were dangerous. Next thing, she'd be looking at him cross-eyed. If she wanted to survive the following days—and nights—alone out here in Nowheresville with this maddeningly tempting man, she'd best make a pact with herself right now.

No matter how strong the tug—no matter what words Jack said, or smiles Jack gave—she'd allow nothing other than these searing outback temperatures to tamper with her body heat.

Composure restored, she straightened and replied, "Babies do a little more than sleep."

"Sure. They eat."

When he cocked a brow and managed to look both naive and sexier still, she couldn't contain a grin. "You know nothing about babies, do you?"

He dropped the glasses back onto his nose. "Not if lambs don't count."

He headed off, his focus hooked on the two-story homestead a walk away. Maddy's step slowed as she took a moment to drink in the place that Jack called home. Or, perhaps, a better word might be *palace*.

Leadeebrook Homestead was an impressive structure that radiated both elegance and a proud sense of endurance. Skirts of yesteryear lace ironwork surrounded both levels of veranda. Bordered by decorative masonry arches, large stately windows peered down at her. The lower floor sprawled out on either side in grand style. Maddy envisaged lavish drawing rooms, perhaps a ballroom, definitely a contemporary office, equipped with every convenience and littered with sheep stud memorabilia. The overall picture substantiated what she'd heard about the days when the country's wealth and glory had ridden on a sheep's back. Maddy could imagine the menagerie of characters who'd frequented its floors and the thrilling early settler stories they could tell.

A flock of pink galahs squawked overhead. She cast another resigned glance around the sun-scorched scene and hurried to catch up.

When a churning tunnel of disturbed dirt appeared in the near distance, Maddy wasn't certain what it meant. She shaded her eyes and narrowed her focus. A rangy dog was tearing up the track toward them leaving a swirling plume of dust in its wake.

A dart of panic hit her in the ribs.

Dogs were unpredictable. They could be savage. She didn't like being around them and she liked Beau being around them less. But this was a sheep station. Why hadn't she thought ahead? Of course there'd be a sheep dog. Maybe two or three.

As the dog sped closer, a hot-cold chill rippled up her spine. Maddy's fingers began to tingle and her breathing shallowed out. She hadn't had a full-blown panic attack in years. Now she recognized the signs and took measures to control them.

Regulate your breathing. Think calm thoughts.

But that comet of a dog kept coming. When the space between them shortened to within feet, she clenched her muscles, ready to dive and shield the baby. If someone was going to be slammed, it wouldn't be Beau.

At the last moment, the dog peeled away. Maddy's soaring adrenaline levels dipped and she slumped with relief—until a shiver fluttered up her limbs and her senses heightened again.

She carefully turned.

Head low, the dog was crouching up behind them. They were being stalked, like deer by a practiced wolf.

Jack growled out a playful "Git here, you," and, ears alert, the dog shot up to her master's side, her dark eyes blind with adoration and anticipation as she waited for the next order.

Shuddering out a shaky breath, Maddy worked to gather herself and force her leaden feet forward while Jack hoisted the baby higher against his chest.

"Meet Nell," he said.

Maddy preferred not to. Nevertheless she nodded curtly at the dog with the lolling pink tongue and penetrating brown eyes while keeping her distance. "Hello, Nell."

Jack paused to give her a dirty look. "You don't like dogs?"

"Let's say dogs don't like me." She had no intention

of explaining further. "She seems to hang off your every word."

"Nell's a working dog." A muscle ticked in his square, shadowed jaw. "Or she was."

Maddy tilted her head. *Was* a working dog. Had Nell had an accident? God knows she seemed agile enough. But Maddy had a more important question to ask.

"Is Nell good with children?"

Jack picked up his pace. "How should I know?"

As they moved toward the house, Nell trotted wide circles to manage her human flock, every so often darting up behind to nose their heels. Although Maddy remained outwardly calm, suffocating tendrils twined around her throat. But clearly this Border collie was well-trained. There was nothing to fear, for herself or the baby. Her falling blood pressure—her tingling brain—was an automatic physiological response to past stimuli. Just because she'd been mauled by a dog many years ago didn't mean it would happen again.

Breathe deeply. Calm thoughts.

As Nell flew past, the dog's tail brushed her wrist. Maddy's anxiety meter lurched again and she coughed out a nervous laugh.

"I have to say, I'm feeling a little like a lamb chop."

Jack flattened his lips and a sharp whistle echoed out over the plains. When he nodded ahead, Nell tore off. Maddy spluttered as more dust clouded her vision and filled her lungs. Fine grains of dirt crunched between her teeth. She needed a bath *and* a drink—a big fat Cosmopolitan with an extra shot of everything.

His broad shoulders rolling, Jack glanced across and measured her up. "There's reception for your cell phone if you need it."

"That's nice to know. Thanks."

"You bring any jeans?"

"Of course." The new season's latest cut.

"Good."

Goosebumps erupted down her arms. Something in his assured tone worried her. "Why good?"

"You can't ride in a dress."

She blinked. *Ride?*

Then she laughed. "Oh, I don't ride." Certainly not horses. She hadn't even swung a leg over a bicycle since that day when she was twelve.

Jack's brows fell together. "You don't like horses either?"

Her brows fell, too. "I didn't realize it was a federal offense."

Then again she was "out west." He probably slept with his saddle tucked under one arm and his Akubra glued to his head.

While she smacked another fly, Jack sucked air in between his teeth. "So you're not a fan of animals."

"Not up close."

He grunted. "What *do* you like?"

"I like the theater. I like chocolate custard. I like rainy days when I know I don't have to get up."

"Are there many days you don't get out of bed?"

She gave him a narrow-eyed look. Was he serious? His tone and expression were so dry, she couldn't tell.

"What I mean," she explained in an overly patient tone, "is that I love to prop myself up against a bank of pillows, snuggle down and read when rain's falling on the roof."

He grunted again—or was that growled—and kept his strides long while she wiped her damp brow and cringed as sweat trickled down the dent in her back. Up ahead, the homestead shimmered like an extravagant desert mirage.

A few minutes yet before they reached shade. But the sun was behind them, the baby seemed settled and the dog had disappeared. On his own turf, Jack seemed to be opening up, a little. Time to get to know more about Beau's legal guardian.

"What about you?"

"What about me?"

She rolled her eyes. She would *never* be able to talk to this man.

"Do you read, Jack?"

"No," he stated in a deep and definite voice. "I don't read."

Maddy blinked. She might have asked him if he wore pink stockings on a Saturday night. "But you do ride." He kept striding and she gave a skip to keep up. Okay. Obvious answer. No need to reply.

"I imagine you'll teach Beau to ride, too, one day," she tried again.

"Imagine I will."

Maddy nodded slowly, let the words sink in, and for the first time the finality of this situation truly hit.

The moment she'd stepped off the plane, she'd begun counting the seconds until she could flee this desolate place. But when she left she would also be leaving Beau behind, her best friend's beautiful gift to the world. When, if ever, would she see Beau again? There must be occasions when Jack flew to Sydney. Perhaps he could bring Beau, too,

Maddy was busy planning when they rounded the side of the homestead. A woman was moving down the wide front steps, winding her hands over a white apron, which was tied at the nape as well as around her ample girth. Her glossy hair was cropped short, polished jet threaded with silver. Soft lids hung over inquisitive cappuccino eyes, and as she rolled down each step, Maddy's nose picked up the mouth-watering smell of scones fresh from the oven.

Negotiating the last step, the woman extended both her hand and a cheery grin. Maddy smiled at the dab of flour on the woman's cheek and the aura of hominess and good humor she gave off.

"You must be Madison." The woman's grip was firm though not at all challenging. "I'm Cait." She nodded heartily, wiping her free hand down the apron. "Welcome to Leadeebrook."

"Jack's told me all about you."

Not exactly true. He'd provided minimal detail and only after some solid pressing. Cait Yolsen had been Leadeebrook's housekeeper for ten years. She was a widow with two children and two grown grandchildren. Maddy had been there when Jack had rung Cait to let her know to expect visitors. Afterward he'd relayed that Cait's cooking was exceptional. Maddy could taste those buttery scones now.

Cait moved close to Jack and the baby. Maddy's heart dissolved as Beau peered up at the stranger, eyes wide and intelligent, while he lay nestled in the crook of his uncle's arm.

Work-worn hands went to Cait's mouth as a hiccup of emotion escaped. "Oh, my, my, my." A tender smile glistened in her eyes. "Isn't he the handsome one." Her gaze darted to Maddy. "Did he sleep the whole way?"

"He was an angel—" Maddy turned to Jack "—wasn't he?"

Jack made a noise of affirmation, but the ghost of an approving smile lifted one corner of his mouth. *No colicky kid here.*

"He'll need a diaper change," said Cait.

"Absolutely," agreed Maddy.

Then they said together, "I'll take him."

But Jack rotated the baby away from two sets of eager hands.

Above those mirror glasses, his brow wrinkled. "Do I look helpless?"

Maddy blinked. "You want to *change* him?" In response, one wry dark brow rose. She rephrased. "I mean, don't you want a lesson or something first?"

"I've shorn over two hundred sheep in a single working day." He sidled past the women and up the steps. "I think I can shake a little talc and do up a couple of pins."

There *were* no pins; Dahlia had put Beau in disposables. That was what filled one of her big bags back on the plane. But Maddy held her tongue. If Jack wanted to assume the reins straight away—if he needed to dive in to prove himself—who was she to argue?

The man could shear two hundred sheep in one day.

At the top of the steps, Maddy noticed Nell, her dark eyes super-glued on Jack's every movement.

"You must be parched," Cait was saying as she ascended the steps, too.

When Nell padded into the homestead after Jack, Maddy followed the housekeeper. "I am a little dry."

"How's a cup of tea sound?"

"I'd prefer something cold, if you have it."

Still climbing, Cait gave a knowing, wistful sigh. "My husband was a stockman. We dated for two weeks and next I knew we were shacked up, working in the Northern Territory. Rugged land. Crocodiles, you know. Never thought I'd get used to the heat and the bull dust and the flies." The corners of her mouth swept up. "But you do."

Maddy blew at the hair clinging to her forehead. "I won't be here long enough to find out."

She had a career back in Sydney…friends…an exciting

full life. Needing to say goodbye to Beau until she saw him again would hurt terribly—she slapped another fly—but she already knew she wouldn't miss this place.

Halfway up, Cait stopped and touched the younger woman's hand. "I was sorry to hear about poor Dahlia. You must have been fast friends to help her out this way."

Maddy remembered how she'd made it through the chapel service yesterday with Beau asleep in her arms and a run of tears slipping quietly down her cheeks. Whenever the raw ache of emotion had threatened to break free, she'd concentrated on the pastor's calming words and the soft light filtering in through serene lofty windows.

Jack had sat beside her in the front left-hand pew. In an impeccable black suit, the set of his shoulders hadn't slipped once. Dahlia's university friends had recited prayers, poems or anecdotes, but her brother had kept his lidded gold-flecked eyes trained dead ahead.

Funneling down a breath, Maddy brought herself back and nodded. "Dahlia was the best friend I ever had."

Never too busy to listen. Never judgmental or rude. She was the easiest-going person Maddy had ever met. Which begged the question: how had two siblings with the same parents ended up with such different natures? Jack must be the most ornery person south of the equator.

Cait resumed her climb. "The bairn is lucky to have you."

Maddy smiled. Bairn as in baby.

"Dahlia wanted Jack to raise him," she explained. "I promised I'd help with the transition."

Cait dropped her gaze. "I'm sure she knew what she was doing."

Maddy's step faltered. Cait had reservations about Jack's suitability as a guardian, too? Dahlia hadn't got along with Jack; Maddy felt certain she, herself, would never penetrate his armor. Nell, on the other hand, idolized him. But Nell was a dog.

How had Jack treated his wife?

A curse blasted out of a nearby window and both women jumped. Maddy's palm pressed against her stomach. *Jack*. Was he having trouble opening the talc bottle?

Nausea crept up the back of her throat.

Oh Lord, had he dropped the baby?

Cait bolted, flinging open the front screen door, and when she sped into a room to the right, Maddy quickly followed. Her gaze landed on the baby, lying bare-bottomed on his back on a changing table, which was set up against a side wall. Jack stood before the table, his posture hunched, hands out, fingers spread, his expression darker than usual. He was gaping at a wet patch on his shirt while Beau kicked his feet and cooed. A bemused Nell was backed up in the corner, her head angled to one side.

When Jack had taken off the diaper, the baby must have squirted him.

Maddy cupped her mouth to catch the laugh. Why were the strongest men sometimes the biggest babies?

Struggling to compose herself, she sauntered forward. "I see you had a waterworks accident."

"*I* wasn't the one who had the accident." He touched the wet patch then flicked his hand. "At least he's a good aim."

Cait's chuckle came from behind. "I'll leave you both to do damage control," she said then asked about the baby's formula. Maddy handed her a bottle and can from a separate segment of Beau's bag. Cait called, "C'mon, Nell." The dog skulked out the doorway behind the housekeeper and Maddy gave a sigh of relief.

When Beau was cleaned up and in a fresh diaper,

Maddy slipped him carefully up and nuzzled her lips against his satin soft brow.

"I'm amazed he didn't freak out when you yelled like that," she said, rubbing the baby's back the way he liked. "I thought you might've dropped him."

When Maddy pivoted around, her mind froze solid while her response systems went into overload. His frown deep, Jack was grumbling, wrestling out of that soiled shirt.

Bronzed. Breathtakingly broad.

The walls seemed to darken and drag away at the same time the breath left her lungs and a sizzling, marvelous current swept through her body. Maddy unconsciously licked her lips.

Jack Prescott's chest was better than any she'd seen, airbrushed billboards included. His shoulders were sculpted from polished oak, his biceps were naturally, beautifully pumped, and the knockout expanse in between was dusted with the quintessential amount of coal black hair. She knew his flesh would be hot to the touch. Knew the landscape would be bedrock hard.

Maddy's gaze dropped.

And if that was the *top* half…

Cursing under his breath, Jack tore the sleeves from his arms and dumped the damp shirt at his feet.

He'd helped birth lambs more times than he could count. In comparison, this was child's play—literally. Being hosed by a baby wasn't a big deal. Three years ago he'd have done anything to have experienced just this kind of scene…to have been given the chance to care for his own little boy.

Raw emotion torqued in his chest. But he beat the pain

down before black memories took over. Feeling nothing was better than feeling angry.

Feeling helpless.

When he glanced up from the shirt, Maddy was standing stock still, jaw hanging. Holding Beau tight, she was staring at everything between his neck and his navel. Then her gaze dropped lower. Taken off guard—*again*—his muscles contracted as a coil of dark arousal snaked up his legs.

Inhaling, Jack set his jaw.

He'd already acknowledged his feelings for Madison Tyler. She was a looker, obviously intelligent. She also had guts. When Jack Prescott drew his pistols, most people had the good sense to run, but back in Sydney she'd stood her ground. She'd insisted she do right by his sister. He admired her for that. Frankly, his curiosity was piqued by the whole package.

But this physical attraction was headed nowhere. He was as good as engaged. Practically set to marry. Even if he *were* free, this woman wasn't what he needed. And vice versa. Clearly she was not the least impressed by what he held most dear—this rugged, sprawling land. Hell, she didn't even like *horses* whereas Tara was the only female he knew who could give him a run for his money galloping full bore down a straight.

So why was his gaze pinned to this woman's legs?

A growl of appreciation rumbled in his chest.

Because they were shapely, *that's* why. Long and milk white, and his fingers itched to know if they were as fine and silky smooth as they looked.

The baby squeaked and Jack came back to earth with a jolt. Shoving a hand through his hair, he shifted the thickness from his throat. He had no business indulging those images, particularly the vision of his houseguest in a negligee…the filmy, sultry kind that might wave and swirl around her slim ankles on a breezy summer night.

When heavy footfalls sounded down the timber floors of the hall, the full quota of Jack's senses came reeling back. Needing a distraction, he swiped his shirt off the floor and wadded it up while Maddy, seemingly needing a distraction, too, spun back to the changing table, busying herself with the baby's bag.

Jack had assumed a cool mask by the time Cait appeared and chimed, "Bottle's ready. I'd be happy to give him his feeding. It's been a long while." Cait extended her arms and Beau put out one of his. Sighing happily, she took and jiggled the wide-eyed baby. "Seems I haven't lost the touch." Then her attention skated over to his state of undress and her lips twitched. "Can I get you a fresh shirt, Jack?"

He held the wadded shirt higher and replied in a low, even voice. "S'right. I'll get one."

On her way out, the housekeeper tossed over one shoulder, "There's a pot of tea on the back veranda and a cool pitcher, too."

Maddy thanked Cait, flicked him an anxious glance, then, for something more to do, performed a fidgety finger comb of her flaxen hair behind each ear.

The entire "checking each other out" episode had lasted no more than a few seconds. They were a man and a woman who'd experienced a moment where natural attraction and physical impulse had temporarily taken over.

Jack drew up tall.

It wouldn't happen again. He hadn't brought city girl Madison Tyler here to seduce her. She was on his property only for the baby's sake. He owed that to his sister. But in two weeks, Maddy would be gone from Leadeebrook. Gone and out of his life. No use getting tangled up in it.

He headed for the door and didn't stop when her voice came from behind.

"Cait'll be a big help with Beau," she said, conversationally.

"She'll take good care of him."

"So you won't be hiring a nanny?"

"Won't need one."

Tara wanted a family. Now, ready or not, they had one. But there was time enough to tell Maddy about Beau's future stepmother. Time enough to let Tara know she was about to become an instant parent. After the news sank in, he couldn't imagine Tara would be anything other than pleased. But that wasn't the kind of information one shared over the phone. He'd tell her in person, in private.

Tomorrow was soon enough.

As he sauntered down the hall, Jack felt Maddy's gaze burning a hole in his back. Not meeting her eyes, he jerked a thumb toward his bedroom doorway.

"I'll grab a shirt and we'll get to that pot of tea."

A moment later he stood in front of his wardrobe, retrieving a button-down from its hanger. Out of the corner of his eye he spied movement—probably Nellie-girl keeping tabs on things. But when he checked, it was Maddy who hovered in the doorway, and this time her gaze wasn't fused on him. Her attention was riveted on the chest of drawers to her immediate right. On the photo he kept there and never put away.

Her face visibly pale, her round gaze hovered over to his.

"I—I'm sorry," she stammered. "I had no idea. I thought you must be going to the laundry. I thought the main bedroom would be upstairs."

Jaw tight, he drove his arms through the sleeves then, leaving buttons undone and tails hanging. He took her arm and ushered her out into the hall. Did she have to follow him around like a newborn calf? Was she purposely trying to get in the way and whip up his blood?

Once in the hall, he released his hold and told himself that would be the *last* time he'd feel her skin on his. If looking was bad, touching was a million times worse. Or was that a million times better?

Growling, he shook that unwelcome thought from his brain and headed toward the veranda, purposefully fastening each shirt button, then rolling the sleeves to the elbow. "Cait'll have set the tray out here."

Out on the veranda, he fell into a chair, lifted the food net and nodded at the spread of scones and cupcakes. After she accepted a scone, he grabbed a cake. He chomped off a mouthful and chewed, studying the plains and daring her to ask the question that must be tingling on the tip of her tongue. He could hear the words rattling around in her head.

The lady in the photo...was she your wife?

But Maddy didn't ask. Rather she sat quietly on the other side of the small square table, her chair backed up against the wall, as was his. She poured one glass of lemonade and one cup of tea and passed it over.

After a tense moment, he flicked her a sidelong glance. She was sipping her drink, surveying his favorite stretch of land—the dip between what was known on the property as Twelve Gum Ridge and Black Shore Creek. The knot binding the muscles between his shoulder blades eased fractionally. A moment more and he crossed an ankle over the opposite knee.

As three full-grown red kangaroos bounded across the shimmering horizon, Maddy sighed.

"I can't get over the quiet." She craned her neck, trying to see farther. "Where do you keep the sheep?"

He uncrossed his ankle and sat straighter. "Don't have any."

She tossed him a look. "Sorry. I thought you said you don't have any sheep."

"I got rid of them…three years ago."

She blinked several times then offered a nod as if she understood. But she didn't. Unless you'd lived the nightmare, no one could understand what it meant to lose both your wife and your child in one day. The world had looked black after that. As black and charred as his heart had been. He hadn't cared about sheep or money.

About anything.

"What do you do on a sheep station with no sheep?" she asked after a time. "Don't you get bored?"

He set down his cup and said what should have been obvious. "Leadeebrook is my home."

Urban folk weren't programmed to appreciate what the land had to offer. The freedom to think. The room to simply be. As much as his father had tried to convert her, his mother had never fully appreciated it either.

Besides, there was plenty of maintenance to keep a man busy if he went looking for it.

He dumped sugar into his cup. "It's a different way of living out here. A lot different from the city."

"A *lot*."

"No smog."

"No people."

"Just the way I like it."

"Don't you miss civilization?"

His face deadpanned. "Oh, I prefer being a barbarian."

She pursed her lips, considering. "That's a strong word, but in a pinch…"

He had every intention of staring her down, but a different emotion rose up and he grinned instead. They might not see eye to eye, but she was…amusing.

Seeing his grin, a smile lit her eyes and she sat back more. "How many acres do you have?"

"Now, just under five thousand. Back in its heyday, Leadeebrook was spread over three hundred thousand acres and carried two hundred thousand sheep, but after World War II land was needed for war service and agricultural settlement so my great-grandfather and grandfather decided to sell off plots to soldier settlers. The soil here is fertile. Their forward planning helped make an easier transition from grazing to farming. That industry's the mainstay of this district now. Keeps people employed."

"I take it back." Her voice carried a sincere note of respect. "You're not a barbarian."

"Save your opinion until after you've eaten my brown snake on an open spit."

She chuckled. "You do have a sense of humor." Her smile withered. "You are joking, right?"

He only spooned more sugar into his tea.

One leg crooked up under the other as she turned toward him. "Did you have a happy childhood growing up here?"

"Couldn't have asked for a better one. My family was wealthy. Probably far wealthier than most people even realized. But we lived a relatively simple life, with some good old-fashioned hard work thrown in for good measure."

"Where did you go to school?"

"Went to the town first off then boarding school in

Sydney. I came home every vacation. I'd help with dipping, shearing, lambing and tagging."

Her smile wistful, she laid her elbow on the table between them and cupped her jaw in her palm. "You make it sound almost romantic."

Almost?

He forced his gaze away from her mouth and let it settle on the picturesque horizon.

"Have you ever seen a sunset like that? I sit out here, lapping up those colors, and know this is how God intended for us to live. Not rushing around like maniacs on multilane freeways, chained to a computer fourteen hours a day. This is paradise."

Sue had thought the same way.

They sat saying nothing, simply looking at the rose-gold pallet darken against a distant smudge of hills. Most nights he took in the dusk, soaking in the sense of connectedness it gave. Sometimes, for a few moments, he felt half at peace.

"Will you ever stock up again?" she asked after a time.

He had plenty invested in bonds and real estate around the country. Despite the wool industry having seen better days, he was more comfortable financially than any of his ancestors, and had harbored dreams of reshaping Leadeebrook to its former glory. He and Sue used to discuss their ideas into the night, particularly during the last stages of her pregnancy. There'd been so much to look forward to and build on together. Now…

His stomach muscles double-clutched and he set his cup aside.

Now he was responsible for Dahlia's boy. He would give the lad every opportunity. Would care for him like a father. But that feeling…?

He swallowed against the stone in his throat.

He wished he could be the man he'd once been. But when his family died, that man had died, too.

"No," he said, his gaze returning to the sunset. "I'll never stock up again."

She was asking another question but his focus had shifted to a far off rumbling—the distant groan of a motor. He knew the vehicle. Knew the driver.

Lord and Holy Father.

He unfolded to his feet and groaned.

He wasn't ready for this meeting yet.

Four

The white Land Cruiser skidded to a stop a few feet from a nearby water tank, dry grass spewing out in dusty clouds from behind its monster wheels. A woman leaped out and, without shutting the driver's door, sailed up the back steps.

Maddy clutched her chair's arms while her gaze hunted down Jack.

He'd heard the engine before she had. Had pushed up and now came to a stop by the veranda rail, his weight shifted to one side so that the back pockets of his jeans and those big shoulders lay slightly askew. When the woman reached him, no words were exchanged. She merely bounced up on tiptoe, flung her arms around his neck and, her cheek to his, held on.

Maddy pressed back into the early evening shadows. This scene was obviously meant for two. Who was this woman? If she wasn't Jack Prescott's lover, she sure as rain wanted to be.

Maddy's gaze tracked downward.

The woman's riding boots—clean and expensive by the emblem—covered her fitted breeches to the knee. She was slender and toned; with a mane of ebony hair, loose and lush, she might have been the human equivalent of a prized thoroughbred. Her olive complexion hinted at Mediterranean descent and her onyx eyes were filled with affection as she drew back and peered up into Jack's— passionate and loyal.

Maddy's mouth pulled to one side.

Seemed Jack had indeed moved on since the death of his wife—the auburn-haired woman whose photo she'd seen on that chest of drawers. When they'd come face to face earlier in the nursery and she'd copped an eye full of Jack's all-male-and-then-some chest, she'd imagined he'd felt the moment, too. She'd told herself that's why he'd been particularly brusque afterward. The lightning bolt—the overwhelming awareness—had struck him, as well, and, taken aback, he hadn't known how to handle it.

But clearly that fiery, unexpected reaction had been one-sided. He'd seemed vexed by the scene in the nursery because he was embarrassed over her ogling. Embarrassed and annoyed. He was spoken for, and this woman in front of her might capture and hold any man, even I-am-an-island Jack Prescott.

With a fond but strained smile, Jack unfastened the woman's hold and her palms slid several inches down from his thick neck to his shirt. She toyed with a button as she gazed adoringly into his eyes and sighed.

"You're home." Then she tilted her head, that ebony mane spilled over her shoulder and her smile became a look of mild admonition. "I wish you'd have let me come to Sydney with you. It must have been so hard facing the funeral on your own. I shouldn't have promised that I'd stay behind."

Jack found her hand on his chest and carefully brought it to her side. "Tara, I brought somebody back with me."

The woman slowly straightened, blinked. Then, having dialed into her personal radar, she honed in on Maddy. The woman's thickly lashed eyes darkened more while her complexion dropped a shade. As their gazes locked, Tara surreptitiously found and held the veranda rail at her back.

Maddy's face flushed hot. She knew what this woman, Tara, was thinking. The accusation blazed in her eyes. But she and Jack were not an item. They weren't even friends, and from the venom building in this woman's eyes, the sooner she knew all the facts the better.

Maddy found her feet at the same time Jack beckoned her over.

"This is Madison Tyler," he said, then nodded to the woman. "Tara Anderson."

An uneven smile broke across Tara's face. "Madison. We haven't met before—" her eyes narrowed slightly "—have we?"

Jack stepped in. "Maddy's staying at Leadeebrook for a couple of weeks."

"Oh?" Tara's practiced smile almost quivered. "Why?"

Before anyone could answer, Cait appeared at the back doorway, holding Beau. The housekeeper's jovial expression slid when she recognized their visitor.

"Tara, love. I heard the truck. I thought it was Snow."

Tara's hand slipped off the rail and when her startled, glistening gaze slid from the baby to Jack, Maddy's heart sank in her chest. Tara's thoughts were as loud as war drums. She thought the child belonged to them—to her and Jack. Yet everything in Tara Anderson's stunned expression said she couldn't let herself believe the worst. She wanted to trust the man she so obviously cared for.

As if afraid he might vanish, Tara tentatively touched Jack's hand and her voice cracked when she asked, "Jack…?"

"This is Dahlia's son," he said in a somber tone. "The father isn't on the scene. Maddy was Dahlia's friend. She promised my sister she'd help the baby settle in here."

Drawing back, Tara audibly exhaled, then touched her brow with an unsteady hand. She shook her head as if to dispel a fog but her expression remained pained.

"Dahlia's son…" She breathed out again before her gaze pierced his. "You agreed to this, Jack? To a *baby?* I thought you said—"

His brows tipped together. "We won't discuss it now."

"When *were* we going to discuss it?" she asked. "How long have you known?"

But the line of his mouth remained firm. Turning, he set his hands on the rail and peered out over the barren landscape.

The anxiety in Maddy's stomach balled tighter. Hearing that Jack was responsible for a baby had been a massive shock for Tara Anderson; she wanted answers. Without knowing their history, Maddy couldn't help but think she deserved them. And yet Jack kept his shoulders set and his gaze fixed on something in the distance. He could be so bloody stubborn sometimes.

It wasn't her place to interfere, but if she could ease the tension a little by extending the hand of friendship, Maddy decided she would. If Jack and this woman were as close as this scene suggested, Beau would be seeing more of Tara…more than he would see of his aunt Maddy.

She edged closer. "Do you live in town, Tara?"

Tara's bewildered gaze whipped around, as if she'd forgotten they had company.

"I own the adjoining property," she said absently. Then a different emotion filtered over her face and she exhaled once more, this time with an apologetic smile. "Forgive me, please. I'm being rude. It's just…" She sought out Jack's gaze. "I've been worried these past days."

"Will you stay for supper?" Cait asked from the back door, giving Beau, who had half his fist in his mouth, a jiggle. "There's always plenty."

At the same time Tara quizzed Jack's face for his reaction, Maddy felt a brush against her leg. She lowered her gaze. Nell had taken up a seat between herself and Jack.

Stiffening, Maddy rubbed the goosebumps from her arm and slid a foot away. A mime act made more noise than this dog.

When Jack rotated away from the rail to face Tara, the familiar furrow between his brows was gone. Accommodating now, he reached for her hand. "Yes, of course. Stay for supper."

But Tara stole a quick glance between the baby and Maddy then, put on a lighthearted air and shook back her ebony hair.

"I would've liked to, but I'm staying in town tonight. Taking a buyer to dinner."

Jack eased back against the rail and crossed his arms over his chest, interested. "Which horse?"

"Hendrix." She addressed Maddy. "I breed Warmbloods."

Maddy raised her brows. And she was supposed to know what that meant? But she imitated Jack's cross-armed stance, pretending to be interested, too.

"That's…great."

"Warmbloods are bred for equestrian sports," Jack explained. "Tara's trained a stable full of champions, mainly Hanoverians."

Maddy tacked up her slipping smile. If she'd felt inadequate before…

No wonder Jack was involved with this woman. Beautiful, ultimately gracious under pressure, and a proven breeder of champions to boot. What more could a man want?

With an elegant, slightly possessive air, Tara looped her arm through Jack's. "Will you walk me down to the car?"

As Jack pushed off the rail, Maddy piped up, "If I don't see you before I head back to Sydney, it was nice meeting you."

Tara's lips tightened even as they stretched into a charming smile. "Oh, you'll see me."

As she and Jack meandered down the steps, Maddy couldn't help but notice—Tara didn't say goodbye to Beau.

Later that evening, Maddy went to join Jack in the yard. With his back to her, he didn't seem to hear her approach, so she cleared her throat and asked, "Don't suppose you want any company?"

When Jack turned his head—his eyes glittering in the evening shadows, his face devoid of emotion—Maddy drew back and withered in her shoes. She shouldn't have left the house and come outside. Standing amidst the cricket-clicking tranquility, it was clear Jack didn't want company. Particularly not hers.

After that awkward scene three hours ago with Tara Anderson, Jack had taken a vehicle out to the hangar to bring the bags in. Then he'd mumbled something about heading off for a while. From the window of her guest bedroom, Maddy had caught sight of a big black horse cantering away. With an Akubra slanted low on his brow, the rider looked as if he'd been born to rule from the saddle.

As he headed off toward the huge molten ball sinking into the hills, her chest had squeezed. She might have been watching a scene from a classic Western movie. Talk about larger than life.

While Cait prepared dinner, Maddy had enjoyed a quick shower. Then it was Beau's turn. He'd splashed and squealed in his bath until she had a stitch in her side from laughing and the front of her dress was soaked through. She didn't want to dwell on the fact that someone else would be enjoying this time with Beau soon.

Would that someone be Tara?

She neither saw nor heard Jack return, but when Cait called dinner, as if by magic he appeared in the meals room. With his gaze hooded and broad shoulders back, he'd promptly pulled out a chair for her at the table. She'd grinned to herself. Jack might be a lot of things, but Beau would learn his manners in this house.

The baked meal smelled divine, but Jack's masculine just-showered scent easily trumped it. His wet hair, slicked back off his brow, was long enough to lick the back of his white collar. He'd shaved, too, although the shadow on his jaw was a permanent feature…an enduring sexy sandpaper smudge.

When the baby was settled in the playpen beside the table, Jack had threaded his hands, bowed his head and said a brief but touching grace about missing loved ones and taking new ones into their home. Maddy had swallowed against the sudden lump in her throat. There was a deeper, more yielding side to this seemingly impenetrable man. There *must* be. In that moment, Maddy regretted she wouldn't come to know it.

As they sat down to dinner, Cait told Maddy of Leadeebrook's main dining room, with its long, grand table and crystal chandelier set in the center of a high, molded ceiling. But that room was kept for special occasions. She and Jack mainly ate here, in the meals area off the kitchen. After promising to show Maddy around the house the next day, Cait flicked out her linen napkin and asked to hear all the news from the city.

Jack didn't seem to care either way. The gold flecks gone from his eyes, he seemed more distracted than ever. While he cut and forked his way through the meal, the ladies chatted, watching over the baby who played with his bunch-of-keys rattle.

When Beau began to grumble, Maddy left to put him down. After firmly taking charge earlier, she was interested that Jack didn't say boo about helping with Beau's first bedtime in his new home. Maybe the memory of that wet shirt still haunted him, but Maddy suspected thoughts of Tara and her reaction to his guardianship of the baby weighed heavily on Jack's mind tonight. How would he handle the divide?

Beau had drifted off without a whimper. After laying a light sheet over his tiny sleeping form, she tiptoed back into the kitchen. That's when Cait had suggested she join Jack outside here in the cool.

Maddy had grown warm all over at the thought, which only proved that being alone with Jack under the expansive Southern Cross sky was not a good idea. But she'd made the effort. She didn't want to provoke any fires—physical or anything else—but neither could she afford to leave here, for the most part, a stranger. Jack had to know that if he needed her, for Beau's sake, despite any personal hiccups, she would always be there. Dahlia would've wanted that, and Maddy wanted that, too.

She and Jack needed to be able to communicate, at least on some level.

She'd found him here, one shoulder propped up against an ancient-looking tree, while he rubbed a rag over a bridle.

"Is the baby down?" he asked.

With nerves jittering in her stomach, she nodded and inched closer. "Now he's down, he shouldn't wake up till around seven."

Stopping at his side, she joined him in taking in a view of the hushed starry sky while that rag worked methodically over the steel bit. A horse's whinny carried on a fresh breeze. A frog's lonely croak echoed nearby. And Jack kept polishing.

If anyone was going to start a conversation, it'd have to be her.

She shifted her weight. "How long have you had the black horse?"

"From a colt."

"Bet he was glad to see you back."

"Not as glad as I was to see him."

She raised her brows. Well, a cowboy's best friend was supposed to be his horse.

She leaned against another nearby tree, her hands laced behind the small of her back. "Where did you ride off to earlier?"

"I needed to catch up with Snow Gibson. He lives in the caretaker's cabin a couple miles out."

Maddy recalled an earlier conversation. "Cait said Snow's quite a character."

A hint of a smile hooked his mouth and they both

fell into silence again…tangible and yet not entirely uncomfortable. Guess there was something to be said for the advantages of this untainted country air.

Giving into a whim, she shut her eyes, tilted her face to the stars and let more than the subtle breeze whisper to her senses. She imagined she felt that magnetism rippling off Jack Prescott in a series of heatwaves and her own aura glowing and transforming in response. She imagined the way his slightly roughened hands might feel sliding over her skin…sensual, stirring. Enthralling.

Opening her eyes, willing away the awareness, she shut off those dangerous thoughts and focused on a heavy star hanging low on the horizon. She wasn't here to indulge in fantasies, no matter how sweet or how strong. She was here to do a job and get back to where she belonged.

Besides, Jack's affections were spoken for. Tara had made her position on that clear: *Hands off.*

Suddenly weary, Maddy pushed off the tree.

She shouldn't have come out here. Talking with Jack was like trying to push an elephant up a hill. She needed to accept this situation for what it was. She needed to chill out and let things between herself and Jack unravel naturally. Right now, she needed to say good-night.

She was about to take her leave when Jack's deep graveled voice drifted through the night.

"This property's been in my family since 1869." He angled his head toward a long stationary shadow to their left. "See that trough?"

He began to walk. Maddy threw a look at the back door then inwardly shrugged. Slapping the impression of bark from her palms, she followed. If he was making an effort, she would, too.

"This trough was a wedding gift," Jack was saying. "My great-great grandfather suggested to his wife he should cut a hole in the bathroom wall and they could use it as a tub as well as to water the horses in the yard."

Maddy blanched. She had a feeling he was serious. *Thank heaven for modern-day plumbing. How had women survived out here back then?*

"I carved my initials here when I was six," he went on and swept one long tanned finger over an etching in the wood. "Our dog had just had pups." He pointed to several nicks—One, two, three... Seven pups. He straightened and, studying her, weighed the bridle in his hand. "You never had a dog?"

"I had piano lessons and lots of dresses."

"But no dog," he persisted.

"No dog."

Something rustled in the brush nearby at the same time he lifted and dropped one shoulder. "You missed out."

Focused on the brush—was it a snake, a dingo?—she admitted, "I was attacked by a Doberman cross when I was young."

His expression froze before he blindly set the bridle down on the trough. "Maddy...God, I'm sorry."

Weeks spent in hospital, years of fighting the phobia. She made herself shrug. "Could've been worse."

He held her gaze for several heartbeats then slipped her a wry smile. "I got the shakes once. I broke my arm jumping a stallion over a creek when I was ten. He was the most cantankerous horse I've ever known."

Maddy openly grinned. Quite the confession coming from Crocodile Dundee.

He walked again, a meandering comfortable gait that invited her to join him.

"Piano and dresses," he murmured. "So you were a mummy's girl."

"My mother died when I was five."

His step faltered. She almost saw the shudder pass through his body. "Wait a minute. I need to take that other foot out of my mouth."

She wasn't offended. He couldn't have known.

"I have one perfect memory of her tucking me into bed. She had a beautiful smile." Her favorite photo she kept in her wallet—a candid shot of her mother laughing and holding her first and only baby high against a clear blue day.

"Your dad still around?"

The snapshot in Maddy's mind faded and she squared her shoulders. "Uh-huh. He's great. Really energized. I work for him at Tyler Advertising."

"I've heard of it. Well-respected firm." He kicked a rock with the toe of his boot. "So you're a chip off the ol' block?"

"Hopefully. I have my first big deal coming together soon."

"In for a big bonus?"

"I guess."

In the moonlight, his lidded gaze assessed her. "But that's not your motivation."

"Not at all."

"You want to make your father proud," he surmised and she nodded.

"That's not so unusual. Besides I really like the industry," she added. "Lots of exciting people and events. It's where I belong."

She believed that and finally her father was believing it, too. She'd seen the look in his eyes when she'd told him at sixteen she wanted to be an account executive with the firm; he didn't think she had it in her. He'd said the words, *You're more like your mother,* which meant she wasn't strong enough. Her mother had been a gentle person and, no, she hadn't been able to beat the leukemia, but she and her mother were two separate issues, two separate people. And once she had the client's signature on the bottom line…

"You must be chomping at the bit to get back," Jack said, coming to stand beside a weathered post and rail fence.

Her lips twitched. "I won't deny I'll be happy to leave the flies behind."

"They don't eat much. It's the bull ants you have to worry about."

"So I'd better not stand in one spot for too long."

He chuckled—a rich easy sound that fit him as well as those delectable jeans. She couldn't think of another man with more sex appeal…the energy he expelled was as formidable and natural as thunder on a stormy night. On the *What Makes a Man Maddeningly Irresistible* list, Jack got double ticks in every box.

When she realized their shared look had lasted longer than it ought to, a blush bloomed over her cheeks. As the heat spread to her breasts and belly, Jack rubbed the back of his neck and moved off again.

"How did you meet Dahlia?"

"A university friend," she said, willing the husky quality from her voice. "Dahlia was a couple of years younger than me. We were enrolled in different majors, but we met at a party and hit it off. She had the best laugh. Infectious." *Kind of like yours,* she wanted to say, *only not so deep.*

Looking off, he scrubbed his temple with a knuckle. "Yeah. I remember her laugh."

Maddy stayed the impulse to touch his arm—to offer some show of comfort. Men like Jack were all about strength, intelligence and making decisions. Jack was a leader and leaders didn't dilute their power with displays of emotion, either given or received. In an emergency, he would act and act well. Even standing in the uneventful quiet of this night, Maddy found a sense of reassurance in knowing that. Some silly part of her almost wanted to admit it out loud.

Instead she said, "You must have missed that sound when she left here."

A muscle ticked a strong beat in his jaw and he let out a long breath. "My wife begged me to go after her but I was determined not to. Some sorry home truths came out that last night. I figured if Dahlia wanted to find her own way, I wouldn't stop her."

But his tone said he regretted it.

"She didn't like Leadeebrook?"

"She liked it okay," he said, crossing his arms as he strolled, "but she didn't feel the same way I feel. The way my father felt, too. She didn't want to stay here, 'shrivel up and die,' as she put it. She'd said she'd had enough of station existence to last a lifetime."

Which would have cut her brother's loyal Prescott heart in two.

"And your wife…how did she feel about the station?"

He searched the sky as if she might be listening and looking down, and Maddy knew in that moment that he'd loved his wife very much.

"This was Sue's home. Always will be." His thoughtful expression sharpened then, frowning, he angled toward the house. "Was that the baby?"

Maddy listened then shook her head. "I didn't hear anything. Cait said she'd keep an ear out." They walked again, toward a timber structure she thought was the stables. When next she spoke, Maddy put a lighter note in her tone.

"Tara Anderson is obviously a big fan of the land, too."

His gaze caught hers and as his look intensified, Maddy's skin flared with a pleasant, telling warmth. The way he was looking at her now, she could almost fool herself into believing that she, not Tara, was the woman with whom he was involved…that the primal heat smoldering in his eyes was meant for her and her only.

When a different, more guarded light rose up in his eyes and he broke the gaze, Maddy's shoulders dropped and she told her pulse to slow down. Dynamic in every sense of the word, he was more of a man than any she'd known. That was the reason she imagined heat waves rippling off him and wrapping themselves around her. Not because this moonlight was affecting him as it was clearly affecting her.

"Tara and I have known each other a long while," he said. "Her uncle and my father were friends. Sue and Tara became good friends, too. They shared similar values, similar interests. So do we."

"Are you going to marry her?"

A red-hot bolt dropped through her middle at the same time her eyes grew to saucers and she swallowed a gulping breath. Had she actually said that? Yes, she'd been wondering—a lot. But to *ask*…

She held up both hands. "I'm sorry. That is so none of my business."

Beneath the star-strewn sky, Jack's gaze held hers for a protracted moment. Then he set his hands low on his belt and tracked his narrowed gaze over to the distant peaks of the Great Dividing Range.

He nodded. "There's been talk of it."

Maddy let out that breath. So Tara had good reason to be so demonstrative this afternoon. She saw Jack as her future husband. A husband who'd gone to a funeral and had brought back a baby.

Maddy chewed her lip. She shouldn't ask—she might not like the answer—but she couldn't keep the question down.

"Does Tara like children?"

He scratched the tip of his ear. "That's a sticking point. Tara wants a family very much…"

He'd been slow to accept responsibility for Beau. He approached his guardianship as a duty to be performed rather than a gift to be treasured. Now he was admitting that he didn't want a family.

Maddy knew one day she wanted be a mother. Caring for Beau had only heightened that knowledge. She couldn't imagine why any person wouldn't want to have their own family—to give and receive unconditional love. What had Jack's first wife to say about his aversion to fatherhood? More importantly, what did that admission mean for Beau?

She'd hoped, she'd prayed, but did Jack have what it took to be a good father to that baby? And there was Tara. She hadn't shown an interest in Beau other than out of shock and suspicion yet she wanted children of her own. If she and Jack married—if they had children together—would Tara see Beau as a nuisance or inconvenience when her own brood came along? If that were the case, what sort of family would poor Beau grow up in? What sort of damaged self-image would being an add-on leave him with?

A whinny sounded in the night and Maddy was brought back.

"Herc can hear us," Jack told her and jerked a thumb at the stables. "Want to meet him?"

Deep in thought, Maddy absently agreed but before

long the scent of horse and leather pulled her up. With a sneeze tickling her nose, she made an excuse.

"It's getting late. We probably shouldn't disturb him."

Jack laughed and kept walking. "Herc won't mind the company."

She pinched her nose. "I think I might be allergic."

That got his attention and he angled back around. "Have you been around horses before?"

"A real one?"

He grinned—a breathtaking, cheeky smile—and Maddy's breasts tingled with unbidden desire.

"You know, Maddy, there's nothing quite like the rhythm of a strong dependable horse rocking beneath you."

Rhythm…strong…rocking. Maddy blew out a breath. She wanted to fan herself. Did he have any clue how fiercely attractive he was?

"Thanks," she announced, dabbing her brow, "but I'll pass."

That smile widened and she imagined the fire in his eyes had licked her lips.

"Why not broaden your horizons? There's more to life than a wardrobe of pretty dresses."

"Or a stable of horses."

"You're right."

He sauntered over to stand, shoulder to shoulder, beside her as he checked out the trillion-star lightshow dancing over their heads. His innate energy—the physical pull she felt when he was this close—was as tangible as his body heat. She wished he hadn't moved nearer. And, dammit, she wished he'd moved nearer still.

"There's a cool breeze after a long muggy spell," he said, "and the dependability of a vast rich land like this. There's the satisfaction that comes with a hard day's work, and the lure of a full moon on a still night just like tonight. And then…"

His dark brows nudged together as if an odd idea had struck. When he turned his head, his expression had softened with an emotion she hadn't seen in him before. He blinked once then, as if he'd read all her earlier thoughts, he cupped her cheek and she stopped breathing.

"And then," he said, "there's this."

The pad of his thumb raised her chin and as his head dropped over hers, Maddy's faculties shut down. She might have wondered, might have dreamed, but having Jack Prescott's undivided smoldering attention focused only upon her had seemed beyond reason or possibility.

And yet now…

Maddy trembled, leaned in and pressed up.

With his mouth closed so perfectly over hers and his hard muscular frame pressed in tight all the world seemed to spiral away. With her heart beating high and hard, she couldn't think beyond the thrill of this moment, beyond the wonder of his fingertips working against her nape… the heavy throb low in her belly…and a fiery internal pulse that whispered to her about the promise of a slow, hot night spent in Jack Prescott's bed.

His thumb ran down her throat as he sipped and tasted and explored. When his mouth reluctantly left hers and her heavy eyelids opened, his eyes were smiling into hers. A delicious full-body quiver ran through her blood. She was light-headed, dizzy. Had Jack truly just kissed her? Had she truly kissed him back? On one level she couldn't digest the reality. The possibility that he would embrace her, gift her with the world's steamiest kiss, didn't compute. And yet as she stood now looking up into the shadowed perfection of his face, improbability faded into another understanding.

Her belly felt heavy with a need that acknowledged only deep physical desire. She wanted his mouth on hers again. With a longing she hadn't known she was capable of, she wanted his lips on her neck, on her breasts.

He stole another light, lingering kiss from the side of her mouth before his lips skimmed her jaw. "See what I mean about that full moon?"

His hand slid down her spine to circle the sensitive dip low in her back and the urge to coil her fingers up through his hair and mold herself against him became overpowering. Every labored breath compounded the desire building in her blood. Every thought confirmed that this felt way too good to let go.

How a bit of common sense survived the fire ripping through her veins, Maddy couldn't say. She didn't want to listen to reason. She only wanted to know his kiss again and again. And yet the danger…the *dishonesty* of this situation was as apparent as the aching desire. As much as she wanted to, she couldn't ignore the harm this kind of scene could and would do.

Finding her strength and her breath, she angled her head away. "This isn't right."

With a knuckle, he coaxed her mouth back to his. "This is *very* right."

When he drew her bottom lip into his mouth and the shaft behind his zipper flexed against her belly, her resolve slipped like hot wax spilling down a candle. The urge to give in was so sweet and so strong…but she couldn't ignore what was most important.

She pushed against his sturdy chest. "Jack, what about Tara?"

They needed to keep this complicated time as uncomplicated as they could. Yes, she was physically drawn to Jack—she'd like to meet a woman who wouldn't be. But a kiss would lead to more—to dark heady places she wasn't prepared to go. She wanted some kind of future with Beau. The last thing she needed was an ill-planned night hanging over her head and a stepmother who would then have good reason for suspicion.

He'd been so intense, so driven, she half expected him to ignore the obvious question. But he surprised her. Comprehension dawned in his eyes. His head pulled slowly back and his gaze searched hers as if he were coming out of a daze. When the horse whinnied again, he took a step away and his previously insistent palm left her back. His hand found the V at his opened collar and his gaze speared through her, as though he were seeing someone else.

His deep voice rumbled through the shadows.

"You should go inside."

A shiver chased up her spine. His face looked changed… almost vulnerable. Gingerly, she touched his strong hot arm but his intense expression didn't change.

He said again, "You should go."

Then he wove around her toward the stable.

Later, as she lay awake in bed staring at the ceiling, she heard the retreating beat of hooves. Still glowing from the feel of him, still buzzing from the high, she rolled over and lightly touched her lips.

She thought she'd been kissed before. Thought she knew what desire was…how it felt to be on fire.

She'd been wrong.

Five

The next morning, Jack drove into Hawksborough, a town that pretty much consisted of a main street lined with Leopard trees, a federation-style library, town hall and courthouse, and a series of fading shop fronts which led to the Shangri-la Motel.

Parked in front of Bruce's Barber's, a residence which co-let to Hawsborough's only bank, Jack swung out of the driver's side of his four-wheel drive and absorbed the town's aura of timelessness. Sue had loved this place almost as much as she'd loved the station. If he ever came in, Sue would, too, to catch up with the locals then veg out in the town square, working her way through one of her tomes. Sue had been as laid back as supper on Sundays.

Sophisticated Madison Tyler, on the other hand, fit in more with canapés and cocktails at five. She would find Hawksborough's sole set of traffic lights and single movie theater gauche. Possibly unsettling. Maddy cared about what happened to Dahlia's baby—he respected her for that—but as soon as her job here was done she'd be gone, back to the city and "civilization". Thirteen more days.

And nights.

As he removed his hat and crossed into the Shangri-la foyer, Jack knew he could fool himself and say he understood why he'd cast off proper conduct last night: he'd wanted to sample an intriguing wine, just a taste. He'd kissed Maddy. Had enjoyed the act immensely. Curiosity supposedly done and dusted. Trouble was, while all this rationalizing had been taking place, he'd forgotten about Tara. About the commitment he'd made to her. And that just wasn't him.

That Maddy was so different from Sue, from Tara— from any woman he'd known—might be a reason for his behavior but it wasn't an excuse. He felt off-center around her. Couldn't seem to shake her from his thoughts. At four this morning he'd finally figured out what needed to be done and how he should do it.

Now he strode up to Mrs. Claudia, the friendly gray-haired receptionist he'd known all his life. She slid the *Life* crossword to one side of the mahogany desk and they exchanged pleasantries about her aging canary and the lack of rain. Then he dialed up to the room Tara took whenever she stayed in town.

When she picked up on the second ring, Jack braced his shoulders. "Tara, I need to see you."

There was a moment's pause before a sigh came down the line. "Jack, it's you. Thank God. Come up."

From her thready tone, something wasn't right in her world. He could guess what. But as he set off for the vintage elevator, Jack knew he couldn't let any bad news delay his own.

When Tara opened her door, her hair was as glossy as

usual but her eyes didn't hold their normal fire. She lifted a large envelope and gave a jaded smile.

"Hendrix's X-rays. There's a small cyst on his hock. In my opinion, and the vet's, nothing to worry about." She flung the envelope on the TV stand. "But the buyer wants a cut in price."

"Three hundred G's is a lot for a horse," he said, hanging his hat on the hatstand.

"Not for a brilliant jumper." Then her dark eyes softened and an inviting smile curved her lips. "But let's not talk about that."

She took his hand and led him toward the bed. Jack kept his eyes straight ahead but even a blind man couldn't miss her attire: a short, pale pink silk wrap. From the outline, she was naked underneath.

She drew him toward the foot of the unmade bed. Positioning herself close, she wove her hands up his shirt front then, closing her eyes, she reached on tiptoe to rub her nose with his.

"It's so good to see you." Her fingers flexed in his shirt as she murmured, "Will I order up some breakfast?"

"I've eaten."

She opened her eyes at his tone and angled her head. "I need to apologize for the way I acted yesterday. But, you have to understand, I was taken aback. The last thing I expected to see was a baby—" she lowered to sit on the rumpled sheet "—or another woman." Twining her fingers with his, she urged him to sit beside her. "But I should've shown more control. You're right. We need to speak about this in private." She pivoted toward him, her wrap slipped but she didn't cover her thigh. "How do you feel about raising Dahlia's son?"

He set his jaw. "Committed."

"There is one big positive."

"You mean besides giving my nephew a home."

"Of course that baby deserves a home." Her touch filed over his thigh and settled on his leg. "And now there's no reason why *we* shouldn't start a family. I understand how you feel about losing your own. Jack, I can't imagine how much that must hurt, even now. But being given this baby is like being given another chance. We could give that little boy a brother or two." Her hand squeezed. "A real family, for us all."

He pushed to his feet and her hand fell away. "We need to talk."

"If you're worried about inheritance—that I might be biased toward the children we have together—I'm more than fine with all the children having equal shares..."

"I can't marry you."

She recoiled as if bitten by a snake. Her slender throat worked up and down as moisture welled in her eyes. His gut twisted around a heavy knot of guilt. There'd been no easy way to say it. But the admission had sounded blunt even to his ears.

"You can't marry..." She carefully unfolded to her feet. "We've discussed this. Gone through it." She stepped closer and a note of desperation lifted her voice. "What about the land?"

"I don't *care* about the land."

He cursed under his breath and scrubbed his brow.

Of course he cared, but...

Decided, he met her gaze. "I can't think about that now."

"It's that woman, isn't it?" Her slim nostrils flared. "How long have you known her?"

He told her the truth. "I met Maddy the same day I learned about Dahlia."

"Then she's a quick worker, getting you to agree to have her stay here."

"It wasn't like that."

Tara might have more reason than she knew to be jealous but it hadn't started out that way. Maddy hadn't set a trap to ensnare an eligible bachelor. She'd made a vow and had come to Leadeebrook when she would rather not have. Her loyalty to his sister, her indignation toward him, hadn't been an act.

Neither was the passion he'd felt break free when he'd held her last night. His palms had itched to shape over her curves. Conscience hadn't been an issue. The primal need to know every inch of her had overshadowed everything.

Tara was imploring him with her eyes.

"Tell me nothing's going on, Jack. Tell me and I'll believe you. You've made mistakes before." The passionate look wavered. "You don't want to make another one."

His eyes narrowed. He'd forget she said that.

"Tara, you and I are friends. I'll always think of you as a friend."

"Friendship can turn into love." She held his jaw and hitched up to slip her lips over his. "It did for me."

He found her hand and held it between both of his. "It's better this way."

He'd married once. He should have known that would do him a lifetime. The ring he wore around his neck would always live there.

But as he threw his hat back on and left the motel a few minutes later, he reminded himself that physical intimacy was another matter. No license was required to satisfy sexual needs. Needs every man had. Natural, instinctive. In this instance, fierce.

The chemistry was right between Maddy and him.

Yesterday under the stars, it had been near uncontainable. Whether this fever was due to the upheaval of emotion these past days—the lasting bond he and Maddy had shared with Dahlia—he couldn't say. All he knew with absolute certainty was he'd been attracted to Madison Tyler from the start. The attraction had grown to a point where, no matter what excuse he made, he couldn't deny it.

He wanted her in his bed.

The primal urge was a force unto itself, demanding release, stoking his mind like a stick at a fire every other minute of the day. He'd never felt this intensely about a woman, not even Sue. He'd never gone there with Tara, neither in mind nor in body.

After the way Maddy had held onto him in the moonlight, her fingers twisting in his shirt, her mouth opening under his, inviting and welcoming him in…

Inhaling, he slipped into his vehicle, ignited the engine and pulled away from the curb.

It was foregone. Maddy felt the same way. She wanted what he wanted. Before the week was through, he would convince her they should take it.

Call back. Urgent re Pompadour account.

Biting her lip, Maddy shifted her gaze from the text message to baby Beau lying, happy and energetic, on a nearby blanket.

Beau had had his lunchtime bottle but had been too restless to go down. She'd done some research; babies' routines changed all the time—teething problems, going to solids, natural decline in naps—all shook up what might seem like a set schedule. Rather than fight the tide, she'd spread a blanket out beneath the sprawling umbrella of a Poinciana tree and for the past twenty minutes had watched him kick and coo to his heart's content.

Although everyone back home knew she was unavailable, out of habit she'd brought along her BlackBerry. While her father had been frosty about her request for this unscheduled break, he wouldn't have left that message without good reason.

Maddy set the phone against her chin as her stomach flipped over.

Urgent…

Had Pompadour Shoes pulled the plug without having seen the campaign? Had another agency stolen their business? Or worse…had her father's disappointment turned to action? Had he replaced her on the account?

Her thumb was poised over Redial when Nell appeared out of nowhere and sat herself down a few feet away. Maddy's blood pressure climbed and she reached for Beau who, unconcerned, gnawed on a length of his rattle. But Nell's attention was elsewhere…fixed on the hazy distance, her ears perked high.

Maddy breathed—slowly in, calmly out.

If the dog wanted to sit around, okay. She didn't have dibs on this square of lawn, as long as Nell didn't get any ideas about wanting to socialize. But when Beau began to grumble, Nell trotted over and the hairs on the back of Maddy's neck stood up straight. Thankfully the collie didn't stop and soon Maddy knew why. The sound of an engine. The same sound she'd heard leaving the property early that morning.

Jack was home.

Maddy's heart began to thud. How would he tackle the subject of last night? Maybe he wouldn't bring up that kiss at all, which was fine by her. During the hours before dawn, she'd reflected enough on the blissful way his mouth had worked over hers. Useless thoughts had wound a never-ending loop in her mind, like what if Cait had discovered them? Where would it have led if she hadn't pulled away?

Maddy shuddered. The fallout didn't bear considering. If not another word was mentioned about that accident, she'd be happy. Surely Jack—a man considering marriage—felt the same way. As far as she was concerned, that caress never happened.

Nell belted a path out into the open space and a few moments later reappeared, ushering in the late model four-wheel drive. The vehicle braked and when the door opened, Maddy's limbs turned to jelly. Setting his Akubra in place, Jack angled out, looking taller and more formidable than she remembered.

Everything about him spoke of confidence and ability. Raw outback masculinity and pride. Good thing he *was* practically engaged or she might forget her resolve about last night's embarrassment and launch herself at him.

He made a motion. Nell rolled over and he rubbed her belly with the toe of his big boot. Patting her damp palms on her khaki pants, Maddy pasted on a nondescript smile. When Jack's gaze tracked her down, she gave a business-as-usual salute. He acknowledged her with a short nod and headed over. With each long, measured stride, her heart beat more wildly. She looked at those strong, large hands and felt them kneading her nape, pressing meaningfully on her back. She saw the shadow on his jaw and relived the delicious graze against her cheek, around her lips.

The next thirteen days would be tantamount to torture—not wanting to say goodbye to Beau, yet having to get back to Sydney. Needing to leave the memory of that kiss behind yet craving to know the sensation again. Talk about chronic inner turmoil.

Jack hunkered down beside the baby, his boots dusty and blue jeans stretched at the knee. When Beau's rattle slipped from his tiny grasp, Jack picked it up and shook the plastic keys until Beau grabbed and stuck one back in his mouth.

A side of Jack's mouth hiked up. "Guess he's hungry."

"He's had lunch. I think he's ready to be put down."

Jack tickled Beau's tummy and, enjoying it, the baby squawked and threw the keys down. Jack chuckled softly. "He looks like Dahlia. Same cheeky grin."

Maddy smiled. *Cheeky grins must run in the family.* Whenever Jack smiled at her that certain way, whenever his gaze dipped to stroke her lips, she could dissolve into a puddle, no problem at all. Guess he'd worked that out last night.

Cait called from the top of the stairs. "Want some lunch, Jock?"

Still on haunches, he swiveled around on the toes of his boots. "I'll get something later."

Cait nodded. "Can I put the bairn down for you, Maddy?"

"I can do it," Maddy called back.

But Cait was already on her way. "You can indeed. But he hasn't been out of your sight since seven this morning."

Jack scooped the baby up and gave him a little bounce in the air before handing him up to Cait.

Beaming, Cait brought him close. "Now it's my turn for a wee cuddle."

Beau looked so at home in Cait's arms, Maddy had no reason to cut in…except, after Cait and Beau's departure, she and Jack would be left completely alone. The idea set her pulse hammering all the more.

As Cait and the baby vanished back into the house,

Maddy gathered her highly-strung nerves. She'd simply have to deal with this situation in an adult-like manner. She'd offer a sentence or two while keeping communication friendly but unquestionably aboveboard. Then, after a reasonably short amount of time, she could follow Cait inside. Distance, and safety from possible humiliation and regret, accomplished.

With a blithe air, she collected her BlackBerry off the blanket. "Interesting that Cait calls you Jock."

"Jock. Jack. Jum. All short for James."

Maddy's insides clutched. Jack was James?

She remembered his reaction—the flinch—that first day she'd told him the baby's name. He and Dahlia hadn't spoken in years and yet she'd named her baby in part after her big brother—Beau James. Maddy could only imagine the stab of guilt when he heard. The gut wrench of regret and humility.

Her voice was soft. "It must've meant a lot to know Dahlia remembered you that way."

He removed his hat and filed a hand through his thick hair. "It was our grandfather's name, too. A family name. But, yeah, it was…nice."

Staring at his hat, he ran a finger and thumb around the felt rim then pushed to his feet. Squinting against the sun sitting high in the cloudless sky, he glanced around.

"Great day. Not too hot." He cocked a brow at her. "How about a ride?"

Maddy couldn't help it. She laughed. He never gave up. Which could be a problem if he applied that philosophy to what had happened outside the stables last night. But he hadn't needed convincing; when she'd put up the wall, reminded him of a couple of facts, he'd promptly taken his leave.

At his core, Jack was an old fashioned type. He'd had

an emotional wreck of a week. Their talk beneath the full moon—the comfortable, dreamy atmosphere it created—had caught them both unprepared. Now, however, they were fully aware of the dangers close proximity could bring. He was involved with another woman. Maddy had no intention of kissing Jack Prescott again.

She had less intention of jumping on a horse.

With a finger swipe, she alleviated her phone's screen of fine dust. "Think I'll leave the rodeo tricks to the experts."

"You don't have to leap six-foot fences. We can start off at a walk. Or we could double."

Maddy guffawed. With her arms around his waist, her breasts rubbing against his back… After seeing reason so soundly last night, surely he knew that suggestion was akin to teasing a fuse with a lit match.

"I'll get you riding," he went on, setting that distinctive hat back on his head, "even if I have to seize the moment and throw you on bareback."

The oxygen in her lungs began to burn. Quizzing his hooded gaze, she knew she wasn't mistaken. He wasn't talking about horses anymore and he wanted her to know it.

"In the meantime—" he offered her his hand "—what say I take you on a tour of Leadeebrook's woolshed."

Her thoughts still on riding bareback, Maddy accepted his hand before she'd thought. The skin on sizzling skin contact ignited a pheromone soaked spark that crackled all the way up her arm. On top of that, he'd pulled too hard. Catapulted into the air, her feet landed far too close to his. Once she'd got her breath and her bearings, her gaze butted with his. The message in his eyes said nothing about awkwardness or caution.

In fact, he looked unnervingly assured.

* * *

After a short drive, during which Maddy glued her shoulder to the passenger side to keep some semblance of distance between them, they arrived at a massive wooden structure set in a vast clearing.

"It looks like a ghost town now," Jack said, opening her door. "But when shearing was on, this place was a whirlwind of noise and activity."

Maddy took in the adjacent slow spinning windmill, a wire fence glinting in the distance and felt the cogs of time wind back. As they strolled up a grated ramp, she imagined she heard the commotion of workers amid thousands of sheep getting the excitement of shearing season underway. Sydney kept changing—higher skyscrapers, more traffic, extra tourists—yet the scene she pictured here might have been the same for a hundred years.

When they stepped into the building, Maddy suddenly felt very small and, at the same time, strangely enlivened. She rotated an awe-struck three-sixty. "It's massive."

"Eighty-two meters long, built in 1860 with enough room to accommodate fifty-two blade shearers. Thirty years on, the shed was converted to thirty-six stands of machine shears, powered by steam. Ten manual blade stands were kept, though, to hand shear stud sheep."

"Rams, you mean?"

"Can't risk losing anything valuable if the machinery goes mad."

She downplayed a grin. *Typical man.*

Their footsteps echoed through lofty rafters, some laced with tangles of cobwebs which muffled the occasional beat of sparrows' wings. Through numerous gaps in the rough side paneling, daylight slanted in, drawing crooked streaks on the raised floor. Dry earth, weathered wood and, beneath that, a smell that reminded her of the livestock pavilion at Sydney's Royal Easter Show.

Maddy pointed out the railed enclosures that took up a stretch of the vast room. "Is that where the sheep line up to have their sweaters taken off?"

He slapped a rail. "Each catching pen holds enough sheep for a two-hour shearing stint. A roustabout'll haul a sheep out of the pen onto a board—" he moved toward a mechanism attached to a long cord—powered shears "—and the shearer handles things from there. Once the fleece is removed, the sheep's popped through a moneybox, where she slides down a shute into a counting pen."

"Moneybox?"

He crossed the floor and clapped a rectangular frame on the wall. "One of these trap doors."

"Must be a cheery job." She mentioned the name of a famous shearing tune, then snapped her fingers in time with part of the chorus and sang, "'Click, click, click.'"

When his green eyes showed his laughter, a hot knot pulled low at her core and Maddy had to school her features against revealing any hint of the sensation. A wicked smile. A lidded look. Being alone with Jack was never a good idea.

"A great Aussie song," he said, "but unfortunately, not accurate."

Reaching high, he drew a dented tin box off a grimy shelf. Maddy watched, her gaze lapping over the cords in his forearms as he opened the lid. Her heart skipped several beats as her eyes wandered higher to skim over his magnificent shoulders, his incredibly masculine chest. When that burning knot pulled again, she inhaled, forced her gaze away and realized that he'd removed something from the tin—a pair of manual shears, which looked like an extra large pair of very basic scissors.

"A shearer would keep these sharper than a cut throat," he told her. "The idea wasn't to *snip* or *click*—" he closed the blades twice quickly to demonstrate "—but to start at a point then glide the blades up through the wool." He slid the shears along through the air.

"Like a dressmaker's scissors on fabric."

"Precisely." He ambled over to a large rectangular table. "The fleece is lain out on one of these wool tables for skirting, when dags and burrs are removed, then it's on to classing."

He found a square of wool in the shears' tin and traced a fingertip up the side of the white fleece. "The finer the wave, or crimp, the better the class."

When he handed over the sample, their hands touched. She took the wool, and as she played with the amazing softness of the fleece, she was certain that a moment ago his fingers had indeed lingered over hers.

"After the wool is classed, it's dropped into its appropriate bin," he went on. "When there's enough of one class, it's pressed into bales. In the beginning, the clip was transported by bullock wagons. From here to the nearest town, Newcastle, was a seven month journey."

Maddy could see Jack Prescott living and flourishing in such a time. He'd have an equally resilient woman by his side. As she gently rubbed the wool, Maddy closed her eyes and saw herself standing beside a nineteenth-century Jack Prescott and his bullock wagons. She quivered at the thought of the figure he would cut in this wilderness. Confident, intense, determined to succeed. That Jack, too, would conquer his environment, including any woman he held close and made love to at night.

Opening her eyes, feelings a little giddy, Maddy brought herself back. She really ought to stay focused.

"What do you plan to do with this place now?" she asked.

He looked around, his jaw tight. "Let it be."

"But it seems such a waste."

"The Australian wool industry hit its peak last century in the early fifties when my grandfather and his father ran the station, but that's over for Leadeebrook." His brows pinched and eyes clouded. "Times change."

And you have to move along with them, she thought, gazing down as she stroked the fleece. *Even if your heart and heritage are left behind.*

His deep voice, stronger now, echoed through the enormous room. "There's a gala on this weekend."

Her gaze snapped up and, understanding, she smiled. "Oh, that's fine. You go. I'm good to look after Beau."

"You're coming with me."

He was rounding the table, moving toward her, and Maddy's face began to flame.

They were miles from anyone, isolated in a way she'd never been isolated before. No prying eyes or baby cries to interrupt. That didn't make the telltale heat pumping through her veins okay. Didn't make the suggestion simmering in his eyes right either.

What was this? She'd wanted to believe he was a gentleman. An enigma, certainly, but honorable. Yet, here he was, blatantly hitting on her.

She squared her shoulders. "I'm sure your fiancée wouldn't approve of your suggestion."

His advance stopped and his jaw jutted. "I spoke with Tara this morning. I was wrong to consider marrying her. I said we should stay friends."

Maddy's thoughts began to spin. Clearly he'd broken off plans with Tara not only because of their embrace last night but because he had every intention of following that kiss up with another.

Whether he was spoken for or not, it wasn't happening. She hardly knew this man. While she was physically attracted to him—shamefully so—she wasn't even sure she *liked* him. And if he thought she was the kind to cave to temptation and fall into bed with someone for the hell of it, he was sadly mistaken.

"Jack, if this has anything to do with what happened between us last night…I mean, if you're thinking that maybe—"

"I'm thinking that while you're here, you might as well experience everything there is to offer. This is Beau's new home and you're our guest."

Was she a guest or, more than ever, a challenge?

Even as the consequences of such a thought burrowed in to arouse her, she shook her head.

"I'm sorry but I won't be attending any gala. I'm not here on vacation. It's not fair to leave Cait with Beau."

"You're going to have to leave Beau soon enough."

His thoughtful look—that fundamental statement— knocked her off balance and her hand, holding the wool, flattened on the table to steady her tilting weight.

Soon enough she *would* be gone. Depending on what lay behind her father's ominous text message, perhaps sooner than expected. Her pragmatic side said she should be grateful that Cait was so good with the baby and happy that Jack seemed to be resolved to forge a relationship with Beau. Happy her life would be going back to normal… back to Sydney at this crucial stage in her career.

"You'll need to pack a bag," he said. "It's a half hour flight from here."

Maddy's thoughts skipped back to the present. But he'd

lost her. Half an hour's flight? He was still talking about that gala?

"Why would I need a bag?"

"Simple." He stepped out from the shadows and a jagged streak of light cut across his face. "You and I will be staying the night."

Six

She'd been wrong. Jack wasn't self-assured. He was plain-and-simple arrogant.

To think he expected her to not only attend this gala affair with him, but also stay the night, made Maddy more determined than ever to stand her ground. She wasn't going. Fantasizing about throwing self-control to the wind and submitting to Jack's smoldering advances was one thing. Agreeing to spend the night together was quite another.

If it'd been any other man, she'd have laughed in his face. Or slapped it. But Jack wasn't any other man. He was a man of action who didn't see a thing wrong with going after what he wanted.

And it seemed he wanted her.

Thankfully during the drive back to the house he didn't bring the subject up again, although she was certain he hadn't taken her objections seriously. He kept sending out the vibes…lidded looks and loaded phrases that left her half dizzy and, frankly, annoyed. Yes, she'd let him kiss her—deeply. *Thoroughly.* That did *not* mean she had any intention of acting impulsively and stealing away with him…even if part of her desperately wanted to.

After dinner, Jack took Beau out onto the veranda for some cool air while Maddy stayed behind to help Cait.

"I'm good here," Cait told her, frothing soapy water at the sink. "You go keep Jock company with the bairn."

Not on your life. She'd copped more than enough of Jack's company—and sex appeal—for one day. Maddy flicked a tea towel off its rack.

"I'm sure he'd like time alone with Beau." She rescued a dripping plate from the drainer and promptly changed the subject to something safer. "I've been meaning to say… the nursery's beautiful. So fresh and the colors are just gorgeous." Pastel blues and mauves with clouds stenciled on the ceiling and koalas painted on the walls.

Dishcloth moving, Cait nodded at the water. "I washed all the linen and curtains when Jock let me know."

"Has that room always been the nursery? I mean, was it Jack's and Dahlia's room when they were babies?"

Cait's hands stopped milling around in the suds. "Jock and Sue…his wife…they did it up."

Maddy digested the information and slanted her head. "I didn't think Jack wanted a family."

"Did he tell you that?"

"In not so many words." When Cait kept her focus on the sink, a dreadful goosebumpy feeling funneled through Maddy's middle. What wasn't the housekeeper telling her?

"Cait?" She set the tea towel aside. "What is it?"

After two full beats, Cait slumped and hung her head.

"Sue wasn't the only one who was taken from Jock that night three years ago."

Maddy absorbed the words. When her mind settled on a plausible explanation, her hip hit the counter and a rush of tingles flew over her scalp.

Oh God. She closed her eyes and swallowed. "There was a baby, wasn't there?"

"A baby boy who was wanted very much. And to have that happen just a year after his parents' passing and Dahlia running off... He'd given up on the idea of family. Having a baby here at Leadeebrook...well, it's hard for him."

Maddy pressed against the sick feeling welling in her stomach. She could barely absorb it. "I wish I'd known."

"He doesn't talk about that day, though I'm sure he thinks about it often. Poor love, he blames himself."

Jack exuded the confidence and ability of a man who could defeat any foe or would die trying. Having to face that he hadn't been able to save his wife, his child...

Maddy swayed. She couldn't imagine the weight on his conscience. Perhaps it was similar to the guilt she felt about pushing Dahlia out the door that day to have her nails and hair done. Would she ever forgive herself?

Maddy dragged herself back to the here and now. Knowing this much about Jack's loss, she felt compelled to know more. More about how Jack's past might affect his relationship with Beau. More about the steel cowboy who was very much a flesh and blood man underneath.

Before she could ask, Maddy's senses prickled and she felt a presence at their backs. Heartbeat hammering, she rotated to face him.

Jack's impressive frame filled the doorway. The baby lay asleep in one arm. His other hand was bunched by his side.

"Beau's asleep," he said.

Maddy secretly gripped the counter for support. He'd come up on them so quietly…how much had he heard? She was so taken aback, she could barely get her lips to work.

When she'd gathered herself, she came forward and with her arms out to take the baby, she managed a smile.

"I'll put him down."

With a single step, Jack retreated into the hall. "I can do it."

Maddy's arms lowered. When they'd met, she didn't believe he had the wherewithal to care for this child beyond a grudging sense of duty. She certainly hadn't envisaged him being hands-on, wanting to change and feed and put Beau to bed. Initially, when they'd arrived here, she'd placed his insistence to help in the 'male pride' slot—he'd once run a sheep stud empire, therefore looking after an infant should be a piece of cake.

But she'd seen a shift in his attitude, like when he'd spoken about the baby's cheeky smile this afternoon, and when he'd lifted Beau out of the playpen to take him outside into the cool night. There'd been true caring in his eyes, a look that had touched a tender, hope-filled place inside of her.

Was he beginning to see Beau as a replacement for the child he'd lost? If so, wasn't that a healing move for Jack as well as a good outcome for the baby? Her head said yes.

Yet something niggled.

Jack moved off down the hall to put Beau to bed and Maddy returned to the sink. Whether he went to his room later or out to the stables, she didn't know but she didn't see Jack again.

Afterward, she went to her room and sat on the edge of her downy bed. She'd experienced a gamut of emotions these past few days. Guilt and deepest sadness over Dahlia's death. Fierce protectiveness toward Beau. Anger then curiosity toward Jack, followed more recently by acute physical desire and ultimately, tonight, empathy.

Slipping off her shoes, she took in her surroundings.

She didn't fit here, but Beau would—or did. The walls of this homestead contained memories, connections, history that were a part of who he was and Dahlia had known it. But this cozy quiet room, with its lace curtains, white cast iron headboard, patchwork quilt and rustic timber floors, was so not *her*. Madison Tyler was tailored suits and classic jewelry, multiple meetings and hardnose decisions. At this point in her life, Madison Tyler *was* the Pompadour account.

Exhaling, she studied her BlackBerry on the bedside table. Good or bad, she couldn't put that phone call off any longer.

Her father picked up with his usual abbreviated greeting. "Tyler here."

Maddy held the phone tighter to her ear. "Hey, Dad."

He groaned a sigh of relief. "Thank God. I need you back here *yesterday*."

Holding her brow, she fell back against the quilt. Worse than she'd thought.

"What's wrong?"

"Pompadour wants to look at the campaign at the end of next week."

Her eyes flew open while her heart sank. "That's two weeks earlier than scheduled."

"They're eager to see what we have. I'm eager to show them." His voice cooled. "What about you?"

She visualized her big desk in her corner office suite even as she gazed at the vintage molded ceiling and felt today's soft fleece beneath her fingers. Then she heard Jack's plea...*you and I are staying the night.*

Her stomach knotted.

Her father wanted her to leave straight away?

"Maddy, you there?"

Thinking quick, she sat up. Today was Tuesday.

"The Pompadour proposal is polished and printed," she told him. "There's only the Powerpoint to tidy up and a final briefing with the staff involved. If I get back mid-next week, say crack of dawn Wednesday, that'll be plenty of time to pull those last strings together."

Tension crackled down the line. "Honey, I've been patient. I understand what good friends you were with that girl. But you've done what you promised. You've delivered the boy to his new home. Now it's time to get back to looking after you. Looking after your own future."

Maddy drew her legs up and hugged her knees. He was right. Absolutely. Given the circumstances, it was only logical she get back to her life, pronto.

Still...

She gnawed her bottom lip. "Dad, can you give me until Monday?"

She imagined her father shutting his eyes and shaking his head.

"You have a choice to make," he said, not unkindly. "Either come back and finish the job or I'll have to give it to someone who can."

Her throat closed. "But I've put so much work into that campaign." Storyboards, multiple media schedules, months spent on research both in Australia and overseas.

"This isn't about being fair. I love you, but that's personal. This is about business. You're either with Tyler Advertising a hundred percent or you're not."

She let go of her knees and straightened. "I understand."

She really did. And yet leaving Beau here after only one day seemed…worse than heartless.

As if reading her thoughts, her father sighed the way he used to when she was young and had pleaded for another scoop of ice cream after dinner.

"If you really think you can pull it off…all right. I'll give you 'til Monday to get back."

She pushed to her feet, beaming. "Really?"

"Monday eight a.m.," he decreed. "Not a minute later."

She said goodbye and thought over how thirteen days at Leadeebrook had dwindled down to five. At least she didn't have to hop on a plane back to Sydney as soon as tomorrow. But now she needed to make the most of every minute she had with Beau.

She crept the short distance down the darkened hall and when she reached the nursery, the door was ajar. After tiptoeing in, she waited for her eyes to adjust to the shadows and moonlight streaming in through the partly opened window. The outline of the crib grew more distinct as the smell of baby powder and Beau filled her lungs. Feeling the cool timber then soft center rug beneath her feet, she inched closer until her fingers curled over the sturdy cot rail. She smiled. Beau was sound asleep.

She stood there for she didn't know how long, simply drinking in the angelic form, filing this memory away for later. In this wedge of time, Sydney and Tyler's Advertising were another world away. Another universe.

And she was more than okay with that.

A creak came from behind. Heart zipping to her throat, Maddy spun around. A hulking shadow in the corner took on shape as it straightened out of a chair and edged toward her. She smothered a breathless gasp.

An intruder?

But as the figure drifted closer, its build became unmistakable. Of course it was Jack. Saying not a thing the whole while she'd been there.

"Why didn't you let me know you were in the room?" she whispered, hoping the irritation showed in her voice. No one liked to be spied on.

"I didn't want to disturb you." He came closer. "But when you stayed…"

He stopped beside her and his simmering magnetism at once drew her in. It was as if she were a planet being sucked into the heat of the sun, or the day needing to surrender to the unconditional blanket of the night.

Bracing herself, Maddy locked her weakened knees.

She needed to get out of here, away from him, before she did something foolish like let him kiss her again. She had to keep *focused*. But she needed to say something important—something that couldn't wait—before she left this room.

"I spoke with my father tonight," she told him. "He needs me back in Sydney early."

The dark slashes of his brows swooped together. "How early?"

"Monday morning."

His frown lowered to Beau. "How do you feel about that?"

She batted a reply around in her head and decided on, "I don't have a choice."

"Doesn't give me much time to get you in a saddle."

When he grinned, she gave in to a smile, too. *You wish.*

"But it *does* give us time for the gala," he went on. "Do you have a dress?"

Her jaw dropped and an exasperated sound escaped her throat.

"I seriously cannot believe you." The baby stirred. Gathering herself, she pressed her lips together and hushed her voice. "I'm not going anywhere with you, particularly not now that I only have five days left with Beau."

Even if, admittedly, when she'd spoken on the phone with her father and had asked for more time, going to the gala with Jack had been something of a consideration.

"Five days, yes," Jack agreed. "But that doesn't mean you can't come back."

The words hit her, caressed her, and she could only blink. Just days ago he'd barely wanted to know her and now...

She half smiled. "You want me to come *back?*"

"Now don't be shy. I know you're secretly attached to the Mitchell grass and the dust."

She almost laughed. Never, *ever* would that happen. But...

"I would like to come back and see Beau," she added to be clear.

"That can be arranged. On one condition."

She narrowed her eyes at him. "Is this going to be an offer I can't refuse?"

"Hope so." He turned to her and held her with his eyes. "Come away with me, Maddy. One night. Just one. Don't make me beg."

They'd known each other such a short time. But she was convinced of his strength and confidence and, above all else, his pride. The idea of him begging...

She touched her forehead.

He made her feel vulnerable. Desirable. *Hot.* How a woman should feel with a man. He almost made her feel too intensely.

"What are you afraid of?" His head angled and a lock of hair fell over his furrowed brow. When he moved closer, his height, his overpowering presence, seemed to curl over and absorb her.

"Once I thought I had all the time in the world," he murmured into the dark. "But we both know life isn't always that way. If we had more time, I probably wouldn't have suggested this." A corner of his mouth hooked up. "Then again, maybe I would have."

Her heart squeezed so much that it ached.

She was physically drawn to a ruggedly handsome man who wasn't hiding the fact that he was seriously drawn to her. He'd told her in the plainest of terms—he wanted them to spend the night together. He was saying he wanted to make love.

What did *she* want?

Not the girl who'd grown up without a mother, or the cosmo-chick who lived for her decaf soy latte each morning at eight. What did Madison Tyler, the woman, want?

He seemed to read her mind. His big hand threaded around her waist and brought her close. "This might help you decide."

His lips met hers, a feathery, devastatingly gentle caress. The steam in his blood found a way into hers and, in that mist-filled instant, she burned white-hot from the inside out. She told herself to keep her wits…to try to find her feet. Useless. Her defenses fell away and any remaining doubt drifted off like weightless wisps from a dandelion ball.

His mouth reluctantly left hers but the hold on her waist remained firm. When her eyes fluttered open, she didn't have the strength to even pretend she was annoyed. She understood the arguments. She barely knew him. She wasn't a leap-in-think-later type. God, what would Dahlia have thought?

And yet suddenly none of that mattered.

For so long she'd wanted to feel as if she truly belonged, without pressure, without fear of disapproval. Right or wrong, for one night she wanted to belong to Jack Prescott.

Siphoning in a much-needed breath, she sorted her thoughts.

"I'll go with you," she said, "but I have a condition of my own. That you don't do that again while we're under this roof."

His grin was lazy. "Was the kiss that bad?"

Her brows knitted. This wasn't a joke.

"I won't deny that I want you to kiss me again, because I do." At this moment more than she could ever have dreamed possible. "But if we start stealing kisses in every darkened corner, where does that leave Beau? The days that I'm left here, he deserves my attention. All of it." Maddy thought of Dahlia's trust in her—that sacred promise—and her throat swelled and closed off. "The least we can do is give him that much."

Jack's gaze turned inward before falling to the baby. A moment later, his hand left her waist. A muscle ticked in his jaw as he nodded.

"Agreed."

"But I will go with you on Saturday," she continued, "if we leave after he's gone down for the night and we arrive back early. Can you live with that?"

Jack studied Beau for a long moment before his gaze found hers once more. His expression changed. A knuckle curved around and lifted her jaw and for a strangled heartbeat Maddy thought he might kiss her again.

But he only smiled a thoughtful smile and murmured, "I can live with that."

Seven

The next day, back from his early ride, Jack headed for the house, remembering Maddy's words from the previous night. They'd rattled around in his head all morning. Had made him smile and made him wonder.

I won't deny that I want to kiss you again, because I do.

Maddy had agreed to go to the gala. In effect they both knew she'd agreed to more than that. Knowing he would soon take to bed the woman he'd been physically attracted to from the start left him with an acute sense of anticipation that released a new and vital heat surging through his veins. But their connection was more than physical. Had to be. He'd been intimate with women over the past three years. The acts had left his body sated, but not his mind. Not his heart. Something about Maddy affected him…*differently*.

Striding up the steps, he chided himself.

Of course he didn't kid himself that making love to Maddy could compare with what he and Sue had shared. It wouldn't, and that was as it should be. Neither could he pretend that he wouldn't have the hardest time keeping his promise not to touch Maddy again until Saturday evening. She wanted no distractions from her time left here with Beau. Commendable. But when they arrived in Clancy for the gala, he'd have to make up for lost time.

Stopping at the kitchen, Jack expected to see Cait by the sink or the stove, but the room, gleaming in the early morning light, was empty. Further down the hall, Maddy's door was closed. In passing, his pace slowed. He wanted to invite himself in. To break his promise and be done with it.

Scratching his jaw, he growled and moved on.

This situation was getting ridiculous. He shouldn't be so preoccupied with speculations over how Maddy would feel beneath him, her thighs coiled around his hips, her warm lips on his neck, on his chest. Family—now that he had one again—was what mattered.

He approached the nursery, confirming again in his mind that he wouldn't fail this boy. Not like he'd failed Dahlia when he hadn't brought her back all those years ago. But, hell, had rescuing his sister ever been possible? He might have been bigger. He might have been right. Staying at Leadeebrook was far safer for a girl—for Dahlia—than trying to survive on the outside. The rape, her death, proved that. But when Dahlia had left Leadeebrook, she'd been over eighteen. The law said she'd been old enough to make her own decisions, even if they ended in tragedy.

He stopped outside the partly closed nursery door and took stock. Life was known for irony, and that tragedy had also produced a baby, the only surviving link, other than himself, to the Prescott bloodline. Beau was more than

Dahlia's legacy, he was the Prescott future. Beau would grow up, find a nice woman, settle here at Leadeebrook, have a family of his own.

Jack pushed open the door, a smile curving his lips. He felt a great deal of comfort knowing that.

Kicking his heels, Beau was wide awake in his crib. After changing his diaper, Jack decided it was high time he took the boy on a tour. He bundled Beau up and headed for what had been known at Leadeebrook as the portrait hall.

"This is your great-great-grandfather," Jack said, stopping before the first portrait, which looked particularly regal in its gold-leaf gilded frame. "He was a determined and clever man. He and great-great-grandmother Prescott were responsible for making this homestead into the stately residence it is today."

Sitting quietly, gathered in his uncle's arm, Beau stared at the stern-looking gentleman in the frame before Jack moved further down the hall.

"And this," he said, pulling up in front of the next portrait, "is your great-grandfather. He taught me how to shear." Jack studied the baby then smiled and tickled his chin. "I'll have to teach you."

On the opposite side of the wide hall resided portraits of the Prescott women. He stopped at his late wife's and clenched his free hand to divert the familiar ache of loss that rose in his chest. The finest artist on the eastern coast had been commissioned for this piece, and the man had captured the loving shine in Sue's soft brown eyes perfectly.

At the same time Jack's throat thickened, Beau wriggled and he bypassed the other distinguished portraits until he reached the part of the house he visited often but always alone. After turning the handle, he entered the library—what had become Sue's library when she'd been alive. An extendable stepladder resided at the far end of the massive room. Numerous shelves, laden with all kinds of reading matter, towered toward the lofty ceiling. Designer crimson-and-yellow-gold swags decorated the tall windows. The cream chairs and couches bore the subtle sheen of finest quality upholstery.

This room upheld the Prescott promise of old money and impeccable taste, yet Sue had managed to make the library look cozy, too, with fresh flowers from the garden and bundles of home décor magazines and crossword puzzles camped out on occasional tables. The flowers were long gone, but the magazines he'd told Cait to leave.

Jack studied the baby studying the room. Beau was a smart kid. Even at this age, Jack could see it in his eyes.

"Will you be a reader or more a hands-on type like your uncle?" he asked his nephew, crossing to the nearest bookshelf. "Maybe both. Your mother was good at everything." He grinned, remembered when they'd been children. "Not that I ever let her know that."

He strolled half the length of the room to the children's section and eyed the spines that Sue might've read to Beau when he was a little older, as well as to their own son, had he lived.

Wincing, Jack inhaled deeply to dispel the twist of pain high in his gut. Every waking minute of every day, he missed her, missed what they'd had. And then Maddy had appeared in his life. When she was around, he didn't feel quite so empty, and he wasn't certain how to process that. Should he feel relieved or guilty?

The polished French-provincial desk in the corner drew his attention. He carried Beau across the room and slid open a drawer on the right hand side. The book was there…Sue's memory book.

Jack laid it out on the leather blotter and flipped through

the pages, pointing out Sue's relatives to a fist-sucking Beau. She had spent hours making the pages pretty. On the last page, a blue-and-yellow heart hugged a black-and-white image…a scan of their unborn child.

His eyes growing hot, Jack gently pressed his palm next to the eighteen-week-old shape that was his son.

"Sue wanted to name him after her father," he told Beau, in a deep, thick voice. "But I told her, no disrespect to her dad, that Peter Prescott sounded dumb. I'd wanted to name him after *my* father—"

A bitter nut of emotion opened high in his throat. Dropping his gaze, Jack swallowed hard and reached again for the drawer. He drew out a platinum-plated rattle, not a family heirloom but a gift Sue had bought for their baby a week before she'd died. The inscription read *Love forever, Mum and Dad*.

His chest tight, Jack smiled at the galloping horses etched down the cool handle. He shook the rattle and was rewarded by a sound similar to sleigh bells. At the noise, Beau pulled his ear then threw a hand out.

Lowering the rattle, Jack sank into the chair and, feeling empty again, searched his soul.

He examined first the scan image in Sue's book then Beau. Then he looked at each again. The pain behind his ribs intensified to a point where he almost lost his breath. But then, remarkably, the ache eased to a warm sensation rather than something bleak and cold and sour. He didn't want to feel that way anymore.

As the tension between his shoulders loosened, Jack bobbed Beau high on his arm and, pressing his lips to the baby's forehead, handed the rattle over.

Later that day, Jack was back in the stables, preparing to brush down Herc. But he was more interested in what was happening outside.

Beau was in the yard on a prickle-free patch of lawn and garden near the house. He was enthralled by the motion of the baby swing, which his uncle had hung from a tree branch that morning. Maddy pushed the swing, carefully—not too high. Her face was a portrait of joy. Of contentedness.

Smiling, Jack absently threaded Herc's brush strap over his hand.

Hell, no matter her mood, Maddy was attractive. Perfect symmetry, graceful movements. In his humble opinion, this landscape was the ideal foil for her skin and flaxen hair, particularly given the denim shorts and blousy blue top she wore today…the same color as her eyes. He itched to go join them in the dappled shade of that cypress. But simply looking from a distance raked the reawakened coals that smoldered deep in his gut.

True, they both felt the same fire. Both wanted the chance to turn the heat on to combustible high. But as much as it needled, he reminded himself yet again that she'd been right last night and he, in turn, meant to keep his word. He wouldn't crowd her. Foremost, she'd come to Leadeebrook to keep a promise not to begin an affair.

Jack turned to Herc and, frowning, swiped the bristles down his glossy black neck.

Affair wasn't the right word. Affair implied some sort of ongoing relationship and neither of them was immature enough to think that was a possibility. They lived thousands of miles apart. He didn't like the city. She was not a fan of the country. She might take up his offer and come back to visit once or twice. But she was a young woman with a life, and who she was and what she aspired to be wasn't here.

When Herc's flank twitched and his rear hoof pawed the ground, Jack swiped the brush again.

Good thing really. He'd considered taking on a more serious relationship with Tara and had concluded it would be a mistake. He'd had no choice but to take responsibility for Beau. After the initial king-hit shock, he was at peace with the arrangement. He'd do everything in his power to protect him, keep him close. Maddy, on the other hand…

Jack stopped brushing.

Well, Maddy was another matter.

Nell breezed by his leg, trotting out the door with a boomerang-shaped stick in her mouth. Curious, Jack crossed to the window in time to see Nell drop the stick at Maddy's feet.

It'd be a cold day in Hades before Maddy got chummy with a canine. Given her past, he couldn't blame her. He, however, couldn't imagine *not* having a dog around his feet. Not so long ago he'd owned five.

Her nose wrinkling, Maddy waved Nell back and Jack heard her say, "Shoo. Get away." But Nell kept sitting there, every few seconds nudging the stick closer to Maddy's city sneakers with her nose. Nell wanted to play. She could catch a stick for hours if anyone was silly enough to throw it. Nell thought Maddy was a good candidate.

Jack grinned.

And he'd thought Nell was smart.

He was about to rescue Maddy when she did the most remarkable thing. She stooped and, as if she were handling a stick of dynamite, lifted the no doubt slobbery stick between a single finger and thumb. With a move that reminded him a little of Swan Lake, she kicked out a leg at the same time she flung the stick away. With a visible shudder, she wiped her hand down her shorts' leg but before she could give Beau's swing another push, Nell was back, the stick between her jaws, eyes drilling her new playmate's.

When Maddy shrank back in alarm, Jack chuckled and set down the brush. Poor Maddy didn't know what she'd started. She was so much 'the lady.' Not prim, but rather manicured, French-scented, lipstick-in-the-morning female.

He liked that about her.

When Nell's ears pricked and she shot off into the western distance, Jack reached for his hat. Only one reason she'd leave her sport. Visitors.

By the time Jack had washed his hands and moved out into the true heat of the day, the familiar engine groan was unmistakable. Snow's Holden truck. Snow knew about Beau. The other evening, Jack had mentioned Maddy. Guess Snow'd gotten tired of waiting for an introduction.

Maddy had scooped Beau out of the molded swing seat by the time Jack joined her and Snow was alighting from his vehicle. Jack hadn't had time to explain to Maddy who their visitor was, although, from the white of Snow's beard, she might've guessed.

Snow didn't close the car door but rather clapped the thigh of his faded jeans. A lamb leaped out, landing in a spray of Mitchell grass with a scramble. Nell sniffed around the lamb but realizing the relationship between these two—this was not a sheep to be worked—she trotted back to her stick. But now Maddy seemed oblivious to Nell's insistent stare. Her own gaze wide, she clapped one hand over her mouth to catch an enchanted laugh. The lamb was prancing after Snow as if the crusty caretaker were his mother.

Snow offered his hand to Jack then announced in his tobacco-gruff voice, "Seeing you got a guest at your sheep station, Jum, I reckoned she might want to meet a sheep." Snow cordially touched his hat. "Snow Gibson at your service." He dropped a glance at his woolly companion. "This tagalong's Lolly."

Maddy introduced herself to Snow then, holding Beau on her hip, hunkered down. "Hello, there, Lolly." She combed her fingers between Lolly's fleecy ears and sighed. "You are the prettiest little darling ever."

Snow stroked his beard. "I see you got one of your own."

Maddy pushed up and spoke to Beau. "Say hello to Mr. Gibson, Beau."

Snow took the baby's tiny hand between a rough thumb and a stained knuckle. He sent Jack a hearty look. "He's like Dahlia."

His chest tight, Jack returned the smile. "Same grin."

"Think he'd like to see this other one fed?" Snow retrieved a bottle from his inside vest pocket. When he handed the bottle to Maddy, eyes sparkling, she sucked in a breath.

"Me?"

Wrinkles concertinaed down the side of Snow's face when he winked. "She'll be thirsty. You gotta hang on to this real tight."

Jack took Beau and both he and Maddy knelt down again. Lolly almost wrestled her over when she nuzzled up for the teat. As the lamb latched on, Maddy clung to the bottle with both hands while Jack considered a warm stirring emotion he had trouble naming.

He'd grown up with orphaned lambs as pets. Sue's parents had been farmers; livestock had been part of everyday life for both of them. He hadn't seen this kind of awed reaction over an animal in…he couldn't remember how long.

The emotion, he realized, was satisfaction.

With milk disappearing at a rapid rate, Maddy asked, "I didn't think there were any sheep left here?"

"I got a few," Snow expounded, "justa keep a hand in."

"You're a shearer?" she asked.

"Among other things, yes, ma'am."

"You'll have to give me a demonstration."

Snow shucked back his shoulders. "That would be my pleasure."

Beau squealed and thrust out an arm, fingers spread toward the lamb.

Snow chuckled. "The Prescott genes coming out."

Snow's Australian Services badge had lived on the side of his Akubra for decades. Now the metal glinted in the sun as he straightened his hat and put a question to Maddy.

"How you liking Leadeebrook?"

Jack's ears pricked. He'd like to hear her answer, too.

But, with a big smile, Maddy dodged the question with a throwaway comment. "Jack thinks he'll get me on a horse."

"Does he now?" Snow eyeballed Jack, who cleared his throat. Just because a man wanted to show a lady how to ride didn't mean anything, even if in this instance it did.

The lamb had finished his feed so Jack hooked a thumb at the house. "Might be time to get Beau out of this heat."

"Babies've got sensitive skin," Snow reflected, taking the drained bottle from Maddy. "But won't be too many summers before this one'll be flying off that tire swing hanging over Rapids Creek."

Maddy snapped a look at Jack. "There's a creek nearby?"

Snow confirmed, "Fulla water, too."

Snow wasn't being smart. There'd been times, and recently, when the creek bed had been bone-dry.

As they moved toward the stairs and the shade of the veranda, Maddy took the baby and slipped Jack an aside. "I won't bother asking if the creek's fenced."

Jack wasn't sure how to respond. Of course the creek wasn't fenced.

"By law, pools have to be," she told him. "Where children are concerned, I don't see why creeks should be any different."

Guess he wouldn't tell her about the dams then.

He assured her, "My father taught me to swim before I could ride."

"There are some excellent swimming schools and coaches in Sydney," she countered in an encouraging tone.

He adjusted his hat and picked up his pace. "Beau doesn't need to be an Olympian, Maddy. I can teach him everything he needs to know right here."

"Everything?" She surveyed the endless plain with a lackluster air. "Here?"

He strode up the steps, half a length ahead. He wanted to tell his guest to let him worry about Beau. She was the go-between. He'd decide what needed to be done and he'd do it his way.

No mistakes this time.

Eight

Maddy hadn't known what to expect.

Hay stacks in every corner? Corncob bobbing contests? A country band wearing plaid shirts, plucking at banjos? Instead, that Saturday evening when she and Jack entered the Clancy City Gala Ball, she was more than pleasantly surprised.

Clancy was a Channel country community in Queensland's deep west. It boasted the usual small town landmarks. Nothing to write home about. But the exceptional establishment in which they now stood shone like an oasis in a desert. She might have been back in Sydney.

Amid the soft strains of tasteful pre-dinner music, uniformed wait staff breezed around classic timber decor surrounded by exquisite gold-plated fittings and waterfalls of fragrant floral arrangements. Best of all, their fellow guests alleviated any concerns she might have had about being overdressed.

Maddy's suitcase had presented nothing even remotely suitable to wear. Rather than rely on Hawksborough's sole boutique—Lindie's Labels—she had her assistant express courier a gown and accessories she'd purchased from a recent fashion show for an upcoming event. The alizarin-red chiffon sheath made her feel like a goddess.

The pleated shoulders were sheer with the waist gathered high under a cupped bodice, which created an elegant fall of fabric through the middle down to her silver-heeled toes. If her Bulgari crystal earrings added the perfect touch, Jack Prescott was the perfect escort.

As he took her arm to guide her through the mingling black-tie crowd, she enjoyed a thrilling rush of pride. The word hadn't been invented to describe the hold-onto-your-thumping-heart factor Jack oozed in that tailored dinner suit. Beneath the custom-made jacket, powerful broad shoulders rolled with every smooth measured step. His bearing was confident yet also casually relaxed. Movie producers cried out for masculine looks as dramatically chiseled as his.

Others in the room noticed, too. Women camouflaged their interest behind elevated flutes. Men stepped aside to give this naturally masterful guest right-of-way. Maddy had never felt more envied, more singled out or...*more special* in her life.

And this event was only the beginning of their evening. At the regional airport Jack had organized for their bags to be transported to an apartment he'd let for the night—a night she both anticipated with relish as well as with dread. A prude she was not, however, in her book, sexual intimacy wasn't something to be taken lightly. There was so much to consider. Her philosophy had always been that if it was going to happen, there was no need to rush.

Yet every time Jack looked at her she felt his gaze on her skin like a steamy caress. Every time he smiled, she wanted to surrender her lips up for his to take. Since Tuesday night when they'd made their pact to keep a respectable distance, the pressure to succumb had built until her anticipation surrounding tonight had tipped the scales toward flash point.

With his guiding arm through hers, she clasped her hands over her beaded pocketbook. As much as she'd lain awake in her patchwork quilt bed these past nights, staring at the ceiling and imagining what making love with Jack would be like, the imminent reality—the trip wire tight expectation of how this evening would end—now threatened to overwhelm her.

She'd bet her life he was a natural in the bedroom. Maddy was sure that as far as Jack was concerned, making love was an art form, a living masterpiece to be crafted with liberal amounts of sultry skill. She, on the other hand, wasn't entirely free of certain inhibitions. She wasn't the type to swing from chandeliers or even leave the lights on.

Would she disappoint him?

Through a break in the chattering crowd, a waiter appeared carrying a silver tray. Jack selected two flutes and offered one over. Maddy sipped the bubbles and sighed at the crisp heavenly taste.

He smiled. "You like champagne."

"A weakness, I'm afraid."

"Let's see…so that's chocolate custard, rainy mornings and French champagne."

She laughed. Tonight the deep timbre of his voice alone

was enough to leave her wonderfully weak. "I like books, too, don't forget."

His gaze skimmed her mouth. "I haven't forgotten anything."

"Jack, good to see you."

Maddy was snapped from her thrall when a man with a steel gray shock of hair thrust his hand out toward Jack.

Jack shook heartily. "Charlie Pelzer. How are you, mate?" His hot palm settled on Maddy's back. "You haven't met my date."

Maddy's smile wobbled. She wasn't sure if she liked being referred to as Jack's date. Or perhaps she liked it a little too much.

"Madison Tyler," she said cordially.

"Maddy's visiting from Sydney," Jack said. "She's in advertising."

Charlie's bushy brows fell together. "Your father's not Drew Tyler? He's a huge sponsor of one of my benefactors." He named a charity.

Maddy nodded, smiling. "I've heard him speak of it."

Charlie leaned in conspiratorially. "Perhaps you can bend his ear about sponsoring this cause."

He went into a spiel about The Royal Flying Doctor Service, how it was the largest and best aeromedical organization in the world and that without its dedicated staff and services, much of the outback would be uninhabitable. She hadn't realized that while the RFDS was government subsidized to a point, donations were needed to help replace aircraft and purchase supplies and equipment.

Knowing that they were here to support such a great cause alleviated some of the guilt she felt at leaving Beau for a few hours.

Charlie Pelzer and Jack discussed the position Japan

currently played in the Australian wool export market while Maddy happily sipped her champagne and enjoyed the lively atmosphere. She didn't dislike the quiet of the outback, per se. There was something undeniably peaceful about it. But this buzz felt like home.

When Charlie spotted another friend, he bowed off and Jack ushered her over to a long stretch of white clothed tables, upon which rested numerous prizes to be auctioned. Maddy's heartbeat fluttered as she inspected the nearby bidding sheets.

"I love silent auctions."

Jack gave an obliging shrug. "Then we'll have to do some real damage."

Holidays, boats, paintings, gym equipment. Maddy pulled up at a bizarre display. "Five cartons of beer?" Small glass bottles of the premium Aussie XXXX label.

Jack had signed many sheets. Now he swept a flourishing signature on this sheet, too, along with a ridiculous amount. Had the champagne gone to his head?

But his look said not to worry. "It's a tradition. A bit of fun."

The master of ceremonies called for guests to be seated. Maddy soaked up the conversation with their dinner companions, which included a criminal lawyer and a geologist recently returned from areas surrounding Uluru, or Ayers Rock as it was still known to many.

Guests continued bidding until the lot was officially closed and the highest bidder announced. The room erupted with applause when Jack was awarded the five cartons of beer. He also scored a painting by a well-respected indigenous artist. After a dessert of strawberry and passion fruit-topped Pavlova, the lights dimmed more and the music lilted into a familiar dreamy tune.

Jack pushed out his chair and offered his hand. "You like dancing, I presume."

Arching a bow, she accepted his hand. "I can hold my own."

But when he gathered her close on the dance floor beneath the slow spinning lights, it was clear who the expert was. Once his strong warm hand was wrapped around hers, he rested them both against his lapel while his other hand lightly pressed on the sensitive small of her back. As he began to lead, Maddy breathed in his delicious woodsy scent and, trying not to sigh, happily followed. She was so relaxed after the champagne and conversation at the table that she instinctively went to rest her cheek against the shoulder of his jacket.

His breath stirring her upswept hair, the magic of his body as he held her close and moved…it all felt strangely surreal. As if every one of her feel-good hormones had been released and her brain had no room for anything other than wondering how she could possibly get closer to Jack's unique brand of hard heat.

In time she pulled herself back.

Dangerous. They were in a room full of people who were clearly interested in the relationship between widower Jack Prescott and this new woman. To give them more to talk about wouldn't do, particularly given at least one of them knew her father. She didn't want it getting back that she was romantically involved or Drew Tyler could assume that romance was her reason for requesting those few extra days away.

Still…

Jack's chest felt so safe and his hand around hers felt so right. If she didn't want to stir any pots, her own included, it might be time to change the tone. A subject came to mind that had lain between them these past days. Now seemed the right moment to clear the air—as well as make her point clear.

"I hope you didn't think I overreacted the other day when I heard about the creek."

His step faltered almost imperceptibly before he continued to slow dance her around in a tight circle among other couples on the floor.

"I assure you," he said. "There's nothing to worry about."

Maddy chewed her lip. His wife and child both had died. She didn't know the specifics because Cait was reluctant to discuss it further. The last thing she wanted was to sound thoughtless, but the bottom line was that Beau's well-being had to be her main concern.

"I was only trying to point out that drowning can happen in a creek as easily as a suburban pool. Obviously nothing could be done to border off a creek," she rationalized. "As long as a good eye's kept on him at all times, I'm sure you're right. There'll be nothing to worry about." She couldn't help but add, "It's just that kids are known to wander off."

Which brought to mind a movie she'd seen long ago where a little boy had been lost in a desert. His lips cracked, blinded from scorpion venom, he'd wandered around, close to death, for days.

Feeling as if ants were crawling over her skin, she shuddered, then quizzed Jack.

"Does Australia have scorpions?" She had the biggest feeling it did. "I know we have snakes." Some of the deadliest in the world.

"Yes, we have snakes," he confirmed. "Scorpions, too, but in the bush we're down on murders and police car chases and high on helping each other out."

She took in his wry expression and let out that breath.

Yes, she should keep things in perspective. Growing up in the country wasn't necessarily a bad thing, or more hazardous than being raised in a city. She needed to keep telling herself that Beau would be happy in his new home after she had left and slipped back into her own life. This is what Dahlia had wanted for him...even if she hadn't wanted it for herself.

"You look beautiful in that gown," Jack murmured against the shell of her ear, clearly wanting to move on from that subject, too. "Everyone in the room thinks so."

Her heart swelled so much she didn't know if her ribs could contain it. Usually she was gracious in accepting compliments, but everything about Jack affected her more deeply. As her cheeks heated, she offered silent thanks for the muted lighting. She felt like a sixteen-year-old at her first dance with the boy every girl wanted to date.

Trying to make light of it, she shrugged.

"The color's quite striking."

"That's what I thought about your eyes when we first met."

A simmering kernel of want began to pulse in her core and she fell deeper into his mesmerizing eyes. He was so sexy, so handsome. Fatally hypnotic. With every passing minute, Sydney seemed farther and farther away.

With his thumb circling low on her back, he nodded at a point above her head. "Notice all the fairy lights."

She nodded. They gave the room an incredibly romantic feel, although that was more likely due to her dance partner's smoldering attention.

"Over there—" he tipped his head "—they've made a replica of the Southern Cross."

Arcing around, she took in the five larger lights which were patterned to reflect the star formation that was synonymous with Australian skies. She noticed some hazy, larger lights that seemed to hover upon the horizon of the room. "What formation are those meant to be?"

"You've heard of Min Min lights?"

She grinned. "Sure." The strange appearance of those lights in the outback was legendary.

He cocked a brow. "But did you know that Min Min light sightings are more prevalent in this district than any other?"

Her blood pressure spiked. In the fast-track world where she lived, Maddy didn't admit it often but she believed that not everything could be explained by science.

"Min Min lights were part of Aboriginal folklore long before modern day sightings made them famous," Jack said. "Experts agree the mysterious lights that show themselves to travelers at night aren't imagination. They appear in the distance, sometimes hazy, sometimes brilliant enough to light up objects around them. When you think you're getting closer, they can disappear only to reappear at your back, speeding up behind you, or at the side, seeming to watch."

Maddy involuntarily swallowed then tried to shake her dark fascination off.

"You're trying to scare me."

He chuckled and squeezed her hand. "Don't worry about them. I'm here."

Her blood flowed like hot syrup through her veins. But she straightened her shoulders and cast a casual glance around. Had anyone heard their conversation? Could anyone see her blush?

He tilted her face back toward him. "And I plan to keep you as close as possible all night."

Her breasts tingled and swelled, and she couldn't quite catch her breath. He was openly seducing her—*here,* amid hundreds of people. And the longer she drank him in, the more light-headed she became.

Giddy from the dance, from the music and from his charm, she dragged her gaze away.

"I…I don't know…"

His polished shoes stopped moving. With a firm hold of her hand, he headed for a set of glass doors and didn't stop until they stood on an otherwise vacant balcony surrounded by a dark velvet dome which held all the stars in the sky.

He faced her and his big palms sculpted over her shoulders, winging them slightly in as he held her still with a penetrating gaze.

"The last thing I want," he said in an earnest tone, "is for you to go through with something you're not entirely comfortable with." His intense hooded gaze lowered to her mouth. "So if you're uncomfortable—" he purposefully, slowly angled his head and his lips grazed hers "—even a little—" his lips brushed again and the hold on her shoulders tightened "—I can always stop."

Maddy's nerve endings shorted out. She couldn't get enough air. Her heart was smashing so madly against her ribs that surely he must have heard the wild thumping.

She'd made the decision to come tonight. She couldn't go back and yet she didn't know if she had the strength—the courage—to go forward. She felt small, unremarkable, like she had the day she walked into that woolshed. Jack was a thousand times more than any man she'd known. And despite the confident act, she was just Maddy.

And Maddy was less than perfect.

But when he drew her close and his mouth slanted possessively over hers, the trillion stars in the sky joined with the stars in her head. Sensations, glorious and absolute, spiraled through her, around her, and she dissolved then surrendered.

Her acceptance and commitment was complete. There would be no turning back. Now the only question seemed to be…

Would she ever want to stop?

He and Maddy arrived at their suite twenty minutes later.

During the cab ride, he'd held her hand in the back seat while she'd chatted on about how much she'd enjoyed the evening. Despite succumbing to him on the balcony—assuring him with the honesty of her caress of how she felt—she was nervous, and he wondered…

She was a city girl, mid-twenties, and worldly with it. He'd assumed she was practiced where men were concerned. Was it possible she was a virgin?

He *did* know that she looked incredible in that gown, particularly with her pale silky hair loosely swept up off her neck. Sensuous flowing fabric and glittering gems were her territory. She shone so brightly, she might have stepped off a New York runway. He'd had trouble keeping up with the conversation at the table, he'd been so bewitched by her grace and her beauty, and he didn't give a damn who'd known it.

Tara Anderson had appreciated glamour to a degree but she'd preferred breeches. He could identify. He was no stranger to tuxedoes but nothing topped the comfort of a pair of jeans and worn-in boots. Escorting Maddy tonight in that spectacular designer dress, however, had him revisiting that long held truth. He'd happily don a stiff collar if it meant having Maddy on his arm.

But, he had to remember, this wasn't an ongoing thing.

Inside the suite, she moved to the center of the expansive living room and rotated to face him. With her hands clasped high at her waist, the hem of her gown floated out and settled again around her slim ankles.

"Do you usually stay here for the gala weekend?"

"Always."

Although not in this room. He hadn't been to Clancy in three years. Hadn't been anywhere much at all. When he wasn't at Leadeebrook, he felt irritable. Out of sorts. Home was the only place that seemed to give him any reprieve from the constant rumble of regret that tagged him.

Rubbing his jaw, Jack crossed to the wet bar.

Did no good to let his mind wander in that direction. He'd loved his wife and where she was now, he was certain that she knew it. Long and hard he'd thought over his feelings for Madison Tyler. Hell, he'd over-analyzed them into the ground.

But he was happy with his decision. He wanted her here with him tonight. He only regretted that their time alone would be so brief. No use thinking about her next visit though—if there was one. Women of Maddy's caliber didn't stay free for long.

From the overhead rack he retrieved wine glasses.

Maddy's gesture caught his attention.

"You go ahead," she said. "But I'm fine."

He slid the glasses aside. He didn't want any more to drink. What he wanted was Maddy raveled up in his arms. He wanted to enjoy that heady, high altitude buzz she consistently whipped up inside him.

He wanted to feel her body, naked, beneath his.

Every minute they spent on small talk was one more precious minute wasted.

Intent, he moved toward her, tugging his bow tie free. When Maddy's eyes widened and her bodice rose on a silent breath, his step hesitated. What the devil was she afraid of? That he'd throw her down and take what he wanted? He didn't operate that way. If she'd only relax he'd be more than willing to show her.

He was an arm's length away when she spun on her heel to face the view of the town lights visible beyond the wall-to-wall window.

"I wonder if we'll see any Min Min lights tonight," she said. "You said they bob up around these parts all the time."

Jack rubbed the back of his neck. More than instinct said she wanted to be here. The way she'd danced with him, clung to him, wasn't manufactured. Yet something kept touching on her brakes. He'd assured her every way he could. With words, with affection.

Flicking back his jacket, Jack set his hands low on his hips. There were two ways to handle this…slow and ultra steady, or cut to the chase and let this push and pull game be decided upon once and for all.

He wound around to block her view before he folded his hands over hers. Bringing her cool knuckles to his lips, he warmed them with a heartfelt vow.

"Whatever you're worried about, believe me, Maddy, you don't need to be."

He meant that promise to the depths of his soul. He wouldn't hurt her for the world. He never wanted to cause harm to anyone again, consciously or otherwise.

She rolled her teeth over her bottom lip and Jack frowned. After coming this far he wondered if she might tell him now that she'd been wrong. That she didn't want to be with him as much as he wanted to be with her.

When she sucked in a breath and finally nodded, relieved, Jack smiled and nodded, too. At the same time, his glance dropped to her lips. Lips he'd remember forever.

His gut kicked with a familiar pleasant tug. This was right. *She* was right. Beyond ready, he lowered his head and claimed her.

Heat rose up his thighs, igniting a trail of flash fires over his skin. The urge to probe deeper, savor more, was alarmingly powerful, near impossible to resist. They were alone. His blood was booming. In his mind she was already writhing beneath him.

Kissing her still, his hands ironed up the curves of her waist. When he reached the bodice of her gown, his fingers encased her sides while each thumb stroked the underside of her breasts. As the kiss grew in intensity, his thumbs circled higher. While she whimpered in her throat and leaned in, he clenched every muscle to stop from satisfying the primal urge to pry those red cups apart.

Instead his mouth reluctantly left hers.

Her eyes were closed, her breathing labored. Her fingers dug into his biceps for support. The delectable burn smoldering below his belt expanded. These past days—watching her, wanting her—had been a bittersweet torture.

Angling, he scooped her off those dainty silver heels and up into the cradle of his jacketed arms. Her lashes fluttered open and his chest grew as she peered up at him with large, dewy eyes. Beyond a set of opened interior double doors, the master bed was in full view. The covers were turned down as he'd instructed. He'd find protection in the bedside drawer. With every cord in his body wound tight, he delivered her into the bedroom.

The room was dark, its open glass slider doors inviting in a cool breeze. Standing in shadows, he was vaguely aware of the moon's silver claw hanging in the sky, the night song of cicadas and a faint rustling of leaves. He set her on her feet, released his dinner shirt's top buttons and then stepped forward to find the zipper at her back. His hot gaze fused with hers, he eased the zipper down.

He felt her slight tremble as he edged one gossamer light sleeve off a slender shoulder then encouraged the next. The gown fell over her curves and landed in an airy puddle at her feet. Hungry, but patient, he soaked up the ethereal vision of her porcelain frame…her high full breasts, scanty red panties, long milky legs ending with sexy spiked heels. He inhaled to the bottom of his lungs then his gaze went to her hair.

"Let it down."

She hesitated only a heartbeat before reaching with both hands to release the pins. Her hair cascaded but she didn't shake out the kinks. Rather she looked to him as if waiting for his next move…or approval.

Stepping into the space separating them, he skimmed both sets of fingers up the column of her warm slender neck, carrying the hair high enough to leave ample access. Then he lowered his mouth to her throat and flicked her fast-beating pulse with the tip of his tongue.

She sighed and melted enough that he had to grip her upper arms to save her from slipping. With patience disintegrating, he carefully backed her up.

As she lowered to sit on the side of the bed, he studied her unwittingly erotic form. With his gaze slipping down the hair shimmering over one shoulder, he shucked back his shoulders and began to undress. Jacket first, shirt, and the rest. Then he knelt at her feet and slipped off her shoes.

Listening to her heavy breathing, high on the scent of her perfume, he closed his eyes and trailed his lips—moist, famished, lingering kisses—up her satin smooth shins, and higher…over her thighs, across her bikini line, around one hip—

He felt a lump. And another, like a welt. Frowning, he pulled back and jumped at the light switch. Dear God, had something bitten her?

The soft glow faded up at the same time he asked, "Maddy, what's wro—?"

The question stuck in his throat.

The scars were white, many and raised. Straight, jagged. Some were dots, reminders of deep puncture wounds. As his heart fisted in his throat, he found her pained face—cheeks red, eyes downcast.

Sick to his stomach, he ground out, "From the attack?"

She dragged the sheet up to cover what she could. Her hair fell in a pale blanket over her brow as she shook her head then shook it again.

"I know. They're ugly. Please…" She blindly flipped a finger at the switch. "Turn off the light."

But he found her free hand and pressed her palm to his cheek. Now it was clear. Now he understood. This why she'd seemed so uncertain.

He brushed his lips over her inside wrist.

"Maddy, do you think that could make a difference to how I feel?"

She slowly looked at him, question marks in her searching gaze. He gave her time to absorb the honesty in his eyes then she let him ease the sheet down.

He kissed the marks. Each and every one. After a time, when her fisted hands relaxed and her stiffness eased, he continued up until his mouth found and captured hers. He maneuvered her back until she lay flat and as she wound her hands through his hair, he pressed in, kissing her as desperately as she was now kissing him.

His descending touch found her more ready than he could have hoped. She was swollen, so wet. He wanted to explore her, enjoy her, with everything she might crave and he so badly needed to give. He lowered her panties as his mouth trailed a seductive line down her neck to her breasts.

His fingertip drew tiny pressure circles round the bead above her folds while his tongue twirled over her nipples. Her nails alternately skimmed or dug half moons into his back. Every so often she made little noises that shot flaming arrows to his groin. Soon she was grinding her hips into the sheet or curling them up to intensify his touch.

The second she tensed and her hand came over to hold his in place, he drew back and saw to protection before he joined her again. Searching her eyes in the shadows, he opened her with his fingers then eased partly in.

She tightened around his tip. As she squeezed around him, her hands filed up the plane of his chest, her fingers fanning and winding over his muscles. Something tinkled. The wedding band on his gold chain. He stopped, visualized the ring and what it stood for but when she began to breathe again, that image faded and he continued to move…a little deeper, a little harder.

Every inch of him was steamy and his heart was a fast-pumping piston by the time he brought her leg high over the back of his thigh. Her calf clamped down to hold him firm. Reading the sign, he drove in all the way.

The fit was glorious, the impulse to give in was mind blowing. The mighty force to reward physical necessity was an avalanche crashing on his back. Clenching every muscle, he tucked in his chin until it met his chest, but it was no good. This was way beyond control.

When she stilled, too, she set off a chain reaction he couldn't prevent. She gave a breathy pant of air, a delicious, full body shudder. Then she threw back her head and her hips jutted off the mattress. Double-gripping the sheet, Maddy cried out and Jack's long-anticipated landslide pushed through.

The release was so complete it seemed to tear his every fiber apart at the same time a primal sound squeezed from his chest. Circling his arm above her head, he swallowed her sigh with a penetrating kiss. Lost in sensation, soaring on the high, Jack scooped his other arm beneath her back and dragged her closer still. Deeply physical, gloriously fierce. This was a passion the likes of which he'd never tasted before. And must taste again.

Nine

Later, still floating from the effects of their lovemaking, Maddy lay with the sheet draped over her legs, drawing lazy circles through the crisp dark hair that dusted Jack's chest. With his arm around her and fingertips trailing up and down her side, she thought over the amazing time they'd spent together in this bed. Her anxiety had been unwarranted. He'd discovered the scars but hadn't been revolted. In fact, she'd never felt more adored.

Her hand wandered higher, into the warm beating hollow of his throat, and her fingers met with the cool of the chain he wore and the circle of the ring threaded through it.

A gold ring.

Maddy stilled, then her palm flattened and slid down to rest on the hard ridges of his abdomen. She'd seen the wedding band before, when he'd taken off his shirt that first day in the nursery, but with so many other things crashing through her mind, she'd thought little of it.

Did he ever take the ring off? If he hadn't tonight, when making love with her had been his intention, she guessed not. Did he wear it around his neck to keep it close to his heart?

Although he didn't show his feelings often, Jack Prescott was a man capable of deep emotion. Of deep loyalty. Some people gave their heart to only one person in their lifetime. Jack had obviously found his soul mate. Had found her and then lost her three years ago.

Maddy's brow pinched and her stomach knotted.

Where did that leave *her* in his affections?

But she shook herself. Tonight wasn't about eternity. He'd never intimated that it was. After knowing each other a week, how could it be?

The ring around his neck was an acknowledgement as well as a sign that couldn't be mistaken. What they shared was a mountain above wonderful but their time together here was based on physical attraction. The electricity that crackled between them was real, was strong. But, where it counted, that ring said he would always belong to someone else.

She breathed in his woodsy masculine scent and snuggled closer.

Still, she couldn't regret agreeing to this arrangement. He wasn't wearing that ring to hurt her. The simple truth was that she wouldn't have missed these past hours for anything.

She'd read about men who made love the way Jack did. Unselfishly. Finding so much pleasure in giving. He'd lifted her to another sphere of awareness, of passion, where more than bodies had joined. She'd never felt closer to another human being. The feeling of absolute rapture would live with her long after tonight was over. So would his reaction after his lips had grazed her hip.

He'd been so supportive when he'd discovered her scars. The last man she'd come close to being intimate with had recoiled in horror. She'd dated that guy for five months. She thought she'd known him. Had wanted to trust him.

Did anyone ever truly know someone else?

Heck, when it came down to it, maybe Jack was just a really good actor.

Easing the sheet higher, she murmured against his chest. She had to ask.

"Those scars are pretty scary, huh?"

"The scars aren't scary." His chest hardened more as he craned to brush his lips over her crown. "What you must have gone through would've been."

A cold shaft whistled through her center and Maddy shut her eyes. She didn't like to think about that day. Whenever the memories surfaced she pushed them down as far as she could. But now she lifted the lid a little and dared to let them rise.

The images were fuzzy.

What had she been wearing? She'd been riding to the shop, but to buy what? Milk, perhaps. Bread. She thought harder but didn't shudder, not like she used to whenever memories had crept up and caught her unawares. The nightmares had been the worst.

"I fell off my bike," she said and realized she'd spoken aloud. "The dog was on me before I could find the handlebars. The real pain didn't hit until later. There was no internal damage."

He tugged her close and spoke against her hair. "Something to be grateful for, I suppose."

Other recollections swam up.

"The doctors and nurses were great. I was a long time in

the hospital. When he visited, my dad's face was lined with guilt. He'd given me the bike. Said with lots of practice I'd get better. I was a bit of a klutz."

"You wouldn't know it now. You move like a vision."

She laughed softly. "I do not."

"Believe me, you're not that klutzy kid anymore. You're a very desirable woman."

She laughed again. "*Very* desirable."

"Very, very desirable. That's something that comes from inside."

In the shadows, she pushed up on one elbow. When she found his eyes, she sent him a mock chagrined look. "You're such a charmer."

"Are you doubting my sincerity? Because if you are—" he shifted until his nose was an inch from hers "—I should show you how serious I am."

His kiss was tender and at the same time held more meaning and passion than any other. At that moment Jack wasn't Dahlia's brother, or Beau's uncle, or even an enigmatic, sexy-to-a-fault grazier. He was the man who'd transformed her into the most beautiful woman in the world. And the feeling was fairy tale fabulous. It was also almost sad.

No one would ever be better than Jack.

When her throat closed off and emotion pricked behind her eyes, Maddy broke from the kiss and wriggled out from beneath him.

Hormones. One minute she was floating, the next she wanted to cry. Too much excitement. Too much emotion. She needed to take a few deep breaths and focus on something else.

When her feet sunk into the soft carpet, she dragged the sheet along with her. "I wonder what Beau's doing now?"

"Sleeping. Where're you going?"

"To get some fresh air."

She moved out onto the balcony where the smattering of town lights twinkled below and mournful curlews cried out in the distance. She was still thinking about Beau when something soft and warm wrapped around her shoulders. Then big hands raveled the blanket around her middle and pressed in.

Jack's deep voice was at her ear. "It can get chilly out here at night."

"I hope Beau's warm enough. Maybe I should have put him in his fleecy PJs."

Chuckling, he grazed his chin over her hair. "You're quite the mother hen, aren't you?"

"He's a cute kid." She smiled into the night, remembering way back. "He reminds me of a life-size baby doll I used to have."

"Dolls, huh? Dahlia liked skipping. One summer she skipped so much I thought her brain would get shaken out of her head."

"And she liked horses?"

"Sure." There was a pregnant pause. "You should try it."

Grinning, she wrestled the blanket more firmly around her. "The day I get on a horse, Jack Prescott, is the day I change my name and dance the polka."

His smile grazed her temple. "My mother didn't like horses much either, even though she'd ridden since she was five."

"How did your parents meet?"

"At a dance. My mother was visiting a cousin. My father fell in love with her on sight." He grinned. "Or that's what he told us kids."

She imagined a couple thirty-odd years ago locked in each other's gazes and an intimate embrace while they moved around a dance floor. The man she imagined looked a lot like Jack. A heart-warming glow filtered through her and she smiled.

"I bet your father treated her like a queen."

"He'd have given her anything she wanted," he said, "But she didn't want a lot." He exhaled and his tone changed. "She had a dream of taking a long vacation on an island. She had a thing for that movie *Endless Love*. Dad booked the flight without her knowing. They'd only been gone a week when she went out swimming and got in trouble. He went out to help."

Maddy held her sinking stomach and pivoted to face him. So that's how he'd lost his parents.

"Jack…I'm so sorry."

Even sorrier that she'd spoken up so strongly about that creek. After losing his parents to a drowning accident she was sure he would rather die himself than risk placing Beau in similar danger. Or any danger, for that matter.

Her palm fanned over his hot bare shoulder. "It must have been hard losing them both."

His eyes glistened in the shadows. He didn't seem to be looking at her but rather through her. "Dahlia didn't take it well."

"Is that why she left for Sydney?"

That bronzed shoulder lifted and fell. "She said she didn't want to be stuck at Leadeebrook like Mum had been all her life. She wasn't going to be trapped." A humorless smile tugged one side of his mouth. "My sister didn't get that if Mum and Dad had stayed on the station they'd still be alive."

Maddy angled her head. Had she heard right?

"Jack, you can't look at it like that. Your parents were on vacation, a well-deserved one, I'm sure. It was an accident."

"An accident they could've avoided."

The line of his mouth hardened and he didn't say the rest although Maddy could guess. *Like Dahlia's accident could've been avoided if she'd stayed at home.*

She had to know for Beau's sake.

Taking his hand, she turned so he held her again while they gazed out over the peaceful outback view. A falling star trailed through the star-studded sky.

"I was speaking to Cait about the nursery," she began. "She told me that you and your wife decorated it."

When his silence stretched out, Maddy cursed herself. She shouldn't have brought it up. If he told her not to speak of it again she wouldn't blame him. Three years was a heartbeat when you were trying to get over a tragedy. She knew.

She'd accepted that he wouldn't reply when his deep voice rumbled over her head.

"The contractions started at three in the morning. She was so excited and anxious. I reminded her that we were a month from the due date. On our last visit the doctor explained about Braxton Hicks. Basically false alarm contractions. A storm was raging outside. The contractions eased but she wanted to go into town and check with the doctor. Her own mother had died in childbirth and now she couldn't seem to think of anything but that. I tried to calm her. Told her we'd wait until light. When she started to cry..." He groaned and exhaled slowly before ending. "I packed her up and headed off. A tree came down on the car. I lived. Lesson learned."

Maddy was holding her stomach, her moist eyes shut. She couldn't bear to think of his pain.

"What lesson is that?" she finally got out.

"Don't tempt fate."

"But no one could guess such a terrible thing would have happened."

"Terrible things seem to follow me around."

Maddy's heart fell. She'd never felt more pity for anyone in her life. He'd lost everyone he'd loved including his unborn child and he blamed himself because he couldn't control the uncontrollable. No wonder he wanted to lock himself away from the world, somewhere he believed he and his memories could be safe. He so desperately wanted to go back in time and make everyone else safe there, too.

But he'd ventured beyond Leadeebrook boundaries tonight. He'd wanted to share an experience with her, the gala, dancing…making love.

"None of those things were your fault," she said, wishing he could lower his defenses for a moment and see.

"Doesn't change the fact that the people I loved most are gone."

She turned in the circle of his arms and held his gaze with hers. "If I was in trouble, if I needed someone to be there to rescue me…I'd choose you."

His gaze softened only to darken more. "And if I failed?"

"Then no one could have saved me."

Maddy thought of her mother, how the leukemia had won; Helen Tyler had accepted her fate even when her husband had begged her to fight. By being strong now— for her father, for her future—in some weird way Maddy felt as if she was making her mother strong, too, and fixing what no one could fix back then.

She'd never admitted those feelings to anyone. Would Jack understand if she told him?

When she shivered, he scooped her close and whispered in a deep sexy drawl, "Come back to bed."

After they moved inside, they made love again, and this time was even better than the first. Then they talked. Talked until dawn. About school days and old friendships. About far-reaching hopes and some of their dreams. When she told him about her father and then her mother's illness—how she wanted to be strong for her now—he brushed the hair from her cheek and with the softest smile said he understood.

When she and Jack arrived at Leadeebrook at seven the next morning, Maddy was bleary-eyed from lack of sleep. She was also pulsing with new energy and heartsick about leaving the next day.

The time had gone too quickly. Even the dry heat and the dust were somehow welcome today. A part of her was even glad to see Nell darting out to greet them.

As they made their way up the front steps, the bold eastern sun warming their backs, Maddy was gripped by an overwhelming need to have this day stretch out like an endless piece of string. She couldn't think of another way to put off the flight she'd booked for herself for Sydney.

Jack had offered to fly her but she'd declined. Saying goodbye here would be tough enough. If he flew her home, she'd be tempted to ask him to stay. Or to ask if she could fly back with him.

Ridiculous.

She'd had one heck of a week at Leadeebrook Station and, to top it off, an unbelievable time last night. The hopeless romantic inside her wanted to be swept up into that spell again. But the responsible woman knew a rerun wasn't possible.

Or was it?

The notion of spending more time here with Jack ribboned around her like a bright new promise and Maddy's face flushed with hope and shame. The basis of Jack's offer for her to return to Leadeebrook had been to visit Beau. She'd been so happy and relieved when he'd suggested it. She'd dreaded the thought of not knowing when she'd see the baby next. After the incredible hours spent in Jack's arms last night, was it wrong to speculate on other advantages?

But if she *did* come back, and she and Jack had another fling, how would she define their relationship? They wouldn't be a couple. She wouldn't be a friend. Maybe a "friend with benefits."

The less contemporary term was mistress.

They reached the top of the steps at the same time that Cait brought Beau out.

The bright-eyed housekeeper held the baby, his back to her front, so that Beau could see all the action. His little legs in their Mickey Mouse cotton PJs pumped with excitement when he saw them. They might've been gone a week.

Cait laughed. "He must've heard the plane. He just woke this minute."

Maddy's arms, but more so her heart, reached out. She'd missed him—his chubby cheeks, his soft curly top. Now she realized how much.

"Did he sleep through?" she asked, taking him from Cait, reveling in his beautiful baby smell while he gazed up into her face and she smiled lovingly down.

"Not a whimper, the little pet." Cait stepped aside to let Jack by with the bags. "How was the gala?"

Before Jack could answer, Maddy piped up, "It was *wonderful*."

Too late, she zipped her lip.

The sparkle in Cait's eyes confirmed what Maddy had feared. Her abundance of enthusiasm at having spent the night alone with Jack had come across loud and clear.

But she wasn't in love. People didn't fall in love after a week.

Did they?

Maddy wasn't sure if it was her imagination but when the hands of her watch reached four and she hadn't seen Jack since scones and morning tea, she was certain. He was either letting her have quality one-on-one time with Beau or he was avoiding her.

In the kitchen, absently sealing the top on Beau's bottle, she wondered. She didn't want to consider the possibility but…did he regret last night?

She rotated toward baby Beau and kissed his tiny fist as he sat patiently in his reclined baby chair.

Jack's feelings couldn't have changed. What she'd felt and what he'd given hadn't been a lie. There was a good explanation for his absence today. Maybe Snow had got in trouble in some distant paddock. Perhaps Jack had fallen off his horse. He could've broken a leg.

She set the bottle on the table, failing to swallow the prevailing sense of doom rising in her throat. Today was her last here. After the intimacies they'd enjoyed, the words they'd said, Jack *must* want to share these remaining hours with her.

As much as she wanted to share them with him.

Maddy lifted Beau. Once nestled against her, with a happy mew he latched onto the bottle and his perfect dimpled hand curled over it. Maddy cradled the baby, drinking in his innocence and, at the same time, holding her breath to stop the spiral of doubt from winding any higher.

She'd been in Beau's life from the moment he was born. She'd been there with Dahlia when he'd come into the world. She'd rocked him and burped him and played "little piggie" long before coming here.

She *loved* this little boy. She would give her life for him in an instant. And when someone loved a child, that love didn't disappear. This kind of love was forever; her heart of hearts told her that. She may not be Beau's mother but that didn't change the way she felt. He was the most precious person in the world to her.

And Jack?

Closing her eyes, Maddy sighed remembering his smile, his woodsy scent, the thrilling rush that flooded her body whenever she saw him. Whenever he held her. Had she fallen in love with this ruggedly handsome man when a week ago she wanted to throttle him? She hadn't understood a thing about him then. She hadn't wanted to.

But here she'd come to know a different side of Jack Prescott—a side that was dedicated to his nephew, had cared deeply for his sister, had been a loving husband and was a heartbroken widower.

In Clancy she'd learned more. They'd spent amazing hours, laughing, talking, making the most blissful kind of love. His kisses sizzled with soul-soaring passion and yet each caress was defined by the purest strain of tenderness. The sensation of his hard, long body locking with hers… the reality of just how effortlessly he brought out every hidden, wanting part of her…

She'd been lifted to the clouds.

Would any woman feel differently, or did she and Jack share something truly special?

She opened her eyes and searched out the kitchen window.

Why wasn't he back?

* * *

Beau was still down for an afternoon nap when Jack rode in near sundown. Through a sitting room window, Maddy tracked his rolling stride as he led Herc to the stables. The horse's nostrils flared from exertion, and his coat was glossy with sweat. Jack would be out there with him for some time yet.

A startling urge leapt up inside of her and she gripped the window sill.

How would Jack react if she appeared at the stable door and asked what had kept him? After these hours of waiting and worrying, she needed to see for herself if the affection that had shone in his eyes last night had dimmed. Could he block out, as easily as this, the way she'd murmured his name?

Fifteen minutes later, she was chewing a thumbnail, pacing the hall, waiting for Beau to wake. She was stir-crazy. An unraveling ball of frazzled nerves. Over a man she'd known a few days and who hadn't chosen to spend these last hours with her.

Clearly she needed to get back to her friends and throw herself back into work. Remember who she was and where she belonged, which wasn't here in this barren wilderness.

She stopped at the front door, hands bunched at her sides. She flicked a glance at the still-quiet nursery, heard Cait's saucepans' distant rattle in the kitchen. The sinking sun washed pails of luminous orange, red and mauve across the hushed horizon. The night was fast approaching. Soon the morning would be here.

Maddy's hands bunched tighter.

Would he *ever* come in?

Her frayed patience snapped. She marched down the stairs and cut a bee-line to the stables.

Jack sat at a small table, dusty boots balanced on one end, ankles crossed. He was rubbing down some leather strap or other, but now the action stopped. His head turned and his wary gaze met hers.

Quivering inside, she stepped forward. In his stall, Herc shook his mane. Her stomach jumping, she pulled up abruptly then scolded herself.

Don't let him know your knees feel like water. Don't let him see you're upset.

Manufacturing a smile, she tipped her head in the homestead's direction. "Dinner's almost done."

His boots swung off the table and the front legs of the chair smacked the wood. "Great. I'm starved."

With that smooth rolling stride, he moved into the tack room and emerged several minutes later. When he didn't acknowledge her but rather crossed to flick his hat off a peg, she cleared her throat quietly, just enough to be sure her voice wouldn't crack.

"There's rhubarb pie for dessert," she said. "Smells delicious."

He dusted off the brown felt then gifted her a tight smile. "Can't wait."

"In a couple of month's Beau'll be tasting solids. I wonder if he'll have a sweet tooth."

"You must leave me your address." He fitted his hat. "I'll let you know how it goes."

When he continued to stand several paces away, the chiseled planes of his face so impassive, her heart contracted and then slid to her feet.

She couldn't stand the tension a moment longer. They needed to talk, sort this out, whether he liked it or not.

"Jack, I'm confused. Have I done something wrong?"

His brows flew together. "Of course not."

"Then where have you been all day?"

He removed his hat, glared at its well while he shoveled a hand through his thick black hair. "I had things to do."

"What things?"

"You wouldn't understand."

"What wouldn't I understand?"

His hat dropped to his side as he heaved out a breath. "Do you really want to know? You're going back tomorrow." He threw a glance around the stable walls. "This'll all be a dusty memory in a month."

Maddy's breath double hitched in her chest.

What was going on? Why was he suddenly so cold? So hurtful? Because she was leaving? He'd always known that.

She moistened her dry lips and reminded him, "You invited me to come back."

"You can come back any time you like," he said blandly.

The room tilted. Had she *dreamt* last night? This Jack was like a different man.

"Can I get this straight? You're saying you're not bothered either way? Whether I come back or not?"

"It's up to you. You have your life. You know what you're doing with it." He glanced at his watch. "And we'd better have tea so you can pack and get back to it."

He headed for the stable door but his pace slowed when she didn't follow.

Her feet were lead blocks. Her insides were roped with heavy knots. She could barely stop the corners of her mouth from bowing. Where was the man she'd shared so much with last night?

Was she supposed to nod politely now and eat dinner at the table as if nothing had happened? As if he hadn't nuzzled and stroked every inch of her? As if he hadn't opened up each hidden part of her soul and invited himself into her heart?

Dammit, if he thought he could walk away from this that easily, he was wrong.

"I need you to answer me. Do you want me to come back?"

His eyes didn't meet hers as he growled over one broad shoulder, "Of course I'd like you to come back."

"Jack...*look at me*."

His broad back in the sexy chambray shirt expanded as he inhaled. He slowly turned. Rubbed his jaw. Met her eyes.

A muscle popped in his darkly shadowed square-cut jaw. "I'm not sure what you want."

She didn't give herself time to think. She walked straight over to cup his face. Then, bouncing up on her toes, she kissed him.

For an instant she felt that same fire, the spark-to-gas-leak explosion that had ripped through and released her again and again last night. She imagined she heard a rumble of satisfaction deep in his chest, felt the vibration rise in his throat and tingle with crystal clear meaning across her lips.

But as suddenly as it appeared, the scalding tension slid away and the kiss...his mouth on hers...lost its life.

The fire was gone. Snuffed out. Or had he simply locked it away behind a steel door? After the heartfelt promise he'd made—that whatever she was worried about, she didn't need to be—could he hurt her that way now?

Gutted, she let go of his jaw, found her feet and stepped back. But before she looked into his eyes, she willed all emotion from her face. She thought of scorpions and snakes. Of barren dusty miles she would soon say goodbye and good riddance to forever. The alternative was to break down and cry and...

She eased out a breath.

She'd rather be strong.

He'd said he didn't know what she wanted.

Shaking back her hair, she pasted on an unaffected smile and formed the necessary lie in her head.

"Oh, Jack," she began, "be fair. All I want is for you to know how much last night meant. Every girl dreams of having a real cowboy." She raised a playful grin. "And you're as real as they get." When tears stung like acid behind her eyes, she smiled harder and rubbed her nose. "I'm going to have to get out of here before I have a sneezing fit."

She brushed past before the tears caught up and beat her down. Damned if she'd let him see her cry.

"Maddy, *wait.*"

Spinning around, she theatrically pinched her nose. "I sincerely hope you're not going to ask me to help clean out that stall or brush down Herc."

They shared a gaze for a torturous moment and just when the emotion seemed about to break free—just when she thought she would crumple and tell him the truth—his shoulders came down.

"No, I wouldn't ask you to do that." He sauntered toward the stall. "Tell Cait to set my place. I'll be along soon."

Returning to the house, Maddy kept her pace steady. *Don't think about what just happened. Don't give in to the tears.* But she *couldn't* keep her mind blank or the sense of devastation from creeping higher, tighter. She simply couldn't believe it. It was as if all her life she'd known every shade of blue and today she'd discovered she was color-blind. How had she gotten it so wrong? She'd been slow to come around, but last night...last night she'd *trusted* him. Truly believed there was so much more to Jack Prescott than arrogance and irresistible blistering charm.

But it seemed he'd meant what he said literally.

One night. Just one night.

That his conscience bit a little—that he couldn't quite meet her eyes—didn't mean his dismissive treatment of her hurt any less. With her blinders off, she shouldn't be surprised.

He'd kissed her in the moonlight when he'd been involved with Tara. No doubt there'd been women before his attractive neighbor. Who would come after *her?* She still believed he'd loved his wife but, clearly, now he was a rich, handsome bachelor, doing what rich, handsome bachelors did best.

Entertaining himself. Filling in time.

Inside the house, Maddy dragged herself to the nursery. When she pushed the partly-opened door the rest of the way, her blood froze in her veins. She'd walked into her worst nightmare.

Beau was awake, cooing in his crib. Nell was up on her hind legs, her black-and-white back hunched and front paws on the lower rail. Her long nose was thrust through the rungs.

Beau squealed and, horror-daze broken, Maddy rushed forward, all those faded memories from half a lifetime ago suddenly pulsing and hideously real. Discovered, Nell dropped and, tail between her legs, trotted off to the far corner before Maddy could rip her away.

"Get out of here," she growled through bared teeth.

Her heart was smashing through her ribs, her fingers tingled, her hands, her arms…they were losing their strength. As she glared at the dog, ready to physically throw her out of the room, Maddy tried to catch her breath.

She clung to the crib before her legs could give way. And still the collie stalked her with those deadly dark eyes.

Maddy hissed, "What are you staring at?"

Like a prowling wolf, Nell inched forward and, remembering those scars, Maddy exploded. "Get out! *Get out!*"

The baby wailed. Cait rushed in, Jack a heartbeat behind. The housekeeper threw a frantic look around while Jack strode to the center of the room, his fists clenched and gaze killer fierce.

"What the hell's going on?"

Maddy flapped her hand at Nell. "That-that *dog* shouldn't be in here alone with the baby. Her teeth were an inch from his arm. Dogs are unpredictable, Jack." Sometimes they were savage.

While Maddy scooped Beau from the crib and held him close, Cait's flushed face calmed and she came slowly forward.

"But Nell wouldn't hurt the bairn, Maddy."

Maddy's heart was bursting through her chest. "No one knows that."

The dog that had attacked her had been a family pet. She'd told Jack last night. He'd seen the scars. He'd said he'd understood—understood everything.

Or would he pretend as if none of that had happened, the same way he'd wanted to ignore her in the stables just moments ago?

But when he moved forward—when he put his hand over hers where she held the baby's head close—a static flicker of what they'd known together only hours before zoomed back.

His deep voice was low and gentle. "Maddy…honey… you're overreacting."

Maddy wanted to laugh. *She* was overreacting? He was

the one who wanted to lock everyone away behind these beastly remote station walls.

When he brought her close and urged her hot cheek to rest against his chest, she blinked several times. Concentrating on her breathing, on slowing her heartbeat, the dots before her eyes dispersed and, after a short time, most sped away. Nell lay in the corner, tail to the wall, ears down and head flat on her paws. Maddy swayed, leaned more against Jack and the tingling in her limbs began to fade.

She was stressed. Too much emotion. Too many memories stirred. Didn't change the fact that she would never allow Nell to come so close to Beau again, particularly when the baby was alone. Nothing would change her mind about that, and if anyone thought that was paranoid—tough luck.

But as Jack eased the baby from her arms and Cait called Nell out of the nursery, Maddy filled her lungs with a shuddering breath and the harrowing truth descended.

What could she do about it? If Beau was her child...

But he wasn't. She had as little say in Beau's life now as she had a week ago. *Less.* And the longer she stayed and had to swallow that reality, the more frustrated and upset she'd become.

Jack had been blunt but also spot-on. The decision was up to her but maybe it would be better better for everyone if she left and never came back.

Ten

In his lifetime, Jack had been to hell and back. Determined to find and sustain the strength he'd needed, most of the day he'd ridden the endless Leadeebrook plains on Herc's back. He'd returned to the homestead calm, cold and resolute.

But moments ago, when he'd taken Beau from Maddy and left her to wash her face and settle down before dinner, he'd been shell-shocked. The weight of the realization was like a stake being thrust into the heart. He was responsible, no one else, for her meltdown.

If she thought she'd fooled him in the stables into thinking their night together had meant little more than an adventurous fling on the side, she was mistaken. If she thought he didn't understand about Nell tonight in the nursery, after seeing those scars, of course he did. But, as harsh as he might've sounded, he meant what he'd said.

Soon her time here would be reduced to a quaint story

retold over Friday night cocktails. *He* would be the one left to make decisions for Beau and, damn right, he trusted Nell. More than he'd trust the drug addicts and pimps who trawled Sydney's King's Cross in broad daylight.

Forget about meltdowns and hurt feelings. Madison Tyler would always find fault with his world and he with hers. Fair enough, she was locked into her life and her future. She wanted to leave here to get back to it. Pity was she couldn't see what she set her compass by.

After their talk last night in Clancy, it was clear her main motivation in her job was her desire to prove herself to her father. Maddy wanted her father, as well as herself, to know she was strong. Strong enough to battle and survive anything.

Hell, who was he fooling? He was no better. He was as stubborn as she was. Worse.

Grumbling to himself, Jack carefully lay the baby down on the changing table. Beau wasn't his usual chirpy self either. After making a silly sound, Jack blew a raspberry on the baby's tummy and was rewarded by having his hair pulled by its roots. Little monkey.

Yep, he and Beau James would be happy here. People might call him a wealthy recluse behind his back, but so what? He wasn't budging, just like Maddy wasn't giving up Sydney or her dad.

Jack sprinkled powder, slipped on the diaper, smoothed over the tabs.

When an hour later, Maddy hadn't emerged from her room, Cait ventured in with a small plate of supper. Jack wasn't too hungry either, but he made a show for Cait's sake then took Beau out onto the veranda. He settled down on a chair with the baby on his lap. They were both keeping watch over another peaceful night when Snow Gibson rode up.

With that notorious bow-legged stride, Snow ascended the steps, found a beer in the outside fridge, tickled Beau's chin then pulled up a seat.

Jack said, "Missed you at supper." Snow had always joined him and Cait for Sunday dinner at the homestead.

"I sent word to Cait I wouldn't make it tonight."

"She said. What's up?"

Snow chugged on his beer then concentrated on the horizon.

"When I was your age, Jum, I was hop scotching around the place. Got all the way over to Western Australia one year. Sold carpet in Adelaide for a spell. Alice Springs was blasted hot but I wouldn't give it back for a row of Sundays. My only regret is that I didn't find a good woman, one to have that family with." He grinned over. "Maybe it's not too late."

Rearranging Beau, Jack shifted up in his chair. This sounded serious. "What's going on?"

"The bush is in my blood, but I'm too young to hide away, dig a hole and die just yet."

Jack caught on and he grinned. "And I am, too, right?"

"What you have here won't go away." Beau received an earnest tip of his head. "You want to take that boy of yours and do some living. You're a rich man. Some'd say filthy rich. Put that money to good use. Get a life."

Snow stood, finished his beer, hitched up his jeans and headed down the steps.

Jack watched his friend mount and ride away. When he looked down, Beau was asleep. He eased up and headed for the nursery.

He appreciated the concern but Snow didn't have his facts straight. He wasn't *dying* here. His aim was to give

Beau a safe upbringing. And he wasn't about to marry Maddy and have a family, if that was the hint.

Sure, the attraction that zapped between them couldn't be mistaken and, certainly, Beau loved Maddy. But the gulf that ran between them was as wide as the Murray. He was done thinking about it. Done mulling over the things that were better left to lie.

The kitchen was empty. Cait must've taken herself upstairs to bed. Jack entered the darkened nursery but stopped when he saw Maddy curled up in a corner sofa chair. A light blanket was cocooned around her chin. Her wrist, drooped over the arm of the chair, as well as her breathing, said she was sound asleep.

Her hair was a pale shimmering river spilling over her shoulder and he had to curb the impulse to settle Beau down then quietly carry her off to his bed and make love to her the way his body begged him to. But that wouldn't change the fact she'd be gone tomorrow.

Would she come back?

After today? Not likely.

He'd make sure she saw Beau if ever he landed in Sydney. But one day—and probably soon—Maddy would have her own family. She would be a prize for any man. She'd remember Dahlia's child fondly. Hopefully remember their night fondly, too. He always would.

Jack laid Beau in his bed and headed for the door. But then he stopped, frowned and turned back.

He couldn't say where the thought sprang from. He was certain in no possible way would it work. But she did love that baby, and last night proved that they were compatible, in the bedroom as well as intellectually. He knew deep down that advertising wasn't her thing, it was her father's.

What if he asked her to stay?

* * *

When Maddy's eyes dragged open, she wasn't sure of the time.

Rubbing her face, she sharpened her gaze and honed in on the window. Still dark, although a streaking mist hinted at the coming dawn. She straightened, winced. Someone had used her back as a pretzel.

The outline of Beau's crib cleared out of the shadows and her mind slotted up a gear. Twenty-four hours ago she'd been in Clancy, drifting off in that big beautiful bed, a satisfied smile on her face. Jack's arms had kept her so warm and close. Yesterday afternoon the illusion had been shattered.

Clenching her teeth against the crick in her spine, she moved to the crib.

She'd made a fool of herself over Nell. She had no say, no power here. Now there was nothing left for her but to escape. And yet what she wouldn't give to be here with Beau. To be here for him. There were women who'd had to give up their children at birth, or lost them in custody battles or to illness. To accidents. What Jack had endured when he'd lost his unborn baby had to be far worse than this.

On the brighter side there was every likelihood she'd see Beau again. When things settled between her and Jack, she'd contact him, ask when he was coming down to Sydney next. And if he stuck to his agoraphobic routine and refused to leave this place...

Well, she'd simply have to set pride aside and knock on his door. But the dust needed to settle first. Her mission had been to deliver Beau and make certain he was happy. She had and he was. As much as it tore her in two, it was time to move on. The text she received last night from her father confirmed it.

See you tomorrow. First thing.

After tugging the blanket up around sleeping Beau's back, she moved to her room next door to pack. She started to toss her ruined Keds in the wastebasket. She didn't want them dirtying up her suitcase. Instead she slipped them on. She'd get rid of them when she got home.

Dressed in jeans and a simple T-shirt, she'd finished swooping her hair up in a high ponytail when she heard something in the next room. Beau. At least an hour before he usually woke. Did he sense something off-kilter this morning?

He was crying softly by the time she collected his warm little body in her arms. Patting his back, she crooned close to his ear. "Hey, little guy. You hungry already?"

Beau's brow lowered, he tried to smile but he rubbed his eye with a tiny fist and grumbled again.

Jack appeared in the doorway. His alert gaze shot from the baby to her. He held up a bottle.

"I was up. It's warm."

She smiled and a part of her knew in the end everything would be all right. It had to be, for Beau's sake. She couldn't afford to blubber or be sullen or even cringe at the performance she'd made last night. Beau would sense the vibes and his welfare counted way and beyond anything else.

Maddy's insides clenched as she held him tighter still.

Ten minutes from now the cab would be here. But this wasn't like saying goodbye to Dahlia that black morning. Not like her mother telling her to be good before the bedroom door closed and she heard her father cry.

Maddy nuzzled into Beau's softness and baby scent and swallowed the tears.

I'm going to see you again. I promise, it won't be forever.

Jack's deep voice broke into her thoughts. "Sure I can't drive you in?"

"I'd rather—" Her words choked off and she cleared her throat. "It'll be easier."

He exhaled. Nodded. "Want a coffee? Pot's brewed."

"I'll get one at the airport."

He nodded again. Slid a foot back. "I'll get your bags."

She siphoned in a calming breath. A few minutes and then she'd be gone. From Beau. From Jack. From this place she hadn't liked yet over time had grown, in some way, attached to.

When Beau whimpered, Maddy sucked it up and put a carefree note into her voice.

"It's okay, baby." She pressed her lips to his brow. "Everything'll be okay. I promise, I promise."

She stopped. Frowned. Her head slowly drew away before she kissed his brow again. It was warm. Warmer than warm.

Jack had moved off down the hall. Striding out, she called him. "Jack!"

He spun around and must have seen the worry on her face and shot straight back.

She ran a hand over the baby's brow. "He's hot. Feel." He cupped Beau's face and his eyes darkened. "Maybe he's teething early. I have baby Tylenol in his bag."

At the same time Jack's gaze shot to the changing table, to the bag, Nell materialized out of nowhere. When the dog leaped up on the table, Maddy's stretched nerves snapped clean through. But before she could act and chase the dog out, Nell gripped the bag handles between her teeth, jumped down and trotted over.

Maddy's jaw dropped. "How did…?" She gaped at Jack. "She knows what we said?"

"Sometimes I think she has a better vocabulary than I do."

Beau began to grizzle and cry, his dear face crumpling and turning beet-red. A bizarre thought struck but Maddy couldn't shake it. Had Nell sensed Beau wasn't well last night? Was that why she'd poked her nose in? To check? Maybe she was trying to tell them something now.

Maddy reached to grip Jack's arm. "We should get him to a doctor."

But he was already halfway down the hall. To get the keys to his truck? She examined Beau, checking his face, his neck for rashes or spots. There were so many deadly viruses around.

Hearing Jack's muffled voice, she edged down the hall. He paced the kitchen, cell phone to his ear.

"Dr. Le Monde?" He drove a hand through his hair and, frowning deeply, nodded at the floor. "Yes, it's urgent."

Eleven

Help arrived within the hour.

Dr. Le Monde took Beau's temperature, checked for rashes and other signs of bacterial infection. He concluded Beau's fever was due to a viral infection. A common cold.

From a separate bag, the doctor revealed a piece of equipment—a vaporizer.

Standing beside the crib, Maddy watched over Beau, who was drifting off to sleep after a dose of medicine.

"I had one of those when I was young," she said. "It moistens the air. Helps your nose and lungs keep clear."

Le Monde's kind brown eyes glowed with approval. "Correct. It'll make things a little easier for him these next few days." The doctor put his hand on her shoulder. "Keep up his fluids. Cool boiled water in between feedings. Acetaminophen every four hours. He'll be irritable but fine soon enough." He spoke to Jack. "Call if you have any concerns—" he lifted his bike helmet off the floor by the door "—and I'll race straight back out."

Jack saw the doctor off. The bike roared away while Maddy patted Beau's head with a cool cloth. Her fingers brushed his flushed cheek and a fountain of love drew a soft smile across her face.

She would do anything to take his pain. He could never know how much she cared. How much he was loved.

Jack returned and set up the vaporizer. Beau was almost asleep by the time he switched the device on and stood beside her, gazing down on the baby in his crib as did she.

After a comfortable moment, he said in a hushed voice, "He seems better."

Beau's heavy eyes had drooped closed a final time and Maddy exhaled. "Thank heaven. But we're in for a sleepless night or two."

His hand shifted on the crib rail, brushed hers, and a frisson of awareness set light to her nerve endings, reminding her of everything she was so desperate to forget. She demanded that her feet move a little to the left. They didn't listen. If she weren't so stern, they might have moved to the right, closer to Jack's natural heat.

The whir of the vaporizer filtered through the room and she drew the sheet over Beau's shoulder at the same time Jack brushed a curl from his forehead. Their hands touched, lingered, before they each drew away.

"You've missed your flight," he said.

"Guess I have."

But she wouldn't think about Pompadour Shoes or her father's disappointment. She only wanted to soak up the vision of Beau slipping into a peaceful sleep and the knowledge that his illness wasn't serious. She hated to think of the time they might've spent in a city triage unit in similar circumstances. Not that Jack might not resort to putting his fist through a wall if he thought it'd get someone's attention.

Now, however, he was almost meek, although she sensed that intense inherent power rippling beneath the calm.

His thumb tapped the crib rail. "You want to call your father?"

"Soon."

"What'll you tell him?"

"That I couldn't get away." She tried to dredge up an appropriate emotion but in the end she shrugged. "He'll need to hand over the account to someone else."

Jack rolled back his shoulders. "I can get you there in—"

"I'm staying." But she tempered her determined tone with a smile. "No arguments." And before he could insist, she added, "I'm sure."

After three days and nights with little sleep for the adults, Beau's temperature was back to normal, his chest was clear, and his cooing and laughter once again filled the house. Maddy glowed inside when she heard it. Again she was reminded how very precious it was to know that those you loved were well.

Thursday, as Maddy gave Beau his evening bath, she pondered over the Tyler Advertising presentation scheduled for the next day.

Was she sad she wouldn't be there? Mad? Disappointed in herself?

Ultimately she was proud she'd made the right choice. The only choice. These past few days her place had been here with this child. His health and happiness were the only things that truly mattered.

When Cait came in, Beau kicked his heels, splashing water over the table and floor. Chuckling, Cait rustled a towel out from under the table.

"He's certainly got his energy back."

Maddy scooped him out of the baby bath and Cait pat-dried every inch of him. When Maddy took over with the talc, Cait asked, "Have you heard from your father?"

Maddy sighed and shook her head.

Cait had become something of a confidante. Maddy had confessed a little of her feelings for Jack, more about Beau and had also admitted how disappointed her father would be that she'd stayed when she'd promised to go home. Cait had been so supportive, like Maddy imagined her mother would have been. She would never forget this woman's kindness. She would be sad to leave it behind.

Cait flicked out a new diaper. "Well, we all three thank you for staying. It was a brave move. One you didn't need to make and yet you did. Give him time. Your father'll see that, too."

Jack tiptoed in on his socks. When he saw Beau awake and ready for some fun, he cruised over and pumped his little legs, making him giggle. Maddy stepped aside while Jack prepared to fold Beau into his PJs. He'd gotten pretty good at handling those tiny snaps.

Cait put away the talc then laced her fingers over her waist.

"Now everyone's here," she said clearly to get their attention, "I've been on the phone to Beatrice Claudia. She runs the hotel in town," she explained for Maddy's benefit. "Her poor canary fell off his perch this morning and she's beside herself. I offered to come stay the night. Share some sherry. Maybe talk her into buying another bird. No one wants to live alone."

Maddy thought she saw something more flash behind

Cait's eyes but then the housekeeper straightened and cleared her throat.

"Anyways," Cait went on, "the crisis here is over. Dinner's cooked, so if you don't mind, Jock, I'll take the truck to town tonight."

"You know where the keys are," he offered. "Give my condolences to Mrs. Claudia."

Cait caught Maddy's eye before she headed off. "Don't expect me home before noon."

Two hours later Beau was asleep.

Maddy enjoyed a long soapy shower then found Jack, equally exhausted and freshly scrubbed, sprawled out on a sofa in the living room. Maddy fell back into the cushions alongside of him.

She sighed. "I could sleep for a week."

Jack groaned. "Starting now."

Maddy was zoned out, eyes closed, remembering the rosy tint in Beau's healthy cheeks tonight, when Jack's question took her by surprise.

"When will you be heading back?"

She blinked across at him. "You're that eager to get rid of me?"

Jack sat straighter, ready to deny it, but when Maddy only grinned, his shoulders went down and he smiled, too.

These past days the atmosphere had changed between them again. He was still dynamic and gorgeous—nothing could ever change that. But they'd worked so closely to make sure Beau was comfortable and on the mend. There'd been no time or energy to hold grudges over what had gone before.

She wanted to move on from their awkward discussion in the stables and had all but convinced herself that Nell would only ever protect the baby; she certainly seemed tuned in to the humans around her and, rather than let the past cloud the present, Maddy decided she should take some solace in that.

Strange to admit but, after these few days, Maddy felt almost at home here and felt close to comfortable again with Jack. He'd done everything he could to help and she appreciated it. Maybe it was time to put her changed feelings into words. No time like the present.

Sitting an arm's length away, she turned to him. He turned at the same time. Their eyes connected and Maddy felt drawn to him as she had been so many times before. It was as if her body knew the danger to Beau was past and now it was time to get back to other unresolved matters.

But that wasn't happening. To go there again with Jack would only complicate what had been settled well enough. They'd shared one night. She wasn't about to make it two, even if she suspected Cait had made herself scarce for precisely that reason.

When his gaze dropped to her mouth, she felt more than saw him lean nearer. A violent tug of war kicked off in her mind, in her heart, and, panicking, she flung up both hands.

"Jack, please…let's not do this."

He stopped, nodded gravely. "You're right." He slid over. "Let's do this."

He dragged her against him and his mouth claimed hers. Astonished as well as instantly, unspeakably aroused, she pushed against his chest but Jack didn't budge. In fact, he drew her closer, kissed her deeper, and soon, rather than pushing, her hands were flexing and rubbing, wanting to get beneath his shirt.

She was barely aware of being carried from the lounge to his room. When he set her on her feet, their clothes came off in a flurry while they twirled and stumbled their way over toward his bed. His mouth on hers, he blindly threw back the covers and, breathing labored, swept her up and laid her down, not in a gentle way.

Curled over her in the shadows, his shoulders expanded as he inhaled a hungry breath and apologized. "I'm being too rough."

She hauled him down. "I won't break."

Their mouths crashed together again, and every time his tongue swept around hers, it stroked and teased the wild surge building inside her, a delicious quickening of her blood that left her panting and clinging to his arms, to his hips. When his erection stabbed her belly, she threw him off and swung on top, her thighs spread and clenched over his. Hair spilling across her face, she slowly arched above him and, teasing, grazed the sensitive tips of her breasts over his chest.

It was as if she were acting outside of herself. Released from their cage, her animal instincts had taken over and every part of her could focus only on satisfying the spiraling aching need he stoked so deep inside.

She'd never felt like this before. On fire. Everywhere. Incinerating.

His hot hands cupped her hips and shifted her up then ground her back down. His expression was an uneven mix of darkest lust and burning appreciation.

He craned up and wrapped his lips around one nipple. He tickled the tip with his tongue and, sighing, she gripped his head.

"Guess it's been building up," he murmured, tugging at her tender tip with his teeth.

She groaned and writhed. "Only to atomic proportions."

They rolled again and he pinned her beneath him.

When he entered her—when she felt him fill her until he hit that throbbing unstable spot only he knew about—she gasped then bit her lip and focused. How could that wave reach so high so fast?

He moved again and she gazed up into his eyes with a helpless, keen fascination. All the fine pieces of the universe were hurtling toward her core. The sublime pressure was contracting around that single, bright pulsing light. When he hit that spot again—when he unleashed the critical power that made her so completely, purely his—she drove her spine into the mattress and cried out. A heartbeat later, he followed her over the edge.

When the stars faded, they were both damp with perspiration and out of breath. Yet, as she brushed the hair from her eyes, still humming all over, she had the urge to laugh. She'd never been so out of control in the bedroom. Never so out of control in her *life*. What a racket they'd made.

Thank God Beau was fast asleep and Cait wasn't around. Maddy hadn't known lovemaking could be so raw. So beyond anything she'd ever experienced.

After kissing her again—long and slow this time—Jack blew out a satiated breath. "We won't be able to get away with that kind of noise when he's older."

She went to agree but then the deeper meaning behind that statement soaked fully through. Fazed, she glanced across. His expression was easy yet half speculative.

He'd known what he said. How was she supposed to respond? Especially now when every fiber that made up her mind and body buzzed with such bone-deep satisfaction.

Where did they go from here? *How* did they go from here?

A noise filtered down the hall. They both stilled then sprang up.

"Beau." She flipped back the sheet. "I'll go check."

"You've barely left his side today. It's my shift." His finger stabbed the air. "That's an order."

She nodded and watched him drag on his shorts and stride away. She heard Beau squeak, the muffled rumble of Jack's voice. Then nothing. Slowly her muscles relaxed and she lay down again. Put her hand behind her head. Eventually closed her eyes.

She woke with a start and squinted at the luminous digital clock. After midnight.

She looked across and found she was alone in the bed. Where was Jack? How was Beau? She strained to hear. Had the baby had a relapse?

She swung Jack's shirt off the floor and, in a hurry, punched her arms through the sleeves. But the room was dark and unfamiliar. On her way to the door, she tripped over something that might have been a boot and landed hard against the drawers.

Pressing her lips together, she swore under her breath. *Damn.* Her little toe felt broken.

Rubbing her foot, gritting her teeth to control the pain, she slowly straightened. A stream of moonlight was beaming in through a crack in the curtain. On top of the drawers, illuminated, that silver framed photo leaped up to greet her. At the frame's base, a gold circle shone in the moonlight. Holding her breath, Maddy reached to touch…

A wedding ring.

She'd seen this photo the day she'd arrived but everything had moved so fast tonight, she hadn't thought about it when he'd swept her in here earlier. How would things have played out if she had remembered? Because now she didn't feel the least bit sexy or impulsive. She felt like an intruder, particularly given that Jack still wore the matching gold band around his neck.

His words echoed in her mind.

When he's older… Next time…

She wanted there to be a next time. And a next. But she didn't know how she felt about making love with a man who still considered himself married the way Jack so clearly did. She certainly wouldn't go there again with this photo watching over them.

A glow way off down the hall drew her eye. Giving her toe a final rub she limped toward it and eventually found herself in a room she hadn't entered before… A large and lavish yet strangely cozy library, with a vast collection of spines highlighted in crafted wood bookcases.

In the far corner, Jack sat on a couch holding a book. She recognized the cover. She had the same edition at home.

He glanced up and found a smile. "You were sleeping so soundly, I didn't expect you to wake."

"So you thought you'd catch a few chapters of *Jane Eyre?*"

He grinned. "Sue loved reading, like you." His gaze grew distant. "I figured I'd spend the rest of my days riding the plains during the day and looking over these spines at night."

Her gaze filtered over the rows and rows of books. All Sue's. Would she have liked Jack's wife? Maddy tugged the oversized shirt around her naked body more firmly. She wouldn't think about that just now.

She wandered over and took the book. "This is one of my favorites. The ending stays with you forever." The fierce patriarch had been reduced to rely upon the loyal governess.

When she flipped to the back cover, scanned the lines

and handed it back, he drew her down onto his lap and concentrated on the motion of curling hair behind her ear.

"Something Snow said the other night…it's making a lot of sense. We're good together, Maddy. Way better than good. And Beau needs a mother."

She predicted the bombshell about to hit. Overwhelmed, she lowered her lashes to hide her shock.

He was going to ask her to *marry* him? It was too amazing to contemplate. Just now she'd confirmed again in her mind that Jack still considered himself to be married. That he would always consider himself to be married to his deceased wife. Had she been wrong?

With a knuckle, he raised her chin and willed her to meet his somber gaze. "Maddy, I'm asking you to stay."

The words took a moment to sink in. *Not* a marriage proposal. He was asking her to move in. He'd said Beau needed a mother. He wanted her to pull up pegs in Sydney and replant them out here?

Her voice was a hoarse rasp. "You want me to live at *Leadeebrook?*"

An image of that photo sitting on his bedroom drawers swirled up and her mind's eye tunneled in on the delicate gold ring. Its larger twin lay shining on Jack's bare chest now.

Her gaze jumped from the ring to the wall of books— Sue's library. Sue's room. Sue's house.

She swallowed against a tight ache in her throat. "What about your wife?"

His eyes narrowed, as though he suspected she'd suffered a memory loss. "Sue's dead."

"But she isn't to you. Not here." Her palm covered the left side of his chest, her fingers brushing the wedding band.

The questions in his eyes cleared even as his jaw tightened almost imperceptibly. "You want marriage?"

"Oh, Jack, it's not about that." The way she felt—the problem this "offer" posed—it wasn't that simple.

Although she couldn't deny that the past few days, when she'd seen Jack being so good with Beau, she'd imagined them as a family. Perhaps with another child or two. But the more she'd thought about it, the more ridiculous it had seemed. First up, where would they live? His world or hers?

Yet in Jack's mind he'd settled that point. He'd asked her to stay here. With the dust and the horse hair and the flies. Of course, there was a lot to like, as well…the history, the sunsets, the peace. But her life was so firmly entrenched in the city, she could think of only one response to his question.

"Why don't you both come and live in Sydney?"

He winced. "You know the answer to that."

She pushed off his lap. "Explain it to me."

"Sydney's fine. Beautiful city, as far as cities go. But it's not home."

"Not your home, but it's mine."

He stood, too. "I'm offering you a new home."

She didn't want a new home, not in the country a million miles from the nearest mall. Away from her friends. Her job. Her father.

She stopped and, torn in two, squeezed shut her eyes.

But Beau was here. Jack, too.

Her stomach knotted and she covered her hot face. Oh God, she had to think. And her thoughts came back to that little boy. Jack was Beau's legal guardian. This was his home, like it or not. But one day he would grow into a teenager with a mind and a will of his own. Like Dahlia had.

"What about Beau?" she asked, dropping her hands. "What happens when he wants to see and live and experience life beyond these fences?" Did Jack want Beau to follow in his sister's drastic footsteps and run away?

"When the time comes, he'll have the best higher education available and that means Sydney." His hands found hers. "But Beau is a Prescott. A male descendant. I won't need to insist he stay because he belongs here, same way I do, like his grandfather and his father before him."

She barely contained an astonished huff. "And the women don't get a choice." When he released her hands as if they'd burned, she hurried on. "I want to be with you and Beau. But how can I say I'll stay when I have a whole life back home?"

He didn't look impressed. "A whole life."

"A job. Friends. You know." She shrugged, exasperated. "A life."

His shoulders squared and his eyes dulled. "Then you've answered my question."

A deep dark cavern open up inside her. Damn his arrogant streak. What made him think the world revolved around him? Didn't anyone else's feelings or background count?

"Why is it okay for you to dig your heels in and not me?"

Detached now, he collected the book off the couch. His voice was a low drawl. "You can do what you please."

Her mouth dropped open then she slowly shook her head. His about-face was so swift and definite, it left her dizzy. "I thought I could talk to you. Thought we were at last somewhere on the same page. But you haven't heard anything I've said." He was only prepared to listen to the voices of tradition and the past. All the ghosts that kept him here and wouldn't him let go.

He slotted the book away, ran his finger down the spine. "If your job is more important—"

"That's not fair."

He spun around. "It's not about being fair."

Maddy staggered back.

He was just like her father, implacable, and just as hard to please. She was sick of trying. Tired of playing everyone else's games.

"You might've put up your feet and retired, Jack, but I have a job, and it's full time."

He crossed his arms. "Is working for your father where you want to be?"

The question took her aback but she recovered. "It's no different than you insisting you belong here."

"I belong here because this is where my heart is. Is your heart in Tyler Advertising?"

"You grew up with shearers. I grew up with jingles and slogans. It's all I know. My father took the time to groom me." It's what she'd told herself for years, and yet now she knew she was trying to convince herself.

"Your father will still love you whether you work for him or not. You don't stop loving someone because they choose a different path from the one you'd wanted them to take."

"But you might stop talking to them." *Like you stopped talking to Dahlia.* And suddenly she had to know. She'd believed it a few days ago. Had things ever changed?

Despite shaking inside, she injected a note of calm into her voice. "Would you cut me off, Jack, if I walked away now?"

His eyes turned to ice. "You'd be the one leaving. Not me. I have no control over that."

Maddy held her stomach. How could she argue? It seemed useless to try.

Every day he lived regretting that he hadn't been able to control certain situations and people, and yet he'd let her walk away now without an argument. And if he thought that way, surely that validated what was obvious. Dreams were nice, but that's all they were. She didn't belong here. Even as much as she loved and wanted to be with Beau, there was simply too much against it.

Obviously Jack was of the same opinion because he drove both hands through his hair, holding them there before his arms dropped to his sides. When he looked at her again, his face was blank.

"So what about Beau?" he asked.

Her gaze landed on the Bible on a shelf behind him and a well-known story came to mind.

"Say I did stay. Beau and I would grow even closer." When she waited, he conceded with a curt nod. "If it didn't work out between us and I decided to leave, would you consider sharing custody?"

His presence seemed to swell and intensify before her eyes, like an otherworldly force taking on immeasurable power. But as quickly as it had surfaced, that tension left his body and a different strain appeared.

Stubborn pride.

"No," he said, no hint of remorse in his voice. "I'll never give him up."

Twelve

Jack was not in a good mood.

Two nights ago, he and Maddy had come to an understanding. Of sorts.

He'd dealt his hand and had asked her to stay. She'd countered with the obvious: she couldn't give up her lifestyle. Why was he surprised? You could take the girl out of the city, but…

He kicked his heels into Herc and the horse galloped harder.

Dammit, he was better off without her.

The sun was rising as he rode Herc into the yard. He yanked up so hard on the reins, hooves ploughed up a swirling cloud of red dust that filled his lungs. He swung out of the saddle and his boots hit the ground with a thump.

If he were lucky he'd have missed Maddy's early departure. That would be best. Everything there was to say had been said. He had Beau. His memories. His station. If he had to say goodbye to her… Ah hell, he'd said goodbyes before.

He clapped Herc's flank and the horse reared off into the stables.

When he spun around, she stood at the bottom of the steps. Jeans, white top, pale hair pulled off her flawless beautiful face…so beautiful, he could barely breathe.

Emotion—both raw and bleak—booted him in the chest. Coming back to earth, he stuck his hat more firmly on his head and strode over.

"Thanks," he said formally, "for staying with Beau when he needed you."

"Thanks," she said, just as blandly, "for letting me stay."

Neither looked away. It was as if whoever broke first, lost. Or maybe it was because this was truly the end but there was still that maddening urge to carry her back inside and lock her in until she came around. A hundred years ago he might've done it.

The thought was still hovering when the sound of an engine in the quiet morning pulled his head around. A dusty Yellow cab groaning up the ruts.

Cait appeared at the top of the steps, the baby propped in one arm. She descended as if she were performing a funeral march. On top of everything, he didn't need that. The cab braked at the same time Cait joined them.

She tried her best to smile. "Baby Beau wants to say goodbye."

Maddy's slim nostrils flared but she managed to smile over the moisture filling her eyes. She cupped the baby's face, her hand pale against his cheek, and brushed her lips over his brow. "Be good, Beau darling." Jack caught her barest whisper, "Remember me."

She didn't look at Jack as she turned toward the opened cab door and slid inside. And then she was gone. In the cab, down that endless track. She didn't look back. Not once.

Cait lifted sympathetic eyes to his but Jack only growled beneath his breath. He wanted to take Beau from her, comfort him—feel the connection—but he wasn't sure that was such a good idea right now.

Instead he stormed up the steps. He strode into his room and slammed the door, so hard that the walls rattled. The photo on the drawers wobbled and crashed to the floor. The ring fell, too, bouncing with a tinkle on the wood. Then it rolled over the timber boards until it stopped and dropped at his boots.

A burning arrow tore through his heart and he flinched. Hunching over, Jack pressed the butts of his hands hard against his stinging eyes. Every muscle in his body felt wound tight enough to snap. He wanted to yell. Wanted to put his fist through that door.

He wanted back what he'd lost.

After a few moments, he blew out a shuddering breath and hunkered down. He reached for the wedding band. The gold felt warm, felt familiar. Keeping it close to him these past years…was it commitment?

Or was it time?

Jack wasn't sure how long he sat on the end of the bed, holding that ring and working through things in his mind. When Cait tapped on the door and asked if he was okay, he told her not to worry.

His hands were steady when he unclasped the chain from around his neck. He moved across the room, collected the photo off the floor and slid open the top drawer. Closing his eyes, remembering and cherishing it all, he kissed the frame then put the photo and both rings safely away.

Thirteen

Maddy's cell call connected at the same time the regional airport loudspeaker announced her flight was ready to board.

She'd checked in her luggage, had grabbed that coffee. Now she needed to do something that would lift a great weight. She was tired and done with carrying it.

Her father's smooth voice filtered down the line from Sydney.

"Madison, you said it was urgent. I meant to get back to you sooner." Papers shuffled. "I've been busy."

On Monday she'd left a message that she didn't know when she could get back, that the baby needed her and he should find a replacement account executive for the Pompadour account. A lot had happened since then.

"Dad, I need to resign."

"I've already taken care of that. Gavin Sheedy's taken on the Pompadour account—"

"I need to resign from Tyler Advertising."

Maddy pressed her lips together as the silence at the other end stretched out.

Drew Tyler's voice was deep and wary. "You're in love with that man, aren't you? I spoke with a colleague the other day. He said he saw you at a—"

She cut in again. "Jack Prescott has nothing to do with my decision." And as the words left her mouth she knew it was true. "Daddy, you love what you do. I wanted so badly to make you proud. I wanted to prove to us both I could make it." Be strong. Survive. No matter what. "But since I've been gone…" There was no easy way to say it. She sucked in a breath. "Advertising isn't what I'm meant to do. It's not who I want to be."

"I see." His tone was reflective, calm. "And what is it you do want to do?"

Her gaze wandered around the busy terminal, people arriving from exotic destinations, families flying off to find new adventures. She saw the shining opportunities and experiences glowing around them like auras.

She shucked back her shoulders and felt herself grow. "I want to travel."

When her father laughed, not in derision but an uncommonly merry sound, she almost fell over.

"Sweetheart, that's a marvelous idea. I wish now I'd had time off when you were younger to take you myself. And when you get back—"

"You're not angry?" Maddy shook herself. He'd spent so much time helping her, coaching her.

"Honey, advertising can be cutthroat. At least it is at Tyler. It's not you. Never was."

The rest of his words faded. Maddy had pivoted around. Now her attention was hooked on the terminal's automatic sliding doors—or rather, on who was striding through them.

The air left her lungs in a whoosh.

"Jack...?"

His purposeful gait pulled up. Long denim-clad legs braced apart, he cast a hawkish gaze around. The thunder in his face said he was ready, and able, to tear the place apart if need be.

Maddy swallowed to wet her dry throat. "Dad, I need to call you back."

She didn't hear the reply. The phone dropped from her ear at the same time Jack spotted her. He marched over with such masterful purpose, Maddy almost wanted to hide. What was the matter? What on earth had she done? Was something wrong with Beau?

He stopped a foot away. Before she could think, he drew her in hard against him and kissed her—kissed her with what felt like everything his soul could gather and give.

One hot hand cupping her neck, the other winging her shoulder in, his caress penetrated every aching, wanting layer—of her mind, of her heart, of her spirit. She'd schooled herself to accept she would never feel the divine skill of his mouth on hers again. She'd fortified her willpower and was determined not to break and go back.

But as the kiss deepened and the pounding of his heartbeat melded with hers, Maddy couldn't bury the truth. She loved this man. Like no woman had ever loved a man before. Every day, every minute of her life, a part of her would be with him. How she wished she'd met him first.

As thrilling as this hurricane display of affection was,

a man couldn't be in love with two women at the same time. Although she couldn't think badly of Sue, it broke her inside to know she wasn't the blue ribbon one.

The kiss broke softly. She went to speak, but his fingertip touched her still-wet lips.

"I've tortured myself," he said. "I can't count the times I've asked why people I love keep leaving me. Maddy, you had the answer."

"Jack, I *so* don't have any answers."

She tried to wiggle free—nothing could change her mind, make this work—but his hold remained firm.

"You told me that night in Clancy. What happened in the past was out of my hands. This isn't. I've made mistakes before. No doubt I'll make more in the future. But letting you walk out of my life won't be one of them." He lifted her chin and scanned her eyes. "I love Leadeebrook. But I love you a thousand times more. Whatever it takes to keep you in my life, I'll do it. If you want to live in the city, we'll do that. And we'll live every day to the fullest. We have enough money to live three lifetimes in luxury."

Maddy's jaw unhinged. Her brain was stuck way back.

"You'd *sell* Leadeebrook?"

"If it means having you—" he smiled with his eyes "—in an instant. I'd shut down. Closed myself off. You and Beau opened me up again—to hope. To *feeling*. To all the things that make living worthwhile."

When Maddy grew dizzy, she remembered to breathe.

He was *deluded*. Must have fallen off his horse and bumped his head. He couldn't know what he was saying.

"I—I can't let you sell." That sheep station was a part of him, as much as an arm or a leg.

But he seemed to think her confusion was funny. He chuckled. "Don't worry. I've never thought more clearly in my life." His smile changed. "Driving here I wondered... Do you think Dahlia might've hoped for something like this?"

"You mean for us to—"

She couldn't say it. If she did, this wild wonderful dream would dissolve and she'd wake up.

But he nodded and said the words for her. "For us to fall in love. Maybe Dahlia could see the three people she loved most in the world finding happiness together."

Tears raced from the corners of her eyes as her gaze slipped to the open V of his shirt. The chain was gone. She honed in on his naked left hand, just in case, and a sob caught high in her throat.

He'd put away the ring. He wanted to move on? Could he honestly, truly give his heart to another woman...to her?

Another possibility came to mind and her throat swelled.

"Are you doing this for Beau...so he'll have a mother?"

Somehow she couldn't hate him if he was.

He came close and his warm breath murmured against her temple. "I love you, Maddy. Please...let me love you. Say you'll marry me."

Something in his voice, in the way his lips brushed her skin, told her it was safe. Not just for now but forever. And suddenly it didn't matter where they lived or what they did. As long as they were together. The three of them together from now on.

Her cheeks were hot and wet. Her voice was a desperate, elated whisper needing to be heard.

"Yes, I'll marry you. I love you, Jack." Her breath caught

on a joy-filled laugh. "I want to be with you so much. Wherever that is. Every day. Every night."

When she answered him again with a kiss that was created from deepest faith and sealed with the promise of everlasting love, smiling into her eyes, Jack swept up his bride-to-be.

And took her home to Leadeebrook.

Epilogue

Maddy's silk gloved hands tugged back on the ribbon reins and Herc's brief journey came to an end.

Pink-and-white petals littered the outdoor aisle, which led to a gazebo laced with climbing roses and gold satin bows. Friends, seated on either side, kept their rapt, so-happy-for-you faces turned her way. But Maddy's gaze was drawn to only one.

Jack's shoulders in that crisp dark jacket had never looked broader. She already felt the rasp of his freshly shaven jaw, could already smell the masculine scent that made her feel so warm and prized. His eyes were dancing. Dancing with love. The same unique love she'd felt thrive these past nine months. Today she could barely hold back from shouting and telling the world.

Drew Tyler, in his morning suit, took her hand and helped the bride from her sidesaddle onto an elevated platform then down two steps to the lawn.

"I've never seen you look more beautiful." Her father's eyes glistened as he smiled. "I'm so pleased for you, sweetheart. Your mother would be, too."

Emotion filling her throat, she squeezed her father's hand while three bridesmaids fussed to arrange her sweeping train. Her wedding gown's white silk and organza bodice hugged to the hips before flaring out into a fairy-tale skirt, which was highlighted by scatterings of sequined leaves gold flecks that echoed her fiancé's eyes.

Adoring eyes that were pinned on her.

The music swelled. Her father looped her arm through his and Maddy closed her eyes. Her mother and Dahlia were close. She felt their wishes for happiness drifting over her.

Her father whispered near her ear, "You ready?"

Smiling, she opened her eyes and together they took the first measured step.

Standing beside Jack, Snow looked splendid in a black-tie dinner suit. He'd even trimmed his beard. As he winked at her, Maddy's gaze, through the fine net of her veil, tracked over to Cait, sitting up front. Year-old Beau was perched quietly on her lap, his big eyes glued on "Mummy." Nell sat beside them, well-behaved, too, wearing a pale pink tutu Cait must have organized for the occasion.

Then the music was fading and she was standing beside Jack, tears of pure joy misting her eyes. He'd never looked more handsome. More proud. Carefully he folded back her veil and the minister raised his book.

When the vows and rings were exchanged, Beau clapped harder than anyone. He jumped off Cait's lap and, blond curls bouncing, scampered up in his tuxedo playsuit to hug his parents' legs extra-tight.

The wedding breakfast was served in a twinkling marquee with a billowing white silk ceiling. When Jack led her to the dance floor for the bridal waltz, Maddy wanted to warn her husband that she hadn't forgotten her promise: today she'd ridden a horse and changed her name. He needed to get ready to dance the polka.

But she had far more important news and she couldn't hold back a moment more.

Her gaze on his bow tie, she ran her hand down his satin lapel. "There's something I need to tell you."

"News? I wonder if it's as good as mine. But you first."

She met his gaze. He looked so enthused, she smiled and tipped her head. "No, you."

"Snow and I've come up with an idea to turn Leadeebrook into a sheep station museum. We can dress it up for the public, have sheepdog shows, shearing displays, outback extravaganzas. You were right. This place is too special, has too much history, to let lie around and decay."

Maddy beamed and hugged his neck. Jack was kept busy enough with his investment portfolio as well as being a great dad to Beau, but some days she caught the restlessness in his eyes. This museum plan was exactly what he needed.

But they spent a good deal of time in Sydney now, coming back here to Leadeebrook for quiet times in between. It wasn't a compromise on either one's part. They were simply enjoying the best both their worlds had to offer.

"Does that mean we'll be spending more time here than Sydney now?" she asked.

He dropped a kiss on her inside wrist. "We'll spend as much time here as you want." He grinned. "Although

Beau's social calendar is pretty full in Sydney. Play groups, swimming classes."

"He's a popular kid."

"With a popular and extremely beautiful mother." His forehead rested upon hers but as he rocked her around to the music, the laughter faded from his eyes. What replaced it made her heart swell and cheeks heat with that familiar desire she could never get enough of.

"Thank you for bringing me back to life," he murmured as wedding guests danced around them. "I love you so much, I just want to grab on and never let you go. In fact…" Taking her by surprise, he gripped her high on her waist and swung her in a circle so that her feet left the ground and her train flew out in a glittering white river around them.

She was laughing, out of breath, when he set her down. Giddy, she righted her diamond-and-pearl tiara. "We might need to go a little easy on that kind of spontaneous stuff for a while." When his brows knitted, questioning her, she teased, "Just for seven or eight months."

Jack's pupils dilated. Then his chest expanded to a breadth and width she hadn't witnessed before. He drove a hand through his hair and again.

"You mean you're…" His Adam's apple bobbed up and down. "You and I…Maddy…we're having a *baby?*"

She bit her lip but couldn't contain the ear to ear smile. "Uh-huh."

He whooped then dipped, about to grab and spin her around again. But he stopped then stepped back.

His smile disappeared. "Do you need to sit down?"

A flicker of unease brushed her stomach but she quickly assured him. "I'm fine. Fantastic. The doctor says everything's better than good." She held his hands, searched his eyes. "But if you want to postpone our honeymoon in Paris… I mean, if you're worried about me flying right now or anything…"

I'll understand.

He blinked slowly and a line creased between his brows.

"We've been to New York," he said, "Hawaii and New Zealand with Beau. I don't see why this little one can't experience France—" he settled his warm palm over her belly and grinned "—even if it's from in here."

Maddy flung her arms around him. He wasn't going to wrap her in cotton wool? Wasn't going to even hint that they should hibernate here at the station, at least until after the birth?

She pulled back. "Are you sure?"

"No. I'm positive." His strong arms gathered her in. "Know what I love most about you?"

"I think I do." Playful, she craned up and skimmed her adoring lips over his.

He chuckled and the rumble vibrated through to her bones. "Besides that."

"Tell me."

"I love that every day I discover something new and wonderful that only makes me love you more."

A surprise tear escaped and rolled down her cheek as his head slanted over hers. Their lips brushed again and again. After she murmured how much she loved him, too, she rested her cheek on his chest and contemplated their fabulous future together.

A cry of *"Dad-da!"* brought them to attention.

They turned. Cait was holding Beau. "Your son wants to dance."

Laughing, Jack scooped Beau onto the swing of his sleeve and Beau clapped his hands while Maddy welcomed the wonderful sense of completeness.

Contentment.

She'd always wanted to belong, but no one belonged to a job or address. Dancing with Jack and their son on their wedding day, with another beautiful baby on the way, Maddy knew exactly who she was and where she needed to be.

With her heart.

With her family.

Wherever their love was, God willing, so was she.

* * * * *

"You said sex can be simple."

Nick peered at Brooke with assessing eyes, his gaze flowing over her lacy white gown that bared more cleavage and legs than she'd ever let him see before.

He swung his legs off the bed and stood. "It can be."

He looked like sex personified in a pair of jeans and nothing else. His body tight and muscled, his skin a golden-bronze.

"I need simple, Nick. With you."

He walked over to her and took the wine bottle from her hand. "You want to tell me what changed your mind?"

She closed her eyes. "No."

He set the wine bottle down and then the glasses. "I've been waiting for you," he said, then brushed his lips to hers gently, teasing, stroking with his tongue until she whimpered his name.

Dear Reader,

When I began writing Nick Carlino's story, I knew I wanted my reckless "ladies' man" to find love, not only with the heroine, but with a small child, as well. Having been born of a ruthless father, Nick is the ultimate bachelor, leaving the pursuits of fatherhood to his two other brothers.

But a midnight car crash in the hills of Napa and a promise made change all that the minute Nick is reunited with his school friend Brooke Hamilton and her sweet baby, Leah.

I've been moonlighting as a childbirth educator in a local hospital for many years and I love all things "baby." So writing this story was a complete joy for me. I have to admit I fell in love with baby Leah first and I think you will, too. Add a hunky reluctant hero into the mix and a determined woman struggling not to fall for wealthy Nick Carlino again, and we have *The Billionaire's Baby Arrangement*.

I'm sorry to leave Napa Valley with this, but I promise you an enjoyable read. In fact, it's my solemn vow!

Cheers!

Charlene Sands

THE BILLIONAIRE'S BABY ARRANGEMENT

BY
CHARLENE SANDS

All the characters in this book have no existence outside the imagination of
the author, and have no relation whatsoever to anyone bearing the same name
or names. They are not even distantly inspired by any individual known or
unknown to the author, and all the incidents are pure invention.

Published in Great Britain 2011
by Mills & Boon, an imprint of Harlequin (UK) Limited,
Eton House, 18-24 Paradise Road, Richmond, Surrey TW9 1SR

© Charlene Swink 2010

ISBN: 978 0 263 88312 1

51-0811

Harlequin (UK) policy is to use papers that are natural, renewable and
recyclable products and made from wood grown in sustainable forests. The
logging and manufacturing processes conform to the legal environmental
regulations of the country of origin.

Printed and bound in Spain
by Blackprint CPI, Barcelona

Award-winning author **Charlene Sands** writes bold, passionate, heart-stopping heroes and always…really good men! She's a lover of all things romantic, having married her school sweetheart, Don. She is the proud recipient of the Readers' Choice Award and double recipient of the Booksellers' Best Award, having written twenty-eight romances to date, both contemporary and historical Western. Charlene is a member of Romance Writers of America and belongs to the Orange County and Los Angeles Chapters of RWA, where she volunteers as the Published Authors Liaison.

When not writing, she loves movie dates with her hubby, playing cards with her children, reading romance, great coffee, Pacific beaches, country music and anything chocolate. She also loves to hear from her readers. You can reach Charlene at www.charlenesands.com or PO Box 4883, West Hills, CA 91308, USA. You can find her on eHarlequin's Desire Blog and on Facebook, too!

To Jason and Lindsay and Nikki and Zac.
May your lives always be filled with love, devotion and
joy. The four of you have made our family complete.
Here's to pizza dinners and game nights,
friendly competitions and traditions.

One

Nick Carlino hopped into his Ferrari and drove out of the Rock and A Hard Place parking lot, gravel crunching under his tires as he turned onto the road that led him to his Napa Valley home. He could really use a smoke right now and cursed the day he quit for good. Rachel Mancini had had that look in her eyes tonight, the one that told him she was getting serious. He'd seen that soft half-lidded expression a dozen times in the women he'd dated and each time he'd been wise enough to back off and let them down easily.

Nick liked Rachel. She was pretty and made him laugh and as the owner of the successful bar and nightclub, she intrigued him with her business smarts. He respected her and that's why Nick had to break it off with her. Rachel dropped hints like bombshells lately that she needed more. Nick didn't have more to give.

Moonlight guided his way on the dark patch of highway with vineyard columns on either side of him, the pungent scent of merlot and zinfandel grapes heavy in the summer air. He'd been called back to Napa after his father's death to help his two brothers run Carlino Wines and according to the will they had six months to decide which of Santo Carlino's three sons would become head of the empire. None of his old man's sons wanted the honor. So it was win by default. Yet Tony, Joe and Nick had pulled it together for the past five months and they had one more to figure out who'd run the company.

As Nick rounded a hilly curve, oncoming headlights beamed straight at him. He let out a loud curse. The car skidded halfway into his lane as it took the turn. Those beams hit him straight in the eyes and he swerved to avoid a head-on collision, but not enough to avoid impact. The two cars collided with a loud smack and his Ferrari whipped around in a tailspin. The jolt jarred him and his airbag deployed. He found himself sitting at a perpendicular angle to the car he'd just collided with.

"Damn," he muttered, barely getting the words out. Pressure from the air bag crushed his chest. He scooted his seat far back and then took a deep breath. Once he was sure all of his body parts were in working order, Nick got out of the car to check on the other driver.

The first thing he heard was a baby crying. Holy crap, he thought, fear gripping him tight. He moved quickly, glancing at the damage to the dated silver Toyota Camry as he strode past. He peered inside the car to find a woman behind the wheel, her body slumped forward, her head against the steering wheel. He opened the door with caution and saw blood dripping down her face.

The baby's cries grew louder. Nick opened the back door and glanced inside. The baby was in a car seat facing backward and looked to be okay—no blood anywhere, thank goodness. The car seat had done its job.

"Hang on, kid."

Nick didn't have a clue how old the child was, not an infant, but not yet at the walking stage, he presumed. He focused his attention on the woman behind the wheel, placing his hand on her shoulder. "Can you hear me? I'm getting help."

When she didn't respond, Nick braced her head and shoulders and gently guided her back, so that he could see her injuries. Blood oozed down her forehead—she had a deep gash from hitting the steering wheel. He rested her head back against the headrest.

Her eyes opened slowly and the first thing Nick noticed was the incredible hue of her hazel eyes. They were a mix of turquoise and green. He'd only seen that spectacular color once in his life. He brushed aside blond wisps of hair from her face, "Brooke? Brooke Hamilton, is that you?"

"My baby," she whispered, straining to get the words out, her eyes beginning to close again. "Take care of my baby."

"She's fine."

This woman he'd known in high school, twelve, maybe thirteen years ago, implored with her last conscious breath. "Promise me, you'll take care of Leah."

Without thinking, Nick agreed. "I promise I'll take care of her. Don't worry."

Brooke's eyes closed as she slipped out of her conscious world.

Nick dialed 9-1-1.

When he was through with the call, Nick got into the backseat of the car. The baby's sobs grew to soft whimpers that tore at Nick's heart. "I'm coming, kid. I'll get you outta this contraption."

Nick could write a book about what he didn't know about babies. He had no idea how to remove the little girl from the straps that bound her into the car seat—hell, he'd never even held a baby before. He struggled for a minute, then finally figured out the release, all the while muttering soft words to the helpless child.

To his amazement, the baby stopped crying and looked up at him, her face flushed and her breaths slowing. With eyes wide, she stared at him in wonderment with her mother's big hazel eyes. "You're gonna break hearts with those eyes," he said softly.

The baby's lips curled up. The smile caught him by surprise.

Nick lifted her out of the car seat, holding her awkwardly in his arms. "You need someone who knows about babies," he said quietly.

Nick shifted the baby onto one arm and got his cell phone out again to call Rena, Tony's wife. She'd know what to do, then he remembered the late hour and how much trouble Rena was having sleeping these days. She was nearly ready to have her own baby. He clicked off before the phone had a chance to ring and dialed Joe's number. Joe's fiancée, Ali, would come running to help and he'd be glad to turn the baby over to her tonight.

The phone went straight to voicemail. Nick left a quick message then remembered Ali and Joe were vacationing in the Bahamas this week. "Great," he muttered, taking the baby in both of his arms now. "Looks like it's me and you. That's not good news for you, kid."

Before the paramedics arrived, Nick managed to sift through the woman's handbag and find her driver's license. In the car's dim overhead light, he saw he wasn't wrong. The woman who'd swerved into his lane and caused the accident was Brooke Hamilton-Keating. He'd gone to high school with her. He'd gone further than high school with her once, but that was ancient history.

Nick sat the baby down on the backseat. "Sh, you be quiet now, okay? I've gotta check on your mama."

The second he released her, she whimpered.

Nick gazed at her and made a slow move toward Brooke. The baby opened her mouth and let out a wail.

"Okay, fine." Nick picked her up again and as soon as she was back in his arms, she quieted. "Let's both see to your mama."

Nick held the baby in one arm and opened the front passenger door. He slid in carefully and adjusted the baby in his right arm, so he could look Brooke over better than he had before. She was out cold, but still breathing. He didn't think the collision had been enough to cause internal injuries, but hell, he was no doctor so he couldn't be sure.

Sirens in the distance sent a wave of relief through him. Nick closed his eyes for a moment. It was late and no other cars were on the road. Napa wasn't exactly a party town and the road they were on led to nothing but residential properties and vineyards.

With the baby in his arms, Nick greeted two paramedics in dark blue uniforms that came bounding out of the van. "The baby seems fine, but the mother is unconscious," he said.

"What happened, sir?" one of them asked.

"One minute I'm driving around a curve, the next this Camry is coming at me head on. I swerved the second I saw her car, or it could have been a lot worse."

"The baby yours or hers?" he asked as he examined Brooke.

"Hers."

He looked at his partner. "We'll take them both to the

hospital." Then he turned to Nick. "How about you? Are you injured?"

"No. The air bag inflated and I'm fine. The Camry doesn't have one, apparently."

The paramedic nodded. "Looks like the car seat saved the baby any injuries."

Within fifteen minutes, the police arrived to take a statement and Brooke's gurney was hoisted into the ambulance. Nick stood by, holding Leah in his arms.

"I'll take her now," the paramedic said, reaching for the baby.

"What'll they do with her?"

"Give her a full exam and then try to reach a relative."

The second Leah was out of Nick's arms, she put up a big fuss. Her face turned red and those big eyes closed as she wailed loud enough to wake the dead. Worse yet, when she opened her eyes, she stared straight at Nick looking at him as if he were her savior.

He remembered the promise he made to her mother.

"Let me have her," he said, reaching for the baby. "I'll ride with you to the hospital."

The paramedic cast him a skeptical look and kept Leah with him.

"I know the mother. We went to high school together. I promised her I'd watch out for Leah."

"When?"

"She opened her eyes and was conscious long enough to make sure the baby was taken care of."

The paramedic sighed. "She likes you a heck of lot better than me. Grab the diaper bag in the car and anything else you see they might need. We've got to get going."

Brooke opened her eyes slowly and even that slight movement caused a slashing pain across her forehead. She reached up to rub it and found a bandage there. She didn't know how long she'd been out, but slivers of sunshine warmed her body.

Her first thought was of Leah and a wave of panic gripped her. "Leah!"

She sat straight up abruptly and her head spun. Her eyes rolled back and she nearly lost consciousness again.

Stay awake, Brooke.

She fought dizziness and took slow, deep breaths.

"She's here," a masculine voice announced softly.

Brooke glanced in the direction of the voice, narrowing her eyes to focus. She saw Leah tucked into her pink blanket, looking peaceful and content, sleeping in the arms of a man. Relief swamped her at first. Her beautiful baby was safe. Tears sprung from her eyes when fragments of the accident played over in her head. She'd gotten distracted by Leah's wailing as she navigated a sharp curve in the road. She glanced back for an instant to check on her and the next thing she knew, she'd collided with another car. She vaguely remembered waking for a moment before all had gone black. Brooke took a minute to thank God for keeping Leah safe in the Peg Perego car seat she'd insisted on when she was pregnant.

Her gaze shifted up to the deep blue eyes and self-assured smile of… Nick Carlino? She'd never forgotten the timbre of his voice that oozed sex or the handsome sharp angles of his face. Or the dimples that jumped out when he smiled. It was enough to make a girl get naked in just under a minute.

She knew. She'd been one of those girls, way back when.

Oh, God.

"Leah is safe," he assured her again.

That's all that mattered to her. "Nick Carlino?"

"It's me, Brooke." Those dimples peeked out for a moment.

She reached out for Leah and the movement rattled pain through her head. "I want to hold my baby."

"She's sleeping," he said, not moving a muscle.

Brooke rested her head against her pillow. It was probably better she didn't wake Leah now, she still felt light-headed. "Is she really okay?"

"She was examined last night. The doctor said she had no injuries."

"Thank God," Brooke whispered, tears once again stinging her eyes. "But why are you here?" She couldn't wrap her head around why Nick was holding her baby in her hospital room.

"You really don't remember?"

"I barely know my own name at the moment."

"You came around a turn late last night and crashed into my car. For a minute there, I thought it was lights out for all of us."

"It was your car I hit?" If she were a cruel-hearted woman she'd say it was poetic justice.

"My *Ferrari*. Yeah."

His *Ferrari*. Of course. Nick always had to have the best of everything. How was she ever going to pay for the repairs? She'd let her insurance lapse when she took off from Los Angeles.

"I'm sorry. I don't know what happened."

"What were you doing driving so late at night?"

"I was looking for my aunt's place and must have taken a wrong turn. The roads were dark and I got distracted. We'd been driving all day and I'd thought we could make it to her place rather than stop at a motel for the night. Are you all right? You weren't injured, were you?"

She still couldn't believe that Nick Carlino was in her

hospital room, holding her baby in his arms like Leah belonged there. A shudder went through her. This was all so surreal.

"I'm fine. The air bag saved my as—uh, butt."

She let go a sigh. "Oh, that's good. What about your car?"

"Needs some repairs."

"And mine?"

"The same. I had them towed to my mechanic's shop."

Brooke wouldn't think about the cost to repair those cars. If she did, the tremors in her head would escalate to a major earthquake.

"You haven't been here all night?" she asked.

The dimples of doom came out on cue and he gave a short nod. Her heart fluttered. "You have?"

He glanced down at Leah then up at her again. "I promised you I'd take care of her last night."

"You did?"

"You were adamant, Brooke. You woke just for a minute to make sure Leah was taken care of. You made me promise."

"Thank you," she said, holding back another round of tears. She didn't need to fall apart in front of Nick Carlino. "I appreciate all you did last night for my baby."

Nick nodded and glanced down at Leah for a second. "Where's her father?"

Brooke blinked. Leah's father, Dan? The man she'd been married to for all of two years, who had told her on her twenty-ninth birthday that he was having an affair with a woman he'd always loved and that he'd gotten her pregnant? He'd left Brooke that night, and one week later she found out that she herself was going to have a baby. That father? "He's not in the picture."

"Not at all?"

Nick seemed amazed by this. Didn't he know how many deadbeat dads there were in this world? Her own father left her mother when Brooke was six years old. She'd rarely seen him, but when he did come around, Brooke would cling to him very tight and beg him to stay longer. He never did. "Daddy's got to go," her mother would say. Brooke never understood why Daddy couldn't live with her any longer. And she cried for him, night after night, praying he'd come home to stay. After she turned ten, he never came around again.

Brooke wouldn't subject little Leah to that heartache and pain. She'd moved away from Los Angeles and Dan, and spent the next months living on her own, managing a small seaside inn on the California coast just outside of San Diego. The little beach town fit her needs at the time. It paid the bills and she liked the cool ocean breezes and smog-free sunshine. It was good for her pregnancy and good for her state of mind.

"No, Dan's not in the picture at all." It felt good saying it. She knew one day she'd have to tell Dan about Leah, but not now. Not yet. She needed to get Aunt Lucy's place up and running and making money before she'd tell Dan about his child. She needed all the ammunition she could get to retain full custody of Leah. That's if Dan would even want his daughter. But Brooke couldn't take any chances. She'd inherited her aunt's eight-bedroom home in Napa Valley and with a little ingenuity she planned to make the place a shining bed-and-breakfast for tourists.

"So, you're visiting your aunt?" Nick asked matter-of-factly, as if he'd already come to that conclusion.

"My aunt passed on three months ago. I inherited her home."

When Nick was ready to pose another question, Leah fidgeted in his arms and made sweet little waking-up sounds. Nick stiffened, appearing confused as to what to do with her.

"She's hungry and probably wet."

On impulse, Nick moved her away from his body, looking at her bottom through the blanket. "You think so?"

"Has she been in the same diaper all night?"

"Yes, no. I think one of the nurses changed her late last night and fed her." He pointed to her suitcases at the other end of the room. "She found what she needed in there."

"Oh, I hadn't even thought about my things. Did you bring them here last night?"

He nodded and stood. She moved her eyes up the length of him and inhaled a steady breath of air. His day-old stubble and wrinkled clothes made Nick look even more appealing, sexier than she'd remembered. She found that he'd filled out his boyish frame to one of a man who could sustain every woman's fantasy.

Good thing he was leaving. "I'll take Leah now. I'm sure I'll be on my way soon," she said.

The doctor walked in at that very moment with a chart in his hands. "I wouldn't be too sure of that." He introduced himself as Dr. Maynard.

Blood drained from her face and her insides knotted. "Why not?"

"While your tests show no damage, you took one nasty bump to the head. You're going to have bouts of dizziness. You won't be able to drive and it's better that you rest for at least two days."

The doctor did a cursory exam, removing the bandage on her head, nodding that it looked better. He checked her eyes with a probing light and used his stethoscope to listen to her heart. "I can release you today into someone's care, though. Do you have help for your baby?"

She shook her head. "I just arrived in town last night."

And what an entrance she'd made. "I can call a friend." She'd kept in contact with Molly Thornton for several years after she'd graduated from high school. Though she hadn't spoken with Molly in two years, she knew she'd lend a hand if needed. Molly was the nurturing type and wouldn't let a friend down.

"Okay, I'll get your release ready. I'm writing you a prescription for pain relievers. Nothing too strong. Are you still nursing the baby?"

Brooke nodded. "Yes."

He glanced at Leah, who was kicking up more of a fuss now in Nick's arms. "She's cute. I have a daughter a few months older than her." Then he glanced at Nick. "I never thought I'd see a baby in *your* arms, Carlino." The doctor glanced back at Brooke. "Next time you come to Napa, I wouldn't suggest you crash into Nick." He winked at her. "It's safer to steer clear when you see him coming."

Brooke had already come to that conclusion, years ago.

Nick twisted his lips. "Funny, Maynard. But you won't be laughing when I kick your butt on the court Friday."

"Keep dreaming." Dr. Maynard turned back to Brooke, his serious face on. "Be sure to have someone pick you up today and stay with you. Take it easy for a few days."

"Okay, thank you, doctor."

When he left the room, she turned to Nick, who had calmed Leah down again. Leave it to Nick to know how to persuade a female. "I'll take Leah now."

Nick walked close to the bed, holding Leah like she was a football tucked close to his body. Her daughter stared at him with wide eyes.

"She seems to like me," he said, mystified. "I don't have a clue about babies. Until last night, I'd never held one in my arms."

"You never had children?"

"No little bambinos for me. I'm leaving that up to my brothers."

She glanced at his left hand looking for a wedding ring and when he caught her, she must have turned a shade of bright red judging by the heat creeping up her neck. Nick always had that effect on her. He'd turn her inside out and then leave her blushing, or worse. The one night they had together, he'd humiliated her so badly she thought she'd die from embarrassment. She must have been the locker room joke of the day for all the jocks on the Napa Valley Victors.

Baseball, girls and partying were Nick Carlino's claims to fame in high school.

Brooke had been crazy to think that Nick would have wanted her. The golden boy, the first baseman with a .450 hitting average, born with a silver spoon in his mouth and heading for great things—Brooke found out just how out of her league she'd been with him.

He'd nearly ruined her seventeen-year-old life. Her self-esteem had hit rock bottom and it had taken her years to recover. All of the negative things she'd believed about herself had been confirmed. And she'd hated him all the more for it.

Now, she glanced at him as he handed over her five-month-old baby. He was looking handsome and sinfully delicious, and she hated the slight trembles invading her stomach. The sooner she got away from him the better. She wanted no reminder of her past and wished she had crashed into anyone else on earth last night but Nick Carlino.

"It's simple, Brooke. You'll stay overnight at my house."

"I can't do that, Nick." Brooke put her stubborn face on

and refused to budge, ignoring the spinning in her head. While he was gone, she'd gotten up and dressed in the hospital room, made three phone calls to Molly to no avail, then nursed Leah on the same leather rocker Nick had sat watch on last night.

When Nick said a casual good-bye earlier, she'd known she'd still have to deal with him regarding the damages to his car, but she hadn't expected him to return to her hospital room two hours later.

She'd found him leaning against the doorjamb, staring at her while she nursed Leah, his lips pursed together in an odd expression. An intimate moment passed between them before he'd started issuing orders like a drill sergeant.

"I'll figure something out," she said quietly, not to disturb Leah. She always had before. She'd supported herself during her pregnancy and managed to deliver a baby without a partner so she could certainly handle this dilemma without a lot of fuss.

"Like what? You're out of options." He could be just as stubborn, she thought, watching him fold his arms over his chest and take a wide stance. "You can't reach your friend and you heard what the doctor said."

"I'll deal with it. Thank you. I don't need your help."

Nick sat down on a chair. Bracing both of his forearms on his knees, he leaned toward her. He looked deep into her eyes and his dark penetrating gaze blindsided her. "Wow, it's been what? Thirteen years, and you're still holding a grudge."

Brooke gasped and Leah stopped nursing. She settled her baby down and waited until she continued sucking, making sure to cover both the baby and her breast with the blanket.

She wanted to be anywhere but here, having this conversation with Nick. It amazed her that he even remembered that night. To her it was a mind-sucking, punched-in-the-gut experience, but she presumed it was business as usual for Nick. He'd probably left dozens of humiliated girls in his wake during his lifetime. "I'm not holding a grudge." It had been so much more than that for her. "I barely know you."

"You know me well enough to accept my help when you need it."

"I don't need it." Even to her ears she sounded contrary. "Why do you care anyway?"

Nick ran a hand through his dark hair and shook his head. "It's no big deal, Brooke. I live in a huge house, practically by myself. You'll stay a night or two and my conscience will be clear."

"You're worried about your conscience?" That sounded like the Nick Carlino she'd known, the one who watched out for Numero Uno first and foremost.

"I promised to take care of Leah last night. And her mother needs a quiet place to rest. Dammit, maybe I'm just sorry I didn't swerve outta your way faster."

Brooke was losing this argument fast and that made her nervous. "You weren't the one in the wrong lane. It's my fault. Besides, who's going to look after us, you?"

Nick shrugged. "I'll hire a nurse for a few days. We'd probably never see each other."

"I can't afford that."

"I can," Nick said point-blank. Not in the cocky way he had about him either. He seemed sincere.

The idea sounded better and better to her, yet how could she accept his charity?

He was right about one thing—she was out of options. With the exception of Molly, she'd broken all ties with her friends from Napa Valley when her mother moved them away right after graduation.

Brooke had never felt like she fit in with the sons and daughters of wealthy winegrowers, landowners and old Napa money. She was one of a handful of students at the school that wasn't of the privileged class. Her mother managed the Cabernet Café down the street from the high school and Brooke had worked there after school and on weekends. It had started out being a wine-tasting room, but after it failed the owner changed the place into a burger and shake joint. The kids at school called it the Cab Café and the name stuck.

When Brooke didn't answer, Nick landed the final blow. "Think about what your daughter needs."

She squeezed her eyes shut momentarily. God. He was right. Leah needed a healthy mother. Having a nurse on duty meant that Leah would be cared for and Brooke would get the rest she needed. Waves of light-headedness had come and gone all morning long. It was barely eleven and she was already exhausted. Every bone in her body seemed to ache at one time or another when she moved. The soreness she could handle, but she needed to be fully alert in caring for Leah.

Damn Nick. While she should be thanking him for his generous offer, she resented that he had the means to provide exactly what she needed. Why did it have to be Nick? It seemed like a very bad, cruel joke.

"Well?" he asked.

The idea of spending one minute under Nick Carlino's roof made her cringe.

"Just let me try calling Molly one more time."

TWO

Nick glanced at Brooke sitting there on the passenger side of his Cadillac Escalade SUV. The only indication of the crash that took her to the hospital last night was the bandage on her forehead. "All set?" He leaned over to give an extra tug on her seat belt and met with her cautious eyes.

"Yes," she said, averting her gaze. After a moment of hesitation, she asked, "How did you get the car seat for Leah?"

Nick looked in the back seat where the baby lay resting against a lambswool cushion. "My mechanic, Randy, has two kids. He installed it for me."

"I think I'm supposed to get a new one now. After a crash, a car seat needs to be replaced."

"I didn't know that."

"How would you?"

"I wouldn't," he agreed, not missing Brooke's impatience. He figured her head ached more than she let on. Lines of fatigue crinkled her otherwise stunning eyes and she appeared exhausted. "My house isn't far."

"I guess we haven't got a choice."

We, meaning her and Leah. Nick caught her drift. "I'll drive slow to the House of Doom and Gloom."

Brooke glanced at him. "Is that what you call it?"

"Me? No. But you, on the other hand, look like you're going to your own execution."

Brooke faced him with a frown. "It just wasn't supposed to happen like this."

"What wasn't?"

"Me, coming back to Napa."

"What was supposed to happen?"

"I was supposed to reach my aunt's house by daylight. Walk in and find an immaculate house filled with antique furniture. Leah and I would spend the night and then in the morning, I'd be making plans to open it to the public."

"Guess what? Life doesn't always work out the way you planned."

"That's cynical, coming from you."

Nick started the engine. "Because I'm wealthy and entitled, right?"

Brooke sighed and blew breath from her heart-shaped mouth. Nick didn't dwell on that mouth. If he did, he'd be knee-deep in babies and beautiful blondes with attitude. He was simply being a Good Samaritan here. But it irked him that Brooke thought it so out of character for him to help her.

"Nice car. Whose is it?"

Nick blinked at her rapid change of subject. "Mine."

She smiled, though he saw what that curling of her lips cost her pain-wise. "I make my point."

Instead of being irritated, Nick chuckled. He hadn't seen that coming. He liked a good sparring partner and

Brooke had just surprised him. "So you think because I drive nice cars and live in a big house, I have everything that I want?"

"Don't you?"

Nick shook his head. He didn't have to think twice. "No." He'd wanted something more than all those things and he'd lost it, just when it was within his grasp. "Not everything, Brooke."

He sensed her gaze on him for a few long seconds and then she laid her head against the headrest and closed her eyes, which gave him a chance to really look at her. Unfortunately, he liked what he saw. Silken lashes framed almond-shaped eyes and rested on cheekbones that were high and full. He'd already decided he liked her mouth. He'd kissed her before, but the image of those kisses had blurred with age.

Long, wavy blond locks tumbled down her shoulders and rested on the soft full mounds of her breasts. Her body was shapely, but he'd never have guessed she'd had a child five months ago from her slim waistline and flat stomach.

Don't go there, Nick warned. He wasn't the fatherly type. He had zero plans to get tied down with a family. His past haunted him daily and reminded him that he was better off single, glorying in bachelorhood than trying his hand at anything more.

He drove the car slowly as promised and made his way onto the highway. "Where's your aunt's place?"

"Just outside of the city on Waverly Drive."

Nick knew the area. It was at the base of the foothills, before the roads led to higher ground and the bulk of the vineyards. "You want to do a drive-by?"

Her eyes widened, lighting up her face. "Yes."

"You're up to it?" he asked, wondering if he should have suggested it.

"I am. I'm curious to see what the place looks like. It's been years since I've seen it."

"You never came back to Napa? Even though you had an aunt living here?"

"No," she said. "I never came back."

Nick looked at her and she once again averted her eyes by looking out the window.

They drove in silence the rest of the way.

Brooke didn't want to tell him that her Aunt Lucy was her father's sister. That after her parents' marriage broke up, her mother never talked to Aunt Lucy again. But her aunt would sneak visits to Brooke, coming around after school to walk her partway home. When Brooke was in high school, Aunt Lucy would ask her to stop by the house. Brooke had little family and she liked Aunt Lucy, even if she was a bit eccentric. Eventually, her mother found out about the visits but she never tried to stop them.

When they moved away, Brooke had fully intended to keep in touch with her aunt, but time had gotten away from her. She'd always feel guilty that she hadn't made more of an effort to see her aunt before she died. Inheriting her house had come as a bolt from the blue and there'd been only one stipulation in the will, that Brooke not sell the place for a period of five years. With her mother remarried and living in Hawaii, it only made sense for Brooke to come back and try to build a life here for Leah and herself.

She glanced at Nick, who'd just taken a turn off the highway. He was part of the reason she'd never wanted to come back here. Thirteen years had dulled the pain and she'd almost forgotten that deep sense of rejection—of not being good enough, of falling for the wrong boy and feeling like a fool, but then fate had a way of intervening and turning Brooke's life upside down.

She'd managed to crash into the very man she'd wanted to avoid at all costs. And now she was his charity case. She was going to live under his roof, accept his help and be beholden to him for the rest of eternity.

Good going, Brooke.

"What's the address?" Nick turned onto Waverly Drive and looked at her for direction.

"It's up half a block on your right. It's the only three-story house on the street."

The houses were sparsely spaced, each parcel of land at least half an acre. If Brooke remembered correctly, her aunt owned slightly more acreage than her neighbors. In fact, it was by far the largest piece of land in the vicinity.

"It's there," Brooke said, pointing to the lot she remembered. Eager anticipation coursed through her veins and excitement bubbled up. This was the start of her new life. She remembered driving up here in her beat-up 1984 Chevy Caprice when she was in high school. "The Victorian that looks like…" she began and a sense of doom crept into her gut. Her heart sank. The wrought iron gates that were once pearly white grabbed the sunlight with golden hues of rust and age. The flower garden once bright with pansies, daffodils and lavender was a mass of weeds and as Nick drove into the driveway that led to the house, Brooke's heart sank even further. The house looked like something from an Addams Family television reunion, the only thing missing were the cobwebs. And Brooke even thought she saw a few of those tangled up on the third story.

"Oh," she said, tears welling in her eyes. "It's not like I remembered."

Nick glanced at her. "Do you want to go inside?"

"I should. Might as well face the music." She smiled with

false bravado. What had she expected? Her aunt had been ill for the last few years of her life. Obviously, maintaining the house hadn't been high on her list of priorities. Another wave of guilt assaulted her. Had her aunt been alone when she died? Did she have anyone to sit by her bedside when she was ill?

She looked at Nick. "But Leah's asleep."

"I'll stay. You go in and check the place out."

When she debated it for a few seconds, Nick added, "Unless you want me to go inside with you?"

"No, no. That's not necessary. If you can watch Leah, I'll go in."

Nick got out of the car at the same time she did. He took her arm and led her up the steps. His touch and being so near as he walked with her mingled with all the other emotions clouding her head. She didn't want to owe him, but here he was, doing her a favor again. And touching her in a comforting way that led her mind to other touches, other days when Nick had surprised her with kindness, only to destroy her in one fell swoop. Today, even in her weakened state, she wouldn't let Nick's touch mean anything. She didn't trust him. Not in that way.

She stepped onto the wraparound porch by the front door and stood a moment, hesitating.

"Are you all right?" Nick asked, holding her arm tight.

"I'm fine. Just can't believe it."

Nick smiled and her heart rammed into her chest. "I'll be right out here. Call if you need me."

She removed his hand from her arm and stepped back.

Nick looked at her skeptically, but bounded down the steps and stood watch over Leah, sleeping in her car seat.

She turned toward the front door and reached into her purse for the key.

Five minutes later, Brooke had seen all there was to see

and it wasn't pretty. The house had been let go for years. The only rooms that were in halfway decent shape were the kitchen and her aunt's bedroom. Those rooms looked somewhat cared for, but the others needed quite a bit of work. It would take a whole lot of elbow grease and some of her hard-saved cash to make it shine, and right now, the whole situation overwhelmed her.

She stood on the porch and found Nick leaning against the side of his car, the open door letting air inside for her daughter. "Well?"

"Let's just say the inside makes the outside look like Buckingham Palace."

"That bad?"

Brooke walked down the steps a little too fast and everything spun. She fought to keep her balance, wooziness swamping her. She swayed and was immediately caught. Nick's arms came around her. "Whoa."

Her body pressed against his. He was rock solid and strong, yet his arms around her were gentle. He pressed his hands to her back and rubbed. "Are you okay?"

"I will be as soon as you stop spinning me around."

He chuckled.

She clung to him, trying to find her balance. Breathing in his sexy musk scent wasn't helping matters. He felt too darn good. She hadn't had a man hold her like this for a year and a half. She'd been deprived of masculine contact for a long time. That was the only explanation for the warm sensations rippling through her body. She'd gotten over Nick Carlino ages ago.

"Bad idea," Nick said softly in her ear.

Oh God. She stiffened and backed away. Did he think she'd thrown herself at him? "I know."

"I shouldn't have suggested bringing you here. You're not up to it."

Stunned, Brooke didn't respond. Clearly, she'd taken his "bad idea" comment the wrong way. She could only look into his eyes and nod. "I think you're right. But I'm feeling okay now, the world's not spinning."

He took her hand and led her to the car. "C'mon. I'll get you home. You need to rest."

Brooke got into the car and closed her eyes the entire way to Nick's house. Partly to rest and partly to block out how good Nick felt when he held her close. He was solid and steady and caring. If he were any other man, she might have enjoyed the sensations skipping through her body, but since it was Nick, she warned them off. He'd been out of her league the first time and nothing had changed, except now she knew better than to take Nick Carlino seriously.

She rubbed her temples and adjusted the bandage, thinking fate had a great sense of humor.

Only Brooke didn't find any of this amusing.

She'd heard about the Carlino estate, driven past its massive grounds in her earlier years many times, but nothing in her wildest imaginings had prepared Brooke when she entered the home for the first time. While she expected opulence and cold austere surroundings, she found…warmth.

That was a shock.

The stone entryway led to rooms of creams and beiges, golden textured walls, rich wood beamed ceilings and living spaces filled with furniture that she would describe as comfortable elegance. A giant floor-to-ceiling picture window in the living room lent a view of lush grounds and vineyards below.

The architecture of the home was more villa style than anything else. It was an open plan on the first floor but the upstairs spread out to four separate wings, Nick explained.

He followed Brooke to the stairway, carrying her bags as she held Leah.

"You doing okay?" Nick asked from behind as she climbed the steps.

"Great, you won't have to catch me again."

"No, I'm not that lucky."

Was he flirting? Boy, she was struggling to keep her head from clouding up and one comment from him had her head spinning again.

When she reached the top of the stairs, she stopped and turned. "Which way?"

Nick stood on the step below her and their eyes met on the same level. He stared at her, then cast his gaze lower to where Leah had clutched her blouse, pulling the material aside enough to expose her bra. Nick flashed Brooke a grin, dimples and all, then looked back at Leah, who seemed absolutely fascinated with him. He poked her tiny nose gently and the baby giggled. "Go into the first set of double doors you see."

Brooke entered the room and then blurted, "This is your room."

She couldn't miss it. His baseball trophies sat on a shelf next to pictures of Nick with his brothers and one family photo from when both of his parents were alive. The entire room oozed masculinity from the hardwood floors covered with deep rust rugs and a quilt of the same color covering his king-size bed. Another picture window offered an amazing view of Napa from the hilltop.

"Yes. It's my room."

She whirled around and narrowed her eyes at him. "Surely, you don't expect..." She couldn't finish her sentence, her mind conjuring up hurtful images of the last time she'd been with Nick.

Nick set her bags down and leisurely looked her over

from the top of her bandaged head to her toes inserted in beach flip-flops. Tingles of panic slid through her.

"It makes the most sense, Brooke. There's an adjoining room where the nurse will sleep." And finally, he added, "I'll take the guest room, two doors down."

Her sigh of relief was audible and so embarrassing that she couldn't face him. What made her think he was at all interested in her anyway? He probably had scores of women dangling, just waiting for a call from him.

She scoured the room looking for a safe place to lay Leah down to sleep. Finally, she glanced at Nick, who was busy taking out a few items of clothing from his dresser. "There was a little play yard for Leah in the trunk of my car."

"It's here."

"It is?"

He nodded. "I got the rest of your things out of your trunk this morning."

"And you brought them here?"

He shrugged. "I figured the kid needed them. I'll bring them up later."

Overwhelmed with gratitude and ready to cry, she didn't know what to say. "I, uh…thank you, Nick."

"No problem. Use whatever you need. There's a great shower and tub. Climb into bed if you want to. The nurse is due in half an hour. I'll send her up when she gets here."

"What about you? You must have had plans today. Don't let us keep you."

"Sweetheart, no one keeps me from doing what I want to do." He winked and walked out of the bedroom.

How well she knew.

"Well, Leah, that was Nick Carlino."

Leah looked around, her eyes wide, fascinated by her new surroundings. She made a cooing sound that warmed Brooke's heart. All that mattered was that both of them were safe and provided for at the moment. She sat down on Nick's bed and bounced Leah on her knee. "Promise me you won't go falling for him, baby girl," she said, clapping their hands together and making Leah giggle. "He's not to be trusted. Mommy did that once and it wasn't good. Not good at all."

"That's a first for you," his brother Joe said, as he toweled off from his swim in the pool. "You're letting a woman and her child stay at the house."

"It's not like I had a choice." Nick glanced at his middle brother with disdain. "What was I supposed to do? She's got a kid. She's injured and has nowhere else to go. I couldn't walk away. Her head's not right."

"Must not be, if she moved in with you." Joe toweled off from his swim and put his glasses back on. He was building his fiancée a house and though he lived at Ali's condo currently, Nick had to put up with his gibes when he came over to do his hundred laps in the pool. Joe was the geek in the family and swimming was his only means of physical activity.

"Good thing you know your way around a computer. You'd never make it as a comedian."

Joe ignored him. "Who is she?"

"Her name is Brooke Hamilton. We went to high school together."

"Brooke Hamilton? That name sounds familiar."

Nick kept his mouth shut. Let his brother figure it out.

"Oh, she's the one who worked at that Cab Café, right?"

Bingo.

"I remember her now. She was the waitress who had a big crush on you."

"Ancient history." Nick didn't want to bring up the past.

It had been the one time in his young life he'd done the right thing. The one time, he'd put someone else's needs above his own. He'd let Brooke off the hook. Still, after all these years, when she looked at him, it was with wariness and contempt. Could it be she still held a grudge over what happened?

"So you're the Good Samaritan now?"

"Something like that," Nick muttered, squinting into the sun. "Like I said, she's here temporarily. A few days at most. Just until Maynard gives her the okay to be on her own."

"Yeah, speaking of that, how is it that my little brother gets in a car crash and doesn't tell his brothers?"

"I tried calling. Then I remembered you were in the Bahamas. Or were supposed to be."

"We got back late last night. If you got our voicemail, it's probably because we were sleeping. So, how are you?"

Nick lifted his arms out wide. "I'm gonna live."

"Amen to that, little brother. How old's the kid?"

"Leah is five months old."

"A baby?" Joe looked at him with suspicion. "You're not—"

Nick shook his head. "I just laid eyes on Brooke last night. I haven't seen her since high school. But thanks for the vote of confidence, bro."

"Hey, don't take offense," Joe said. "But you do have a reputation with the ladies."

Nick couldn't deny it. He liked women and they liked him back. They had a good time together and then Nick would let them down gently and walk away. Or they'd get fed up with not getting a commitment from him and leave on their own. He never led them on or lied to them. From the beginning, he'd always let the women in his life know what to expect from him. It had been that way since he could remember. As a young man, he assumed he'd grow out of it when the right woman came along, but his father had taken that option away from him in his attempt to control Nick. Santo Carlino had wanted one son to take over the family business and once Tony left to race cars and Joe took off to New York to develop software for a global company, the youngest son got the brunt of his father's manipulations.

Santo had done a number on him and Nick had taken a hard fall.

"I'm not interested in Brooke Hamilton. Hell, give me a break, Joe. I'm doing a good deed here, not looking for an instant family."

Damn it! Nick glanced up to find Brooke standing behind Joe. The baby bottle she held slipped from her hand. Flustered, her face turned color and Nick couldn't tell if she was angry or embarrassed.

Angry, he decided.

Joe swept up the bottle quickly and handed it to her. "Here you go. Hi, I'm Joe."

"I remember. Hi, Joe." She took the bottle graciously and smiled at him. Those knock-out hazel eyes, the shade of tropical waters, lit up her whole face.

"Sorry to hear about the accident," Joe said. "I hope you recover well from your injuries."

"Thank you." As if she had forgotten about her head injury, she touched her forehead. "I'm doing okay."

"Shouldn't you be resting?" Nick asked. He'd shown the nurse to their room an hour ago and she'd promised to watch over both mother and child.

She glanced at him and the light in her eyes faded as fast as her smile. "I couldn't calm down so I thought I'd get some air."

"With that?" Nick pointed to the baby's bottle. Seemed she only had a smile for Joe.

"Oh, I was on my way to the kitchen to store this. It's expressed breast milk."

Nick blinked. "Expressed?"

"I think this is my cue to leave," Joe said, adjusting the glasses on his nose. He darted glances at both of them then bid them good-bye and left.

"Sorry to bother you," Brooke said to him, not sounding sorry at all as she turned to leave.

"Brooke?"

She stopped and whirled around. "It's not as if Leah and I have a choice in this, Nick. I don't mean to sound ungrateful, but I don't want to be here anymore than you want us here."

"If I didn't want you here, you wouldn't be here. Why couldn't you calm down?"

Brooke fidgeted with the bottle in her hands. He didn't want to think about how she'd expressed the milk into the bottle. Some things were beyond male comprehension. She glanced away, looking at the pool, then the grounds, and finally back at him. "I, uh, it's the accident. I keep replaying it in my head. Every time I close my eyes, it's there. I hear it. I see it." She took a swallow and her voice cracked then lowered to a bare whisper. "And when I think what might have happened to Leah…"

Nick walked over to her and put his hands on her shoulders. "But nothing happened to Leah. You're going to be fine."

"My brain knows that." She closed her eyes for a second, then when she opened them again, granting him a soft look, something pierced through his gut. It was *something* that he didn't recognize. *Something* that was new and strange to him.

He touched her cheek and got lost in her eyes. He had a need to protect. To comfort. He brought his mouth close and brushed his lips to hers. The kiss was meant to reassure, to help her find some peace, but Nick didn't expect the sensations to rip through him. He didn't expect to want more. Sure, he'd once been attracted to Brooke. She'd been different than the other girls he'd been with in high school. There was substance to her, a depth that other girls didn't have at that age. She hadn't been a party girl. Maybe that's why Nick had been attracted to her. She was unique and special and Nick had realized that during the one night they'd spent together when he'd almost taken her virginity.

For years after, he'd wondered if he'd been really noble or scared that she was the one who could tie him down. And for years after he'd also imagined what it would have been like making love to her. Her first time. He'd wanted it to be with him, yet, he knew enough to back off. He'd done the right thing back then.

Her lips were warm and inviting. Devouring her heart-shaped mouth until she was swollen and puffy would be easy, but Nick pulled away. She gazed at him with a question in her eyes. He circled a lock of her long hair with his finger and tugged gently. "Just so you know, there aren't any strings attached to you staying here."

"I know," she said abruptly. "You're doing a good deed and you don't want an instant family. You're not interested, and buddy, neither am I."

She turned on her heel and walked off. He watched her stop to fight off a dizzy spell before climbing the stairs. He waited until she made it up to the second floor before looking away and smiling. Now he remembered why he liked her so much. She wasn't afraid to speak her mind and tell him off when she thought he needed it.

Three

Brooke lay in Nick's bed as fading sunshine spilled through the window. She'd never been one to sleep away the afternoon, but the doctor ordered rest and she would do anything to get out of the Carlino house as quickly as possible. So with Leah sleeping in her little playpen next to her and Nurse Jacobs in the adjoining room, Brooke punched the pillow and placed it under her head then forced her eyes closed.

But rest wasn't coming easy. Her little episode with Nick down by the pool played over in her mind. *Stupid, Brooke. You let him kiss you.*

Nick Carlino wasn't lacking in the kiss department. He knew what he was doing and always had. He was sexy down to the bone. Even with a dozen internal warnings screaming at her to back away from Nick, the second his lips touched hers, magic happened.

Foolishly, she'd gotten lost in his touch and taste, wanting more. More comfort. More reassurance. More magic. But Brooke wouldn't let the need inside her grow. She might have had a weak moment, but she'd be on guard now.

She took slow deep breaths, calming her nerves and letting all the tension ooze out of her body. The events of the past twenty-four hours had finally caught up to her. Her head ached less and less and sleep seemed possible now.

Nick left his group of friends at the window booth in the Cab Café, and headed her way. The minute Brooke spotted him approaching the counter her heart skipped some very necessary beats. Every time he came into the café with his friends she wanted to run and hide.

She wasn't one of them. The baseball jocks and their cheerleader girlfriends had their own exclusive club. Their friendliness ended with casual hellos. They wouldn't let her inside their circle, even if she wanted to be let in. She worked at the Cab Café and wore a purple and white uniform with an apron decorated with lavender grapes. She lived on the wrong side of town.

"Hi," Nick said, straddling the stool in front of her.

"Hi. What can I get you?" Brooke asked, as she passed him to set down coffee and a slice of peach pie for a customer.

"Would love a vanilla shake, but I'm in training. Just a lemonade." He smiled.

"You got it," Brooke said, trying not to stare at him. Nick Carlino had a set of dimples that made mush of her brains. "How's the team doing?"

"We won last night. I hit home run number twelve."

Brooke poured his lemonade and slid the glass over. "Is that a record?"

"Not yet, but I'm getting close. You should come to the games."

"I, uh, thanks. Maybe I will." Brooke had to work on the weekends. That's when they were the busiest. But Nick didn't know about things like that. He came from the privileged class and she doubted he knew anything about sacrifice or paying the bills.

"I hope so." He stared into her eyes so long, heat traveled up her neck.

Why did he care if she came to his baseball games? "I'll try."

He sipped his lemonade. "How'd you do on the trig test?"

"Got an A, but I sweated that one. You?"

"You beat me, Brooke." His blue eyes twinkled with mischief. "I don't like to lose."

It was official now. It wasn't just her brain melting—her entire body turned marshmallow-soft hearing him say her name. "Try studying. I hear it's a sure way to ace a test."

Nick chuckled and rose from the stool, taking the last sip of his lemonade. He laid down some money on the counter. He was a good tipper for a high school student. She moved on to her next customer at the counter and Nick walked away. When he reached the middle of the café, he turned back around and caught her eye one last time. "I've got a game tomorrow at three."

She nodded her acknowledgment just as the Victors' head cheerleader, Candy Rae Brenner, slipped her hand into Nick's and pulled him along, giving Brooke a dismissive look.

The dream startled her awake. But it wasn't a dream—it was a real memory. Brooke hadn't thought about that day in a long time. She didn't know why that particular scene entered her dreams, but it must have to do with the fact that she'd hit Nick's car and was sleeping in his bed.

She glanced at Leah beside her, all rosy cheeks and dark blonde curls wrapped into a sweet sleeping bundle. Leah made everything possible. She held her mama's heart in those tiny little hands.

Concentrate on her, Brooke. Forget about Nick. And the past.

But Brooke couldn't do it. The dream had been so real, so vivid that it triggered more memories of Nick. Those next few weeks entered her mind with stunning accuracy.

"You didn't come to the game." Nick caught up to her *as she walked down the hall past the chemistry lab. School was out and she had a long walk home.*

She glanced at him. Tremors of excitement erupted inside and she felt queasy from the turmoil stirring her stomach. Why was he walking with her? "I had to work. You know, some of us have to earn a living."

"Little Miss Attitude today, aren't you?"

"Me?" She pointed to her chest then realized her mistake. Nick's gaze followed the direction of her finger and he studied her chest. He raised his brows and stared some more. It figured she'd be wearing a tank top that revealed a modest amount of cleavage today.

She scurried past him but he caught up to her. "Hey, are you working after school?"

"Why?" she asked, curious what he wanted with her. "Need a study buddy for trig?"

Nick laughed. "Hell no. I'm getting a passing grade, that's good enough. As long as I keep my grades up, I'm on the team."

"And that's all that matters?"

Nick was a sure thing for the major league draft. The entire school rallied around him. He was the golden boy who earned okay grades and had a batting record that brought the scouts out in droves.

"For me, yeah. I'm not going to college. And I'm not working for my old man. It's baseball or nothing."

He had dreams, Brooke thought, and he'd probably attain them. He was after all, the golden boy. While Brooke faced community college and working to help her mother pay the bills, others would be off pursuing a life that would mean something important to them.

"So, are you working or not?"

"Later tonight I am," she answered.

"I'll drive you home."

She was ready to say no thanks, but then she looked into Nick's midnight blue eyes and hope swelled in her chest. Her heart wanted to say yes, but her brain got in the way. "Why?"

"Why what? Why do I want to drive you home?"

She furrowed her brows and nodded.

"Maybe I'm going that way." Then he leaned in closer and lowered his voice. "Or maybe I like you."

She laughed, thinking that would be the day, and looked away.

Nick moved in front of her so she had to face him. "Brooke?"

He said her name again in a tone that sounded sincere and…hopeful. It was the hopeful part that swept through her like a hurricane, obliterating all rational thought. She nodded and smiled. "Okay."

His world-class dimples emerged, stealing her breath. "C'mon, my car's in the parking lot."

Those last weeks in June before graduation were a combination of highs and lows. Whenever Nick didn't have practice after school, he'd drive her home and they'd sit on her front porch and talk about everything and anything. She'd learned a lot about his childhood, his baseball dreams and when he spoke of his mother, it was with fondness and love. Each day, Brooke had fallen more and more in love with him. It was a young girl's fascination, but the feelings she had for him were real. He'd never asked her on a date or tried to kiss her, which contradicted his reputation. He'd dated every popular girl on campus, Candy Rae being the latest in the string. Rumor had it that they'd broken up and Nick had alluded to it, but one thing he didn't talk about with Brooke was other girls.

She'd resigned herself to the fact that she was Nick's "friend" who lived on the other side of town. When prom came, Brooke had waited, but Nick never said a word, so she accepted a date with the busboy that worked with her at the Cab Café. She'd shown up in a dress she'd splurged on from her meager savings. Her mother, who had a great sense of style, had curled her hair and helped with makeup. When she spotted Nick at the dance with Candy Rae her heart sank. Though Nick had never promised her a thing, she felt hopeless and dejected, but was determined not to take it out on poor Billy Sizemore, her date. They'd danced and danced, and took pictures under the corny grapevine arbor inside the hall where the prom was held.

She came out of the ladies room and was instantly grabbed by the waist and pressed against the wall of a secluded corner by the bathroom. "Nick? What are you doing?"

"Just wanted to say hello."

"Hello," she droned without emotion.

The dimples of doom came out and Brooke had an uncanny urge to touch her fingertip to one.

"You look amazing." His gaze swept over her hair, her dress, her body and then he looked deep into her eyes. "You have incredible eyes. It's the first thing I noticed about you."

Nick was deadly handsome and so near, she could

hardly breathe. What she couldn't figure out was why he was torturing her.

"I didn't want to bring Candy Rae here," he confessed. "The fact is, she made me promise months ago."

"And you don't break your promises?"

"Try not to. Her mother called my father last week to make sure I'd follow through. He put the old Italian guilt on me."

"Why are you telling me this?"

He looked at her quizzically. "You don't know?"

She shook her head.

He reached out to touch her hair, his gaze flowing over her face. A long moment passed and then he bent his head and kissed her.

Brooke couldn't believe this was happening. His lips were just like she imagined, amazingly warm and giving, a prelude and a promise of more to come. Brooke had waited so long for this, for him, that at first she just remained there enjoying the sensations rippling through her, frozen like an ice sculpture and melting a little at a time.

He wrapped his arms around her and she found herself immersed in Nick Carlino, his touch, his scent, his body pressed to hers. And she was through holding back. She returned his kiss with everything she had inside. He kissed her again, his mouth more demanding now, and a wild sort of frenzy built. Lust combined with the love she held in her heart for him and everything else faded from her mind. He parted her lips and drove his tongue into her mouth. Sensations whirled and she let out tiny gasps as he devoured her, his desire overwhelming.

Overhead, an announcement rang out calling for the last dance.

"I've got to go," he said with a low rasp. He backed away from her but the regret in his eyes bolstered her spirit.

Things had gotten out of control. Wonderfully so and she knew that when she went to sleep that night, her dreams would be of Nick.

Nurse Jacobs entered her room to take her blood pressure and temperature. Brooke waited patiently, sitting upright on the bed, while the older, sweet-faced woman removed the cuff and took the digital thermometer out of her mouth.

"All looks good, Mrs. Keating. Your blood pressure is normal and so is your temperature. How about the dizzy spells?"

She'd told the nurse once already not to call her Mrs. Keating. She hated the reminder of her marriage. "It's Brooke, remember? And I had a slight dizzy spell earlier, but nothing for a few hours."

The nurse looked pleased. "The rest is doing you good. Now, if I could get you to eat something. Mr. Carlino said that dinner would be ready at six. Are you up to going downstairs or shall I bring food up to you?"

"Oh, no. That's not necessary. We'll go down."

Leah began to stir and she knew her baby had enough of napping. She'd want some stimulation and learning about these new surroundings would satisfy her curiosity. Brooke would take her outside later to get some air as well.

"She's a good baby and a good sleeper." Nurse Jacobs smiled at Leah. "My children weren't good sleepers. I tried everything, but they were determined to keep their mom up most of the night. But they were good kids after that. Didn't give me a wink of trouble as teenagers."

"I guess you can't ask for more than that," Brooke said, suddenly curious about the nurse. "Are they grown now?"

"My son is finishing up college at Berkeley. My daughter,

she's the older one, is married and I'm hoping she'll make me a grandmother one day."

Brooke thought about her own mother. She'd had a tough life and was finally married again and living in Hawaii with her new husband, a widower and former naval officer with a kind heart who thought the sun rose and set on her mother's shoulders. Brooke was glad of it and though they missed each other, she knew her mother would spend some extended visits with them once Brooke and Leah settled into their new home.

"My mom is really crazy about Leah," Brooke said. "We saw her last month and—"

Leah fussed, letting out a complaining cry. Brooke stood up to go to her, but the room spun instantly and she reached out for the bed to steady herself. She closed her eyes until the feeling passed.

Nurse Jacobs was beside her quickly and braced her around the waist. "You stood up too fast," she said softly. "Move slow and make each step deliberate. How's your head now?"

Brooke glanced at her. Everything began to clear. "Better."

"Let me get Leah for you. Have a seat and I'll diaper her and bring her to you so you can nurse her."

Brooke did as she was told. The sooner she recovered, the better. She didn't want to be beholden to Nick for anything more. She already owed him for the damages to his car and for room and board, not to mention for the private nurse he'd hired to care for her. Brooke vowed to pay him back once her establishment started making money.

An hour later, Brooke had showered, changed her clothes, put a little blush on her pale cheeks and felt human again. She dressed Leah in a sundress and sandals that matched her own—a gift from Grandma "for her two girls," her mother had written on the gift card. Thankfully, her mom was provided for now and could spend money without pinching pennies and she'd lavished so many wonderful things on Leah.

Brooke smiled.

"That smile looks good on you. Feeling better?"

"Much. I'm ready to go down for dinner."

"I'll take Leah, if you can manage the stairs."

"I'll help Brooke down," Nick said, standing in the opened doorway and nodding at the nurse. He wore a black Polo shirt that displayed lean muscles and tanned olive skin. His pants were beige, expensive and fit his frame perfectly.

"I can manage."

Nurse Jacobs touched her arm. "Let him help you, Brooke. Just in case."

Brooke hesitated, but now wasn't the time to be obstinate. "Well, okay."

Nick waited until they reached the top of the staircase before putting his arm around her waist. She felt the gentle pressure of his touch all the way down to her toes. If nurse Jacobs only knew what a dizzying effect Nick had on her, she wouldn't have encouraged this.

"I'm glad you decided to come down for dinner. I thought you were still annoyed at me from before."

"I'm not in a position to be annoyed. You're being very… gracious."

"So out of character for me, right?"

"No comment," Brooke said, but she smiled and Nick didn't seem to take offense.

Once they made it down the stairs, Nick led them to the terrace where a table was set under a slatted patio roof held up by stone columns. "We're between cooks right now, so I ordered in. You'd end up back in the hospital if I tried my hand at cooking."

"That's fine, thank you," she said, then reached for Leah. "Come here, pretty baby." She kissed Leah's cheek the minute Nurse Jacobs handed her over. She settled Leah onto her lap. The baby was still groggy from her long nap.

The housekeeper, Carlotta, made a big fuss over Leah, offering to hold her while Brooke ate her meal, but she kindly refused. She still hadn't gotten over the accident and what could have happened. She wanted Leah near and she'd eaten this way, with Leah on her lap, dozens of times. It was a ritual that she'd soon have to break. Leah was growing in leaps and bounds and would need a high chair soon.

Carlotta made sure they were served and wanted for nothing. Brooke was amazed at how hungry she was, satisfying her growling pangs with shrimp salad, pasta primavera and creamy pesto chicken. She ate with gusto as Nick and her nurse conversed about growing up in Napa. Nick was a charmer and by the end of the meal, her middle-aged nurse was surely smitten. Every so often, Nick would catch Brooke's eye and they'd exchange a glance. Heat traveled through her body even as she pretended not to notice his effect on her.

Carlotta served a decadent Italian dessert catered from a restaurant Nick's family owned. The oozing lava cake exploded with melted chocolate the minute Brooke touched her fork to the center. Leah grabbed at her fork with her chubby grasp and a spray of liquid chocolate splattered onto Brooke's chest. The baby giggled and swiped at the confection again, tipping it over.

"Leah!" Brooke shook her head as she glanced at her freshly stained white blouse and the puddle of chocolate her child made on the table.

Carlotta and her nurse rushed into the kitchen to repair the damage, leaving Brooke alone at the table with Nick.

"Look what you've done to Mommy." Leah giggled again and Brooke had to smile, unable to feel any anger at the situation. Though she imagined she looked a total mess now. "You're getting me all chocolately and—"

"Delicious," Nick said softly, gazing into her eyes. He slipped a forkful of dessert into his mouth, but his eyes remained on her.

She didn't know how to react. Was he coming on to her? Any embarrassment she might have felt dissolved just seeing the spark of intensity in Nick's eyes. Did she want his flirting, even just for her own deflated ego?

"Here, Carlotta gave me this." Nurse Jacobs returned and handed her a wet dishcloth. "It might not stain if you get to it quickly."

"Oh, I'll probably just take it off upstairs and work on it," she said, holding Leah on her lap with one hand while dabbing at the splashes of chocolate with the other hand.

Carlotta walked onto the patio with a pained expression. "Nick, you have a visitor."

Nick glanced up as a sultry dark-haired woman breezed onto the patio.

"Hi, Nicky."

"Rachel." Nick got out of his seat.

The woman was stunning, even if she was a bit older than Nick. Looking proprietary, she placed her hand on his shoulder and lifted up on her toes to kiss him.

Brooke looked away rather than intrude on an intimate moment. She wondered what Rachel would say if she knew Nick had kissed her just hours ago, on this very same terrace.

"Who are your friends?" the woman inquired, staring at Nick.

He made the introductions without qualms. Rachel followed the direction of Nick's gaze and swept a quick glance at Brooke and the baby, noting her stained blouse without missing a beat.

Brooke had learned not to give in to humiliation anymore. She lifted her chin and greeted Nick's girlfriend with a poise that could win her an Oscar. "It's nice to meet you, Rachel."

"Rachel owns A Rock and A Hard Place," Nick offered.

Brooke furrowed her brow. "I don't remember it."

"It's a bar and nightclub," Rachel explained. "I opened it about three years ago and I guess you could say it's my baby." Rachel looked at Leah. "Until the real thing comes along, that is." She glanced at Nick, who held an unreadable expression, then turned her attention to Leah. "She's adorable."

"Thank you. She's quite a mess at the moment. Both of us are. I should probably clean us both up."

When Brooke rose from the table, Nurse Jacobs stepped up and reached for Leah. "I'll take her for you."

"Thank you," Brooke said, her glance darting from Rachel to Nick. "I'll leave you two alone. Have a nice evening."

Nick met her eyes. "Think you can make it upstairs okay?"

Brooke nodded. "I'm feeling better. Thanks for dinner." She waved her hand over her blemished blouse. "For as much as I managed to get into my mouth, it was *delicious*."

Nick's eyes went wide, then he chuckled and Brooke walked off feeling his gaze on her.

She heard Rachel question him with one word. *"Upstairs?"*

And she scurried a bit faster into the house.

* * *

Nick leaned against the railing that overlooked the valley below, his beer held between two fingers as he took a swig. He'd sipped champagne with the monks in France and enjoyed the best wines in all of Europe, not to mention imbibing from the best-ranked vintages in the family wine cellar, but tonight he needed good all-American beer.

His father would cringe seeing the cases of beer Nick had stocked in the house. Carlinos didn't drink beer. Carlinos were winemakers. His father never came to grips with the fact that none of his sons wanted to be winemakers. They had separate interests, which were, of course, of no concern to the man who'd fathered them. Once Nick's mother died, the boys were treated to Santo Carlino's constant demands on how they should live their lives.

Tony and Joe had escaped relatively unscathed, but Nick hadn't been so lucky. His father had managed to ruin Nick's career, before it had even started.

"I'm pregnant, Nick," Candy Rae cried into the phone right before his debut minor league baseball game. "I'm scared and I need you. Come home."

Nick couldn't come home. He'd been drafted by the Chicago White Sox. He was making his first start on the triple AAA squad on the Charlotte Knights and he needed to perform. He needed to make his mark and prove himself.

While he assured Candy Rae he'd come home and deal with the situation as soon as he could, she wouldn't let up. She'd called him every day for weeks and the calls sapped his concentration on the ball field, so much so that he stopped taking her calls. Next thing he knew, Candy Rae showed up at the ballpark and pleaded with him in person to come home. She was six months pregnant and the evidence of his child growing inside her couldn't be missed. He didn't love Candy Rae, but he'd make sure his child wanted for nothing. He'd have a part in raising the baby but that wasn't good enough for her. She wanted Nick home. She wanted marriage and the white picket fence fairy tale. Candy Rae was spoiled and stubborn and she put up a huge fuss, crying, screaming and stomping her feet. They argued, Nick not giving in to her tantrum and an hour later Nick walked onto the baseball field.

Distracted and pissed off, he'd collided with his teammate trying to make a catch in the outfield. He'd dislocated his shoulder, requiring surgery and a long recovery time.

"Should've been a piece of cake," Nick muttered, sipping his ice-cold beer in the warm Napa night, thinking about that catch *and* the recovery.

The house on the hill was quiet. Only a few stars lit the sky and it was the remote silence surrounding him that brought back his desolation and disappointment. His life could have been so different.

He'd found out late that summer that Candy Rae's baby wasn't his but he'd also found out that his father had put her up to the deception. They'd schemed together to get what they wanted and both wanted the same thing, Nick to come home to Napa. Candy Rae claimed she loved him and Santo wanted a son he could groom to take over the family business.

Nick was released from his minor league contract after that injury and to this day, he'd bet his life his father had his hands in that. Santo was an unscrupulous manipulator. He'd had a reputation for being a ruthless businessman and his business always came first with him.

Nick never forgave him for that…for messing with his dream.

After that fiasco, he'd moved out of the country for many years, becoming the foreign liaison for Carlino Wines in European markets. This was all he could stomach to do, working for the family business—needing time and distance away from Santo. Nick managed other interests overseas, making sound real estate investments. He'd become wealthy in his own right before long.

Nick heard footsteps on the grounds and turned to find Brooke coming out of the house, barefoot, wearing a silky robe. Her long blond hair spilled onto her shoulders. He watched her take a few steps onto the terrace.

She hadn't seen him yet—he was in the shadows—and that was fine with him. He could look at her without her defenses going up. Cascading terrace lamps lit her in a halo of light. Her movements graceful, she stepped farther out onto the terrace, taking in deep breaths of air. She looked troubled, as if searching for peace.

When she spotted him, she jumped back. "Oh, sorry," she whispered. "I didn't think anyone would be out here this late."

"Neither did I. Couldn't sleep?"

"Not tired. I think I got too much rest this afternoon. Looks like you're enjoying the peace. I'll just go back upstairs." She turned and took a step.

"Don't go." Nick cursed under his breath. He was in a dangerous mood and it would be better for her to go inside.

She stopped but didn't turn to face him. "I should go up."

Nick pushed off from the railing and strode over until he was behind her and near enough to whisper in her ear. "You should. But I don't want you to."

Nick put his arms around her waist and brought her close. He'd always liked Brooke. She was unique and fresh with a clever sense of humor. She could make him laugh and he admired her gutsy attitude, while being beautiful and sexy at the same time. She was the girl that got away and she'd remain so, but right now, he wanted her company. And maybe a little bit more.

He felt her trembling in his arms. "What happened to Rachel?"

"She wanted something I can't give her."

Brooke hesitated, then finally whispered quietly, "What's that?"

"All of me."

Nick reached up and took Brooke's hair in his hand. He moved soft strands off her neck and kissed her there. Goose bumps erupted on her nape and Nick drew her closer to whisper, "And you want none of me. Are you holding a grudge?"

"Not a grudge. I told you before."

"Then what, Brooke?"

She turned around to face him. He was hit with an immediate jolt when she stared at him with those beyond-beautiful eyes. "Why does it matter?"

"You were important to me. We were friends once."

Brooke's mouth gaped open then she hauled off and shoved at his chest. Startled by her sudden move, he struggled to keep his balance.

"You are so dense!" Brooke seemed to shout, though it came out in a loud whisper.

Nick looked at her and the absurdity of the conversation struck his funny bone. He laughed. "What the hell are you talking about?"

"You see, you don't even know!"

"So why don't you tell me?" Judging by the look on her face, maybe he didn't want to know.

"You used the 'F' word."

"I did not," he said adamantly and then it dawned on him. He arched a brow. "Oh, okay. So I said we were friends."

Brooke turned to leave. 'I'm not having this conversation," she said as she stepped into the house.

Damn it. The woman was always walking away. He marched after her. "Sit down, Brooke."

She stopped in his living room and glared at him. "Is that an order?"

Nick was through being amused. Why he cared to clear the air with her was beyond him. Maybe it was the mood he was in. Maybe it was hearing Rachel accuse him of using her that got to him tonight. Maybe it was because she'd also accused him of not having a heart. Or maybe it's because he thought he'd done the right thing for once in his life and Brooke was punishing him for it.

He shouldn't give a damn.

But he did.

"Hell, Brooke. Cut me some slack. Talk to me."

Brooke glanced at the sofa and twisted her lips. "I could claim fatigue. I think I feel a dizzy spell coming on."

"Sit," he said, keeping his tone light.

She sat down on the sofa and he took the seat across from her. A glass and wrought-iron coffee table separated them. The room was dark but for the dim lamp light from the terrace filtering inside.

Nick waited.

Then Brooke began. "You were the last person on earth I ever wanted to see again."

"I know that. Now tell me why."

Four

Brooke's memories came rushing back of that one night that had changed her life forever. It wasn't what Nick had done but what he hadn't done that had devastated her young heart.

The pounding on the door startled Brooke out of a sound sleep. She raced down the hallway in her nightie, certain that something was wrong. Her mother was visiting her best friend in San Francisco for the weekend and Brooke feared something terrible had happened to her. Why else would someone be pounding on her door after ten o'clock at night?

She hesitated behind the door, until she heard his voice. "It's me, Brooke. It's Nick. C'mon. Open up." She heard the excitement in his voice and immediately yanked the door open.

He stood in the moonlight, grinning from ear to ear and she came alive right then, as if she'd been an empty shell until Nick appeared to breathe new life into her. She smiled instantly, his obvious joy contagious. "Nick? What is it?"

He lifted her off her feet and twirled her around and around in dizzying circles. "I did it. I did it. I'm going to the major leagues. I got drafted by the White Sox in the fifth round."

Before she had time to react, he set her down, cupped her face in his hands and kissed her with such intensity she thought she was still floating above ground. When he broke off the kiss, the hungry look in his blue eyes held her captivated. "Nick, that's great. It's what you want."

"I know. I know. I'm going to Charlotte to play for the Knights. It's Triple A ball, but if I play to my potential, Coach thinks it won't take long to make it to the majors."

"Oh, Nick. You'll get there. If you want it bad enough, you'll get there."

Without his knowledge, she'd gone to a play-off game and watched him play once. He'd been the star of the team. Everyone cheered for Nick when he stepped up to the plate. He'd hit three home runs in that weekend series and the team had gone on to win the championship.

"I came right over to tell you. I wanted you to know. I wanted to share this with you first."

He'd come to her, before telling his friends? Warmth rushed through her body and when he reached for her again and kissed her, Brooke's world turned upside down.

"I want you, Brooke," he whispered urgently, bracing her waist and tugging her close. Her legs rubbed against his jeans. "I've always wanted you."

He lavished kisses on her forehead, her eyes, her nose, her cheeks and then devoured her mouth in another long, fiery crazed kiss that lit her body on fire. "My mom's out of town," she whispered and Nick wasted no time.

"Where's your room?"

Brooke led him there and stood by the bed. He smiled and in one smooth move, he lifted her nightie and filled his hands with her breasts. The exquisite feel of his palms on her sent a hot thrill through her body. Deft fingers stroked her nipples and she ached for more. When he put his mouth on her, she squeezed her eyes shut from the exquisite, sweet torture.

Nick had her naked on the bed in seconds, then he removed his shirt and joined her. She was glad she'd waited, glad to have her first time be with Nick, the boy who'd been out of her reach for so long. Now, he was here, wanting her.

She loved him with a fierceness that stunned her. His touch sent her spiraling out of control. He kissed her a dozen times, driving her insane with his tongue, as he caressed every inch of her body.

Inexperienced and awkward, Brooke didn't know what to do. What would he expect from her? Should she be touching him back?

"This is a good night…being with you," he whispered, nibbling on her throat. His softly spoken words abolished her insecurities.

His hand traveled lower, his fingers seeking her warmth, and electric shocks powered through her body. She stiffened from the new sensation. She'd never felt anything like it, the intimacy of the act, the way he knew how to find her most sensitive spot and stroke her until she was breathless and mindless.

The sensation built and built and she arched and moaned until only little cries of ecstasy escaped her lips. Wave after wave of release shattered her and Nick stroked her harder, faster, drawing out her orgasm, his eyes dark and filled with desire. He murmured soft words but she didn't hear *him, didn't recognize what he was asking until she felt the last tiny wave leave her.*

"Are you protected?" he asked again.

And she looked at him and shook her head. "I don't have, I mean I don't—"

He stood up and reached into his pocket, then something stopped him. She'd never forget the look on his face, the way he studied her as she lay naked on the bed.

"Nick?" Dread beat against her chest and her stomach coiled.

He stared at her and blinked. His gaze roved over her again and this time she truly felt naked and strangely alone. Then the unthinkable happened. Nick shook his head, closing his eyes to her and taking deep breaths. "I can't do this, Brooke. I'm gonna have to leave."

"Nick?" Panicked, Brooke lifted up to reach for him.

To her horror, he backed away, as if repulsed by her touch. "I gotta go, Brooke. I can't. I'm sorry."

Mortified, Brooke watched him grab his shirt and walk out of her bedroom.

"Brooke?" Nick asked, glancing at her intently.

Sudden anger strangled the words she wanted to say to him. She wanted to blast him with full guns and then walk out of his house and forget she ever laid eyes on him again. But she bit back her remarks and calmed down to a rational level. "You hurt me, Nick. That night. The night you got drafted."

His sharp breath was audible. "None of that was supposed to happen."

That's all he had to say? He'd broken her heart and left her shattered, wishing that she'd been enough for him. The girl from the right side of town. The girl he'd want to take out on a date and introduce to his family, the girl who didn't work at the local diner and sewed her own clothes.

She'd dared to hope, but that hope had been crushed.

She wasn't even good enough to have a one-night fling with. He'd rejected her and left her lying there, exposed and vulnerable and humiliated.

"How do you think I felt when you walked out on me?"

"You should have been relieved," Nick said in earnest, and she wanted to shove him in the chest again.

"Relieved? How can you say that? You…you led me on. You came to my house that night with one thing on your mind."

"Things shouldn't have gone that far, Brooke. I realized that and I walked out before we made a mistake."

"A mistake?" Inwardly she cringed. Now she was a *mistake*. This conversation was going from bad to worse and Brooke wanted to scream out in frustration.

Nick leaned forward, bracing the back of his elbows on his knees. "You were special to me, Brooke and—"

"I was your good buddy," she spit out.

"No, you were the girl I wanted the most and the one I couldn't let myself have."

Brooke shook her head. "I don't get it. Your memory must be failing you. Age does that to a person. You must be old before your time."

"You see," Nick said with a grin. "You're clever and feisty and pretty. Listen, I may have had a reputation back then—"

"Similar to the one you have now," she butted in.

"R-right. But I didn't want to lump you in with the other girls I dated."

"You never *dated* me. Are you going to tell me that's because I was so special?"

"I was afraid of you."

"What?" Brooke sat back in her seat, thunderstruck. Nothing he said was sinking in, but this, *this* was too ridiculous to even consider. "Big, bad Brooke."

"Sweet, special, smart Brooke," he said.

Her anger rose. His compliments meant nothing to her. "Stop! Just stop, Nick," she rushed out. "Why don't you just admit the truth! I didn't measure up to the other girls in your string. You got me naked and decided you could do better. Isn't that what really happened? I was inexperienced and I don't know, maybe I wasn't doing the right things and you—"

"Let me get this straight," he said, between clenched teeth. "You're angry because we didn't screw like rabbits all night long? Here I was trying to be noble, to do the right thing, and you're upset because I didn't take your virginity?"

"I cared about you," she said, raising her voice. "I wanted it to be with you."

"And I didn't want to use you. Damn it, the one time I do the right thing I get kicked in the ass. Listen, Brooke. I wasn't sticking around. At that time, my life, my future was baseball. I was leaving the next week for the minor leagues. And yeah, you scared me, because of all the girls I'd been with you were the one girl who could tie me down. The one girl I'd miss when I took off. It wouldn't have worked. I didn't want to hurt you. I never meant to."

"But you did," she said quietly. "You devastated me, Nick. I never heard from you again. Ever."

I was deeply in love with you.

She opened up to him, finally confessing what she'd held back all these years, "Just think of all the worst things you think about yourself, your secret innermost thoughts that nag at you day after day, that you're nothing, not pretty enough, not smart enough, not wealthy enough, not *anything* and to have those very thoughts confirmed by the one person in the world who can change your opinion. You leaving me there that night confirmed the worst about myself."

Nick came around the coffee table to sit beside her. From the dim lights, she could see into his eyes, the sorrow there and the apology. He didn't try to touch her, but those eyes penetrating hers were like the tightest embrace. "I'm sorry. I thought I did the right thing for you. I've never been one to hold back when I wanted something, but what I did that night, it was for you. I wanted you, Brooke. But it wouldn't have been fair to you."

Brooke had clung to her perceptions about Nick for so long it was hard to let them go. She wanted to believe him and release the bitter feelings that had only dragged her down these past years. She wanted to be done with it. She had a future to look forward to now with Leah. Finally she resigned herself to accept Nick's claim as the truth as he saw it. "Okay, Nick."

It still didn't make up for the months of anguish she'd experienced or for the heartache of loving someone like Nick, but she realized it was finally time to move on.

"Okay?" Nick said. "We've cleared the air?"

She nodded. "Yes."

And they sat in silence for a long while, just absorbing the conversation.

"I think I'm well enough to leave tomorrow," Brooke said finally. "I've got a new life waiting for me." She rose from the sofa. "I should go."

Nick nodded, but his response left room for doubt. "We'll see."

Brooke dressed Leah in a blue-and-white-polka-dotted short set with a ruffled collar and bloomers. She combed her hair and hummed the *Sesame Street* song, laughing as Leah's stubborn curls popped right back up the minute she put the brush down. The morning seemed filled with promise. She'd had a lot to absorb from her encounter with Nick last night and she'd slept on it, waking this morning with a better attitude and ready to put the past behind her.

"It's gonna be a good day, baby girl," she said, lifting Leah up and twirling her around. A wave of light-headedness hit her and Brooke stopped and let it pass, clutching her child tight. "Your mommy is pushing her luck," she whispered.

Nurse Jacobs entered the room, dressed and ready to take over. "Time to take your vitals," she said to Brooke.

Brooke complied, having her blood pressure and temperature taken. When the nurse finished her exam, she gave her a reassuring smile. "You look well-rested."

"I'm feeling much better today."

"You got dizzy just a second ago."

Brooke didn't think she'd seen that. "Stupid of me to spin Leah around. I won't do that again. We're going down for breakfast."

"Okay, I'll hold Leah on the way downstairs."

"Actually, I'd like to hold her."

Nurse Jacobs narrowed her eyes and debated until Brooke added, "You'll be right by my side. We'll go down together."

Once it was all settled, they headed to the kitchen. They heard cupboards being opened and slammed shut and curses being muttered by Nick in hushed tones. The odor of burnt toast filled the air. Brooke walked in with Leah in her arms, took one look at the kitchen in disarray with greasy frying pans on the stovetop, blackened bread in the toaster and Nick, dressed in a pair of jeans and a white T-shirt that hugged his male frame, looking frustrated and out of sorts.

Brooke immediately grinned. "I didn't feel the tornado this morning. Did you, Leah?"

The baby looked at her quizzically.

Nick cast Brooke a quick glance. "Carlotta's got the morning off, not that she cooks anyway, but at least she can boil water and make toast. Looks like I can do neither."

Brooke took in the state-of-the-art appliances and fully functional workstation. "It's a great kitchen. You don't have a cook?"

"Not since my father passed away. The cook retired and we've managed without her up until now. Tony's gone and Joe spends his time at the office or with his fiancée. Which leaves me. I've been fending for myself, not very well I might add, interviewing a little, but no one's worked out." He picked up the phone. "I'll call for delivery. What would you ladies like for breakfast?"

Brooke shook her head. "Jeez, that bump on my head didn't obliterate my cooking skills. I'll fix breakfast. It's the least I can do. I make a mean omelet. Let me at this kitchen and I'll have breakfast on the table in half an hour." Nick put the phone down slowly and Brooke took over. "Here, hold Leah a minute while I raid your refrigerator."

She put Leah in Nick's arms and her daughter snuggled in looking comfortable, while Nick looked anything but. He tried to hand her off to Nurse Jacobs and the wily nurse stepped back and shook her head. "*Brooke* is my patient." She winked at Brooke. Nick sat down at the kitchen table with a twist of his lips and Leah latched onto his shirt.

Brooke opened his double stainless steel refrigerator and

began taking out ingredients. "It's well stocked, which is good news." She immersed herself in her task, enjoying the process. She quickly whipped together three of the lightest, fluffiest omelets she'd ever made, pan-fried potatoes and a fresh fruit salad. Coffee brewed in the pot and while she cooked, Nurse Jacobs set the table.

"How's Leah doing over there?" Brooke asked. She'd been keeping an eye on the two of them.

"Is she always this fidgety?" Nick asked as Leah tried to crawl her way up his chest. She pulled at his shirt and brought her little hand up to swipe at his chin. He set her back down onto his lap. "I think I liked her better when she was sleeping."

Brooke smiled. "She's an absolute *angel*...when she's sleeping. Okay, all set. I'll dish it up. I hope you like lots of veggies and avocado."

There was still tension between them, but she wouldn't have to deal with it too much longer because Brooke was leaving today. She was eager and excited at the prospect of starting her own business.

She served the meal and silence ensued. With Leah on her lap, she dug into the omelet and tasted. Not bad. Then she glanced at Nick's plate to find he'd gobbled up the omelet already and was working on the potatoes. "Want another?" she asked.

"In a heartbeat. Finish yours first. I'll work on what's left on my plate."

A few minutes later, Brooke started cooking Nick's second omelet and Nurse Jacobs took Leah outside for a little stroll.

Nick leaned over the black granite counter, elbows folded, watching her put the bell peppers, onions, bits of ham and grated cheese onto the egg mix and top it off with avocado. "So we're good, about last night. No hard feelings?"

Brooke met his gaze, waiting for the hurt, anger and bitterness to emerge. When it didn't appear, her heart lifted. She and Nick came from different worlds. They were never destined to be together and maybe…just maybe she might believe that he had spared her that night. Yet her initial thoughts from her high school days hadn't changed. He was way out of her league. If she were looking for a man, he wouldn't be last on her list—he wouldn't be *on* it at all. He wasn't a man to stick around. Nick was a player and Brooke had already played the game and lost. And while that might be okay for her, it wasn't all right for Leah. Her daughter's needs always had to come first.

"No hard feelings. But we have to talk about something else. Have you heard back from your mechanic?"

"I have."

"And? What's the bad news?"

He frowned. "Your car might live."

"That's not bad news! That's great."

She flipped the omelet over and lifted it with a spatula then grabbed Nick's plate from the table. "I was hoping it wasn't totaled." She loaded the omelet onto the dish and set it in front of him.

He took his fork and began eating. "How do you do it? This is better than the last one and that one was pretty damn good."

"I'm amazing. I can make an omelet."

Nick scoffed. "You're a good cook, Brooke. Admit it."

"I do okay. So how much is it gonna cost for the repairs?"

"It's taken care of."

She blinked and stood completely still. "No, Nick. It's not. Both of our cars were damaged. I owe somebody, something. I plan to pay. Do you have an estimate?"

"I do."

"Well, where is it? Show it to me," she ordered.

Nick scratched his head and stared at her. She glared back and held her ground. He reached into his pocket and pulled out two pieces of paper from Napa Auto Body Works. Unfolding the papers, he laid them onto the counter and turned them her way.

"Thirteen thousand dollars for your car! You can practically buy a new car for that!" Of course she'd had to collide into *Nick* and the *most* expensive car on the planet.

"My insurance will cover most of it."

Relieved about that, Brooke peered at her estimate. "Forty-eight hundred dollars." She breathed a heavy sigh. That would cut heavily into the money she had saved to start her business, not to mention fixing up the place. The broken interior door would have to wait, and so would the painters and new linens she'd need for the beds. And fixing the bathrooms. Still, she couldn't make *any* repairs without her car. She needed wheels. "When can I have my car back?"

"Maybe you should get another car. Randy said it was borderline. He could fix your car but it's almost not worth it."

"I can't do that. I can't afford a newer car."

Annoyed that Nick would think it just that easy for her to buy a car, she turned away, working out her frustration by scrubbing the frying pan in the sink.

A long minute stretched out in silence.

"Brooke, turn around." Nick was sure bossy this morning. She turned. "Listen, I have a proposition for you. I've got a 2006 Lexus just sitting in the garage waiting to be driven. The insurance is paid up on it for the rest of the year. It's yours if you want it."

She laughed at the thought, shaking her head. "Yeah, you'll just give me a car."

"Not give. You'll work it off."

"Work it off?" Her smile faded instantly. She closed her eyes to small slits. "I feel the need to slap you coming on."

"Cooking," he explained.

"Cooking?"

"You need a car. I need a cook. Correct that, I desperately need a cook. Carlotta's been a pain about who she'll let into the house. The last cook I tried to hire had Carlotta threatening to quit, but she'll jump for joy at having you here."

She immediately began shaking her head. "No, it wouldn't work. I've got a job. I'm going to be spending all my time at my aunt's place. My place now."

"You said yourself, it's in bad shape. You can stay here while you work on your place." The idea seemed to take hold, snowballing as Nick became more adamant. "I'd only need you for breakfast and dinner. You'd have all day to work at the house."

"I'm not staying here."

"You shouldn't have made me that omelet, Brooke. My stomach's involved now. You need the car. I'm tired of eating restaurant food. It'll work out for both of us. Think about it."

She didn't' want to think about it. She didn't, but his offer was too good not to at least give it some thought. "How long before I earned the car?"

"For as long as you need to get your place up and running. A couple of months?"

"That's very generous of you, but I can't—"

"Your car doesn't have air bags," he pointed out none too gently. "You'd be foolish to fix that car."

She squeezed her eyes shut, reminded of what might have happened. The accident could have been far worse.

"Think of Leah," he added without missing a beat.

She was thinking of Leah, constantly. And harrowing thoughts of that accident struck her with fear. She'd actually lost consciousness when they'd collided. What if she hadn't run into someone she'd known? What would have happened to Leah then? She didn't want to take Nick's offer. But Leah's safety came first. She remembered what the flight attendants always said in their little welcome aboard speech about putting an oxygen mask on yourself first, before putting one on for your child. The bottom line, in order to care for your child, you must take care of yourself.

Brooke craved independence and wanted to be indebted to no one. Living under Nick Carlino's roof wouldn't be an option if she were thinking only about herself. But of course, Nick had the upper hand and was on the right side of the argument. Small wonder—he negotiated for Carlino Wines, and knew when to finesse and when to land the crushing blow. This time, he'd used Leah as his weapon and Brooke was defeated.

"That's low, Nick. You know I always have Leah's welfare at heart. What's in it for you?"

"I'm selfish enough to want to eat good meals. And keep the housekeeper from walking out. Do we have a deal?"

Brooke's mouth turned down as she accepted. "Hand over the keys and tell me what you want for dinner."

The dimples of doom came out when he smiled and Brooke didn't find them attractive at all.

Not even a little bit.

"You're joking, right? You've got Brooke Hamilton *living* with you now? I thought it was only temporary." Joe glanced at Tony as they sat at their monthly meeting at the Carlino offices in downtown Napa. His two brothers shook their heads in disapproval. "You're good, little brother," Joe said, "but I didn't know how good. You met her what, twenty-four hours ago?"

Normally, Nick didn't let his brothers get to him, but right now he wasn't in the mood for their wisecracking. He spoke through tight lips. "It was two days ago. And more like she met with the front end of my Ferrari. She's working for me, to pay off her debt." Hell, he made her sound like an indentured servant. With a brisk wave of the hand, he added, "It's complicated."

Tony's laughter filled the air. "Complicated as in a honey blonde with pretty blue eyes."

"You liked her back in high school," Joe said. "You know what they say about the one that got away."

"She's got a baby," Nick said in his defense. "Or are you forgetting about the kid?"

"You think that's gonna stop you?" Tony looked skeptical.

"Hell yeah." Nick wasn't father material. He'd learned from the master. He had enough of his old man in him to know he wouldn't make a good daddy. The blood ties ran thick. He never planned on having children, thus saving some poor child his ruthless tendencies.

"We think not," Tony said glibly, leaning back in his chair and stretching out. He darted a glance at Joe.

"Then, you think wrong," Nick said, ready to change the subject.

After Candy Rae's deception, Nick had lost faith in the opposite sex. Not that he didn't love women, but he wouldn't be foolish enough to place his trust in a female again. He'd lost out on his dream because of Candy Rae's lies and his father's self-serving manipulations. He'd been crushed and trampled on like the precious grapes that his father had loved so much. For that, he hated what he did for a living, feeling his father had won. Nick spent most of his time in Europe, away from the place that caused him such heartache. He'd made enough smart financial investments to break loose of his father's ties forever and was about to do so, but then Santo up and died. Nick came home because his brothers needed him. He was here because of them even though they were a pain in his rear end. Nick liked things simple and getting too involved with Brooke and her bundle of trouble would only complicate his life.

"Want to put money on it?" Tony said, baiting him.

"Damn right," Nick said. "A betting man always likes to take money from suckers. Name your price."

Joe sat straight up in his seat and Nick saw his brother do mental calculations. "What if it's not for cash? What if we wager something more important?"

"Like what?" Nick furrowed his brows.

"Like if you fall for her, you take over the company."

Nick fell back against his seat in shock.

"I like it," Tony said. "The nameplate on the door will read, Nick Carlino, CEO."

"Don't go counting your chickens. I haven't agreed to this yet. Seems this is a little lopsided. What do I get if I win?"

Joe didn't hesitate to answer. "Easy, if you win and you don't fall hard for that gorgeous woman and her little girl, you're completely off the hook. You'll get your fair share of the empire but you won't have to run the company." Joe looked to Tony. "Does that sound fair?"

Tony nodded. "That's right. If you win, it'll be between Joe and I."

"You said if I fall for Brooke. Define *fall for*."

"The whole enchilada, Nick," Joe said. "Love, marriage and baby carriages."

Nick grinned. He'd never been in love before. He didn't think himself capable and marriage to any woman wasn't in his game plan. Ever. Just because the two of them found their so-called soul mates, didn't mean Nick wanted to follow in their footsteps. He wasn't like his brothers. He didn't do long-term relationships. "This is a piece of cake. You've got yourself a bet." Nick stood, eager to shake hands with his brothers and seal the deal. "And thanks for making this easy for me."

Joe looked at Tony and they both smiled smugly.

Nick would relish wiping the smiles off their faces and then he'd be off the hook to go about living his life. There was no way he'd let one woman and her child take him down.

No way in hell.

Five

The Lexus was a really great car, Brooke thought, running her hand along the smooth black leather seat. With dual temperature settings, a CD player and all the other bells and whistles, this was five-star luxury at its finest. She couldn't wait to get behind the wheel and take it for a drive. She sat in the passenger seat glancing at Nick behind the wheel as they drove to Dr. Maynard's office.

He wouldn't let her drive until she got the okay from the doctor this afternoon and she couldn't blame him for that. Still, she hated leaving Leah behind. Though she trusted Nurse Jacobs and Carlotta to watch her baby, she hadn't spent much time apart from her since the moment she'd been born.

"She's okay," Nick said, glancing at her. He had an uncanny way of knowing what she was thinking.

"I know. It's just that I feel lost without her."

"We'll get her a new car seat after your appointment, then you won't have to leave her behind again."

"Thanks for doing this, Nick."

"No problem. I've got a vested interest now." He winked.

She cocked him a wry smile. "I live to cook for you."

"That's the attitude," he said.

"So what would you like for dinner?"

"First, let's see what Steve says. If all is well, you can surprise me."

"All will be well."

Nick looked her up and down and the heat of his gaze made her quiver. "Looks good from where I'm sitting."

Brooke had to remind herself not to melt into a puddle just because he complimented her. It was Nick being Nick. She wouldn't fall for his charm again.

Thirty minutes later, after a thorough exam, Dr. Maynard gave her a clean bill of health. "I'm feeling so much better today," Brooke said, as he walked her out of the room.

"Good, well just take it slow for a while. Don't overdo anything," the doctor said.

"I won't."

Nick rose when Dr. Maynard walked her to the reception area. The two men shook hands.

"Well?" Nick asked her with a hopeful expression.

"I'm fine. I get to pass Go and collect two hundred dollars."

Nick smiled and his dimples appeared. She ignored them, telling herself the thrill she felt was only because she was finally back to square one and she could begin working on the house. Then she turned back to the doctor. "Oh, Dr. Maynard, can you recommend a pediatrician for Leah?"

"Sure can." He walked around to his reception desk,

pulled out a business card and handed it to her. "Dr. Natalie Christopher. She's excellent. And right in this building."

"Thanks for everything," Brooke said, glancing at the card. "I appreciate it."

"You take care now," he said to her, then turned to Nick. "I'll see you Friday."

Nick nodded and when he walked away, Brooke walked up to the desk and spoke to the receptionist, taking out her checkbook. "What do I owe you?"

The receptionist shook her head. "There's no charge."

"No charge? Really? But—"

Nick took her arm and led her away. "It's taken care of."

"You paid for me?"

"Not exactly. The doc owes me and he just settled up the score."

"What? I can't let you do that." Her voice elevated enough to cause stares from the patients in the waiting room.

"It's done, Brooke. Trust me. He's getting off cheap. Come on, we have to go car seat shopping."

Frustration rose and settled in her gut. She didn't want to make a scene in the waiting room, so she marched out of the office. She couldn't figure out why she was so angry with Nick. Ever since the accident, he'd been kind to her, so why did she want to lash out at him all the time? Was it because he could still push her internal buttons with a look or a smile? Was it because he was still the golden boy with all the money, good looks and charm one man could ask for? Or was it because he always seemed to be in control, always took care of things. He was someone she didn't want to rely on and yet, that's all she'd been doing lately was letting Nick make her life easy. It wouldn't last and she didn't want to get used to him being there for her. In the long run, she knew Nick couldn't be counted on.

Once they reached the parking lot, Nick took her hand and looked deep into her eyes. He was amazingly handsome and being near him complicated her life in ways she couldn't begin to deal with. She stilled from his touch, feeling a sharp jab of emotion, knowing she should pull her hand away.

"It's all yours," he said, dropping the keys into her palms.

Brooke stared down at the keys, speechless.

"You want to drive, don't you?" he asked softly.

Brooke nodded, holding back tears. Why had she gotten so emotional? Maybe, because Nick Carlino had just given her a car.

A car.

She wouldn't fool herself into thinking that her culinary skills could have earned her enough to pay for this car. This was the nicest, most decent thing anyone had ever done for her. Her lips quivered. *Don't cry, Brooke. Don't cry.*

But the more she tried to hold back, the more moisture pooled in her eyes. Then the dam broke and tears spilled down her cheeks.

Nick appeared puzzled, then he pulled her into his arms. "Hey," he said quietly, tucking her head under his chin. He stroked her back. "It's just a car."

"It's not just a car," she blubbered, feeling like a fool and hating Nick for being so sweet. Why on earth couldn't he just be the bastard she'd hated all these years and leave her alone?

She clung to him for an awkward minute then pulled away. "It's more than a car…it's safety for Leah and my future, and—"

"Don't cry," he said, lifting her chin and gazing at her. Her eyes were probably red and swollen, her nose all wet and ugly.

He bent his head and kissed her softly on the lips.

It was a warm, sweet, gentle brushing of the lips meant to console and comfort. It did just that, making Brooke feel safe and protected. She sighed deeply and allowed soft feelings for Nick to filter in, just this once. Fighting them would be futile, so she surrendered to her emotions and took what he offered.

When he lowered his head again, ready to do more consoling, Brooke's nerves rattled, not because she didn't want him to kiss her again, but because she did. She turned her head into his chest, denying another kiss, and announced with a whisper, "Men don't like seeing women cry. They think they've done something wrong and don't know how to fix it."

Nick cupped her chin gently and lifted her face to his. "Did I do something wrong?"

She shook her head. "No, you did something…nice."

His gaze lowered to her mouth. "And for the record, that's not why I kissed you."

She didn't want to know why he kissed her.

"I kissed you because you're a brave, honest woman who's been through a lot these past few days and…"

When he stopped speaking, Brooke searched his face, waiting. "And?"

Nick appeared slightly taken aback. He blinked and seemed a little flustered, then he moved away from her. "And, nothing. You looked like you needed a kiss, that's all." He headed for the passenger side of the car. "Are you ready to test this baby or what?"

Surprised by Nick's sudden change of demeanor, Brooke had no choice but to bolster her emotions. She took a deep, cleansing breath. "You bet. I'm ready."

She got into the car, put the key into the ignition and started the engine, then glanced at Nick. He looked at her oddly for a moment as if he were trying to figure something out, then he pointed to the road. "It's all yours, Brooke."

Sudden nerves took hold. Maybe she wasn't ready yet. Apprehension led to fear as she replayed the collision in her mind. The images rushed back to her fresh and vivid. She'd never been one for panic attacks, but she could see one happening now. "This is my first time behind the wheel since the accident."

"First times can be rough. Just do what comes naturally and you'll do fine." Nick sounded so confident.

"Really?" She nibbled on her lip.

"Gotta jump back onto that horse."

"I'm afraid of horses," she said.

Nick shook his head. "We'll remedy that another day. Right now, you're going to hold onto the steering wheel and put the car in gear, then gas it." He was back to being bossy again.

"Okay, don't go getting smug on me. I know *how* to drive."

Nick grinned. "That's my girl. Let's go."

Brooke pulled out of the parking lot and onto the road, doing what came naturally. Nick was right, she was doing fine. It was like riding a bike in some ways, everything seemed to come back to her and she'd overcome her initial fear.

"You've got it, Brooke," he said after a minute on the road.

"Thanks." She breathed a sigh of relief and wondered how she would have done without Nick sitting beside her, giving her courage. She felt more confident with each mile she drove. Now if she could only get the "that's my girl" comment out of her head, life would be peachy keen.

Nick helped Brooke install the car seat and was amazed at how intricate the danged thing was. Pull the strap here, tug there, make sure it fits tight enough and after all their struggles, Brooke finally said, "I'm going to have a professional look at it. Make sure it's safe."

"Doesn't look like it's going anywhere to me." He gave a final tug.

"Just to be sure," she said, staring at the car seat with concern. "Can't be too careful."

Brooke looked cute with her hair pulled back in a ponytail, her blonde curls falling past her shoulder, wearing an oversized T-shirt, jeans and flip-flops on her feet. She'd changed into different clothes once they'd returned home from Napa, calling them her "mommy clothes." It shouldn't be a turn-on, Nick was used to women in slinky clothes that left little to the imagination. But on Brooke, the clothes suited her and he found no matter what she wore, he was more than mildly interested.

"Thanks for helping me get it into the car," she said. "Maybe the experience will come in handy for you one day."

Nick winced. "I doubt it."

"You might change your mind. Don't be too sure of it, Nick." She glanced at her watch. "What time do you usually eat dinner?"

"I'm usually through working at seven."

"Okay, I'm going to surprise you tonight."

"You always do," he said and Brooke's soft laughter made him smile.

He thought back on their kiss this afternoon in the parking lot. That had been a surprise. It was nothing, something to soothe her fragile nerves, but he hadn't expected to be thrown for a loop by that kiss, or by holding her and bringing her comfort. Usually a master of self-control, Nick hadn't been able to stop himself and the rewards he'd reaped were those of protecting and calming her. It had felt good, damn good in a way he hadn't experienced before.

He scoffed silently at the notion. Just hours ago, he'd made the deal of all deals with his brothers. He was so certain he'd win his bet, that he'd started making plans for his return to Monte Carlo in the fall. He had a house there and planned on moving in permanently once the renovations were done, hopefully by late September.

By then, Tony and Rena would have their child. Joe would have married Ali, and Nick would be free to come and go as he pleased.

With no ties and no one to account to but himself.

Nick's stomach grumbled as he admitted to himself that he was ready for home cooking again. His mother had been a great cook and he remembered as a child being lured into the kitchen by pungent aromas of garlic and rosemary and bread baking in the oven. His mother would hum a melodic tune as she prepared the family meals, happy to be nourishing her young family. She'd been a saint to simmer Santo's volcanic nature. When Nick's mom was alive, the house had been a home. Nick had almost forgotten what that felt like.

He'd been smart to hire Brooke for the time being. He was really looking forward to sitting down to a meal that hadn't been boxed up, frozen or delivered from a local restaurant.

At least that was one craving Brooke could satisfy while under his roof.

"I guess it's time to say good-bye to Nurse Jacobs," Brooke said with a note of sadness. Brooke glanced down the driveway to where Leah was being strolled around the garden by her nurse. "She's a sweet woman."

"Are you sure you don't need her a little longer?" he asked.

"I'm sure," she said firmly. Bracing her hands on her hips next to the car, she hoisted her pretty chin. "I just drove you all over town. And installed my daughter's car seat. I'm fine, Nick."

"Correction, *we* installed the car seat."

"Fine, burst my bubble. *We* installed the car seat. But I really hate saying good-bye. And you know what's crazy? I don't even know her first name. She doesn't like it and wouldn't divulge it."

"It's Prudence. I was warned not to call her Pru, Prudy or Trudy. Otherwise, she might walk out."

Brooke's mouth gaped open for a second. Then she tossed her head back, giving way to spontaneous giggles that made Nick laugh too. She braced herself on the side of the car, her whole body jiggling as she tried to stifle her amusement.

Fully caught up in her laughter, Nick watched her breasts ride up and down her chest from underneath that loose shirt. He sidled next to her by the car. Her fresh citrus scent that reminded him of orange blossoms filled the air around her.

"I'm sorry," she said amid another round of giggles. "It just struck me as funny. You should have seen the look on your face when you were telling me that."

Nick smiled along with her. "Pretty unbelievable, isn't it?"

"Why didn't you tell me before now?"

"I forgot all about it. It was on the terms of her agreement."

"It's not a bad name at all," Brooke said, still smiling. Her entire face lit up when she was happy. "I don't know too many women who really like their name."

Nick tilted his head. "You don't like your name?"

She shook her head. "Not really. Brooke sounds so...I don't know, boring?"

"It suits you."

"So you think I'm boring?" Her amusement faded.

Nick winced. He'd stepped in it now. "Hell no. It's a strong name, like the woman. That's all I meant." He wouldn't tell her that her eyes reminded him of streaming clear aqua waters. What better name than Brooke?

Thankfully the conversation was interrupted when Nurse Jacobs approached with Leah in the stroller. "She's ready for a feeding."

"Okay," Brooke said, bending down to lift the baby out. "How's my pretty girl?" Brooke planted a kiss on Leah's forehead. "Did you like your walk?"

Leah clung tight to her mother, then focused her wide blue eyes his way and gave him a toothless smile.

Nick looked at mother and baby and an off-limits sign posted in his head.

"I'll take her inside and feed her, then I'll make dinner."

Brooke walked off with the baby and Nick stood in front of the house with the nurse. "As you know, Brooke got a clean bill of health from the doctor. I want to thank you for all you've done, and on such short notice."

"You're welcome. It was a treat for me too. I don't often get a chance to care for a young family. Leah's precious."

Nick nodded politely.

"Brooke is a determined young woman. It's a hard life, being a single mother. I hope she finds someone to share her life with." Nurse Jacobs cast him an assessing look. "You'll look out for her, won't you? As her friend?"

The "F" word. Brooke wouldn't want that label put onto their relationship. He didn't know how to label it, but they weren't friends. Exactly.

"She'll be working here for a while, so you don't have to worry," Nick replied, sounding as noncommittal as he could.

She nodded. "I'll go inside now and say my good-byes."

He shook her hand and thanked her once again, watching as she walked inside the house, leaving Nick alone with some nagging thoughts.

Brooke nursed Leah, knowing that pretty soon the pediatrician would probably encourage her to begin feeding the baby solid foods. Leah's appetite was growing and she was ready to have more substance in her diet. Brooke gazed down at her daughter—the bond they made through eye contact during this special time touched her heart. She'd miss these daily feedings, when she could forget all else, put her feet up and simply enjoy this special time with her baby.

Brooke's guilt came in sudden waves now when she thought about Leah's father. Her ex-husband didn't know he had a daughter. He didn't know Leah existed. Would it matter to him? A little voice in her head told her he had a right to know, but her fear had always won out. And if she were honest with herself, she'd have to admit that both fear and *anger* were at the root of her holding the truth from Dan.

Their marriage hadn't been perfect, but she would never have guessed that her husband was capable of such deception. Right under her nose, Dan had been carrying on an affair with another woman. He'd been sleeping with both of them.

She'd been blindsided by the betrayal and wasn't in any frame of mind to divulge her own pregnancy to him, not when he'd made it clear that he no longer loved her. But deep in her heart, Brooke knew she would have to confront him one day and reveal the truth to him. One day…but she didn't want that day to be anytime soon.

Brooke took Leah down to the kitchen and set her into her little playpen positioned by the granite island in the middle of the room. "Watch Mommy cook."

Leah looked up with wide curious eyes and picked up a pretzel-shaped teething ring and stuck it into her mouth. She gnawed on the ring with glee, as if it were a one-hundred dollar steak.

Brooke grinned. Her little girl would be cutting her first tooth soon.

"Okay, what shall we surprise Nick with?" Brooke scoured the refrigerator and pantry and decided on her meal. Cooking soothed her nerves. There was something therapeutic about producing a fine meal for someone who would appreciate it. She'd always enjoyed the nearly instant gratification she'd felt when it all came together better than expected. Working as a waitress while in high school, then managing the inn more recently, where she'd lend a hand in the kitchen, had taught her a thing or two about taste, presentation and nutrition.

By seven o'clock dinner was ready and the table was set. When Nick didn't appear, Brooke picked up Leah and went in search. She found him sitting in the downstairs study behind a desk, head deep in paperwork. The room was so masculine, with dark walnut panels combined with warm russet textured walls, massive bookcases and a wood-framed bay window that looked out to verdant vineyards, that Brooke felt uncomfortably out of place.

Leah's little baby sounds brought Nick's head up.

"Hi," she said, witnessing Nick's power and status once again, as he sat in the Carlino office. Sometimes, when he was adjusting her baby's car seat or holding Leah in his arms, she'd forget that he was a wealthy wine magnate with a vintage heritage that went back for generations. "Dinner is on the table."

"Okay, smells great from here." Nick rose and smiled at her. "What's for dinner?"

"It's a surprise. Come and see."

Nick followed her into the kitchen and she filled his plate and set it on the table. "Have a seat."

He glanced at the table set for one. "After you."

"What? No, Leah won't sit still. This is her fussy time. You eat. I'll have something later."

Nick glanced at the baby in her arms. She was peering straight at him with a look of contentment on her face.

Leah, don't make a liar out of your mommy.

"I'd like to have your company during dinner, Brooke. Set yourself a place."

"Why?"

"Why not? You have to eat too. Why should we both eat alone? Besides, how else can I critique your meals?"

"Oh, so you're going to rate my cooking."

"I'd like to *taste* your cooking. Are you going to sit or what?"

"You're grumpy when you're hungry." Brooke moved the playpen closer to the table and set Leah down, then dished herself a plate. She sat across from Nick and he watched her carefully. "Dig in," she said. "It's pork loin with tangy mango sauce. Cinnamon sweet potatoes and creamed spinach. Carlotta said you eat your salad last."

"I do."

"Why?"

"I like to get to the good stuff first," he said, casting her a look so hot, she could have burst into flames.

He dug into his food and Brooke waited patiently for a comment.

"You gonna eat or watch me clean my plate?" he asked after about a minute.

She passed him the basket of warm Italian bread she'd sliced and toasted under the broiler then coated with olive pesto. "I can do both, you know."

Nick looked at her with admiration. He pointed with his fork to what was left on his plate. "This is delicious."

She breathed a sigh of relief. "Carlotta said it was one of your favorites."

"Yeah, but I've never tasted anything this good."

"Helps when you have an amazing kitchen to work with. And good cuts of meat."

Nick shook his head. "You never could take a compliment."

"I didn't get that many from you," she blurted.

Nick smiled. "Now who's grumpy?"

Brooke clamped her mouth shut, hating that she made a reference to their past. She wanted no reminders of that time in her life.

Nick got another plate of food and demolished it before Brooke had a chance to finish her first helping.

"It was hard to say good-bye to Nurse Jacobs." She took a small bite of her potatoes.

"Was it? She could have stayed on longer."

"It wasn't necessary. I'm feeling fine. It's just that I've never really remained in one place long enough to have a lot of close friends. She and I sort of bonded. I'm hoping now that I'm in Napa for good, I'll be able to make some friends."

Leah fussed and Brooke put down her fork to lift her out of the playpen. "You want outta there, baby girl, don't you?"

She set Leah on her lap and continued with her meal while Nick looked on. "I've left another message with Molly and I hope she calls me back. I'd like to reconnect with her. Not that I won't have enough to keep me busy," she said as she tried the spinach. Leah's hand came up and she grabbed the fork from her and giggled. "Leah!"

The next time she tried to get a forkful into her mouth, Leah twisted in her lap, squirming so much that Brooke had to put her silverware down. "What, you want to play now?"

She was just about to stand up, when Nick reached for Leah. "Here, let me have her. Finish your meal, Brooke."

Leah went willingly to Nick, nearly bounding out of Brooke's arms and into his. Leah adjusted herself onto his chest and settled in, her small body against Nick's strong chest. Brooke's heart gave way a little.

"Let your mama finish her meal," he said in a stern tone and when Leah twisted her face, ready to let go big tears, Nick softened his voice. "Okay, okay, Leah." Then he bounced her on his knee.

Brooke smiled wide and Nick shot her an annoyed look. "What? You think I don't know how to bounce a kid on my knee?"

"I didn't say a word." Brooke finished her meal with her head down, refusing to give in to the tender emotions that washed over her as Nick consoled her baby daughter, speaking softly and charming her with sweet words.

That night, Brooke had a slight argument with Nick over their sleeping arrangements on their way upstairs. She wanted to give him his room back, since she'd be staying on for weeks. But Nick wouldn't budge claiming she needed the extra space for the baby's things and the guest room had everything he needed for the time being.

Stubbornly, she wasn't ready to give up until Nick walked over to her in the hallway near the master suite, ready to compromise. "Or we could *share* my room," he suggested with an arch of his brow. He began taking his shirt off.

Brooke froze on the spot, watching one button after another open to his tanned chest. She was very much aware that they were alone in the house. Carlotta, much to her surprise, didn't live in the house. She used a downstairs room for sleeping when the Carlinos had a big party or special occasion; otherwise she went home before dark to spend time with her husband. "Fine, you made your point. I'll take your room. Th-thank you."

Nick backed away then, satisfied.

She entered her room and closed the door. After she bathed Leah and nursed her one last time before putting her to bed, she took a long hot soak in the bathtub and fell into a gloriously deep sleep.

Brooke woke in a great mood. She fixed Nick a breakfast of bacon and eggs and home-fried potatoes, grabbing a quick plate for herself before heading out. Nick had called Randy, arranging for Brooke to drive by his shop this morning so he could double-check the car seat for Leah. Randy had been nice enough to make a few adjustments and she drove away relieved to know Leah was as safe as she possibly could be. Still, Brooke drove five miles under the speed limit all the way to the house, garnering some dirty looks from the drivers behind her.

"Here it is, sweet girl," she said once they arrived. "This is our new home."

Brooke spent the better part of the day making assessments and writing up a list of all the repairs she'd need, setting her priorities. Yesterday, she'd called to have the electricity turned on, and that made her work much easier. She noted the sizes of the beds in each room and checked the bed linens in the closets. There were antique quilts that she could have cleaned but the bed sheets and all the towels would have to be replaced. Thankfully, the kitchen appliances were in working order, though on the old side, their dated look added charm to the kitchen. The dining room was full of dust and debris but the table and chairs were made of fine wood that would polish up nicely.

Brooke contacted a few local handymen and painters in the area by phone and set up appointments, then she called to make Leah an appointment with the pediatrician. She also placed another call to Molly Thornton, hoping her friend was still living in Napa.

She felt an odd sense of belonging here. She'd never owned a home of her own. Even the house she'd shared with Dan had been a rental. At least during their quickie divorce, she didn't have to deal with property settlements; he'd taken what was his and she'd taken what was hers.

But this house was all hers and an overwhelming sense of pride coursed through her system. Tears pooled in her eyes as she looked around the old house, seeing it not as it stood today, but envisioning how it would be one day. Her dream was finally coming true and it had been a long road getting here. Often she'd wondered if this was her aunt's way of making up to Brooke for what her father had done to her. Nothing really could. How can you make up for a man who'd abandoned his family?

But she was grateful for her aunt's generosity. Because of her, Brooke would secure a future for Leah without any outside help. If she didn't rely on anyone, then she couldn't be disappointed. Her ex-husband had taught her that hard lesson.

Yet it was Nick's face that had popped into her mind. It was so unexpected that her breath caught in her throat. Why had she been thinking of Nick? Was it because he'd disappointed her once, or was it because she wanted to make sure he wouldn't have the chance to disappoint her ever again?

"I don't know about him, Leah," she said, sweeping up her daughter and planting kisses on her cheek. Leah was fascinated by her new surroundings and had been quietly curious since they'd arrived, letting Brooke make her phone calls without interruptions.

By mid-morning, Brooke had accomplished what she'd hoped to and decided a trip into town was necessary. She packed up Leah and made their first stop at a hardware store to pick up cleaning supplies, some small appliances and a beginner's tool kit. Next she went to Baby Town to purchase a new playpen for Leah that she could keep in their house, eliminating the need for her to continually cart it back and forth. After picking out a jungle-themed playpen, she drove to the grocery store and bought beverages and food to stock in the kitchen. It was a funny thing, just having milk and bread in the refrigerator made her happy. She smiled the entire way home.

Hours later Brooke glanced at her watch to find it was time to head back to Nick's house. The time had flown by and she was extremely happy with her progress. She'd managed to clean up the refrigerator, wash the kitchen floors and counters and arrange a new toaster, food processor and coffeemaker in strategic places in the kitchen. She'd had a full day and now was off to make dinner for Nick.

She arrived a little later than she'd planned, so dinner was a rush of getting Leah nursed and down for a nap, and creating something wonderful to eat. The something wonderful ended up being a quick stir-fry with shrimp and scallops, scallions, and veggies over brown rice.

"I know I must look a mess," she offered when she heard Nick walk into the kitchen, precisely at seven. "And dinner's going to be a little late today." Steam from the wok rose up and heated her face. She wiped her forehead with her arm, feeling like a slug from the earth. She hadn't had a chance to change her clothes or clean up before starting dinner. "Give me a second and I'll have it all ready."

Nick approached her in a slow easy stride. "Why, do you have somewhere you need to be?"

She snapped her head up. Heavens, he looked like a zillion bucks today. His tan trousers and a chocolate brown shirt brought out the bronze of his skin and accented those dark blue eyes. His appearance made her feel even more a mess, if that were possible. She caught the subtle scent of his musky cologne and knew immediately it probably cost more than her entire wardrobe at the moment. "No, of course not. I'm sorry I'm running late."

She took the wooden spoon and stirred, as if that would make the dinner cook faster.

Nick sidled up next to her and covered her hand with his. Stir-fry steam continued to drift into her face, but that wasn't what caused her body to flame. Having his hands on her was doing a great job of that.

"There's no rush," he said quietly and her heart pounded in her chest. He stroked her gently and she didn't dare look at his face and show him the turmoil he caused her. Instead, she focused and took a deep breath.

"Brooke?"

"What?" she barked out and Nick smiled.

He took the spoon from her and shut off the burner on the stove. "Don't make yourself crazy about this, honey. If you're running late, just tell me. I'm a big boy, I can wait for dinner."

"You said seven."

"Or later. Today it's going to be later. Go up and take a minute for yourself."

"Is that your way of telling me I look like something the cat dragged in?"

"You look fine, Brooke. You've had a busy day. And I want to hear all about it."

"You do?"

He nodded.

She glanced at Leah asleep in her little playpen. "But Leah's down here."

"I've got some reading to do. I'll stay in here and watch her."

Nick had a determined look in his eyes and she decided to take him up on his offer, rather than argue about it. "Okay, I'll be down in a few minutes."

She raced upstairs and tossed off her clothes, jumped into the shower and reveled in the refreshing spray that not only cleansed her, but relaxed her as well. She changed into a pair of clean jeans and a black sleeveless tunic and brushed her hair back, away from her face, letting it fall in curls down her back. Taking a look in the mirror, she liked this image reflecting back at her much better than the harried, uptight woman she'd been just twenty minutes ago.

When she entered the kitchen again, she found Nick standing over Leah's playpen, watching her sleep. The moment caught her by surprise. She walked over to stand beside him and they stood there silently like that for a few seconds.

Finally, Nick looked at her. "She made some sounds. I thought she was waking up."

"Those are her baby noises. She's not a quiet sleeper. You'll get used to it."

Nick glanced once more at Leah, then took a long assessing look at her. "Feel better?"

"Much."

The appreciation in Nick's eyes told her he liked what he

saw. Her nerves went raw and she resumed her position at the stove to finish cooking the meal and ignore the flutters threatening to ruin her dinner.

Nick set the table, putting out plates and utensils and Brooke opened her mouth to stop him but then clamped it shut again. He'd said it point-blank tonight—he was a big boy. If he wanted to set his table who was she to tell him not to?

So she sliced bread and stirred the meal as Nick set the table and Leah slept. For anyone walking in on the three of them in the kitchen, they'd think it a homey domestic scene. Only it wasn't, and Brooke had to remind herself that Nick was her employer and she was leaving him as soon as humanly possible.

Nick ate every bite on his plate and went to the stove to get a second helping. When he sat down again, instead of diving into his food, he leaned back in his seat looking her over. "So how did it go today?" He poured himself a glass of wine and gestured for her, but she shook her head. She couldn't drink alcohol while nursing her baby.

"You really want to know?" She didn't think her day would be of any consequence to him, but if he'd rather make small talk than eat then she would oblige.

"I wouldn't have asked if I didn't want to know." He sipped his white zinfandel thoughtfully.

"I got a lot accomplished. Actually, I'm feeling pretty good about things," and Brooke went on to explain the details of her day. To her surprise, Nick asked quite a few questions and seemed genuinely interested in her progress. In fact she felt so comfortable discussing the subject with him, she asked him for advice. "I was hoping you could help me figure out a good promotional plan to advertise and attract guests, once I get my place ready."

Nick thought for a second, scratching his jaw. "I've made a lot of contacts in the area. I'm sure I could call in some favors."

"I wasn't asking for your help, just a point in the right direction."

"Right, heaven forbid I should help you."

Nick focused his attention on her face then lowered his gaze to her chest and the hint of cleavage her top revealed. He didn't seem to mind that she'd caught him in the act. He merely sipped his wine and continued to look at her until heat crawled up her neck.

"I appreciate you will—"

"Get your place registered with tour books and guides. You'll need a Web site. You'll also need to work out arrangements with other bed-and-breakfasts so that they refer tourists to you if they can't accommodate them. Initially, I'd say to visit local wineries and make your place known. Carlino Wines will put you on top of our referral list for visitors." Through tight lips, he added, "Unless that's against your rules too."

Brooke took offense to that. "I don't have rules, Nick."

He finished off his wine and poured another glass. "Sure you do. You don't want anything from me."

"I don't want anything from any man," she said, her anger rising. She was sorry she'd asked him for advice. "It's not personal."

His brow furrowed. "Is that because of what happened between us in high school?"

Brooke had heard enough. She rose from her seat and took up her plate, unable to hide her annoyance. "Maybe you don't know this, but there is *life* after Nick."

Nick shot up and followed her to the sink. "What is it then? Why are you so damn stubborn? Is it your ex? Did he do a number on you?"

She winced at the mention of her ex. "I don't want to talk about it."

"Hell, maybe you should. Maybe it'll knock off that chip on your shoulder."

She whirled around and faced him straight on. "I don't have a chip on my shoulder. I have a baby to raise by myself and I'm trying my best not to get hurt again. That's all, no chip, just survival. But you wouldn't understand that."

"Yeah, because I've got everything I want."

"Hell, it looks like it from where I'm standing!"

Nick ignored her accusation and wouldn't let up. "Tell me. What did he do to you, Brooke? Why isn't he around for Leah?"

Brooke's defenses fell at the mention of her daughter. Emotion roiled in the pit of her stomach making her queasy. Her heart ached for Leah and all that she'd lost. Dan's betrayal had cut her to the core, because it meant her daughter wouldn't know her own father. It meant, when she did tell Dan about his daughter, he might not care to know her. He might abandon Leah, the way he'd abandoned Brooke. And that would be too much to take. Too hard to deal with.

Brooke lashed out at Nick because he was there, and because he'd asked for the truth. "He isn't around for Leah, because he doesn't know about Leah! One week before I found out I was pregnant, Dan came to me with the news that he was having an affair. She was pregnant with his child. He left me and the child he'd didn't know about. And," she said, her tone and bravado fading, "my beautiful baby girl isn't anyone's castaway. She isn't." Tears spilled down her cheeks and she let them fall freely, shedding her heartache with each stinging drop. "She'll never be. And when I tell Dan about her, it'll kill me if he hurts her the way he hurt me."

Nick ran a hand through his hair. "Christ, Brooke," he said in a low rasp.

"I know," she said, between sobs. She swatted at her shoulder. "Knocked the chip right off."

Nick closed his eyes briefly, then grabbed her around the waist and drew her into his chest. She wound her arms around him and sobbed quietly while he held her, making her feel safe and protected.

"Damn him," he muttered. "The jerk."

"I know," Brooke replied over and over again. "I know. I know."

"Want me to have him killed?"

Even through her heartache, she chuckled. "How would you do it?"

"He would just disappear one day, never to be heard from again."

Brooke nestled into his chest a little more. "I appreciate the thought," she whispered.

"I'm a helluva guy."

"Don't be nice to me, Nick," she pleaded.

"Don't be so damn brave and beautiful and sexy."

"I'm none of those things." She wasn't. She was just muddling her way through life, making mistakes and trying to cope the best way she knew how.

Nick lifted her chin and met her eyes. "You're all of those things, Brooke." Then he lowered his head and kissed her.

It wasn't a consoling kiss, but an all-out Nick Carlino kiss filled with demand and passion. He cupped her face, weaving fingers into her hair and tilted her head to get a better angle, then he kissed her again, his mouth hot and moist and intoxicating. Brooke fell into the sensations swirling down her body in a spiral of heat.

He pressed her mouth open and drove his tongue inside,

taking her into a more intimate place—a place Brooke hadn't been in a long time.

She wanted more. She wanted *him* but she knew it would have to stop. She couldn't do this. Not with Nick. Those thoughts turned to mush when he drizzled kisses down her throat and cupped her breasts with his hands. He groaned with need and backed her up against the counter, their bodies hard and aching for each other. His thumbs stroked over her blouse, making her nipples peak, tormenting her with slow circles that sent shockwaves down her body.

It felt good to be kissed this way by Nick, to have him desire her, and she would die a happy woman if he made love to her now. But Brooke thought about Leah again, and the mistakes she'd already made in her life.

Nick would be another one. And she couldn't afford that luxury.

"No, Nick." She broke off his kiss, and regretted it immediately, but she was determined to stop him. "We can't do this."

He gazed at her with smoky eyes that promised a hot night between the sheets. His hands were halfway up her blouse. He removed them and waited.

"I haven't had sex in a long time," she confessed.

"You haven't forgotten anything."

She squeezed her eyes shut for a moment. "You're good at bringing it all back."

"Somehow I don't think that's an invitation."

"It's not. It's an explanation of why I let things get out of control. My life is complicated right now."

Nick sighed. "Sex doesn't have to be."

She breathed in deep and his scent on her lingered. "I'm not ready."

Nick backed up and gave her breathing room. "When

you are, you have an open invitation. You know where my room is."

She swallowed past the lump in her throat and nodded.

They stared at each other a long moment, then Nick turned away, picked up his keys and walked out the front door.

Brooke stood there, bracing herself against the granite counter, her body aching for completion. She needed the physical act, but she also needed the intimacy of being held and loved and cared for. She wanted the bond and connection that lovemaking at its finest could bring. Knowing she had an open invitation with Nick rattled her nerves and made her imagine things she shouldn't be imagining.

When Leah stirred, Brooke glanced down to watch her daughter's eyes open to the world, her blond curls framing her chubby cheeks and a little pout forming on her mouth. She believed with her whole heart that she'd done the right thing by pushing Nick away tonight.

For all three of them.

Six

The week flew by uneventfully. Brooke got into a routine of waking early enough to cook breakfast and get out the door by nine to work at the house. She'd come back to the Carlino estate in the late afternoon to shower and make dinner. All in all it was working out better than she'd hoped.

Nick came and went as he pleased, and she was grateful there was no tension between them. At least not on the surface. They'd share their meals, talk about their day and have a few laughs. After dinner, they'd head in opposite directions.

She didn't think about Nick during working hours, when her focus was on getting the place cleaned up. She had a handyman there during the week, fixing doors and repairing damage to the walls as well as bolstering the railings that wrapped around the house on three sides. The painters were due next week and Brooke had to begin building a website for her project. She could write the text herself, but she couldn't add photos until the house transformed from the deteriorating Addams Family house to one that looked appealing and inviting. She'd made plans to visit wineries in the area this weekend, reacquainting herself with local vintners and getting the word out about her new establishment.

That would be the hardest part. She'd never felt as though she belonged in Napa and during the night she struggled with old feelings of not being good enough and of not fitting in—only this time, she was able to talk herself out of those nagging thoughts. She'd come a long way since her teen years, having been through some rough patches and learning from them. This was her chance for independence and happiness.

But while she could talk herself out of those old feelings, new feelings had emerged that were harder to keep down. At night, she'd lie across her bed and think about the temptation that lay just a few steps away. Nick had let her know in no uncertain terms that he was available to her if she wanted him. She had an open invitation. And every night since, she'd thought about his offer and him and what it would be like making love to Nick.

The passion they experienced in the kitchen in those few unguarded minutes had been two-sided. She'd opened up to Nick and bared her soul to him and he'd understood her pain. He'd approached her not from self-fulfilling lust, but from shared desire. Each night, as she turned down her covers and crawled into bed, she'd secretly wished Nick was beside her and as the nights wore on, it was getting harder and harder to sleep knowing what she craved, if just in body, was so close to her.

And yet, never further out of her reach.

That afternoon, Brooke stopped work early, deciding Leah needed a break from the drudgery of the old house.

As much as she wanted to accomplish her tasks as soon as possible, she never wanted to lose sight of Leah's needs. She'd stopped off at the store and bought Leah a turtle-shaped inner tube and a two-piece pink bathing suit. Leah loved water, her bath time being one of her favorite activities. Today, they were going for a swim in the Carlino pool.

"Oh, don't you look sweet in your new suit," she said as she dressed her daughter on Nick's big bed. She adjusted the straps on Leah's two-piece swimsuit. "There, all set." Leah giggled and kicked her legs up. "Let's go. Mr. Turtle wants to take you for a ride."

Brooke wore her own two-piece suit covered by a sundress. She grabbed the already inflated turtle—a bad move on her part, she should have blown it up downstairs—picked up the diaper bag full of towels, sunscreen, bottled water, Leah's hat as well as her diapers, then lifted Leah up in her other arm. "Here we go, little girl."

She made it out the door and headed toward the staircase, balancing baby and everything else in her arms, precariously.

"Need some help?" Nick strolled out of his bedroom and didn't wait for an answer. He slipped his hands into the straps of the diaper bag, taking it from her, then lifted Mr. Turtle off her shoulder. "Did you load the diaper bag down with lead?" he asked.

"Not quite," she said, and a chuckle escaped. "It's just a girl thing. Thanks."

Nick followed her down the stairs. "I take it Leah likes water."

"We'll see. She's never been in a pool like this before."

"Really? This I've got to see."

"What are you doing home?" she asked matter-of-factly. It was his home and he could come and go whenever he pleased, but Brooke was really looking forward to having this special time alone with Leah. And if she were honest, she didn't really want to parade around in her swimsuit with Nick looking on. Her body wasn't perfect, not in the way Nick was accustomed to seeing a woman—she had stretch marks still in the process of fading that never really bothered her until now.

Suddenly, the idea of using the Carlino pool lost its appeal, but she couldn't back out now without looking like a complete idiot. Besides, Leah deserved some splash and play time.

Suck it up, Brooke.

"I only work half a day on Friday. It's a guy thing," he said with a wink. "Maynard wiggled out of our tennis game, claiming he had a patient in need." A wry grin spread across his face. "A likely story. He didn't want to get beat again."

"Yeah, and owe you any more favors like treating me for free."

Nick only smiled.

Once they reached the pool, Nick set her things down on the chaise lounge. The day was gloriously warm, the sky a clear blue and the pungent scent of new grapes nurtured on the vine filled the air.

Brooke laid out her towels on the chair, then set Leah down and lathered her with sunscreen before plunking a pink bonnet on her head. "I called Dr. Christopher today and she said Leah could be out in the sun for thirty minutes as long as she was protected."

Nick took a seat in an adjoining chaise lounge and spread his legs out. He was dressed in slacks and a white button-down shirt with the sleeves rolled up. "You're a good mother," he said and she waited for the punch line, but when none came she realized he'd meant it.

"Thank you." She stepped out of her flip-flops. "I never thought I'd be a single mom." She shimmied off her sundress and let it pool down her legs. Then stepping away, she reached down to pick up Leah and the turtle tube.

When she finally glanced at Nick, she found he'd put on sunglasses, which was a good thing because now she couldn't see his eyes measuring her. Thankfully, her suit wasn't a bikini thong. She'd picked out a more conservative two-piece suit, yet there was more skin exposed than she'd like Nick to see.

"I like the suit," he commented immediately.

It suddenly got ten degrees warmer under the direct sun. "I, uh…it's nothing special."

"Leah could be a model for *Baby News* in that pink getup."

Oh, he meant Leah. Now, Brooke wanted to die of mortification.

She turned away and took her first step into the pool. The water felt cool enough to be refreshing, but warm enough to enjoy.

"Brooke?"

She tossed the turtle into the water and watched it land with a little splash in the shallow end. Then she turned to face him, holding Leah close in her arms.

"Your kid looks cute, but I was complimenting you."

"Let's just leave it at, Leah looks cute." Brooke took another step in, and then another. Normally, she wasn't the wait and see type of swimmer—she loved to dive in and feel the unexpected shock of the water, but of course she couldn't do that now. Once she got in up to her waist, she splashed water on her daughter's legs. Leah bent down to touch it. Her chubby fingers reached out again and again and Brooke had to cling onto her tight for fear of dropping her.

Nick sat forward, straddling the lounge, and tipped his sunglasses down. "She's fidgeting again."

Brooke tossed her head back and laughed. "Now I've got you saying words like fidgeting."

Nick smiled and those dimples popped out and caught sunlight. "I guess you do."

He leaned back in his lounge, getting comfortable as Brooke finally managed to get Mr. Turtle to accept Leah's weight. Once she was sitting on the floatation device comfortably, Brooke breathed easier. She pushed Leah around and around, her daughter's big smiles and cackles of delight warming Brooke's heart.

Then a thought struck and she hated to ask, but she also hated to miss this moment. "Nick, a big favor? Since it's Leah's first time in a pool, will you take a picture of her?"

He narrowed his eyes as he made his way over. "Depends, what are you feeding me tonight?"

"Anything you'd like. Name it."

"I'll let you know later. Where's the camera?"

"In the diaper bag."

Nick sorted through her things and came up with the camera. She didn't have to instruct him how to use it—he seemed knowledgeable. He asked for smiles, and Leah obliged immediately, staring straight at Nick. He bent down close to the steps and clicked off a few shots.

"You look hot," Brooke blurted, noticing beads of sweat on his brow.

Nick cast her a charming grin. "I'm taking that as a compliment."

"You know what I mean," she said, spinning Leah around on the tube again.

"Do you swim?" he asked.

Brooke glanced with longing at the long kidney-shaped pool. "Like a fish. I'm a good swimmer."

"Hang on. I'll be right back."

A few minutes later, she heard a quiet splash from behind and turned toward the deep end. Nick swam underwater the length of the pool and came up just inches from her and Leah.

Leah's eyes rounded and she clapped her hands with glee when she saw Nick. He patted her on the head and she followed the course of his hands, watching his every move with fascination. "I'll watch her for a few minutes. Take a swim."

"You don't have to do that." Brooke stood close enough to Nick to reach out and touch the droplets of water trickling down his chin onto his chest. His dark hair was pushed off his face and she noted a small scar cutting into his forehead she didn't know he had. It was just enough of a flaw on a perfectly handsome face to make him look dangerously sexy. Brooke figured it safer to take him up on his offer than stand in the shallow end drooling over a well-muscled hard body.

"Have at it, Brooke," he commanded, pointing to the water. He grabbed hold of the turtle tube and gently pushed it through the water. "The kid and I will be just fine. When you get done, I have a favor to ask you."

"Ah, that makes more sense. You have an ulterior motive."

Their eyes met with amusement.

Brooke turned to kiss her daughter's cheek. "Watch Mommy swim."

"Don't worry," Nick said with a sinister arch to his brow. "We will."

Brooke turned and dove into the water, freeing herself from all worries and simply enjoying her swim. She lapped the pool several times, slicing through the clean rejuvenating water with her breaststroke and several minutes later, she came up to take a breather on the opposite end of the pool.

With a hand on the edge, she glanced at Leah, who was now out of Mr. Turtle and being swirled around by Nick. He held her under her arms and lifted her high in the air, then lowered her feet into the water, letting her kick and splash before lifting her high again. Next, he twirled her around above the water, holding her like a little horizontal helicopter then swooped her down again to let her feet and legs splash through the water.

Leah loved it. Her joyous cackling tore into Brooke's heart. The scene they made, the way her daughter looked at Nick—it was almost more than she could bear to watch.

She swam over to them and Nick turned to her as she straightened up to face him with Leah clinging to his neck.

"She's a swimmer, just like her mama," he said. "Did you enjoy your swim?"

"It was very refreshing."

"For me, too. It isn't every day that I have a gorgeous dripping wet blonde standing in front of me."

Brooke ignored his comment, but it was hard to ignore the earnest expression on his face. "Thanks for the swim. I enjoyed it. Here," she said, reaching for Leah. "I'll take her now."

Nick tried to untangle Leah's arms from around him, but she didn't want to let go. Brooke coaxed her with another ride in Mr. Turtle. After she set her into it and moved her to and fro, she turned to Nick. "You said you had a favor to ask?"

Nick sat down on the pool's step and stretched out his long legs, his face lifted to the sun. "My sister-in-law, Rena, is dying to meet you. Well, actually, she's dying to see Leah and pick your brain about babies and labor and everything else." Then he met her eyes. "My brother Tony said she's going stir-crazy. She's as big as a house, but don't tell her I said that. And she wants a night out. I invited them to dinner tomorrow night."

"That sounds okay," she said with reluctance. She didn't want to enmesh herself any more into Nick's life than necessary.

Nick picked up on her reluctance. "I know it's Saturday night. If you had plans—"

"I'm a single mom with a five-month-old baby. Not exactly hot date material, Nick. I'll cook for your family."

"I wasn't suggesting that. We'll go out for dinner. And then come back here for drinks, maybe some of that blueberry pie you made the other day."

"I don't have a sitter for Leah."

"Not a problem. She'll come along."

Fully surprised by the suggestion, Brooke tossed her head back and a deep rumble of laughter spilled out. "You can't be serious."

"Why not?" Nick looked truly puzzled.

"Leah will disrupt everyone's meal. You see how *fidgety* she is, especially if she's not in her own surroundings."

"So? It'll show Rena and Tony what they're in for." His grin was a little too smug.

"As in, it serves them right for having a baby?" Brooke wasn't sure she liked Nick's suggestion to use Leah as a means to taunt his brother.

"It's not really Tony's baby. At least not biologically, but he's in it for the long haul and no one could be happier about becoming a father than Tony. He'll love meeting Leah. Both of them will and it'll get them off my back. They've been hounding me all week about you."

Brooke's internal alarm sounded. "They don't think that you and I are, uh…"

Those dimples popped out with his sly smile. "You can set them straight."

"Darn right I will."

It shouldn't matter to her what Nick's brother thought about their living arrangements, but it did. She had a good deal of pride. She wasn't one of Nick's bimbo girlfriends that he could toss aside when he was done. She'd never put herself in that position.

"I'll take that as a yes."

"Okay, I'll go to dinner." Did she really have a choice without coming off as sounding ungrateful? She recalled all the questions she had before Leah was born and how nice it would have been to talk to a friend who had gone through it already. And since Molly hadn't returned her calls, Brooke didn't have any female companionship in Napa aside from Carlotta, who seemed to be on the opposite schedule from hers. When Brooke was home, Carlotta wasn't working and vice versa.

Nick's comment about the parentage of Rena's baby spiked her curiosity. She'd left Napa and never looked back and apparently, a good deal had happened during that time. "Is there anything I should know about Tony and Rena, just so I don't put my foot in it?"

Nick shrugged. "The short story is Rena was married to Tony's best friend. Right before David died, Tony promised him he'd take care of Rena and the baby."

"How tragic. She lost a husband and he lost his best friend."

"Yeah, it was rough, but Tony and Rena had past history and my brother worships his wife. They're one of the few happily married couples I know."

"Does the *long* story have something to do with your father?"

Nick drew in a sharp breath and uncharacteristic pain crossed his face. "Santo had a hand in ruining lives and Tony and Rena were drawn into all that."

Leah squawked, letting go a little cry of complaint. Brooke wanted to hear more about Tony and Rena, but it was time to get out of the water. She lifted Leah off the float. "I think it's time to get out or my little girl will turn into a prune. She's ready for a nap."

Nick stepped out first and wrapped a towel around Leah. Together they wiped her down, before he stepped away. "Thanks," she said. It was a simple gesture that lasted no more than a few seconds, but being here with Nick, doing things together was starting to get too comfortable and feel too right.

When Brooke knew in her heart it was all wrong.

Nick hated to admit how much he was looking forward to having dinner with Brooke tonight. Whenever he thought about her, it was with a smile. She made him laugh and he enjoyed her company more than any other female he had or hadn't been sleeping with. She was off-limits in so many ways, yet he found himself drawn to her. Part of that was due to the challenge she posed. She didn't want him and she'd made that clear.

She was also at the root of the deal he'd made with his brothers.

Falling for Brooke was a deal breaker and Nick didn't like to lose.

He showered, shaved and combed his hair, then dressed in a pair of casual beige trousers and a black shirt. They agreed on having an early dinner because of Leah's schedule and so Nick knocked on Brooke's door at precisely six in the evening.

"I'll be right there," she said, her voice hurried. She yanked open the door and rushed off, putting earrings on as she moved to the bed. "Leah took a longer nap today and I'm running late."

She dashed about the room, tossing a few things in the diaper bag and checking on her own purse. While standing before him in a knockout black dress that hugged her curves and reached her knees, she slipped her feet into heels. "I'm sorry."

"Don't be. I'm enjoying the show."

She glanced at him and rolled her eyes, too harried to see his humor. "Okay, what do you need me to do?"

"Stop teasing me, for one," she said.

"Done. What else?"

"Leah needs to be fed."

Nick shrugged, blinking, recalling the time in the hospital when he'd witnessed Brooke feeding her baby. "Sorry, can't help you with that."

"Sure you can." She grabbed a bottle out of her diaper bag and shoved it into his hand. "Give her this. She'll do the rest. She'll take enough to last her until tonight. It'll keep her content through dinner."

Nick sat on the bed and she put Leah into his arms. "Here you go. I've got to comb my hair."

"It's okay if we're a few minutes late you know."

"Good to know," she called out. "Because we will be."

A chuckle rumbled in his chest at her answer. Then he looked down at Leah who seemed happy enough at the moment. "You want this?" he asked. Her big hazel eyes followed the bottle until Nick got it near her mouth. She grabbed hold and tipped it until the thin milky fluid flowed into her mouth. She sucked in a steady rhythm and Nick watched as she drank.

Leah kept her gaze focused onto his eyes as she drained the bottle, her little chubby cheeks working for all she was worth. "You like that, don't you," he said quietly, getting the hang of it. Leah made it easy. She'd taken to him from the moment he'd wrestled her out of the car seat after the accident.

"She looks pretty," he called out, thinking it wasn't a lie. Leah had golden curls, big eyes, rosy cheeks and Brooke had dressed her in a sunny yellow dress that made her look like a sunflower.

Brooke walked out of the bathroom, appearing beautiful and calmer, her blond hair curling past her shoulders in waves and her smile lighting up the room. "Thank you. Compliments to my daughter will always win you points."

"I'll remember that," Nick said, taking a leisurely look at her. "How about compliments to you?"

"I don't count."

"You do to me," Nick blurted, then stood with Leah in his arms, surprising himself for his uncanny appraisal of both of them. "Like mother, like daughter. You both look amazing tonight."

"Thank you," Brooke said slowly, refusing him eye contact. She reached for the baby. "I'll take Leah if you wouldn't mind taking the diaper bag."

"Got it. Toss me your keys. I'll drive. I hope you like Italian. We're going to Alfredo's. We own half the place so there won't be much chance of Leah getting us thrown out."

"Funny, Nick. You'll see. She can be quite a handful. And for the record, I *love* Italian."

Twenty minutes later, Nick walked into the restaurant

holding the handle of the car seat that transformed into Leah's baby seat. Brooke was by his side carrying Leah. "Oh I forgot to tell you, my brother Joe invited himself to dinner and he's bringing his fiancée."

Nick knew Joe and Tony were conspiring against him, trying their damnedest to bring Brooke and him together for their own reasons. Nick was slightly amused at their efforts. He was a worthy opponent and while he might be a sucker for blondes with big eyes and pretty smiles, he wasn't a fool. He might want Brooke in his bed, but that's where it would end.

His brothers underestimated him if they thought they would win their bet.

Brooke glanced at him. "Is this the whole family?"

"Except for a few cousins on my mother's side, living in Tuscany, yeah. This would have been the end of the Carlino line, except now Tony is having a boy."

"I'd like a boy one day," Brooke said quietly and he noted a sense of defeat in her tone. "It's lonely being an only child. I wanted Leah to have a brother or sister."

"Maybe one day you'll get your wish."

Brooke shook her head. "No. That's an impossibility." Her gaze flowed over Leah with softness in her eyes. "Leah's enough."

Nick didn't pursue it. He never talked to women about having babies. He didn't care to know their dreams and hopes for the future because it would never include him. He was destined to be the family's favorite uncle. And that suited him just fine.

Tony and Rena had garnered a large corner table at the back of the restaurant. Fresh flowers adorned the table in cut crystal vases. Flowing fountains lent an air of old European charm with richly appointed stone floors and Italian marble statues.

Nick made quick work of the introductions and helped Brooke to her seat. Rena asked to hold the baby immediately and the two women began a discussion about pregnancy and labor that left Nick and Tony to catch up on some business.

Joe and Ali arrived just as the wine was being served. Nick introduced Ali to Brooke and the three women conversed until their waiter arrived with menus. "The chef will prepare any special entrées you would like."

Nick asked Brooke if she wanted anything special. "I'm sure everything is wonderful. I'll order off the menu."

After they placed their orders, the women took turns holding Leah with looks of longing on their face and talked "baby" for twenty minutes. Finally Nick changed the subject. "Brooke's going to need a Web site for her bed-and-breakfast."

"I don't know what I'm doing really," she offered. "I'm going to start researching what I need beginning next week."

Ali grinned. "Are you kidding? Joe is a computer genius."

"Tell her like it is, Ali," Nick said with a grin. "He's a geek."

"He could probably whip you up a site in less than an hour," Ali said, looking at Joe with adoration.

Joe took her hand and winked at Brooke. "I don't walk on water, but I can help with that, if you'd like. Probably wouldn't take me very long once I had a clear picture of what you wanted."

"Really? That's…well, it's awfully nice of you but—"

"She accepts," Nick butted in, then shot Brooke a warning look. Hell, the woman had trouble accepting help, but there was no one better to get her started on her Web site than Joe.

Brooke shot him an angry glare then smiled at Joe. "Apparently, Nick doesn't think I can speak for myself."

"It's a trait of all the brothers," Rena said. "You'll get used to it. Just stick to your guns and they back down." She smiled sweetly at Tony, who seemed totally unfazed.

Nick sipped his wine and watched as Brooke interacted with his family. When the food came the women fought over who would hold Leah while Brooke ate her meal. It was only when Leah fussed, making frustrated baby noises that she was handed back to Brooke. From across the round table, he watched Brooke handle her child with care and patience. She had loving smiles for Leah even though the baby's complaints grew louder and louder. Finally, Brooke set down her fork and gave up on eating.

Nick stood and strode over to her. "Let me have her. I'm finished with my meal," he said, reaching for Leah. The baby's cries stopped and she lifted her arms to Nick. He picked her up and, having learned not to be stern with the baby's sensibilities, he said softly, "You gonna let your mama eat in peace now?"

Leah's cheeks plumped up, giving him a big smile.

"That's a girl."

Nick didn't miss Tony darting a quick knowing glance at Joe.

"Look at that," Rena said. "Nick's got a way with babies."

"I wouldn't have guessed," Ali said, in awe. "Looks good on you, Nick."

He took his seat as Leah laid her head on his chest and looked out toward the others. "She's a sweet kid, but children aren't in my future. Rena and Ali, it's up to you to carry on the Carlino name."

"We plan to," they said in unison then both laughed.

"Good, then you won't miss me when I'm gone. You'll have your own families."

Brooke's head shot up and all eyes at the table noticed her surprise.

"Of course, we'll miss you," Rena said, glancing from Brooke to Nick. "Where are you going?"

"If things go as planned, I'm leaving for Monte Carlo in a couple of months."

"For good?" Ali asked.

He nodded and when Leah squirmed, he rocked her in his arms to soothe her. "I'm itching to get back there."

"Nick?" Rena said, looking disappointed.

"I'm not going anywhere until your baby is born. And I'll be back for holidays. I'll be your kid's favorite uncle. Promise."

Joe shook his head. "I wouldn't plan ahead too far, bro."

Tony chimed in, glancing at the baby in his arms. "You never know what might happen."

"I'm going," Nick said adamantly. "As soon as we meet the terms of Santo's will."

Nick glanced at Brooke, sitting there, looking beautiful but wearing an unreadable expression. He had no idea what she was thinking. She seemed quieter than usual yet Rena and Ali took to her right away. Both Tony and Joe seemed to like her; Tony offering to help spread the word about her bed-and-breakfast and Joe setting up a date to design her website. Nick knew they had ulterior motives and were trying to trap him into losing the bet. Yet, watching Brooke interact with his family disturbed him on a number of levels, not the least of which being that she fit in so naturally.

Since Leah fell asleep shortly after the meal, they decided to order dessert at the restaurant rather than go back to the house. "Sorry," Brooke said, looking at Leah sleeping soundly in the infant seat, "but with a baby you have to be flexible."

"Oh, we understand," Ali said, "you'll just have to invite us over for coffee another day."

"Once I get my bed-and-breakfast going, I'll invite all of you over for dinner."

"Sounds good to me. Nick says you're a fantastic cook," Tony offered.

"Nick's been staying home nights," Joe added. "Can't say as I blame him."

Brooke blushed, her cheeks turning a bright shade of pink. "If that's a compliment, thank you. But just to make the record clear, Nick and I have a deal. He's been generous to me since the accident and I cook breakfast and dinner for him. But that's all I do for him." She glanced at Tony and Joe, and both men sat back in their seats.

"You tell them, Brooke," Ali said.

"I think we've been properly put in our place," Tony said with a grin. "Are we still invited for dinner?"

"Of course," Brooke said, her eyes going soft again. "I'd love to have you all as my guests."

"Great," Ali said. "I can't wait."

Coffee was served and a variety of desserts were put on the table; cannoli, tarimisu, almond pound cake, pastries and cookies. Nick sipped his coffee and leaned back. Every so often, he'd catch Brooke's eye and they'd share a look.

He wanted her and it was becoming increasingly harder to sleep under the same roof and not share a bed.

Something had to give.

Soon.

Brooke was pleased with the progress she'd made in just a few short weeks. Every day, she spent the morning weeding and planting flowers in her front yard as workmen painted the exterior of the house and a handyman did repairs to the bathrooms and bedrooms. She'd gone shopping for bed linens and fluffy bath towels and bought new curtains for the kitchen.

Joe had helped her with the website—they were now in the preliminary stages of the design. Ali had offered to take her shopping at her favorite out-of-the-way antique shops one day last week. They had a fun time, returning with some really beautiful items to decorate the rooms. Ali's friendship was both unexpected and welcome. By the end of the third week, Brooke felt her bed-and-breakfast would soon become a reality. Her dream was finally within her scopes.

She'd even heard from Molly Thornton, who finally returned her call to say she'd been out of town with her family for nearly a month and she'd been thrilled to hear from Brooke. Molly explained she was a schoolteacher now and had taken the summer off to do some traveling. She'd promised to stop by the house this afternoon.

Brooke had just finished feeding Leah in her new high chair, when a knock sounded at her door. Her daughter had graduated from a breast milk only diet to eating solid foods and managed to get half the jar of carrots anywhere but in her mouth. "Whoopsie!" she said to Leah, wiping clean her mouth and chin. "That'll be Molly. Can't have her meeting your carrot face, now."

There was additional pounding on the door, and Brooke called out, "Coming." She scooped Leah up in her arms. "You're going to like Molly. She's a nice lady."

Brooke opened the door wide, excited to see her friend again after so many years and her heart stopped for a moment, when instead of finding Molly, she came face to face with Dan Hartley, her ex.

A dozen questions entered her mind as her body began

to tremble. How had he found her? Why was he here? She noticed his eyes on Leah and hugged her tighter as she backed away.

He looked from her to the baby. "When were you going to tell me I had a daughter?"

"Dan, what are you doing here?"

"Don't you mean, how did I find you?"

She'd hoped she'd never have to lay eyes on him again. Though she knew she'd have to tell him about Leah soon, she wanted it to be on her own terms, once she'd thought things through, not unexpectedly like this. She didn't want Dan to have the upper hand, ever again.

"How could you do this to me, Brooke? I have a daughter and you don't tell me? You run away and hide her from me?"

"You didn't seem to mind taking off with your bimbo girlfriend, without a thought or care about me."

"You're not denying she's mine."

"I'm not having this conversation with you. I'm expecting someone to stop by at any moment. You want to talk to me, you call me on the phone."

"You want me to *call* you? I'm here to get to know my daughter, Brooke." His gaze roamed over Leah as if memorizing each little detail of her body. "She looks like you."

Leah turned away from him, nestling her face into Brooke's shoulders.

"Let me come inside. I want to see her."

No. No. No. Brooke wanted to scream. "You left us to have a child of your own, remember?"

Dan's expression changed to defiance. "I didn't know you were pregnant!"

"Would it have mattered? Sure didn't seem like it to me. You couldn't wait to pack up your things and get out.

You had something better waiting for you—the woman you really loved and the baby you were having with her. So, why don't you go back to your *something better*."

He winced as his brown eyes went dark. "She lost the baby. Things didn't work out between us."

Brooke's anger rose and her sense of betrayal intensified. Her entire body shook. "So now you want to get to know Leah? So now you want to impose on our lives? I'm sorry for the loss of the child, but that doesn't excuse your behavior. And I'm going to tell you this *just once,* Leah isn't anybody's second choice. Would we even be having this conversation if things had worked out? Would you even care about the child you abandoned?"

"Hell, Brooke, be reasonable. I didn't know you were going to have my child."

"That might be true, but you were having an affair behind my back and you managed to get another woman pregnant while you were married to me."

"I know. I made a mistake."

"You slept with both of us at the same time. That makes you a snake in my book. I don't want you anywhere near Leah, ever."

"You're hurt and angry."

"Damn right I am. But I'm over you and moving on with my life. I want you off my porch right now. If you want to talk to me, call me. You're not coming into my home."

With that, Brooke slammed the door in his face and bolted it shut.

She waited and it was several minutes before she heard him get into his car and pull away. She stood there shaking and wishing this were all a bad dream. She had trouble fusing her thoughts together, trying to make sense of what just happened. She still didn't know how he'd found out about Leah or how he knew how to find her.

Thankfully, Leah went down for her nap without a fuss and she'd just walked out of the downstairs bedroom when another knock came at her door. She nearly jumped out of her skin. She moved to the parlor window, carefully parted the sheer draperies and peered out. Relief seeped in when she saw a woman on her porch.

Brooke opened the door and found Molly's smiling face. She hadn't changed much over the years. Her hair was a darker shade of auburn and she wore it shorter in a stylish cut. "It's good to see you, Brooke. You look exactly the same."

"Molly, come in," she said, trying to hold it together. "It's good to see you, too." A friendly face was exactly what she needed at the moment.

They fell into a heartwarming embrace.

Then Brooke broke down and cried.

Seven

Brooke entered the Carlino home a little later than usual that afternoon, her routine disrupted by seeing her ex and the implications that involved. Thankfully, Molly had been as sweet as ever and lent an ear to her troubles. Just having someone listen, just being able to open up to a friend, made her situation seem more than hopeless. They'd spent the better part of the afternoon talking and catching up. Brooke hadn't had this type of outlet in a long time and it felt good. She had her mother to talk to, but her mother had had enough grief in her life and had finally found happiness. The last thing Brooke wanted to do was burden her with her troubles. So Molly's timing today had been perfect. Brooke didn't know how she would have made it through the day without her.

Now, at the Carlino house without Molly's strong shoulder to lean on, Brooke's fears returned and a knot twisted in her stomach. All she could think about was seeing Dan's angry face. What would he do? She'd literally kicked him off her property and she knew he wouldn't let it go. He'd be back. Deep in thought and worried to death, she cooked the meal quickly and didn't say much to Nick all throughout dinner. She couldn't eat a thing and he asked her three times if anything was wrong, but she denied there was and rushed out of the kitchen and away from him as soon as she could.

Of all nights for Leah to go to sleep early, tonight wasn't the night. Brooke wanted to hold her and play their silly little games and read her a story, keeping her close and feeding off the love they had for each other. Instead, she sat on her bed and watched Leah sleep, worried about her future. When Brooke laid her head down and tried to sleep, old haunting feelings of betrayal, of not being good enough for Dan, of hating him and what he'd done to her, came rushing forth. Her thoughts wouldn't go away, they wouldn't give her peace.

Tears streamed down her face, as Molly's words came back to her. "You've come so far, Brooke." And she had. She wasn't the wilting wallflower from the wrong side of the tracks anymore. It wasn't her, but Dan, who'd done wrong. She shouldn't be torturing herself like this. She deserved better. She deserved more.

She heard footsteps going down the hallway and Nick's bedroom door closing shut.

She was through denying that *the more* she wanted was Nick.

He'd given her an open invitation to join him in bed.

He was the balm she needed to soothe her restlessness.

And why not? They were two consenting adults and he'd made it clear that he wanted her with no strings attached. Her life was complicated enough—she didn't want strings either. He was leaving the country soon and that would ensure no complications.

"He's just down the hall," she whispered into the darkness and rose from the bed. She dressed in a sheer white summer nightie, checked on Leah, who was still sound asleep and tiptoed downstairs. Her bravado needed a little help. She grabbed a bottle of fine Carlino merlot and two goblets and went back up.

Behind Nick's door, she heard the television. She knocked and didn't bother to wait for him to answer. She slowly pushed open the door.

Nick gazed at her from his bed. He clicked off the TV. "Brooke, is something wrong?"

This was Nick Carlino, the boy she'd once loved, the boy she had wanted to claim her virginity. It was too late for that, but she'd never stopped wondering about Nick. She'd dreamt about this moment so many times through the years that she had trouble believing she was actually standing here, offering herself to him. "You said sex can be simple."

Nick peered at her with assessing eyes, his gaze flowing over her lacy white gown that bared more cleavage and leg than she'd ever let him see before.

He stood up. "It can be."

He looked like sex personified in a pair of jeans and nothing else. His body tight and muscled, his skin a golden bronze. Brooke wondered how she'd been able to stay away from him so long.

"I need simple, Nick. With you."

He walked over to her and took the wine bottle from her hand. "You want to tell me what changed your mind?"

She closed her eyes. "No."

"You really want wine right now?"

"No."

He set the wine bottle down and then the glasses. "I've been waiting for you," he said softly, then took her into his arms, bringing her in close. Their bodies meshed perfectly and she ran her fingers across his chest, stroking him before he had a chance to kiss her. She heard his intake of breath.

"It's a long time coming, honey." Then he bent his head and brushed his lips to hers gently, teasing, stroking her lips with his tongue until she whimpered his name.

His kiss went deeper and deeper until they simultaneously mated tongues, the potent sensation sweeping them both up into a hot raging storm of desire. Nick cupped her neck and angled her head to take her fully then he wove his fingers into her hair and muttered quiet oaths between kisses that only spurred her passion further.

He moved his lips lower, to her throat and down her shoulders, planting moist delicious kisses there, his hands riding up and down her sides. She arched for him and he didn't bother getting tangled up in her nightgown, he removed it with one quick yank of the spaghetti straps down her shoulders. The garment slowly dropped down her legs to the floor.

Her breasts sprung out—now her tiny white thong was all that was left on her body. Nick's gaze filled with lust and admiration. "No more mommy clothes."

Throaty laughter spilled out. "Not tonight."

Nick cupped her breasts and stroked with nimble fingers, driving her completely insane. He whispered, "I don't care what you say, those clothes are still a turn-on."

"Are you saying I turn you on, night and day?"

"Pretty much." He bent his head and kissed one breast, then the other. "Whatever brought you here, I'm damn glad." He cupped her behind and pressed her belly to his erection.

"I see how glad you are."

He groaned when she rubbed harder against him.

"Don't tease me, Brooke."

"Why," she said breathlessly. "What will you do?"

He grinned wickedly then picked her up and lifted her until she was over the bed. "This." He dropped her a few inches and she bounced once, before settling in. He didn't give her time to react, joining her on the bed, covering her with his body.

"You feel good."

The heat of his gaze and the hungry look in his eyes told her playtime was over. Her throat constricted and she managed, "So do you, Nick."

She wove her hands into his hair, threading her fingers through the dark locks, gazing into his eyes, then lifted up to brush a quick kiss to his lips. He lowered her down and pinned her hands above her head, then proceeded to make love to her body with his mouth. She was trapped by his hold, but more by the way he touched and caressed every inch of her. Little moans escaped her throat as she closed off her mind to everything but the pleasure Nick gave her.

Nick released her hands then lowered himself down on the bed, and kneeled before her. He lifted her legs and pressed his hand to her core, the heat of his palm creating hot moist tingles of excitement. He rubbed his palm over her several times then angled his head and brought his mouth to her.

She arched and gave him access, feeling every kiss, every stroke of his tongue in her most sensitized spot. The pleasure was exquisite and torturous and Brooke thrashed her head back and forth, absorbing the sensations whipping through her.

Pressure built quickly and she panted out breaths, the tension almost too much to bear.

Nick released her then and lay beside her, unsnapping his jeans. "Let me," she whispered, turning toward him and lowering his zipper. She helped him out of his jeans and then took his manhood in her hands, stroking him lightly.

"You're wicked cruel," Nick said with a smile.

"You're welcome."

He lay back, taking heavy breaths as she continued to stroke him, his erection thick in her hands. She felt so free and open with Nick, the final culmination of years of wondering and dreaming about this night that she wouldn't hold back.

Tonight was all about sex and she couldn't think of a better partner than deadly handsome, dangerous Nick Carlino.

Brooke could be dangerous too and she was about to show him how much. She slid her hand up and down his length, enjoying the contrast of hard muscle against silken skin. He grew harder in her hands and when she rubbed her finger over the tip, a guttural groan emanated from his throat.

A slim path of moonlight streamed into the room casting shadows on his perfect body. "I want you on top," he demanded, his gaze burning hot.

She gulped oxygen and waited while he took care of protection. Then he lifted her over him and she straddled his legs, her back arching slightly.

"Do you have any idea how beautiful you look right now?"

A charmer and a sweet-talker, Brooke often didn't take Nick seriously, but there was a rich sincere tone to his voice now and even though she didn't think her body was beautiful, not after stretch marks and breasts that had lost their ripeness, she peered into his half-lidded, sex-hazy eyes and saw that he believed it.

He took her hips in his big hands and guided her down. She felt the initial touch of his penis and a dam of desire broke as her body opened for him. She lowered down a little more, taking him in slowly, deliberately, absorbing the feel of him inside her.

She closed her eyes to feel the height of every sensation. It was sheer heaven. She'd gone so long without this natural act. At this time in her life, she needed Nick and the sexual satisfaction he could provide for her.

Nick moved his hips and thrust into her, testing her and tempting her to take all of him. She complied easily, her body moist and ready to accommodate his needs. She sunk down deeper and through the dim light, she witnessed his expression change. He whispered words of encouragement as she moved on him, up and down, each intense thrust bringing her closer to the brink of fulfillment.

Nick lifted up and wrapped his arms around her, holding her tight as she moved on him. He cupped her derriere and brought his mouth to hers, slanting fiery hot kisses over her lips. She was ready, so ready.

"Together," he said, between kisses. "We're doing this together."

Brooke understood and when Nick rolled her onto her back, she accommodated his full weight. He adjusted his position and took control. He fondled her breasts as he kissed her, driving her nearly insane. His thrusts were powerful and deliberate, each one meant to arouse and tease until she couldn't hold back her release. Her breaths came fast and hard. Nick was relentless, his body covering hers. She held him around the neck as he drove his thrusts home.

Hot waves swirled and electric jolts coursed through her body. She cried out with little moans, her face contorting as she took on the extreme, heady pleasure. Their release erupted, shattered and consumed. Just as he'd promised, they came at the same time and the notion left her with a breathless smile.

Nick lowered his body down and she breathed in the scent of man and musk and sex. He stroked her face gently and kissed her again before moving off her to roll onto his back. "That might have been worth the wait."

Brooke chuckled. "It's only been a few weeks."

Nick moved onto his side and with a finger to her chin turned her face to his. "More like thirteen years."

Her throat tightened and she tried to make light of it. "Ancient history."

"I wanted you back then, Brooke. I know you don't believe it, but it's true."

Brooke didn't believe it. "Let's not talk about the past."

Nick bent his head to kiss her lightly. "Okay, let's talk about how amazing you are."

The compliment made her uneasy. "I bet you say that to all the girls."

Nick remained silent and Brooke realized that she had really stepped into it now. Her obvious attempt at humor failed.

"Listen," Nick said in a serious tone, "I don't sleep with a different woman every night. That's never been my style. I actually have to like the woman and respect her, before I take her to bed."

"Okay," Brooke said, oddly believing him. He was a man with integrity.

"What happened between us just now was amazing."

Brooke agreed with a nod. "For me, it was."

Nick took her into his arms and laid her head on his chest. "For me too."

She could stay in his arms all night, but thought better of it. "I'd better check on Leah."

She found her nightie and tossed it over her head then made a move to go, but Nick stopped her, taking her hand. "Come back."

"I, uh, we're still keeping this simple, right?"

"Simple," Nick agreed without hesitation, releasing her from his grasp.

"Okay, then I'll be back."

Nick put on his boxers and got out of bed to pour two glasses of wine. He didn't know what brought Brooke to him tonight and he wasn't going to look a gift horse in the mouth. But he couldn't help wondering. She'd been bold and vulnerable at the same time, but it was the underlying trepidation in her eyes that she'd tried to hide that bothered him. Something was up with her—something had changed to bring her to his bed. Maybe he shouldn't want to know and maybe he was better off not knowing but the hell of it was, he did want to know.

Sex with her was better than he'd imagined. And he'd done a lot of imagining over the years. Whenever he was at his lowest points in life, he'd think about Brooke Hamilton and her image would make him smile. But at the same time, it would leave him empty.

He'd done the right thing back then, but it was different now and Brooke seemed to want what he did. Simple and uncomplicated. Two words Nick knew a lot about when it came to women.

He set the bottle down, the Carlino Wines label facing him, a constant reminder of the sacrifices forced down his throat for the sake of the company. He wanted out. He wanted away from here and the sooner the better. His old man wouldn't win. Not ultimately. Nick would win his bet with his brothers and that would be that.

When Brooke reappeared in his doorway, he was swept up by the look in her stunning blue-green eyes. It was a turn-on just seeing her framed by the moonlight, her blond hair tousled and the strap of her nightie falling down her shoulder.

"Hi," she whispered.

"How's Leah?"

She smiled. "Sleeping like an angel."

Nick walked over to her and took her hand. "Come back to bed."

She hesitated and peered at him with eyes that seemed haunted. "This isn't a mistake, is it?"

Nick put his hands on her shoulders and caressed her lightly. Touching her spurred something fierce within him and he followed the path of her slender body, his hands roaming down her sides until he reached her waist. He pulled her close and she squeezed her eyes shut.

"Doesn't feel like a mistake." He brushed a kiss to her lips. "Does it to you?"

She shook her head and those gorgeous eyes caught him in a spell. "No, but it's just that I…"

"Just that you, what?"

"Nothing, Nick." She pulled away from him to pick up the two goblets of wine. She handed him one, then took a sip of her own, her demeanor changing. "I haven't been able to drink wine or anything alcoholic in a while. This tastes delicious."

Nick blinked and wondered about her sudden mood change but not enough to destroy the evening. He had a beautiful woman in his room, drinking wine after a wicked time between the sheets and he wanted her back in his bed. He wasn't through with Brooke Hamilton yet.

She took a few more sips then set the glass on the nightstand. Nick polished his merlot off easily, then sat down on the bed and grabbed her hand. With a tug, he pulled her onto his lap. She fell onto him gracefully and wrapped her arms around his neck.

He nibbled on her throat and his voice took on a low rich rasp. "I want to make love to you all night long."

"That's why I'm here," she answered softly.

Nick's questions were quelled with her response. He gave up trying to figure her out and simply enjoyed the fact she was so willing. He lifted her off him and laid her down on the bed. She reached for him with outstretched arms causing his heart to hammer and his body to tighten instantly.

He made love to her slowly this time, peeling away her clothes and relishing each morsel of her body. He took care and time and enjoyed her as he'd never enjoyed another woman. She was hot and sexy and fun and feisty in bed. She gave as much as she took and as the night wore on, they made love again and again.

Each time was different and better than the last. Nick hadn't had sex like this in a long time. It was almost as if Brooke had been dying of thirst and once she was offered a drink she couldn't get enough. Lucky for him.

Sometime during the late night, Brooke must have tiptoed out of bed, because Nick woke up alone. Oddly, the sense of loss he experienced when he found her gone puzzled him. They'd certainly had a satisfying night between the sheets and it wasn't unusual for him to wake up alone after being with a woman. Usually, he preferred it that way.

Nick showered and dressed and made his way down the hallway. He knocked on Brooke's door softly, and when no one answered, he opened it to find both mother and baby weren't there.

He strode downstairs and found them in the kitchen.

Brooke stood at the kitchen counter feeding Leah her breakfast. The little girl was outgrowing her infant seat quickly. Brooke was so intent on spooning squash into her mouth, she didn't notice him enter the room. He walked up behind her and wrapped his arms around her waist. "Morning," he said. When she turned around, he planted a kiss to her lips.

"Morning," she said, taking only a second to look at him before turning back to her daughter. "Watch out, Leah's in a squash-tossing mood this morning."

Nick patted Leah's head, her loose little blond curls bouncy under his palm. "You need a high chair, kid. I'll order one and have it delivered today."

Brooke put Leah's spoon down and stared at him. "Nick, you will not."

"Why not? She's outgrowing that seat she's in."

"Because for one, she has a high chair at my house, and for two, we'll be moving out in a few weeks. We can make do until then."

"Hey, did you get up on the wrong side of the bed?"

Brooke's defiant expression changed to something more reasonable. "No, I didn't." Then a little smile emerged and she softened her tone. "I got up feeling pretty wonderful this morning."

"You can thank me for that later." He grabbed a cup by the coffeemaker and poured his coffee.

"I thought I showed my appreciation last night."

Nick chuckled and was glad feisty Brooke was back. They drove each other crazy last night, a memory that would stay with him long after she was gone. He sipped his coffee. "What are you doing tonight after work?"

"Cooking for you and then falling into bed. I didn't get a whole lot of sleep last night. Why?"

He shrugged. The thought just popped into his head.

"There's a new pizza place in town and I hear it's pretty good. I thought you'd like to try it. Nothing fancy, sawdust on the floor."

The incredible hue in her eyes softened and just when he thought she'd agree, she turned her attention away and shook her head. "I don't think so."

"We'll take Leah."

"It's not that. I just don't think it's a good idea."

"Pizza is always a good idea."

She wiped her daughter's chin then the rest of her face and removed her from the infant seat. With Leah on her hip, she turned to him. That underlying worry he'd seen last night reappeared. "I've got a lot going on right now, Nick. I…can't."

"What's going on?"

"Nothing." She clammed up and again he wished she'd tell him what had put that wary look on her face. "We're keeping this simple and I really need that right now."

"It's what we agreed on. I'm a man of my word."

She sighed deeply. "Your breakfast is on the stove. I'm not hungry this morning."

Hell.

"Don't cook tonight. I'll bring pizza home."

She turned away from him and busied herself with dishing up his meal. "Okay. If that's what you feel like having tonight. It's fine with me."

Nick spent the morning at the Carlino offices in town. More than once he thought about Brooke and that haunted look on her face. He told himself to butt out, that *simple* meant not getting involved too personally. Leah's face popped into his head and he figured Brooke's worry might have something to do with her baby. If that were the case, she might need his help. But Leah looked like the picture of health. He didn't know much about kids but he knew that Leah was a happy child.

Brooke was a fantastic mother.

After lunch, Nick found himself in front of Brooke's bed-and-breakfast. He had no reason to stop by other than he couldn't stop thinking about her. He got out of his car and the first thing he noticed was how manicured the front lawn appeared. New grass grew along the walkway leading up to the front door. A garden of yellow, pink and lavender flowers sprouted from the borders on either side of the front porch. The exterior walls of the house were painted with a fresh coat of yellow paint and half of the shutters were gleaming white, the other half layered with primer.

Nick knocked on the door. When Brooke didn't answer, he knocked again, louder. He saw her part curtains in a big box window and glance first at his SUV, then gaze at him. The look of pure relief on her face gave him pause.

A second later, the door opened and he grinned, seeing the splotches of cornflower blue paint on her nose and chin. Her oversized T-shirt and denim jeans were splashed with streaks of paint in various colors. In the background, he heard Leah's cries of complaint. "Did you get any paint *on* the walls?"

"Funny, Nick," she said, heaving a big sigh and opening the door wider to allow him entrance. "Come in."

As she waited for him to step inside, he noticed her scanning the street before shutting the door and bolting it. "I'm painting one of the bedrooms and Leah's not happy about it." She headed toward the sound of Leah's cries.

Nick followed her past the parlor and up the staircase. "I don't want her inhaling the fumes, so she's complaining about being out in the hallway."

Once he reached the hallway, the baby gave him a big smile from inside her playpen and lifted her arms out toward him. He bent to lift her up and Leah tucked her little body against him. Nick stroked her soft curls as her baby scent wafted to his nostrils.

Brooke looked at the two of them together and her lips pulled down in a frown. "What are you doing here?"

Was this the same woman who'd been sweet, sexy and loving in his arms last night? Brooke seemed to be out of sorts and jumpy as if she'd lose it at any second. It was exactly why he'd come here today. Something was wrong and she wouldn't confide in him. The truth was, he was worried about them though he wouldn't say it out loud. "I had an appointment with a client. It was on my way and I thought I'd stop in and see your progress. The outside is taking shape."

"Thanks. It's slow going today though. Leah's not cooperating."

"She's fine now." He couldn't help it if the kid liked him, could he?

The furniture was in the middle of the room covered with a big drop cloth. Brooke must have dragged it there and covered it without any help. Hell, he could have a crew of painters out here tomorrow and every room painted to her specifications if she'd allow him. But he wouldn't even suggest it. She budgeted for the exterior to be professionally painted and took on the interior work herself. He had to admire her work ethic and pride. He knew she loved working on this place. *That* was not what was making her edgy.

"She'll be worse once you're gone."

"Then I won't leave."

Brooke glanced at him. "You've got better things to do."

Leah bumped her head against his chin and he flinched

from the hard knock that gnashed his teeth together. He ground out, "Can't think of anything."

Brooke shook her head and laughed. "She's got you conned, Nick."

"I'll help you paint. We can take turns with her."

Brooke scoffed and the look on her face annoyed him. "You're dressed like a million bucks."

"I'll take off my clothes. Anything to accommodate a lady."

"Thanks, but no thanks."

"I'm serious, Brooke. I have a free afternoon. I've got an old pair of sweats in my car."

Before she could answer, her cell phone rang. Nick glanced at it vibrating on the window ledge. One ring. Two rings. Brooke's eyes went wide but she didn't make a move to answer it.

"Want me to hand it to you?" he asked.

"No! Don't get it." Brooke's face froze with fear. She glanced at the phone as if it were death warmed over. "I'm not going to answer." When the phone stopped ringing, her body slumped and she let her breath out.

Nick set Leah down in her playpen and strode over to Brooke. "What the hell's wrong? The phone scared the crap outta you."

"Nothing's wrong." She tried to smooth over her fear by softening her tone, but Nick saw straight through that. "I can't talk right now. I have to finish painting, that's all."

"And you don't want to know who it was?"

"It was Molly," she said without skipping a beat. "You remember Molly Thornton, don't you? She's teaching school now and I told her to call, but I'm too busy to talk. You know how women are, once they get on the phone, they don't stop. I'm really eager to finish this room today."

Nick narrowed his eyes. "You're a terrible liar."

Brooke squeezed her eyes shut. He watched turmoil cross her features. When she opened her eyes to him, she hoisted her chin, her stubborn face on. "Are you going to help me paint this room or what?"

"Yeah, I'll help," he said, angry that she'd lied to him. Why the hell he cared baffled him. She wanted simple and so did he.

He walked out to his car and got his sweats. He couldn't remember the last time he'd picked up a paintbrush.

If ever.

Eight

Nick was true to his word. He helped her paint the bedroom and they took turns with Leah when she fussed. It was a sight, seeing Nick with paint smudging his usually impeccably groomed face. Half an hour into it, his sweats were in no better shape than her clothes. She kept fixating on the speck of blue paint on Nick's eyelid whenever they spoke to keep from thinking about the *call*. She suspected it was Dan but she hadn't listened to her voicemail. It could have been Molly leaving her a message. Wishful thinking, she supposed because from the look on Dan's face yesterday, she didn't think he would give up. Oddly, having Nick with her today calmed her nerves.

By six o'clock they'd finished the room. Both stood back to admire their work. "Looks nice, a soft shade of blue and once I get the furniture back in place, I can call this room ready to rent. Only three more to go."

It was a good thing too, because the money she'd saved

for repairs and renovation, meager as it was, had been stretched to its limit.

"I'll call for pizza and once the paint dries, we'll put the furniture back."

Brooke had a protest on her lips, but Nick had turned his back on her, his cell in hand making the call. "What kind do you want?"

"Vegetarian."

He winced and ordered two pizzas, one with veggies and one fully loaded. "They'll be here in thirty minutes," he said. "Where can I clean up? I need a shower."

"Oh." That caught her off guard. Images of Nick naked in the shower made her mind sizzle with promising thoughts. Making love to him last night had been better than any of her wild imaginings.

Nick grinned as if reading her mind and approached her. "You could use one too."

The dimples of doom emerged on his face in a way that beckoned and brought even more lusty thoughts. After a full day of being shuffled back and forth, played with and read to, Leah had conked out. Her naps usually lasted at least an hour, so Brooke couldn't use her for an excuse.

Not that she wanted one.

Nick came within a breath of her and their eyes met. Once again, she focused on that blue fleck of paint on his eyelid and inhaled sharply. He dipped his finger onto his wet paintbrush coming up with a dollop of cornflower blue and spread it across her throat in a slow caress. "You're gonna need a good scrubbing to get all that paint off." His brows lifted, then he bent his head and brushed a lingering kiss to her lips.

Brooke trembled and her eyes fluttered closed. Every nerve in her body tightened. She couldn't refuse Nick and the promise of pleasure he would give to her. For a few minutes, he could take her away from her troubles and make her forget.

It was simple sex, she reminded herself. She took his hand and led him to the upstairs shower in the corner room. "It's small. We'll have to squeeze in together."

"I like the way you think." Nick lifted his sweatshirt over his head and tossed it in the corner. With his muscled chest bare, she itched to touch every inch of taut skin then devour him with her mouth.

He skimmed the edge of her shirt, pushing it up and over her head, exposing her white cotton bra. His dimples popped out and an appreciative smile spread across his face. "You've changed my opinion of soccer moms."

Brooke swatted at him, but he grabbed her wrist and wound her arm around his neck. He pressed his lips to hers in a more demanding kiss, one that had them pushing and tugging off the rest of their clothes. Nick pulled her into the shower stall, turned the water on to a hot steamy spray then backed her up against the tiled wall.

He was beautiful and sleek and tan, built like a superior athlete and at the moment, he was all hers.

They didn't even try to scrub each other, but allowed the steam to do that job while they kissed and touched and played in the shower. Brooke devoured him with her mouth as she'd planned and he, in turn, did the same. His hands slid all over her—pausing in her most erotic spots long enough to drive her completely crazy.

Nick had expert hands and a mouth that was made for pleasure. He brought her to the brink of climax with just a few exquisite touches to her inner folds, then he bent down and took her into his mouth. She grabbed his hair in her hands when she no longer could hold on and the rush of raining waters drowned out her little cries of ecstasy as her body convulsed.

She lay back against the tile, her gaze hazy and her body sated. Nick smiled at her. "I like that look on you."

"Feels pretty good too."

Nick kissed her again and his massive erection rubbed her belly. She reached down and took him into her hands, smiling when his face grew taut and his eyes closed with pleasure. "Wicked cruel."

"That's me," she said, sliding him through her fingers, his shaft growing even larger. He only allowed a minute of stroking before he stopped her. "No more," he said then lifted her up in his arms and wrapped her legs around his waist. He kissed her hard, stroking her with his tongue, then plunged deep into her moist body, his hands on her waist guiding her movements.

She arched back and he thrust harder and harder. "Brooke," he muttered, his voice deep and primal. His release came shortly after, in hard bursts of power that stirred her to another amazing climax. Her body shuddered for several long seconds and then she went limp in his arms. He held her that way for a long time after he shut the water off.

Nick made her forget her troubles for a short time and gave her more pleasure than any man she'd known. She was grateful to him for that, but reality knocked her hard when Dan's angry face stole into her mind. It was like a splash of freezing cold water on her sated body. "I'd better check on Leah," she said hastily. "And the pizza will be delivered soon." She left Nick standing there, gloriously naked with a puzzled look on his face.

"She's cutting her first tooth," Brooke said to Molly on the phone much later that night in her bedroom. Leah had fussed all evening long requiring all of Brooke's attention.

"I can see the first buds coming through her gums. No wonder she's been out of sorts."

"Oh, I remember that phase. Sometimes they wake up with teeth in their mouth and sometimes it's a major trauma when a tooth comes in." Molly had two children, a six-year-old boy and a four-year-old girl.

"I think Leah is somewhere in between. She's really such a good baby most of the time, but I know her little gums are bothering her."

"Teething rings work well," Molly said. "Do you have one?"

"Yes and she likes it. She gnawed on it until she finally fell asleep." It was ten o'clock, late for Leah to fall asleep. But between a late nap and the teething, it had taken a long time for Brooke to get her down.

That late nap allowed Brooke time alone with Nick, always a risky proposition. He was her guilty pleasure and as long as she thought about him that way, she'd manage okay. No hearth and home thoughts of Nick, she warned herself.

"Brooke, what happened with your ex? Did you hear from him today?" Molly asked, more than mildly curious.

"He called, but I didn't pick up the phone. The voicemail was not pretty. I don't know what to do. He's so angry with me but at the same time, there's an undertone of civility. I think he wants a second chance, for Leah's sake."

"He told you that on the voicemail?"

"It's the impression I got."

"And how do you feel about that? Would you ever take him back?"

"No. Never. I'm not in love with him. He killed that a long time ago. He's Leah's father and I'm going to have to deal with that sooner or later. I'm just so scared."

"Well, you're not alone. I'm here if you need me."

"I know, Molly. Thank you." But it was Nick's image that popped into her mind whenever the fear got to her. She slammed her eyes shut to block him out. She didn't want to rely on him. She wouldn't allow herself to feel anything for him. He was a walking heartbreak and she'd be a fool to fall for him. Yet, she knew in her heart, he'd be there for her, if she really needed him. That's why she wouldn't confide in him about Dan. She couldn't afford the luxury of getting that close to him. She had to be strong and independent. She'd never place her trust in another man ever again. "You've always been a good friend. I'm sorry we can't meet for lunch tomorrow. I don't know how fussy Leah will be."

"That's okay. We'll do it another time. Remember, I'm here if you need me."

"I know and I'll call you soon, I promise."

Brooke hung up the phone and walked over to Leah's little bed. Her baby looked peaceful, sleeping soundly. Instead of undressing, Brooke had something on her mind, something that had occurred to her after two slices of pizza and a beer tonight, in the aftermath of making love with Nick. But this was the first chance she'd had to address it.

She left her room, keeping the door open in case Leah woke, then strode down the hall to Nick's bedroom. She knocked and waited.

He opened the door with his cell phone to his ear and gestured for her to come in. She thought she heard a woman's voice on the other end of the phone and immediately her jaw clenched. A sense of dread coursed through her system and raw jealousy emerged. It hit her hard and she denied it over and over in her mind.

Nick could do whatever he wanted.

She had no hold on him.

Was he making a date with another woman?

He'd told her he didn't see more than one woman at a time. Had he lied? She fought her trust issues, reminding herself that she and Nick had an uncomplicated relationship. Still, her ego would be trampled if Nick were seeing someone else.

"Hi. That was Rena," he said to her, looking thoughtful after the call ended. "She couldn't sleep and needed to talk. Tony's out cold."

"So, you're her sounding board," she asked, ridiculously relieved he'd been speaking with his sister-in-law.

His grin spread wide and stole her breath. "Yeah, I'm willing to listen to complaints about my brothers anytime."

"She was complaining?"

"Venting. Tony's been hovering and protective. She's due in just a week or two."

"It's an emotional time," Brooke offered. "I remember my mood swings were like a roller-coaster ride, up and down, mostly down."

It was ironic that the subject led to this, because that's exactly why she'd come to his room tonight.

"Yeah, that sounds like Rena too."

He glanced at her, as if finally realizing she was there. He focused on her mouth, arched a brow and waited.

Suddenly, Brooke's throat constricted. She'd thought it would so easy to bring this up, but now found herself unbelievably speechless. "I, uh, about this afternoon."

"The best shower I've ever had."

"Nick," she said, glad he was the one to mention it. "We didn't use any protection."

Nick studied her a moment, his gaze roaming from her eyes to her nose, to her mouth and lower still, taking his time. When he lifted his gaze back to hers, once again he appeared thoughtful. "I'm healthy, Brooke. I'd never endanger you."

"Okay." She took a big swallow and nodded. "But it's more than—"

"If you're worried about getting pregnant, don't. I can't have children."

That came out of the blue and was so unexpected, her mouth dropped open in surprise. "You…can't?"

He shook his head. "No, but it was my choice."

"What do you mean, it was your choice?"

Nick took her hand and led her to the bed. He sat down and pulled her next to him. His fingers laced with hers and he let out a heavy sigh. "About five years ago my father pissed me off, as usual. That wasn't new, but I was so angry with him I wanted to do something that would show him he couldn't control me any longer. I fixed that part of my anatomy so I couldn't give him an heir."

"Wow," Brooke said, her brows furrowing together. "You must have really wanted—"

"I wanted to hurt him. It was wrong, but a cocky twenty-something, and my rage at my father made me do some crazy things."

"Oh Nick. I'm sorry. You must regret that."

Nick squeezed her hand. "I don't. I'm not father material. I knew I'd never make a good father. I wasn't lying when I said I'd be happy being the favorite uncle. Joe and Tony will take care of the baby-making in the family."

Brooke felt like crying for Nick. Imagine that, the sexy dangerous and wealthy wine magnate had Brooke's sympathy. "What did your father do when he found out?"

"The hell of it was I never told him. My brothers talked me out of it and I wasn't sure that was the right move, but they convinced me. Now that he's gone, I'm glad I didn't, so I owe my brothers for that."

"Nick, what did he do to make you hate him so much. Was he...abusive?"

Nick smiled with sadness darkening his eyes. "No, never. But he was ruthless when he wanted something. He destroyed my career."

Brooke remembered Nick had told her a few times, he didn't have everything he wanted. Searching her memory, she recalled his one passion. The one thing that he'd wanted above all else. "Baseball?"

He put his head down and dragged her hand to his lap, holding tight. "I was just a kid with a dream." Deep emotion weighted his words. "I was good, Brooke."

"I remember."

"I'd made the minor leagues and was on my way to the majors, but dear old dad wanted his boys to run the wine business. He wanted us to love his legacy as much as he did. None of us did. I was his last chance."

Nick went on to tell the details of the incidents that crushed his baseball career. The lies, the deception and the manipulations. He spoke about Candy Rae and Brooke's spine stiffened when she learned about her part in the deception. Nick had been just a young boy with his whole life ahead of him. How devastating for him to go through that, knowing his father disregarded his wishes to manipulate him into a life he didn't want. Brooke finally understood why Nick wanted nothing to do with the company. It signified all he'd lost.

"Then I had my accident during the game. I know in my head my father didn't physically injure me so I couldn't play again, but he sure as hell put pressure on me and had me rattled enough to make a fool move on the field. I was recovering from the surgery too, but before I knew what happened, the team released me. I know my father had something to do with that."

Brooke had heard rumors about Santo Carlino when she'd lived in Napa as a young girl. He'd been a powerful and ruthless businessman. "I'm sorry."

"Don't be. I'm only telling you this to ease your mind about being with me."

"Is that the only reason, Nick?" She shouldn't have asked. She never knew when to keep her trap shut.

He turned to face her, his gaze piercing hers. "It's been a long time since I've spoken about this. And only to my brothers. I guess I figured you'd understand."

"I do." She smiled and stroked his cheek gently, his day old stubble rough under her palm. "But I'm sorry for more than what you've gone through. I'm sorry for thinking having money and good looks meant you had everything you wanted."

"You like my looks?" he said, in an attempt to lighten the mood.

"Yes, I like your looks," she said, not taking the bait to banter. This was serious and she wouldn't let Nick make light of it. "I've misjudged you and I apologize."

He brought her hand to his mouth and gently kissed the inner skin of her palm. "Thanks."

They sat in the dark, holding hands, the intimacy of the moment more profound than the sex they'd experienced these past few days. Brooke's heart ached for him in a way she'd never be able to justify or explain to another person.

Because this was Nick.

And she was falling in love with him.

"Stupid, stupid, stupid," Brooke muttered, as she gave the dining room table a second polish, the cloth in her hand circling faster and faster, to match the crazy beating of her heart. "How could Mommy do that? How could she fall in

love with Nick again?" she asked Leah, who played with a
Baby Elmo music box on the floor. Leah looked up with a
questioning pout on her little lips. To add insult to injury,
her daughter's eyes rounded and searched the room at the
mere mention of Nick's name. Even her child was smitten
with him.

Her life was in shambles and she didn't have a solution
to either of her dilemmas.

Dan wanted to know his daughter and start over, and
Nick, the man she loved, wanted to be rid of Napa in the
worst way. One man was coming back into her life, another
leaving for good. And it was all wrong.

When her cell phone rang, Brooke didn't jump and she
didn't panic. It was time for her to come to terms with her
life and fix what she could. She noted Dan's number on the
screen and took a deep breath before answering. "Hello."

"It's Dan, honey."

Honey?

"I'm only in Napa for a few more days. I'd like to come
see you. We have things to talk about. Things to work out.
I know I made a mistake leaving you."

"Yes, you did, Dan. But that's over now."

"It doesn't have to be. I want to talk to you, Brooke."

There was a calm and amenable tone to his voice today,
but she still didn't trust it, or him. "I suppose we do have
things to talk about."

"Can I come over?"

"Today's not good, Dan. Come tomorrow afternoon.
We'll talk."

After Brooke hung up the phone, she slumped down in
a chair and put her head in her hands. She couldn't afford
a court battle with Dan, but she'd do anything within her
power to keep Leah. There was no way she'd give him joint
custody. At the very most, she'd allow him the right to come

for a visit every now and then. She'd stick to her guns and not budge an inch.

She glanced at Leah who had rolled onto her back on the pink flowered quilt, her chubby legs kicking in the air, as she nibbled on her teething ring. "He doesn't deserve you," she whispered, holding back tears.

The only good news she had all week was that her mom was coming for a visit in a month. She's promised to help Brooke with her first paying guests and with any luck she'd be open for business by then. With Joe's expertise, her website would be operating soon and she'd managed to meet local merchants, hand out flyers and spread the word about her establishment.

"It's good news," she said to Leah. "I've gotta keep reminding myself that all this hard work will pay off one day."

Brooke got down on the floor and sat cross-legged on the quilt. She put Leah in a sitting position facing her. "Wanna play a game with Mommy?"

She took Leah's hands in hers and spread them wide. "Open," she said, drawing the word out. Then she closed their hands together, relaying in a sing-song voice, "Close them."

Leah giggled with joy. She loved this game. "Open," she repeated. "Close them." Brooke's mood lightened instantly just seeing her daughter's fascinated expression.

There was a sharp knock at the door, a knock she recognized. She braced herself, glancing outside at the parked car, before opening the door. Nick stood on the threshold, looking like a zillion bucks as usual and her heart thumped hard in her chest. He was eye-catching no matter what he wore, but today, he had on a tailored, and from the look of it, very expensive dark suit. "Hi," he said with a sparkling gleam in his blue eyes.

The sight of him blew her away. "Who died?"

He smiled. "You don't like my going-to-San-Francisco-on-business look?"

"You look nice, Nick," she relented, a gross understatement. "You didn't mention your trip this morning, though."

"It just came up. I'll be staying overnight. I came to give you the key to the house, just in case you miss Carlotta when you come in."

She let him in and they walked into the dining room. "Hey, kid," Nick said when he spotted Leah on the quilt. She gazed up at him and immediately lifted her arms for him to take her.

"She cut her first tooth. She's in a better mood today."

"Really," Nick said, taking off his jacket and getting down on the floor. "Let Nick see your tooth." He picked Leah up in his arms. Leah smiled at him, opening her mouth just slightly but not enough for him to catch a glimpse of it. He tickled her chin to make her laugh, then bent his head, searching until he came up with a grin. "Hey, there it is." He kissed Leah's forehead and Brooke's stomach twisted. How this man thought he wasn't good father material, she couldn't fathom. Granted, she'd thought so too, until she'd seen him interact with Leah and gotten to know him again.

Her heart broke thinking he'd never have a child of his own.

He looked up at Brooke, the smile still on his face. "Let's move furniture."

"What?"

"You have three more rooms to paint, don't you?"

"Yes, I was going to start on the next one when Leah took her nap this afternoon."

Nick rose, taking Leah in his arms. He tilted his chin and gestured upstairs. "It'll take me a few minutes."

"You're all dressed up."

"Are you going to stop arguing with me?" He glanced at Leah. "I hope you won't be this stubborn when you grow up."

Her daughter responded with a soft touch to his cheek.

"Okay, fine," she said. It was killing her seeing Nick holding Leah and how easy they were with each other. "Let's move furniture."

Half an hour later, after they'd arranged the furniture in the center of each of the three remaining rooms, Nick glanced at his watch. "I'd better get on the road. My meeting is in a couple of hours."

Brooke walked him downstairs and handed him his jacket. He slung it over his shoulder and strode to the door. "See you tomorrow night."

She nodded and glanced at his mouth.

He inhaled a sharp breath. "Keep looking at me that way and I'll never get out of here."

Heat rushed up her neck to warm her face. He was smooth, a charmer to the umpteenth degree, but he'd shown her a different side of himself last night and she feared she'd never get enough of him.

He took her into his arms and brushed a light kiss to her lips. Then he groaned and pulled her up tight against him, deepening the kiss. It lasted a gloriously long time and when they finally broke apart, both of them were breathing heavily.

"You make a man want to stay home nights," he whispered with a rasp, before turning and exiting the house.

She stood on the porch and watched him get into his car and pull out of the driveway. Then she entered the house and leaned back against the closed doorway. "Damn you, Nick. Don't say those things to me."

Nine

"So how long have you been teaching English at the high school?" Brooke asked Molly as they sat at the bed-and-breakfast's newly spruced up dining room table. It was tea for two with her aunt's Royal Albert English Chintz china teacups looking wonderful on the lacy rose tablecloth she'd laid out.

Molly juggled having Leah on her lap and sipping chamomile tea without the slightest pause. It was clear her friend knew a thing or two about children. She was glad she was finally able to have Molly over for an early brunch.

"This is my fifth year at the high school. I started teaching English and History a year after Adam was born and it's working out very well. We have our summers together and during the school season I'm home early. My husband works out of the house a few days a week, so he's Mr. Part-time Mom."

Brooke chuckled. "Is that what you call him?"

"Yeah, I do. John's got a great sense of humor. We laugh about it all the time."

"It's important to have someone to laugh with. Dan never laughed much. It's a wonder the two of us ever got together."

Molly reached for her hand. "You're doing the right thing by moving on. He wasn't right for you."

"Don't I know it! He'll be here in a couple of hours and I have no idea what I'm going to say to him."

"Just listen to what he says," Molly offered, touching her hand. "Let him speak his mind, but don't give him an answer. Tell him you have to think things over and then do that. There's no rush. You don't have to make any decisions quickly."

Having Molly here soothed her fragile nerves. She'd given her good advice and made her wish they hadn't lost touch with each other in the past. "Thanks, Molly. I will do that. It's the sane, rational thing to do." Then Brooke thought about it some more, shaking her head. "It's hard to be objective. He's such a snake."

A quick smile brought light to Molly's amber eyes. "Take the high road. Only call him a snake behind his back."

"I'll try," Brooke said, arching her brow as she pondered. "It won't be easy."

Brooke rose from her seat to arrange little round lemon pastries she'd made earlier this morning on a plate. She set out a bowl with fresh strawberries and raspberries topped with a special cream she'd prepared and a platter of sliced cranberry bread. "I'm practicing on you. Tell me what you think."

Molly tasted each one of the dishes and nodded. "Excellent. You get an A. The lemon tarts are amazing. When did you have time to do all this?"

"Last night and early this morning. Nick was gone, so I had free time."

Molly grinned. "Nick?"

"I mean, I usually cook him breakfast and dinner and the house was empty so I took advantage of the time to whip these up."

"Okay, I get it. He wasn't home to *occupy* your time, right?" Molly shot her a wicked smile. "What's up with the two of you?"

"He's a fr—" she began, then quickly stopped herself from calling him a friend. The "F" word wasn't a label she wanted between the two of them. "He and I have an arrangement. And no, it's not what you're thinking."

"Oh, so you're not sleeping with him? Too bad. Remember when he won Desert Island Dream in high school? The girls got to pick the one guy they'd like to be stranded on a desert island with."

"I remember," Brooke said with a groan. The girls wouldn't have been disappointed.

When Leah began to fidget too much, Molly set her down in her playpen and gave her a toy. "There you go."

Molly lifted up to stare into Brooke's eyes. "You had a thing for him and now you're living under his roof."

"Just temporarily. We'll be moving out soon. And he'll be off to Monte Carlo. He's got a house there and can't wait to leave the country."

Molly continued to stare at her, narrowing her eyes. "You're in love with him."

"I've got enough problems at the moment, thank you very much."

Molly spoke with gentle regard. "Doesn't change the fact."

"No, it doesn't," Brooke admitted, lowering her tea cup slowly to confess her innermost feelings. Maybe it would help to discuss this with someone. "It just happened. I had my eyes wide open, knowing it was impossible."

"To coin a cliché, love is blind. You can't help who you love."

"But you can be smart about it, can't you?"

Amusement sparked in Molly's eyes when she shook her head. "I don't think so. Intellect has very little to do with matters of the heart. Nick must be more than a hot hunk loaded with money for you to fall for him. The girl I knew needed more than eye candy." Molly was forever astute and that's why they'd gotten along in high school.

"Nick always let me see a side of him he rarely showed anyone else," Brooke said soberly. "I told myself over and over it was ridiculous and impossible, but there he was, opening up to me and being so good with Leah." Tears welled up in her eyes as she glanced at her baby sucking on her fist. Brooke had dressed her for company and she looked so pretty in her frilly flowered dress and bloomers. "Leah adores him."

She sniffed and halted her feelings of melancholy. "It's not going to work with him, Molly. My life is so complicated right now. I just want to have it all simple again."

Brooke and Molly talked for half an hour more and before her friend left she gave her a big comforting hug. "Call me anytime, Brooke."

"Don't worry, I will."

Brooke braced herself for Dan's visit. She didn't want this, any of it. She scooped Leah up in her arms and thought about running away, but it was just a wishful dream. She had to face him today and there wasn't much she could do about it. She sat down on the sofa and rocked Leah, giving her a bottle of formula and hoping she'd be sound asleep when Dan came by.

Less than an hour later, she heard a knock and rushed

to the door to keep Leah from waking up. "Come in," she said the second she saw Dan.

He entered the house. His hair was groomed, his face shaven, and he had on the same type of business casual clothes he always wore; khaki pants and a brown Polo shirt. She looked at him and felt nothing but disdain. At one time she had thought he was handsome, with his angular lines and sharp facial features. "Let's have a seat in the parlor."

She moved ahead of him and sat down in a wing chair that faced the sofa. Dan took the sofa and stared at her. He leaned forward. "You look good, Brooke. Pretty as always."

She refrained from rolling her eyes. "How did you know where we were?"

Dan glanced around the parlor taking it all in with assessing eyes as if doing mental calculations. "There's a lot of antiques in here. Are all the rooms furnished like this? How old is this place? "

"Old," she replied, refusing more information. "Please answer my question."

"Okay, fine, Brooke. I've been searching for you for months. I realized I'd made a drastic mistake. I hired a private detective to find you only to get a report last week that you'd had a baby and moved back to Napa."

"How touching," Brooke said. Was she supposed to cave just because he paid someone to find her?

Dan's face reddened and he looked ready to wrestle a bear.

She hoisted her chin.

"Look," he began. "Let's try to be civil to each other. We have a daughter."

Brooke hated hearing it. She hated that Leah had a drop of his blood and that he did have a legal right to see her. "Her name is Leah Marie and she's a Hamilton."

Dan's lips twisted. "She's a Hartley, Brooke, whether you want to accept it or not. Now, can I see her?"

Brooke's stomach quaked. "Fine, but please don't wake her." Brooke rose and took him into the downstairs bedroom where she'd set up a little crib she'd recently purchased on sale. Slowly, this place was becoming a home to them.

She led him into the bedroom and Dan gazed down at his daughter sleeping in the crib. He stood there a few minutes, just watching her as Brooke studied him. Something odd happened. Dan's expression didn't soften. It didn't change at all. His gaze didn't flow over Leah with loving adoration. Maybe it was because she was a stranger to him, or because he'd already lost one child, but Brooke had expected something more from Dan than the stony face staring down at the crib. Granted, he'd seen her several days ago, but that was for only a few seconds.

After half a minute, Brooke cleared her throat and Dan got the message. He exited the room with Brooke steps behind him.

"I remember you talking about this place," he said as they reentered the parlor and took their seats again. "Now it's all yours. What will you do with it?"

Brooke was taken aback by his question. Didn't he want to know about Leah? When was she born? How was the delivery? What is she like?

"I'm converting the house into a bed-and-breakfast. I have to support myself somehow."

"How many rooms does it have?"

"Eight, but six upstairs that I'll use for patrons."

"You were always good at homemaking, Brooke."

"Funny, but I never heard that from you before."

Dan gritted his teeth, making the words flowing from his mouth seem implausible. "I'm sorry I hurt you."

She wasn't sure that he really was. "That's not enough. Being sorry won't make up for anything. You abandoned me."

"I didn't know you were having a child. You should have told me."

"You shouldn't have gotten another woman pregnant and left me the way you did. You just packed up and moved out the same day I'd learned about it. I was in shock for months and picking up the pieces. I don't owe you anything, Dan."

"We can be a family again."

"That's not possible."

"Anything's possible, Brooke. Give us a second chance."

Leah cried out and Brooke prayed she'd fall back asleep, but the cries continued and she excused herself. "I have to get her. She's probably hungry and wet."

"I'll come with you."

"No. Stay here. I'll be back in a few minutes. I'll bring her in."

And Brooke walked out of the parlor on shaking legs.

Nick stepped onto Brooke's porch, a gift for Leah in one hand, another for Brooke in his pocket. He'd made it back to Napa after his late morning meeting with customers for Carlino Wines in good time and decided to stop by Brooke's house first before heading home this afternoon.

He told himself that Brooke might need a hand putting the furniture back in place after painting for the past two days, but in truth he was anxious to give the girls the gifts he'd picked up in San Francisco.

He heard a man speaking to Brooke from inside the house. The somber tone of his voice had an edge to it that

Nick didn't like. He pushed through the front door, without bothering to knock, and turned toward the parlor.

"Don't be unreasonable, Brooke," the man said. As he held Leah in his arms, the baby's lips turned down in a pout, tears ready to spill from her eyes. "Things could go so much easier if you agree to give us a second chance. I have rights and if you don't think so, I might have to take you to court."

Distressed, Brooke reached for her baby. "Give her to me, Dan. She's upset."

The man backed away from Brooke, refusing her the baby. "She needs to know her father."

"She *doesn't* know you and she's scared." Brooke said, panicked.

Nick stepped farther into the room, his emotions roiling. Seeing Leah in that man's arms and Brooke clearly agitated infuriated him. "Leah's not a pawn in this. Give her back the baby."

Both Brooke and Dan seemed startled to see him standing in the room.

"Who the hell are you?" Dan asked, raising his voice even more. He turned to Brooke, "Who is he and why is he issuing orders about my daughter?"

"Nick Carlino. He's been like a father to Leah, the only one she's ever known. She should be so lucky."

Nick's gaze darted straight to Brooke and from the firm resolve on her face he knew she meant what she said.

"But he's not her father. *I am.*"

The roughness of his voice carried across the room and Leah's face turned red as she burst into tears. The jerk was too selfish to realize he'd upset the baby.

"Give her to me," Brooke said quietly between gritted teeth.

"I will in a minute." Dan tried to calm Leah but it wasn't working, her cries grew louder.

Nick set Leah's gift down and strode up to Dan, his anger barely contained. Immediately, Leah turned toward him and reached out her wobbly arms, her sobs quieting down. Nick put his hands on Leah's waist, her body twisting toward him. He stared at Dan, his jaw tensing. "Let go of her."

The man glanced at Brooke then sighed. He released his hold on Leah. She flowed into Nick's arms. Her baby scent wafted up as she hung on tight, attaching herself to him. He held her for a few long moments and stroked her hair, before handing her back to Brooke. He eyed Leah's father with contempt and spoke with deadly calm. "Don't come in here and threaten them ever again."

"Nick, I can handle this," Brooke said, intervening. He didn't think so, but he backed off for her sake. "Dan was just leaving. We've said all we have to say for now."

"I'm not giving up, Brooke," Dan said. "We can make this work. I want you both back."

Brooke squeezed her eyes shut. "And I told you, that's not going to happen. Just go, Dan."

Dan shot a quick glance at Leah, then his gaze went to Brooke. "This isn't over." He sent Nick a hard look and strode out of the house with Nick at his heels. He waited until the guy was off the property before returning to Brooke, who had collapsed on the sofa with tears streaming down her face.

Nick stood staring at Brooke, his anger dissipating but other emotions clicking in with full force. When he'd walked into the house seeing another man holding Leah, claiming he wanted Brooke and Leah back in his life, surging waves of anger and jealousy destroyed his good mood. He'd never experienced anything like it, this fierce instinct to protect and comfort.

Brooke's defiant words from just minutes ago stuck in his head.

He's been like a father to Leah, the only one she's ever known.

Was that true? Was he getting that close to both Brooke and Leah? Or was Brooke just using those tactics with her ex to drive her point home, that Dan hadn't been any kind of father to Leah? He had walked out on Brooke and never looked back until what? What had happened to make him seek Brooke out?

She should be so lucky.

That comment had touched Nick in ways he didn't want to think about. Brooke couldn't possibly look at him as a role model for her child. Could she? Could she think of him in a way that he'd never thought of himself, as a man who could be a good father?

The *simple* they both wanted was getting real complicated.

His best bet would be to walk away now, but Nick knew he couldn't without helping Brooke one more time. He wouldn't leave until he was sure she and Leah would have the life they deserved. Dan had some rights to see his daughter, he was Leah's biological father, but Nick wouldn't stand by and watch the jerk hurt either of them.

He could be a hard-ass when necessary and this was the time and place for that.

Later that night, Nick watched as Brooke sat cross-legged on the floor opposite Leah in his living room, playing with the music box he'd brought home for the baby. Brooke opened the ornate silver box and a miniature ballerina twirled around to a classical tune that had Leah mesmerized. She kept trying to touch the ballerina and Brooke caught her hand each time. "Let the pretty ballerina dance," she said in a soft sweet voice.

Leah bobbed up and down with excitement from her sitting position and gurgled with laughter at the music box.

"She loves it, Nick."

Nick leaned forward in his chair, bracing elbows on knees, seeing Brooke finally calmed down from today's debacle. "Looks like it."

"Did you pick it out yourself?"

"I did. The ballerina reminded me of Leah."

Brooke's gaze met his. "You're an old softy."

"Just don't tell anyone."

Brooke glanced away for a few moments then turned to face him with regret. "I'm sorry you had to witness that today."

"I'm not. I seriously hope you don't plan on letting that guy back into your life."

"Not if I can help it," Brooke said, closing the music box. "But what choice do I have if he takes me to court?"

"He won't do that." Nick had connections and already had someone on it. He'd managed to memorize Dan Hartley's license plate and coupled with the information he'd gathered from conversations with Brooke, he'd know a lot more about him and his motives very soon. "How much are you willing to give him as far as Leah goes?"

"Nothing, but I have to be realistic. She may want to know her father one day. At the very most, I'd grant him visitation rights with me being there. That's all I can imagine for now."

"That might be doable."

"I'm not that sure, Nick. I'm going to have a lot of sleepless nights over this."

"He's the reason you came to me that first night, isn't it?" It didn't take a rocket scientist to figure that one out. "You were upset."

"That was part of the reason," she confessed with apology in her voice.

Nick arched his brows. "Part? What was the other part?"

"Maybe you're just irresistible."

Nick scoffed at that. "Come on, Brooke. Tell me."

Indecision marred her pretty face as she debated a few seconds before finally owning up. "It was partly because Dan had contacted me and I was frightened, but it was also because I wanted to be reckless for once in my life. I wanted something just for me. I've dreamed about being with you for a long time and well, you were just down the hall giving me an open invitation."

Nick swallowed down hard. He didn't know what to say to that.

"I know you're leaving, and I've got my own plans. I figured no harm could come of it."

"You want simple, I get that," he said. "I've lived my whole life that way."

"Right. Simple is as simple does."

Only Brooke and Leah were complicating the hell out of his life lately.

Nick stood and walked over to Brooke, reaching for her hand and when she placed it in his, he helped her up. He wound his arms around her waist and kissed her gently. "It's late. You've had a rough day. Let's go to bed."

"Together?" she asked.

"I'll be waiting for you."

Brooke's eyes softened and she smiled. "As soon as I get the baby to sleep, I'll be there."

Nick would hold her all night long if that was what

she wanted. He'd never done that with a woman but with Brooke, all his rules were shot to hell.

He picked up Leah and walked up the stairs side by side with Brooke, Nick kissing the baby's cheek before handing her off to her mommy.

He was in deep. But he hadn't changed his mind about anything. Brooke knew the score—he was leaving for Monte Carlo in just a few weeks.

He wanted no ties to Napa at all and that included this beautiful blond mommy with her equally beautiful blond baby.

Brooke got Leah to sleep easily. All that crying today had worn her out. She checked on her one last time, before she donned the oversized T-shirt that Nick liked and went to his room. She knocked softly and Nick was there, immediately opening the door and taking her into his arms. He held her gently and kissed her forehead, cheek and chin before bringing his warm inviting lips to hers.

"I don't think I can leave Leah," she whispered, a sense of urgency she couldn't explain, niggling at her. "I'm sorry. I thought I could, but I can't. It's going to be hard enough for me to fall asleep tonight."

Nick kissed her forehead again. "Then I'll come to you."

She gazed into his eyes.

He winked and pulled her against his chest. "I miss my big old bed."

"I'm not feeling—"

"I know, honey. We'll just *sleep* together. Just don't tell anybody, it might ruin my reputation."

She punched him in the shoulder. "You're so bad, Nick." Then she added, "In a wonderful way."

A chuckle rumbled from his chest. "That might be the nicest thing you've ever said to me."

She turned to go back to her bedroom, but Nick grabbed her hand just in time and she swirled around to face him. "Wait a second." He moved to the dresser and pulled out a black velvet box from the top drawer. "When I saw this, I knew you had to have it."

He handed her the square box. "This is for you."

Her heart pounded and she was totally confused. "What, why?"

"Open it, Brooke."

She held the box with trembling hands and opened it slowly. "Oh, Nick, this is beautiful." She fingered the green-blue oval gemstone surrounded by inset diamonds on a long silver chain.

"It's tourmaline. This stone is the exact color of your eyes."

"I don't know what to say, except thank you…and why?"

Nick shrugged. "Why not? When I saw the necklace it reminded me of you and I wanted you to have it."

"But it's probably worth more than my old clunker car."

"Your point?"

"I don't really have one, except that it's too generous, Nick. You've already done so much for me. How can I possibly accept this?"

He gave her a smoldering kiss, loving her mouth and charming her into submission. "Just say you love it."

She shook her head, ready to refuse his gift even after that mind-blowing kiss. She had pride and Nick had given her so much already, but she couldn't insult him by not accepting such a thoughtful gesture. Happy tears pooled in her eyes. "You're impossible, you know."

"I've heard that before."

She reached up on tiptoes and pressed a sweet kiss to his lips. "I love it. But you shouldn't have done it."

"I do a lot of things I shouldn't do, but giving you this gift isn't one of them."

Nick put out the light and took her hand, leading her back to the master bedroom. Quietly, they slipped in between the sheets and he took her into his arms and held her until she fell asleep.

Brooke woke early in the morning in a better mood. She'd had a good night's rest after all, cradled next to Nick during the night. She breathed in his expensive musky cologne and smiled from ear to ear at the position they were in. He lay on his back, his legs spread out, while she was on her stomach, her thigh thrust over his, and his full thick erection pressing against her hip.

"It's about time you woke up," he said, stroking her back.

Stunned, she let out a gasp. "How long have you been like this?"

Nick groaned a complaint. "Too long. Am I taking a cold shower this morning?"

Brooke kissed his neck and whispered, "Sometimes that can be fun when we do it together."

"Brooke," he warned then he rolled her over onto her back and kissed her until her lips burned from the scorching heat. He gazed into her eyes until she nodded and smiled. He wasn't a man to be denied, not that Brooke could even conceive of that now. She wanted him in all the ways that complicated her life. She wanted him in any way she could have him.

Nick made love to her with slow hands and sexy words that sent her mind spinning and her body aching for more. He was an expert at making a woman feel desirable and beautiful. She relished every illicit touch, every gliding stroke of his hands and every moist sensual thrust of his tongue.

With his encouragement she touched him back, her assault a partial revenge for the tortured pleasure he'd given her. She inched her palms up his muscled chest, through the coarse hairs surrounding his nipples. She kissed him there, then suckled on him until a heavy impatient groan erupted in his throat. She smiled and moved farther up, kissing him hard then outlining his mouth with her index finger, swirling it around and around, then slipping it into his mouth. He suckled her finger and pressure built, his chest heaving as much as hers. Heavy heat consumed her and when Nick held her tight and rolled her on top of him, instincts took over.

He helped her off with her T-shirt and she slid him out of his boxers. Naked now and consumed with lust, Brooke took his thick shaft in her hands and stroked him, sliding her open palm up and down the silken skin. She bent and put her mouth on him, loving him with fiery passion. She sensed when he was at the brink and rose above him. His face was emblazoned with desire, his rough stubble and dark hair tousled. He was the sexiest man alive.

She lowered her body down in a straddle and took him inside her. It felt so right, so perfect that she wanted to cry. Nick watched her ride him, his eyes heavy-lidded. He brought his hands to her breasts and caressed her, sensitizing her pebble-hard nipples even more. She ached for him, wanted him and loved him like no other man before.

Her climax came first and she splintered, her nerves tight, her body convulsing and finally giving up to the intense pleasure of being joined with Nick.

Nick watched her with awe in his eyes and when she was completely through, she rolled off him and accommodated his weight. He filled her again and she welcomed him. He thrust into her hard and fast, his climax coming just seconds after hers. She felt another wave of fulfillment just witnessing the satisfaction she could give to him.

She was so much in love with him her heart ached.

Afterward, they lay in each other's arms silently.

Brooke felt content and happy, but distraught at the same time. She knew this wouldn't last. She knew she was in for a gigantic fall.

When Leah made her early rising sounds, little complaints as she woke, Brooke lifted up to get her. Nick put a stopping hand on her arm. "I'll get her."

Brooke shook her head. "She'll need to be changed."

Nick winced, his lips pulling down in a frown. "Really?"

"Of course, really. She's slept all night in the same diaper."

Nick thought about it for half a second then gave her a quick kiss on the lips, slipped on his boxers and rose from the bed. "I'll take care of it. Just relax."

Brooke laid her head down on the pillow and grinned as she heard Nick struggling with the diaper change, but after a while Nick brought Leah to her. "Here she is."

He sat Leah on the bed between the two of them and Brooke inspected his handiwork. "Well, you're no speed demon, but it looks good."

With a satisfied look on his face, he winked. "I learned from the best."

She hated when Nick said nice things. She hated when he did nice things. And he'd been doing and saying nice things for so long now. Maybe she should have clung to her anger and not let him charm her into liking him. Because aside from being head-over-heels in love, she really liked the man Nick had become.

Deep down in her heart, Brooke knew this wasn't a good idea. Nick hadn't made her any promises. He'd been up front and honest with her. She was the one who wanted "simple."

What she'd gotten was a whole lot more.

Sure, she feared Leah was getting too attached to Nick. But her mommy was already a terribly hopeless case.

Ten

Three days later, Nick showed up unannounced at the bed-and-breakfast just as Brooke had finished dusting the entire house from top to bottom. She met him at the front door, wearing an apron with her hair pulled back in a ponytail. "Hi," she said, looking at him with confusion. "You didn't say you were stopping by this morning."

"I have some news," he said, his face grim. He made his way into the house and walked into the kitchen. Brooke followed him inside the room, curious. He gestured to a chair. "Here, have a seat."

Brooke's heart pounded with dread as he waited for her to sit down. "What is it?"

He sat in a chair adjacent to her. "I had your ex investigated. Don't ask me how or why, but it's done."

Brooke ran a hand down her face, taking it all in. She was more than a little stunned. "Okay," she dragged out, "but I don't understand."

"He's bankrupt. Seems his girlfriend cleaned him out and he's desperate for money. He knew that you'd had his child, months before showing up here."

Brooke blinked and shook her head. "What are you saying?"

Nick studied her face and spoke quietly, "I'm saying that he didn't search for you for months. He found out where you were right after Leah was born. He knew about her almost from the time of her birth. He didn't come for you and Leah, until he found out that you inherited this house. The house is probably worth what, three quarters of a million dollars? He probably figured you'd inherited a huge pile of cash along with it."

Brooke squeezed her eyes shut momentarily. "That bastard."

When she opened her eyes again, she saw the whole startling truth. It hurt to know what little she'd ever meant to Dan, but it hurt worse knowing he didn't really care about his daughter. "He was after my money?" Brooke asked, already certain of the answer.

Nick nodded.

Her heart in her throat and her stomach in knots, she was ready to cry. "It's hard to believe I once loved him. Shows you what a poor judge of character I am."

"Don't beat yourself up too badly. He only showed you a side of himself he wanted you to see."

"He's Leah's father and she deserves more."

"He won't be around much."

Brooke snapped her head up and stared into eyes that didn't meet hers. "What did you do? You didn't make him disappear, did you?"

Nick cast her a crooked grin and scratched the back of his neck. "No, I had a little chat with him. I told him you and Leah were off-limits. You'll decide when and where you want Leah to see him."

"How did you get him to agree…?" Then it dawned on Brooke. "Oh Nick, you paid him off, didn't you?"

Nick kept his expression unreadable. "All that matters is that you and Leah won't be bothered by him from now on."

"It does matter." Brooke rose from her chair. "How much was my little girl worth to him? How could he put a price tag on that?"

Nick stood and cupped her shoulders in his big hands, holding her still while she wanted to throw things. He spoke calmly. "It doesn't matter, Brooke. He was never in Leah's life. You can move on and forget about him. Will you do that?"

Brooke stared at Nick, wondering if she should take that same advice about him. She was a bad judge of character. She'd fallen for a guy who'd flat out told her he didn't want a family—a man who was leaving to live halfway across the world. Was he also telling her to move on and forget about him?

Nick's cell phone rang and he excused himself to answer it. Brooke took that time to check on Leah, then wash her face and comb her hair. She removed her apron and by the time Nick reentered the kitchen, she had new but heartbreaking determination.

"That was Tony. He's a giddy mess. Rena had the baby. They named him David Anthony Carlino." Nick's grin broadened across his face.

Brooke's heavy heart warmed. Babies brought such joy into a person's life. "That's wonderful. Is Rena okay?"

"According to my big brother, she's doing fine. I'm going to see them now. Want to come?"

"No, no. You go. Tell Rena I'll visit her another time. I want to see the baby. But this time is for family."

The thought of seeing Rena, Tony and their new baby, a child that wasn't Tony's biological child but one he'd love like his own, hit a little too close to home. Brooke had wanted that so much for herself, but it wasn't to be. And after the news she'd gotten today about Dan, she couldn't take witnessing the happy threesome with their whole future ahead of them.

Nick cast her an odd look. "She wouldn't mind if you came with me."

"No, Nick," she said with resolve. "I'm not coming with you. I'm not part of your family."

And I never will be.

That night when Brooke entered the Carlino house, her courage bolstered by the words she'd rehearsed all day and knew by heart, she found Nick's suitcase by the front door.

"Hi," Nick said, coming to greet her when she walked in. "You should have seen the size of that baby. He was almost nine pounds." He held two flutes of champagne. "I've been waiting for you to celebrate."

Leah clung to her shoulder, nearly asleep. "I can't right now, Nick. Leah's not feeling well. She's a little warm and her nose is running. I'm going to put her to sleep."

Nick's face fell and she could barely stand to watch his cheerful expression transform. He gazed at Leah with concern, his eyes soft and caring. "I'll go up with you." He set the flutes down, ready to help.

"No, that's okay. She's a little clingy right now. Are you going somewhere?"

Nick glanced at the suitcase in the entry. "I've got a

crisis at the Monte Carlo house. I'm leaving on the red-eye tonight. I hope to be back in three days, tops."

Brooke stopped when she reached the base of the staircase and seized on her chance to say her rehearsed words. "Nick, now's as good a time as any to tell you, Leah and I are moving out. The house is ready for us now. I don't have much more to do before I can open my doors. We'll be gone before you get back."

Nick furrowed his brows. "You're leaving?" He sounded as if it were news to him. This had always been their deal, though it broke her heart to see the look of confusion on his face. Women didn't walk out on Nick Carlino.

"It's time for me to go. I want to thank you for everything. I don't know what I would've done without your help these past few weeks. I promise, I'll find a way to pay you back. And I'm still in shock about how you handled Dan. I don't know what to say about that."

"Damn it, Brooke, you don't owe me anything." His mouth tightened to a thin line. "And you don't have to move out right now."

"Yes, Nick. I do. That was the deal." He was the classic dealmaker in the family, so he should understand. She may owe him a few weeks of work, but he'd just have to make do. She couldn't live in the house with him another day. "This was always a temporary arrangement."

His eyes darkened with anger. "I know that."

"I've learned something since coming back to Napa, Nick. You can't dwell on the past. You have to move on and look to the future. You've helped me see that."

Nick stared at her without blinking.

"Just think, you'll have the house back to normal, no more baby things to trip over."

Nick ignored her little jest. "This is because of what that jerk did to you, isn't it?"

Brooke smiled with sadness in her heart and shook her head. How could she explain that her leaving had nothing to do with Dan and everything to do with protecting herself and her daughter from getting attached to Nick, a man who was bent on running away from his past, a man who wanted a lifestyle that didn't include a ready-made family. "You've given me so much and I want to return the favor the only way I know how. My friend Molly says the high school is in desperate need of a baseball coach for the boys. You should think about it."

Nick looked at her like she'd gone crazy.

"Okay," she said with a heavy sigh. Saying good-bye to Nick was one of the hardest things she'd ever had to do. She summoned all her courage and held her ground, when she wanted to throw herself into his arms. "I've got to go up. Leah and I have a long day tomorrow." She whispered softly, "Good-bye, Nick."

Nick remained silent. She sensed his gaze on her as she climbed the stairs to the room she'd sleep in one last time. When she reached the top of the staircase, she heard him pick up his suitcase and open the front door.

There was a long pause before finally, the front door slammed shut.

Silent tears rained down her face as she carried her precious child to her bed. Brooke had no one to blame but herself. She'd come into this with her eyes wide open yet couldn't help falling in love with him again regardless of her constant internal warnings.

But by far, this time hurt the most.

She'd never get over Nick Carlino.

Not in this lifetime.

Nick sat on the deck of his Monte Carlo home and sipped wine, gazing out at the Mediterranean's classic blue waters.

He had everything he wanted here, a gorgeous view of the ocean, twelve rooms of modern conveniences and old world charm, friends to party with and a world-renowned casino only minutes away.

He'd gambled there last night and had gone out with friends afterward. He had offers from women during his time here, but Nick wasn't interested in them. Somehow their sleek clothes and sultry looks didn't stir his juices as they once had. Images of Brooke in her mommy clothes would seep into his mind instead. But he balked at that.

Thoughts of her stayed with him constantly, but he knew that would pass. Nick wanted an easy life and now that he was away from all that Napa represented, he decided to stay on a few more days.

The Italian marble "crisis" his contractor had called him about had been straightened out and it turned out not to be a big deal after all. The renovations he'd ordered were almost done and not a minute too soon. He was only weeks from winning his bet with his brothers, and by all accounts he'd already won. He'd be through with his father's wine business once and for all and he could come and go as he pleased. He would enjoy rubbing his brothers' faces in the win, smug as they both had been about the bet.

But with those thoughts also came Brooke's words that she'd spoken just days ago. *You can't dwell on the past. You have to move on and look to the future.*

He'd helped her see that?

A smile spread across his face. If he had, then he was damn glad. He couldn't deny that he wanted to see her happy. She'd always been special to him and she always made him smile with her sassy tongue and witty comebacks. She had a chance for a good future with Leah now.

During the next few days, Nick refused more party invitations than he accepted and he refrained from entertaining females at the house. He took walks on the beach, spent a more active role in the renovations and watched sports on television.

After dinner on Thursday night, he placed a call to Rena and Tony. The baby was almost a week old and Uncle Nick wanted to hear how the three of them were doing.

Rena picked up and said hello.

"Hi, it's Nick. I'm checking on my favorite uncle status."

"You're still it, but don't tell Joe I said so. And least *he* isn't thousands of miles away. He didn't abandon the family."

Nick chuckled at Rena's teasing.

"I'll be back in few days and I'm bringing gifts."

"Oh, so you're spoiling my child already?"

"That's the plan. How's the little guy?"

"He's doing fine. Eating like a Carlino and growing like one too. I never knew breast-feeding could be so challenging."

Nick laughed and an image popped into his head of Brooke holding Leah to her breast, the baby nursing until she was good and satisfied. The serene picture they'd made would be forever imbedded in his mind. "I bet you could ask Brooke for advice. She seemed to take to it naturally."

"Brooke?" Rena paused. "That girl's got her hands full right now."

"What do you mean?"

"You haven't heard?"

"No, I haven't spoken with her. We don't have that kind of relationship," Nick said, convincing himself of that fact.

"The baby's in the hospital."

"What?" Nick's good mood vanished. His heart pounded hard and he thought he heard wrong. "Leah's in the hospital?"

"Yes, she had a febrile seizure."

"A seizure?" Nick couldn't believe it. "But she's such a healthy kid."

"It's caused from a high temperature. The baby was sick and her fever spiked really fast. It's pretty scary, but they say it happens to some children. Because she's so young, they're doing tests to make sure it's nothing more serious."

"Damn! It better not be." Nick couldn't fathom that sweet baby having to suffer. "How's Brooke?"

"She's a brave one. She's all alone and I tell you, I don't know how she does it. Ali stopped by the hospital when she found out to check on both of them. She said Brooke is holding up. She has no choice, but it's rough. Her world revolves around that baby."

"Oh man." Nick put his head down and took a few deep breaths. His stomach felt hollowed out, like someone had gone in and scooped out his guts with a shovel.

"You should call her, Nick. She doesn't say it, but I know she misses you."

"I'm not so sure." He couldn't call her. He didn't know what to say to her. He'd walked out on her just like every other man in her life. He'd let her down and he'd done it without realizing it. He should have known better than to get involved with someone like Brooke. She didn't need him in her life. She needed stability. She needed someone who would be there for her, through thick and thin. She needed a man who would love the hell out of her and her beautiful daughter.

He's been like a father to Leah. She should be that lucky.

Had Brooke meant it? Had she seen something in him that he hadn't seen in himself?

Nick hung up the phone and paced the length of his living room, darting glances around his home, noting the textured walls and marble flooring, the pillared terrace with its sweeping vista overlooking the Mediterranean. The place was perfect. He'd gotten what he wanted. He could Pass Go and Collect $200 and as an added bonus he'd received the Get Out of Jail Free card, his prison being Napa and all it signified.

He admitted that he had decided to stay on longer in Monte Carlo to keep as much distance from Brooke as possible. She would have moved out of his house by now. He could go back to living his bachelor life, yet he didn't like what he was feeling about her. He missed her, but he was no good for her. He wouldn't succumb to those emotions. A few more days away would help purge her from his thoughts.

"Hang on, Nick," he muttered to himself. "Don't go nuts because the kid got sick. Brooke's a survivor. She'll be okay."

And to prove to himself that he was better off without them and vice-versa, he went out that night. He gambled in Monaco and had dinner with an acquaintance he'd met months ago at the roulette table. She was beautiful and willing, but he made up an excuse and spent the night alone in his bed.

Nick woke up feeling like crap. If someone had taken a hammer to his head, he couldn't feel worse. The hell of it was, he knew why. He hadn't caught too many winks last night and he had two blond-haired, blue-eyed females to thank for that. He rose from his bed and padded to the kitchen for some aspirin.

Only Nick knew beyond a doubt now, aspirin wouldn't cure what was really wrong with him.

Brooke took Leah out of her car seat in the back of the Lexus and gazed at her daughter with pride. "You're my pretty girl." Leah returned her compliment with a two-toothed smile. She'd dressed her in a brand-new white dress dotted with bright red cherries and green stems. Atop her baby blond curls sat a cherry red bow.

"We're going to visit your new little friend, David Anthony today," she said as she walked up the path to the house at Purple Fields. Brooke had dressed to match Leah. She wore a red and white sundress, minus the cherries. It felt good to dress up for a change and go out with Leah. Since the move into the bed-and-breakfast, Brooke had felt somewhat isolated and lonely, just the two of them in that big house.

Leah's medical episode had taken its toll on Brooke. The febrile seizure had come on so suddenly and had scared her half to death. She'd called the paramedics and they'd taken Leah to the hospital. By the time they arrived, Leah was alert and awake again. The doctor explained that the seizure was the body's natural reaction to such high temperatures and as soon as Leah's body adjusted, she came out of it. They also explained that febrile seizures in themselves were not life threatening.

Thank God for that.

They'd kept Leah in the hospital to do some tests and when they released her with a clean bill of health, Brooke had broken down and cried her eyes out. Now, just three days later, Leah was a happy girl again and both were looking forward to spending time with Rena and the new baby.

She knocked on the door and just a few seconds later Rena appeared, looking beautiful and well rested. "Hi, Rena. Leah and I are so excited to see you and the baby."

"I'm glad you accepted the invitation." Rena smiled at her and patted Leah's head. "She looks happy and healthy, Brooke. Is all okay now?"

"Yes, she's perfect. Thanks for your support and friendship. It means a lot to me."

Rena opened the door wider. "Come in, please."

Brooke stepped into the entrance hall and followed Rena to the living room. Once they reached it, Rena turned to her with apology in her eyes. "I just want you to know this wasn't my idea. I think there's a better way to do this."

Puzzled, Brooke looked at Rena then followed the line of her gaze into the room. Tony, Joe and Ali were there. "Oh, I didn't realize you were having the family over."

Rena sighed and shot Tony a hard look.

"Meet little David Anthony." Tony walked over to greet them and Brooke forgot all else, thrilled to see their new child.

"He's beautiful. You must be so happy."

"We are," Tony said to her, then Rena walked over and Tony put his arm around her. "We're thrilled."

Leah reached a hand out to touch the baby and Brooke made sure she was gentle, helping guide her hand to his cheek. "Isn't he sweet, Leah?" And after they'd fawned over little David, Brooke turned to say hello to Ali and Joe. They inquired about Leah's health and made her feel welcome, then the room became awkwardly silent. Brooke wondered what was up.

"Sorry, Brooke," Ali said finally.

Rena joined forces with Ali. "We didn't know about the bet."

Brooke looked from one woman to the other, sensing their discomfort and feeling some of her own. "What bet? What's going on?"

Nick appeared, coming out of another room and startling her. He stood in a solid stance, his gaze flowing over her from head to toe with hunger in his eyes, then he glanced at Leah and his gaze went heartbreakingly soft. He looked drop-dead gorgeous and dangerously confident about something. Just seeing him again squeezed her heart and coiled her stomach. He'd hurt her when he hadn't called about Leah. He must have known. He must have realized how much agony she'd been in when Leah was sick. He'd taken her at her word when she'd asked for *simple*, but she never thought he'd be so cold and uncaring. He should have called and asked about Leah.

"Hello, Brooke," he said.

She couldn't keep her disappointment from showing. She pursed her lips.

"Tell her," Nick demanded, looking at his brothers.

Joe glanced at Nick. "You're sure? This could spell doom for you, bro."

Nick nodded. "I want her to know the truth, all of it."

Tony handed the baby off to Rena and she shook her head at him. "We were on your side, Brooke. In all of this," Tony said in a defensive tone.

"All of what? What's going on?" she asked.

As soon as Leah spotted Nick, she put her arms out to him and she bounced with excitement until Brooke could barely contain her. "Leah!"

The dimples of doom broke out on Nick's face and he strode over to Brooke. "Let me hold her."

"I can't seem to stop her," she said, disgruntled.

Leah reached out for Nick and when he took her, she clung to his neck. He kissed her cheek and stroked her hair. "Thank God you're all right."

Ali's and Rena's expressions softened.

"Tell her the truth," Nick demanded again of his brothers.

"Why don't you tell me, Nick?" Brooke said, angrily. "Since it's obvious this was all set up and your doing. Tell me what you have to say."

Nick looked at his brothers who refused to speak. "Cowards."

"On that note, we'll leave you two alone." Joe grabbed Ali's hand and walked outside.

"That's a good plan. Let's take the baby for a walk," Tony said to Rena and the three of them left the room.

Once they were alone, Nick turned to her. "Okay, I'll tell you the truth. When you first came to live with me after your accident, my brothers were so damn sure I'd get involved with you. I mean, here you were vulnerable and alone and you had this adorable kid. They were so damn smug about it. I told them what I told you, I don't do permanent and I'm not father material. I was so sure of how I felt," he said, stroking her daughter's hair again, "that I made them a wager. I bet them I wouldn't fall for you and want the whole enchilada. I bet them my stake in the company. If I didn't fall in love with you, I get a free pass with Carlino Wines. I wouldn't have to run the company and I wouldn't have to stay in Napa. I'd be out of the running and it would be between Joe and Tony."

Brooke's mouth dropped open and she was stunned speechless.

Nick went on, "I told you how much I hated it here. How much I wanted revenge against my father. So much so, that I wanted nothing to do with his legacy. So much so, that I couldn't see past my anger. But you made me see things differently, Brooke. You made me realize that I shouldn't live in the past. That's all I've been doing, living in the past and running away."

Brooke regained her composure and finally spoke. "You actually *bet* you wouldn't fall in love with me? Not very good for a girl's ego, is it?"

"I wasn't looking for permanent, Brooke. But man, was I wrong. I lost the bet. I'm the new head of Carlino

Wines. I'm the CEO now and rightfully so. Joe and Tony are staying on too. We're brothers and we're going to help each other. Thanks to you I'm facing my past and moving on to my future."

Brooke swallowed hard. "Nick." She didn't know what to say.

"I put in a call to the high school too. Looks like they might want me to coach the Victors this season."

"Oh, Nick. That's wonderful."

"You've made it all possible, Brooke. You helped me see that I was wasting my life away. This is one bet I was glad to lose. Because I'm crazy about you and Leah. You're all that matters to me. I don't want to lose you and if it means me staying in Napa and running the company, I'll do it. I want you that much. I love you that much."

Brooke got past the initial ego deflation, to hear him, to really hear what he was telling her. He loved her. He loved Leah. It was quite a lot to take in. He was making sacrifices for her and the idea warmed her to the point of melting. "What's the whole enchilada?"

Nick spoke with reverence and a hopeful tone. "Marriage. The three of us being a family, everything I thought I never wanted."

"And now you do?"

"I took the CEO position to prove it to you." He lowered his voice and spoke with sincerity. "With your help, I think I could be a good father to Leah."

Oh my God. That did it. Any anger she felt over the stupid bet he made just faded to nothingness. She couldn't hold it against him. He'd always been honest with her. But hearing him say he loved her and that he wanted to be Leah's father turned her insides to jelly. Tears welled in her eyes and raw emotion overwhelmed her. She struggled to get the words out yet she felt them with every beat of her heart, "You don't need my help being a good father. Leah's already crazy about you."

"What about you, Brooke? How do you feel about me? Still trying to keep it simple?"

Her smile spread across her face and her heart burst with joy. "Nick, you've complicated my life since the day I set eyes on you in high school. I loved you then and I love you now."

Nick breathed in deep. "Then will you marry me?"

Brooke gazed at him holding Leah in his arms. "You don't play fair asking me with Leah looking at you like you could paint the moon."

"I could, with both of you in my life."

Brooke sighed with utter joy and spoke the words she'd never thought she'd ever say to Nick Carlino. "Yes, I'll marry you."

Nick bundled her up close, the three of them in a huddle and Nick kissed her with sweet tenderness. "I've missed you, Brooke. I've missed you both. I promised you that night of the crash that I'd take care of Leah. I want to do that and share my life with you. We'll be a family, the three of us."

"Oh, Nick. That's all I've ever wanted."

Brooke would have the family she'd always hoped for, but she was getting a bonus.

Her very own drop-dead handsome, dangerously sexy Desert Island Dream.

What more could a girl ask for?

* * * * *

A sneaky peek at next month...

Desire™

PASSIONATE AND DRAMATIC LOVE STORIES

2 stories in each book - only £5.30!

My wish list for next month's titles...

In stores from 19th August 2011:

☐ What a Westmoreland Wants – Brenda Jackson

& Stand-In Bride's Seduction – Yvonne Lindsay

☐ Claiming Her Billion-Dollar Birthright – Maureen Child

& Falling For His Proper Mistress – Tessa Radley

☐ Sweet Surrender, Baby Surprise – Kate Carlisle

& The Secretary's Bossman Bargain – Red Garnier

☐ The Billionaire's Bedside Manner – Robyn Grady

& Her Innocence, His Conquest – Jules Bennett

Available at WHSmith, Tesco, Asda, Eason, Amazon and Apple

Just can't wait?

0811/51

MILLS & BOON® Book Club

2 Free Books!

Get your free books now at
www.millsandboon.co.uk/freebookoffer

Or fill in the form below and post it back to us

THE MILLS & BOON® BOOK CLUB™—HERE'S HOW IT WORKS: Accepting your free books places you under no obligation to buy anything. You may keep the books and return the despatch note marked 'Cancel'. If we do not hear from you, about a month later we'll send you 4 brand-new stories from the Desire™ 2-in-1 series priced at £5.30* each. There is no extra charge for post and packaging. You may cancel at any time, otherwise we will send you 4 stories a month which you may purchase or return to us—the choice is yours. *Terms and prices subject to change without notice. Offer valid in UK only. Applicants must be 18 or over. Offer expires 28th February 2012. **For full terms and conditions, please go to** www.millsandboon.co.uk/termsandconditions

Mrs/Miss/Ms/Mr (please circle)

First Name

Surname

Address

Postcode

E-mail

Send this completed page to: Mills & Boon Book Club, Free Book Offer, FREEPOST NAT 10298, Richmond, Surrey, TW9 1BR

Find out more at
www.millsandboon.co.uk/freebookoffer

Visit us Online

0611/D1ZEE

The World of Mills & Boon®

There's a Mills & Boon® series that's perfect for you. We publish ten series and with new titles every month, you never have to wait long for your favourite to come along.

Blaze.
Scorching hot, sexy reads

By Request
Relive the romance with the best of the best

Cherish™
Romance to melt the heart every time

Desire™
Passionate and dramatic love stories

Browse our books before you buy online at
www.millsandboon.co.uk